THE THREE EMPERORS

A NEW MAP
OF
BOHEMIA
AND
MORAVIA.
FROM THE LATEST AUTHORITIES
By JOHN CARY, Engraver
1800

THE THREE EMPERORS

EMPERORS

An Ethan Gage Adventure

WILLIAM DIETRICH

HARPER

www.harpercollins.com

HarperCollins books may be purchased for educational, business, or sales promotional use. For information, please e-mail the Special Markets Department at SPsales@harpercollins.com.

FIRST EDITION

Designed by William Ruoto

Map designed by Nick Springer for Springer Cartographics, LLC

Library of Congress Cataloging-in-Publication Data has been applied for.

ISBN: 978-0-06-219410-7

14 15 16 17 18   OV/RRD   10 9 8 7 6 5 4 3 2 1

*To Heidi, Charlie, and newcomer Isaac Mills,
beginning their own adventures*

There is no such thing as accident; it is fate misnamed.

—Napoleon Bonaparte

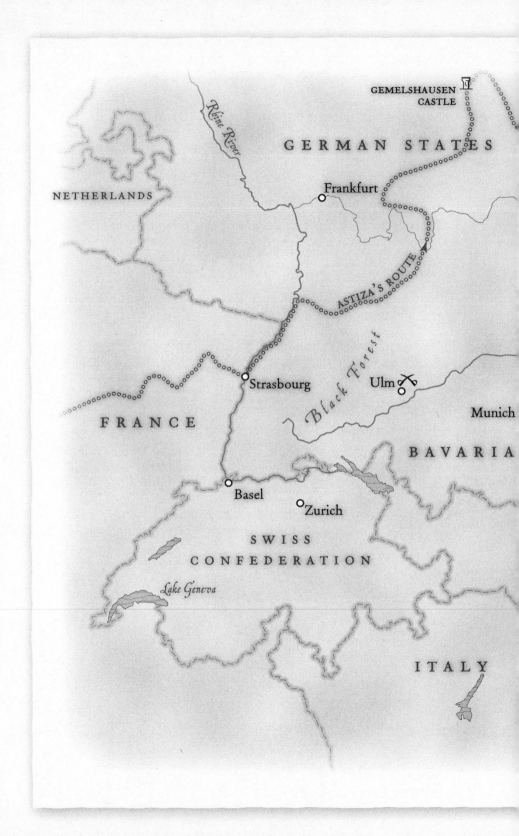

GEMELSHAUSEN
CASTLE

GERMAN STATES

Rhine River

NETHERLANDS

Frankfurt

ASTIZA'S ROUTE

Black Forest

Strasbourg

Ulm

Munich

FRANCE

BAVARIA

Basel

Zurich

SWISS
CONFEDERATION

Lake Geneva

ITALY

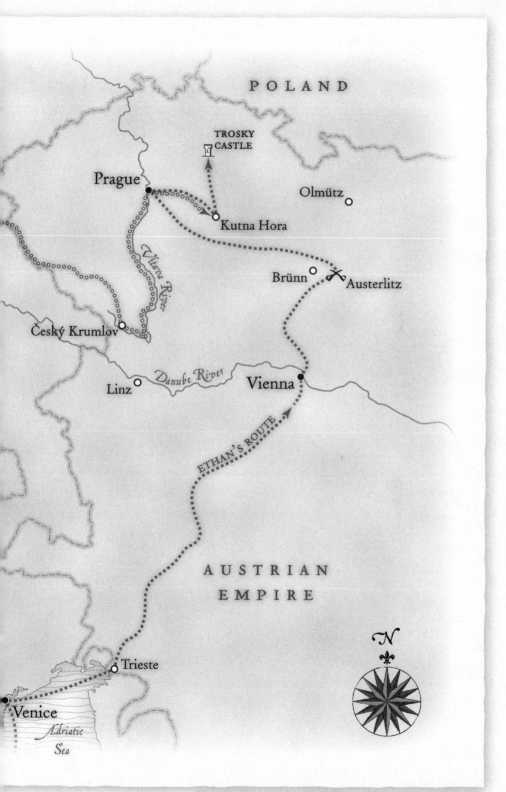

POLAND

TROSKY CASTLE

Prague

Olmütz

Kutna Hora

Vltava River

Brünn

Austerlitz

Český Krumlov

Danube River

Linz

Vienna

ETHAN'S ROUTE

AUSTRIAN EMPIRE

N

Trieste

Venice

Adriatic Sea

CHAPTER I

It is remarkably convenient to be dead.

As I studied my opponents at a Venetian casino, I marveled at the advantages of my temporary demise. One's debts and obligations disappear. Projects can remain unfinished. Enemies are permanently avoided. Failures are forgotten. Even people with nothing good to say while you are alive might spare a word of sympathy at your passing.

If you are Ethan Gage, the American sharpshooter, savant of electricity, treasure hunter, spy, diplomat, and mercenary, this is all to the good.

So I enjoyed my decision to stay missing after narrowly surviving the epic naval battle of Trafalgar. I traded the problems of Gage for temporary reinvention as Hieronymus Franklin, a distant cousin of the famed American philosopher Benjamin Franklin. I'd fled the battle's aftermath in a captain's boat cut loose from the sinking *Bucentaure*, been storm-pushed through Gibraltar, sold the gig for passage on a swift ship on its way to Venice, made an end run round Napoleon's empire by sea, and arrived at the most beautiful, corrupt, decaying, polluted, and elegant city on earth.

I had died and gone to gambler's heaven.

"I'm a confidant of President Jefferson and scholar of civilization who hopes to combine republican virtue with your venerable wisdom," I said when introducing myself to every well-dressed notable I encountered after stepping ashore, since I needed invitations to dances and card games. "The whole world can benefit from Venetian industry." Never mind that Venice hadn't been industrious for two hundred years: if you wish to be believed, flatter.

The fact that I'd actually been a young protégé of the late Franklin helped me cheerfully lie about him, and myself. I was aided by the Venetian habit of wearing disguises at carnivals and casinos. Since medieval times, the anonymity of the mask has meant freedom for nobles hobbled by rank and protocol. They can gamble, flirt, test outrageous ideas, negotiate agreements, and debate. Liaisons can be arranged, dance partners traded, courtesans hired, bribes taken, and class lines crossed.

I purchased an eye mask of foppish silver filigree worn under a purple tricorne hat, with golden breeches and embroidered waistcoat better suited to the recently passed eighteenth century than to early November of 1805. My cape was midnight blue, its lining white silk, and its piping gold. In short, I looked ridiculous, but safely disguised as a fool.

My missing wife has fondly called me the Fool, the madman of the tarot deck, in search of experience and crazed wisdom. She'd have laughed and called me dressed for the part, and I miss her desperately. Now I had to win enough money to find her. My costume and a stake in our games had consumed the twenty gold guineas I'd been paid by English spymaster Sir Sidney Smith, plus the remainder of what I'd earned from selling the stolen captain's gig and posing as a physician during my passage.

Hieronymus Franklin, professor of medicine. Yes, I'd pretended to be a doctor who "cured" the seasickness of a Hapsburg countess and her lady-in-waiting by mixing a tincture of sugar, rum, and poppy seeds I'd bought from a Moroccan spice peddler in Gibraltar. The opium eased my own aches after battle. I advised my patients to rest amidships for a minimum of two days and talked importantly of phlegm, bile, and the four humours. It didn't hurt that I shamelessly flirted with a lady of too little chin and too much nose, remembering Franklin's advice that the plain are more grateful for attention than the pretty. I clasped hands, stroked forehead, and made a bawdy joke or two while the drug did its work.

Like any medical expert, I took full credit when the pair awoke with their sea legs, and I suggested they someday visit my clinic in Boston, which doesn't exist. *God heals, and the doctor takes the fee*, my mentor Benjamin Franklin observed.

Such enterprise padded my purse, but I needed more money to complete my quest. Almost a year before, I'd been separated from my wife and son at Napoleon's coronation at Notre Dame, they fleeing east as I fled west. My enemy Catherine Marceau wrote shortly before Trafalgar that my wife was captive in Bohemia and in danger of being burned as a witch. Confined with Astiza was my four-year-old son, Horus, or Harry.

Almost as alarming was wicked Catherine's proposal that we ally. The pretty spy had tried to woo me a couple of times in my family's apartment in Paris. Couldn't blame the woman, given my dash, but she was persistent as a pox. Rather than get tangled with that seductress and her plotters in France, I'd flanked Napoleon's empire.

All I needed was enough money to hurry on to Vienna and Prague. In the meantime I'd avoid uncomfortable questions about my job as spy and peripatetic diplomat by letting Ethan Gage temporarily rest at the bottom of the Atlantic.

I said not a word about the naval battle, since I'd outsailed official news of it, deferring instead to card players hundreds of miles from any real information. Ignorance always fortifies certainty.

"This time Bonaparte is finished," prophesied a red-masked opponent across the table from me. Lord Frederick Ramsey was a seedy English aristocrat who avoided London creditors by gambling away the last of his fortune in a foreign place. "There are half a million soldiers arrayed against him, he will recklessly advance too far, and Emperors Francis and Alexander will hand him his usurper head. And with that, my friends, the world will return to normal."

"Normal" meant England triumphant and royalism secure. That country had succeeded in assembling a Third Coalition that enlisted Austria and Russia against France's new emperor. Napoleon had been forced to abandon his plans to invade Britain and was marching east to meet this new threat.

I studied my cards, decorated with the Italian suits of wands, cups, swords, and coins, and reflected on my life. In the previous two years I'd spied for both Britain and France, lost my savings, let Catherine make a fool of me, and misplaced my family. I've achieved more notoriety than fame, and accumulated more experience than money. Now I pondered my purpose. Armies tramp, fleets thunder, and new aristocracies of strivers swirl to the waltz while Bonaparte broods in one corner, looking at his watch.

My savant friends take the long view. The earth is indescribably old, scientists inform me, and we are gnats in the gusts of time. These intellectuals live for knowledge, the only achievement they deem eternal.

My less learned companions, such as adventurers Pierre, Jubal, and Ned, think great men waste today to pursue tomorrow. They let the future go hang.

My women have a different strategy yet, living for love, children, and home. Their immortality is their descendants.

I share all these goals and another as well, my own cantankerous freedom. However life is judged, I want to be responsible for it and yet unfettered. So I married a priestess, sired an adventurous little boy, and when I steered the Gibraltar storm and asked myself what I desired most, it was for us to live independently and stop chasing the fool's gold of fame.

However, it takes real gold to make anything happen in today's violent world. I needed an oracle to give me answers, and Astiza was on a quest to find a mechanical one built in medieval times. This was the Brazen Head, constructed by Albertus Magnus and reputed to foretell the future. Some said Saint Thomas Aquinas had destroyed the automaton as evil. Others said the mystic Christian Rosenkreutz had spirited it away to a hiding place in Bohemia.

The future! Any king would rejoice at such advantage. Or would he go mad from foreseeing the inevitable tragedies that await us all?

I shifted uncomfortably in my casino chair, its legs carved like griffins and its back topped by the wings of the falcon god Horus. The hilt of a mysterious broken sword I'd been given by Talleyrand was uncomfortably tied to the small of my back, because he'd claimed it might prove a clue to finding the Brazen Head. When I rubbed my itch like a bear, the others thought I was fidgeting, and I was counting on their overconfidence. I needed a thousand Venetian sequins to find my family.

"Is something causing you discomfort, Franklin?" Ramsey boomed.

I smiled wanly. "Only a little indigestion."

"Damned foreign fare. Travel exacts its indignities."

"Not enough fruit at sea."

"Do my best thinking on the privy!" He laughed.

The women redirected the conversation. "You give the Corsican so little military credit, Lord Ramsey?" asked the self-described Marchesa Antonia Rinaldi, the curving feathers of her mask adding to the high plumage of her hair. Venetians love to dress up.

Whether Antonia was really a marchesa we'd no idea, but it was charity to call her one, since time had roughened her beauty. She still had an imposing bosom and corseted waist, and in dim candlelight the years faded away. A half mask allowed her to display wide lips and liberally sample the casino's prosecco and cognac. The thrice-widowed marchesa usually found a man to go home with, and thus paid more attention to Ramsey's opinions than he might otherwise get.

"Napoleon is a lucky general, but he hasn't faced the full might of the Austrian and Russian nobility," the Brit said. "The French army draws its leadership from the mob and its manipulators. The aristocrats of the Continent ride into battle with five hundred years of breeding." *He that speaks much is much mistaken,* Franklin taught.

The marchesa nodded, however, since agreement is always seductive to a man. I avoided comment, lest I resurrect Ethan Gage too early. Despite my good heart, I've accumulated a ball and chain of enemies.

Certainly the strategic situation was complex. The French marshal Masséna was marching toward Venice as we spoke, while Austria's Archduke Charles maneuvered to block him. The British were organizing expeditionary forces at Naples in the south and Hanover in the north. The Russians were marching west to join the Austrians. The allegiance of the Bavarians was uncertain.

My battlefield was considerably smaller. I couldn't afford the stakes at Palazzo Vendramin Calergi, with its Murano glass chandeliers, silk wallpaper, and fireplaces as ornate as altars. The venerable and fraying Casino dei Nobili fit the purse of down-at-heel aristocrats, of which Venice had a surplus since Napoleon ended their thousand-year republic in 1797. The carpets were stained, the dusty chandeliers were trimmed of a third of their candles, and the floors pitched from the mansion's settlement into the lagoon. Age-spotted mirrors reflected dim light, felt cloths hid chipped tables, and powdered wigs topped clumsy servants. The players were greedy as bankers and rootless as gypsies. Our hands had the gambler's twitch, and risk was our refuge. The drapes were heavy, the clocks stilled, and the stacks of Venetian sequins, British guineas, Spanish doubloons, fresh new napoleons, and German talers were thick with golden light.

Our bravado fit the city. Venice had passed from French rule back to Austrian, and was so thoroughly looted in the process that all it had left was atmosphere. This it retained in abundance. The houses and churches shimmered above the lagoon like jewelry on a lacquered table, their baroque decorations a frozen music. Rascals and strumpets from a dozen nations rode gondolas like plumed birds, dressed for display while scrounging for opportunity.

Napoleon had bullied the city into surrender eight years before, threatening to be "an Attila to the state of Venice." The invading French troops had erected a Tree of Liberty in Piazza San Marco, ordered the Jews released from their ghetto, and hung revolutionary banners between old Roman columns. They also levied an indemnity of three million livres, three ships of the line, twenty paintings, five hundred manuscripts, and thousands of diamonds, rubies, sapphires, pearls, and amethysts, all pried from the gold and silver settings in the Treasury of St. Mark's. Then, thinking better of it, they took the settings, too. Napoleon made war pay for itself.

Now war had erupted again, and I turned to my skills as a gambler in the particularly risky game of brelan, matching the city's mood. The languor of Venice, its decay of mold and peeling paint,

its wines and campo suppers, and its nightly concerts all emphasize the brevity and beauty of life and the need to take chances.
Travelers come to risk love, the love pox, commerce, and wagers,
because existence is precarious and time fleeting.

I must turn this to my favor.

Thus far, I'd had a minor triumph in biribi, a game of pure
chance similar to roulette in France. The player bets on one of
thirty-six figures placed like chessmen on a sumptuous cloth. The
figures were painted to resemble the war's generals. To curry favor, I resisted the temptation to bet on Napoleon, who I knew was
the best of the lot, and wagered instead on Austria's Archduke
Charles. I electrified my audience (I am a Franklin man, have generated sparks at parties, and enjoy the fashionable metaphor) by
luckily selecting the ball representing Charles from a leather bag.
I thus won thirty-two times my wager.

I pocketed half my 320 sequins and left the rest on the table,
in the remote chance that the next player might pluck Charles
again, making me a fortune. Alas, pulled from the bag was General Mack, who commanded in Bavaria. So I lost that bet and
turned with the rest of my winnings to brelan.

This is a game dependent on one's ability to judge an opponent's character. A "brelan" is a triplet in a game of thirty-two
cards. What makes the match intriguing is that the player with
the highest card can take all the cards in that suit, winning decisively if he captures many, or still losing if few cards of that suit
have been dealt.

The dealer also turns a final card, called *la retourne*, claimed
by the player holding a brelan or the highest card in the *retourne*'s
suit.

The skill is reading opponents to know when to bluff and
when to fold. The luck is the cards dealt.

Lord Ramsey and the countess were drunk enough to be impulsive. Across from me was the younger and watchful Countess

Nahir de Lusignan, a beauty with Astiza's dusky sculpture. She even claimed to have been born in Alexandria, where I'd captured my bride. Nahir's golden mask was trimmed to reveal attractive cheekbones, her lips were gilded, and her black hair was a complicated macramé that fell down her back. We had met at a dance when I entered the city two days before, and playing her was a dance as well.

Our fifth player was Baron Wolfgang Richter, a professional gambler of intimidating reputation as cardsharp and swordsman. He didn't drink at all, because his mouth was hidden behind a full face mask the color of bleached bone, painted with a devilish black grin. When Richter shuffled, the staccato of cards was quick as rasping an ivory comb. He'd be my cleverest rival, I judged, and like any fierce competitor, he sought to dent my own confidence. His Apollo's head of curly, sand-colored hair suggested youth, but there was something aged and anxious in the tension of his shoulder muscles. He was a man of mysterious torment, the whispers went. His masked eyes moved as quickly as a bird's, their color the dark of a gun barrel. Then they settled on me.

"Welcome, Monsieur Franklin. I hope you can afford to lose."

CHAPTER 2

I understand you're Bohemian, Wolfgang."

"My friends call me Wolf, Monsieur Franklin. Prussian on my father's side and Czech on my mother's." As was the custom of the higher classes in Europe, we were speaking French, the universal language of travel. "But people of our sort are really men of the world, are we not?"

"I've crossed the Atlantic several times." Best to remain vague.

"The truly sophisticated person is stateless," said the marchesa. "I've danced in St. Petersburg and worshipped in Madrid."

"And which did you find more satisfying?" Lord Ramsey asked.

"Drinking champagne in Strasbourg and bedding a Polish lancer in Berlin." She brayed, leaning forward to give him a good view.

"Did you have a role in your famous relative's experiments?"

Richter asked me. "Franklin was Prometheus, was he not? Lightning from heaven?"

Clever as the devil, I'd judge, though by the time I served Ben, he napped, farted, and recycled tiresome stories like any old man. "No. His genius didn't extend to my bloodline."

"Yet you're a traveler on an intellectual mission?" The baron cocked his head slightly. The full mask must be stifling. "To bring Old World wisdom to the New? What do you wish to look at?"

"Ruins, I think. We've little history in the United States. I understand there are glorious castles in Bohemia. Dungeons and prisons, too."

"In decay." Richter gave a dismissive wave. "Prague itself is a beautiful city, however, and scholarly." His dark eyes studied me as if I were a specimen. "Old books, dusty relics, medieval secrets. Narrow alleys and secret rooms."

"Hadn't thought of going there," I said, lying. Could Richter be of help on my quest? Dangerous men have uses. I wished I could see his face.

"And you're an electrician like your famed relative?" Nahir asked.

"A dabbler." I liked the excuse to turn and look at her. "I experiment."

"And what do you seek, scholar?" She gave me a promotion I decided to accept.

"Beauty."

The marchesa snorted.

"I do research myself," Richter said. "Civilization has forgotten half what it once knew. We can relearn secrets from the ancient past."

"Boatloads of books go to your Ca' Rezzonico," Ramsey put in. "Old histories full of legend and speculation, I hear. It's an imposing address, Baron. And a big one."

"I'm merely renting. And I have the leisure to read."

"You travel alone, Monsieur Franklin?" Nahir persisted. I'm wary when strangers are too inquisitive. And susceptible when they're too pretty.

"Temporarily."

"Intriguing to meet an American in Venice in time of war," Richter went on. "But then I've heard stories of Americans caught up in European affairs. Spies, diplomats, and soldiers of fortune, scattered from Moscow to Paris. Some are dashing, others disloyal. They flit to conspiracies like moths to flames."

"I can't imagine they're very effective." By Thor's hammer, had this gambler somehow heard of the rascal Ethan Gage? I'm at the dimmest edge of notoriety, but he could have heard my name at gambling tables, as I'd heard of his. "We Americans are rustics when it comes to European politics. And your allegiance, Baron?" Too many questions to me, so I'd volley to him.

"To live life to the fullest, by enriching myself on the follies of my companions." His fingers spat cards like seeds.

"You wish the world to be normal, Lord Ramsey?" Nahir said, referring to his earlier comment. "Whatever for?"

"So that every man know his place, and all the bloody head chopping and church sacking and mob fighting of the past fifteen years finally stop. When radicals rise, it means chaos. Is that not so, Baron Richter?"

"It means opportunity, my lord, which is why I'm less certain than you that Bonaparte will lose. The Corsican has risen to become emperor of the French, so I see no reason why he cannot become emperor of us all, if we're not careful."

"Absurd. His marshals are tradesmen and smugglers. His foreign minister is a fallen bishop. His wife is a whore."

"Ante," Nahir reminded.

There was a steady clink of metal.

Ramsey addressed me. "I suppose, Franklin, that you believe in mob democracy, given your American heritage."

"We prefer to call them citizens," I replied. "If wars were won by hereditary rank, we wouldn't have won independence from England. Nor would Napoleon have won the 1797 and 1800 campaigns here in Italy."

"Touché," said Nahir.

"Those were skirmishes," Ramsey countered, "and my point is the courage and character that comes from birth and training. You see it on the stud farm, and you see it on the battlefield. The Austrians and Russians have entire brigades of counts and princes."

"I have a female acquaintance that preaches much as you do," I said, thinking of Catherine Marceau and her treacheries. "However, she prefers a winner and has joined Bonaparte."

"If the Prussians join us, Bonaparte is finished."

"You may pick up your hand," Nahir said. Her masked eyes regarded me over the fan of her cards. Damnation, how she reminded me of Astiza! I hadn't had wifely company for nearly a year, meaning my heart ached with loneliness and another organ stirred from temptation. I straightened instinctively, even while ordering my body to behave itself. "Prussia has not joined," she added.

"They're stalling to pick the winner," Richter said. "They lust for Hanover, and can get it from either the French or British."

"And you're stalling, too, Wolf?" the marchesa asked impatiently, gesturing to the pot in the middle of the table.

"Ten more sequins."

My hand was weak, so I folded. I matched the bets of the next hand and lost anyway, and folded again on a third. I was down to thirty-five sequins. Ruinous, as I've said.

But I'd learned that Ramsey trusted capricious luck, Nahir was cautious, the marchesa pursed her lips slightly when she received high cards, and Richter was competitive to a fault. The deal passed to him.

"It's not your night, American."

"The game can turn on a card."

He dealt me three, of which the highest was a ten. I tried to catch him cheating. He tilted his mask as if to taunt, fingers hummingbird fast. His skill was the barrier between my wife and me, so I set up my bluff.

I bet with deliberate abandon, the others viewed me warily, and they laughed when I took a modest pot with my ten.

"Well played, Yankee Doodle!" Ramsey boomed.

Now I had some breathing room.

The baron's voice was even. "Can we double the ante?" His mask fixed on me. "I like to play until I'm rich or bankrupt."

"I prefer to stop when I'm rich."

The laugh had an edge. Each hand was a battle in a greater game of war. I bluffed with a triplet.

Even though my hand was strong, I allowed a blink when I viewed it, so quick that I couldn't be certain anyone saw it. A finger trembled until I willed it still. I shifted, almost imperceptibly. The others kept their heads down, masks shielding, but we were all studying one another. They were hounds with a scent, gauging American impetuosity, and when I bet big, they followed to crush me.

I was Alexander, I was Hannibal, I was Caesar. When the sequins were a shoal, I revealed my three of a kind, pounced on *la retourne*, raided for my suit of coins, and swept in my winnings like a pirate. Ramsey managed a dismayed laugh, the marchesa moaned, and the baron conceded a nod of respect. Nahir studied me with her great dark eyes through a visor of gold with silk headdress like a turban, lips parting just enough to give me a glimpse of teeth and tongue.

Still not enough. Besides, I didn't want to just beat Richter, I wanted to crush him. Any conceit challenges my own.

So I lost the next hand, folded on two more, and lost yet again.

It was the darkest time of night, my family as distant as stars. I was still laying my trap while trying to avoid the snares of the others. I deliberately gambled away half my winnings, Richter recovered his loss, and the other three won enough to keep them in the game. There were shouts of consternation and sharp laughter. Brelan is as capricious as life.

"We're evenly matched," Richter commented, more generously than he had to. "You've the skill of a Florentine banker, Mr. Franklin. I hope not the ruthlessness."

"Never been to Florence."

"London? Paris?"

I was tiring of his persistent curiosity. "Yes."

"For business?"

"Opportunities."

"Do you know the French emperor? I hear he's a useful patron."

"Certainly not," I said, lying again. "A minister here or there. Tedious trade matters, mostly. Talleyrand and the like."

"The grand chamberlain! The lame bishop is one of the most powerful men in Europe. If there is one thing the French foreign minister is not, it is tedious."

"But ghastly," said the marchesa.

"As is the Corsican," Lord Ramsey put in.

Talleyrand's odd stub of a sword dug into my back again, reminding me of the need to end this interrogation. I'd tentatively joined the foreign minister's cause, and then fled with his cloak. I'll send cutthroats in competition, he'd warned.

I upped the ante, raised again as the bets circled, and began to force a dizzying pile of sequins, ducats, guineas, and talers onto the felt.

"He's bluffing again," the countess scoffed.

"Unless he isn't," Lord Ramsey said, peering at my three unturned cards as if concentration would make them transparent.

I shifted a shoulder, as subtly as a woman in a ballroom gown. I wanted them to deduce I was nervous, but about the size of the pot, not my hand.

Nahir folded, giving me a flutter of her lashes. "I'm afraid my resources have become thin."

"You are conservative, madame."

"Prudent. And realistic." Her pile was indeed small.

I am ever gallant. "I can advance a small loan."

The marchesa snickered.

"I would be reckless to take it, Mr. Franklin."

"I'm a lenient creditor, having been a debtor myself. Your beauty as collateral, perhaps. Should I need to collect, you will remove your mask."

"Only my mask?"

"I am a gentleman."

"Bloody fool, sounds to me," Ramsey rumbled.

But Nahir accepted, they bet, and I matched.

Ramsey raised—"There's a broadside!"—and then Richter followed, his mask and manner as imperturbable as the Sphinx. I prayed they couldn't hear my heart hammering. I matched again, but this time with hesitation quick as a candle flicker. No one saw it. Or did they? My goal was to confuse them.

The marchesa tapped her cards contemplatively. The baron was still as a cat.

"Damn it all, this game has gotten too rich." Ramsey folded.

"No. The American is a fraud," the marchesa said. "He's not who he says he is." Yet there was a tremor of doubt. She bet again, and then the baron, and then Nahir with my money, and then I raised the stakes once more. My wife and son were in that pile of coins. I didn't hide my sweat. You could see the sheen on my neck.

The marchesa cupped her hand around the last of her sequins. "I want to challenge you, Mr. Franklin. But I can't afford it, unless you want to loan to me as well."

"I'm afraid my resources are stretched to the breaking point." My voice was so even that it could have leveled a beam.

Her mouth set. "By the young."

I shrugged.

Nahir sat back, too. "I cannot take your generosity anymore, either, Monsieur Franklin. This is the richest hand I've ever played. I'll pay my debt with my face, as you've demanded."

"Only should I win. And only when you're comfortable doing so."

Richter stretched, glanced at the casino clocks that never ticked, and considered his cards. "It's growing late, or at least I'm growing tired. You're forcing everyone out. So I think I'll end this game now." He matched and then raised once more, his bearing poised as a duelist's. "One way or another, we'll see what you're made of, Franklin."

The marchesa leaned back from the table as if it were hot, fanning herself. Her cleavage was damp.

The battle was at a crisis, and it was time to commit my strategic reserve. "And you, Baron." I shoved in every sequin, my fingers jumping ever so slightly, except one I pocketed for luck.

Wolf Richter studied me. I was stone, I was vacuum, I was the collapse of time. My breath was the only sound in the room.

"You give every sign of bluffing, which means you aren't," the baron tried. "Unless you are."

"It's your turn to bet."

The air was cloying. His hand strayed to his depleted pile, my pulse thudded, the game was up . . .

And then it paused, trembling. "Damn you. I've still got money."

Silence.

"You fold?" Nahir demanded.

"Perhaps." It was bitter. His hand hovered. It did not tremble. "But I'm tired of this. I match." He shoved the rest in. "Let's see your artillery."

I froze.

"Monsieur Franklin?" Nahir demanded.

My highest was a nine.

"Brelan," Richter said. He laid down a triplet.

Had he cheated? I told myself he must have. Yet it was I who'd recklessly bluffed. My ploy had failed, and my mission was bankrupt. I felt dizzy. My rival hauled with both arms, the money to find my wife and child receding like a tide.

"A loan to keep playing?" I was ashamed of my plaintive tone.

His reply was cold. "I'm no banker, and have no need to see your beauty, monsieur. I suspect I already know the kind of man you truly are."

The others regarded me with pity from behind their masks. I stood, swaying from defeat and confusion. "Meaning?"

"That you're an American who might win in Philadelphia but can't prevail in Venice." He turned to dismiss me. "Lord Ramsey, will you deal?"

New cards arced across the table.

I bowed, awkwardly. "Ladies. Lords."

They ignored me entirely.

I departed with my mask on, threading through a casino that smelled of cognac, sweat, and pipe smoke. I hailed a gondola. The canal stank.

The boatman demanded I show him payment before departure. "You fools gamble it all away."

I gave him my last coin.

Why had Richter asked so many questions? How had he crushed me with such assurance? Did he know I was Ethan Gage? He'd mentioned my hometown of Philadelphia, which I had not. Yet once he had emptied my purse, he ignored me.

"Signore!"

A footman hurried from the casino to hand me a note written by a male hand, titled in English. "From a gentleman to a cousin."

Ramsey. He'd dabbed it with sealing wax. I sat by the craft's charcoal brazier, pulled off my mask, broke the seal, and read as we rowed into the canal and passed under the casino's red lamp.

"His brelan included a card I'd already discarded."

So Richter had cheated. I was embarrassed not to have caught him at it. And annoyed that Ramsey hadn't the courage to accuse him openly.

"Caution. He is deadly."

Not to a man who is already dead, I thought.

CHAPTER 3

Theft is not theft when one steals something that has already been stolen. But Richter's mansion, Ca' Rezzonico, was guarded like a fortress.

The gondola took my last coin, so I experienced the humiliation of removing my meager belongings through a window of my inn to escape payment. Included were some medicinal supplies I'd accumulated in my brief imposture as a doctor, which I now intended to put to ruthless use. I napped in an alcove in the Campo San Polo until being kicked awake at dawn by a member of La Forsa, the local police, who shouted something in Italian that translated roughly, I believe, into "damned foppish sot." I stood with as much dignity as I could muster. My silk cape and tricorne had kept me from freezing, but I needed something more practical than gaming clothes. So I sold my fancy attire at the Burano market, bought a plain dark traveling outfit, and had enough left over for breakfast and dinner. My curious sword hilt remained tied to my back.

I had planned to start journeying north to hunt for my family by now. Instead I was spending precious time salvaging fortune and pride.

The afternoon was spent making a small profit more shamelessly than I prefer, playing *les trois perdants*, which I'd learned in Paris. It's a three-card confidence game, and I used a deck I'd peevishly pocketed in Casino dei Nobili. The goal is to shuffle the three cards on a table—I used a tray on my crossed legs, "borrowed" from a taverna—and convince the mark that he can spot the ruse and win. By sleight of hand, you trick the victim into following the wrong card from the beginning. The farce depends on the player's greed.

I beat one man and gave him his money back, in order to persuade him to join me as a partner to help distract new players. I did the same with a second, and then took profit from the next dozen men and two women. When the growing crowd finally summoned the courage to accuse us of cheating, I shouted "La Forsa!" and everyone scattered from imaginary police.

I'm not proud of this devilry, but I needed to buy a few props to liberate my purse from the cardsharp Richter.

The mansion of Ca' Rezzonico is at a hairpin turn of the Grand Canal, its three-story pillared facade having a view down both arms. The edifice is grand as a London bank and white as frosting, festooned with balustrades, rosettes, plump cherubs, plumed knights, palm fronds, watchful lions, and Venetian notables no one remembers. The mansion proclaimed ancestral fortune spent on hired taste. A troop of black-caped guards made it forbidding. There were at least two poltroons on the roof, two at the entry, and two more pairs on gondolas in the canal, but a full count was surprisingly difficult. Rather than strut in bright costumes like Swiss Guards, these sentries had the curious ability to blend in and out of the shadows as if temporarily invisible.

Richter was no ordinary tourist. And why hadn't he shown his face? Did I know him? His voice had been unfamiliar.

Getting into Ca' Rezzonico would be easier than getting out, so I contemplated escape while drinking a glass of wine in the winter sunlight of Campo San Angelo. I noticed coffins leaving the adjacent cathedral, recalled a policy imposed by Napoleon, and got a macabre idea. There was a convent to one side of the church and, I noted, a brothel to the other: convenience all around. I visited the bordello to access the roof, tipping a whore for the privilege. Stepping out on a sea of red tiles, I mapped my strategy and liberated a clothesline. Then I waited past midnight so that most of Ca' Rezzonico's inhabitants would be asleep.

Moon, stars, and lights coated the city with silver. Venice has none of the experimental lamps of London and Paris, but torches reflect off the canals and candles glow in the windows of decaying palaces. Gondola lanterns are fireflies, and violins sigh across the canals.

It's much easier to be invited into a fortress than to breach it, so with my three-card winnings I had purchased an empty keg, a wine-spotted vintner's sash, a low slouch hat to hide my features, a pewter flask, and passage on a gondola. I was rowed to Richter's palace at the witching hour and sprang onto its stone quay as if expected. "A delivery for your master."

The sentries had cloths pulled around their lower faces like Arab bandits and displayed the pompous hostility that lackeys rehearse everywhere.

"At this hour, tavern keeper?"

"And a tip for you." Dogs will quiet for meat, and guards for a florin.

A ground-floor pòrtego led to the inner courtyard, the house rising high as a ship's mast. My good friend Tom Jefferson dreams of an egalitarian society of yeoman farmers, but he takes architectural inspiration from European monuments to brutal economic inequality. The rich fantasize, their architects envision, and laborers mine, log, and mortar. Beyond the Grand Canal's palaces are teeming tenements, flea-infested wineshops, beggars like herds of sheep, families twelve to a room, and cripples displaying stumps and leprosy in hopes of pity.

I asked a butler for the kitchen, slipped into a pantry, and watched out its door until the mansion's central marble staircase momentarily emptied. Then I galloped up to the first floor under a hanging lantern big enough for a flagship's stern. I strode boldly through an empty ballroom, its chandeliers gold and the ceiling as gaudy as a queen's coach. Half-naked goddesses cavorted between whipped-cream clouds, boxed in turn by moldings made of noble coats of arms, all of it requiring a neck ache to be admired. Since my boots clacked on the waxed parquet, I slowed and pondered. If Richter could afford these surroundings, why was he playing cards in a shabby casino like Nobili? And where did his money come from?

All was quiet. I passed through red, blue, and green salons, overcast by a perfect storm of cherubs, angels, chariots, sunbeams, and flapping robes. The cacophony made me cringe, as if a rearing stallion or half-draped nymph might accidentally drop on my head. Priceless Chinese vases, ebony African statues, and inlaid Italian furniture dared me to break them. Persian carpets were soft as moss, and divans were embroidered with silk. None of it looked especially comfortable, but then that's not the point.

I jumped when a sentry challenged me from behind. He was wearing a uniform the color of the room and blended with his background as skillfully as a deer.

"Who are you, shopkeeper? Where are you going?" He accosted me softly, his paste-white face blank, but there was menace in the way he'd materialized, with arms cocked like an ape's. He also wore a rapier.

"Baron Richter, fool." Always reply to a challenge with arrogance. At the mention of Wolf's name, the guard's eye flickered to the paneling of a sitting room beyond. I guessed there might be a hidden door there. I gave the man a contemptuous look up and down. "You're dressed as wallpaper?"

"The baron has no need for a tradesman in the middle of the night."

"But perhaps he has for a purveyor of pleasure. In this keg is the ambrosia of the gods, ordered by your employer at great expense, with extra offered if I climbed out of bed at this godless hour to deliver it. You interfere?"

"You don't sound like a wine merchant."

"Wine is puddle water compared with what I have on my shoulder." I didn't have to feign my impatience, but I pretended to great weariness. "Here, try a drink if you must. I have charity for the slow-witted."

He scowled, but he had a soldier's familiarity with abuse, and I was relief from the boredom of standing guard. He took my pewter flask warily, glancing about lest a supervisor see him drinking.

"A big swallow, to allow the flavors to come through."

He nodded, threw his head back, drank, squinted, and grimaced. "What in Hades? It tastes like piss!"

"Swish it in your mouth, like wine."

The idiot did so. Then his eyes bulged and he reeled, staggering backward. I'd expected a sentry, and needed something to put one on his back. The guard opened his mouth to bellow, and nothing came out, since his tongue had turned to stone. I helped things along with a rap to his temple from the butt of my broken broadsword, and then graciously helped him down.

My Moroccan spice peddler had sold me more than opium seeds. The hairs of the Mediterranean's processionary caterpillar are more venomous than nettles and cause tissues to swell almost to the point of suffocation. I'd bought a snuff tin's worth of the creatures, carried them ashore in Venice, and added their remains to some limoncello. The man gasped blindly, incapacitated but alive. I left him to it.

A minute's investigation revealed that the paneling he'd eyed indeed had a concealed door, its latch behind some books on a case. This led to a secret spiral stone staircase that climbed to a floor with lower ceilings and tighter rooms. I wound down a passageway to an apartment that would overlook the canal, hearing romantic moaning and chuffing within. Normally I respect privacy, but not when I've been cheated. I picked the lock with a twist of a copper nail I'd brought, slipped inside, latched the heavy entry behind me, and quietly braced a heavy chair against it. Then I crept.

A sitting room first, and then a boudoir in blue, with Chinese basin and feminine combs. The bedchamber beyond was where the noise was coming from.

Two candles and the coals of a fireplace cast yellow light on a sumptuous bedroom with maple armoire and marble mantel. My eye was drawn to the four-poster canopied bed. Richter galloped against Countess Nahir's well-sculpted derriere, the baron still dressed in evening shirt and silk breeches, unbuttoned only for the part in vigorous use. Must be in a terrible hurry, which is seldom a good idea. Even more oddly, he still wore his ivory-colored mask with its painted smirk, giving a mechanical look to the proceedings. Nonetheless, the lady's translucent chemise was pulled up to her waist, and she matched the rhythm just as lustily, with encouraging noises. Lady Nahir clearly was not waiting for her husband's return from his travels. A bedside candle silhouetted the glory of her form.

The tableau was arousing, but not as much as the small iron chest I spotted on an inlaid table. It was just the kind of treasure box to contain Richter's cheatings from the game. I'd hoped the baron would simply be asleep, but the lovers seemed preoccupied enough for me to retrieve my share anyway.

So I advanced on all fours, kneeled at the table, eased out the old sword, and used the jagged edge of its broken blade to jimmy the latch. The lid opened to a pleasing pile of gold and silver coins. I began easing the plunder into my empty leather purse, heart hammering as its weight increased.

Alas, Richter and Nahir were people of the casino, their ears attuned to the clink of money. She swiveled her head to gasp warning, her lovely hair flying like a flag, and the baron quickly disengaged. "Like a fly to sweets," Richter said calmly. He pulled a pistol from under a pillow and rapped a bell on the wall with the muzzle. It gonged with doom. "I'd almost given up waiting for you, Gage." He hauled up his breeches with one hand and pointed the gun at me with the other.

I had frozen in surprise. This Bohemian noble knew who I really was? How?

Boots pounded on the parquet below.

Richter yanked off his mask to take better aim, and it was then that I truly started. No wonder he made love in disguise! Beneath the covering was one of the most hideous faces I'd ever seen.

Someone had melted it. His cheeks and lips were a mass of scars, as if ravaged by acid, a hole in one spot giving a glimpse of a tooth. The color was an angry red, and one eye squinted against the pull of scar tissue.

"I think you will share everything you know," he said, face muscles straining to enunciate past the damage. The man was a monster, and had set a trap.

But so had I.

CHAPTER 4

Astiza

The language of angels is Enochian, and the language of gods is the stars. I cannot see the sky's fire from my alchemical laboratory, its vaulted stone ceiling the weight of divine silence. I've heard nothing from Ethan in nearly a year. Our son, Horus, is pale and withdrawn, his hands pitifully wrapped in rags. We are prisoners, and Harry's unhappiness is my greatest torture. I keep us alive by agreeing to do Satan's work, mixing brews that promise gold and immortality for my captors. Penelope held off her suitors until her husband Odysseus's return by asking them to wait until she completed her weaving, and then unspooled her progress each evening. I delay by skittering globules of silver mercury and glints of copper to conjure a miracle, and then concoct slag at midnight to convince them of another failure. They cannot kill me until I succeed. Yet each experimental mistake makes them surly. Our cell stinks of fumes, our eyes strain from inadequate candlelight, and our joints ache from damp.

Alchemists John Dee and Edward Kelley received revelation from the angels in the language of the patriarch Enoch, great-grandfather of Noah. Enoch learned it when he was lifted up to tour heaven. There are books in my prison written with the angelic script, such as *Mystic Sevenfold Rulership, The 48 Angelic Keys,* and the *Book of Earthly Knowledge, Help and Victory.* Their meaning, alas, remains a riddle to all but the angels. I'm ensnared in webs of mystery, my only hope that pursuit of the rose will lead me through its labyrinth of petals to truth at the bud. I'm devising an escape but need the help of my husband. Ethan, where are you?

Has my quest for understanding led me to earthly damnation? Or was it merely my impatience to flee Napoleon's coronation at Notre Dame without waiting for my mate, thinking I could discover a bargaining chip that would protect us all? He doesn't know that when searching the bedroom of Catherine Marceau in Paris, I found a cache of her romance novels, that I brought three of them in my bag to the coronation at Notre Dame, and that they made a fine weapon to sling against the head of the giant policeman Pasques in order to escape. It was the first useful service Catherine did for my family. The blow gave Horus and me time to run from the cathedral with the letters of recommendation that Talleyrand had given me. The French minister wanted us to search for the fabled Brazen Head.

Now I kneel on flagstones, palms on the rock, to feel the Goddess mother. But the womb of the earth is only half of what sustains us. I'm buried from the sky, and thus robbed of male power. All things are dual, and burial keeps me half a priestess.

My jailers know this. I beg for a tower. They fear me too much to allow one. If I don't cooperate, I'll be tied to a stake and burned. Or so they threaten. And then the dwarf eyes my son . . .

My name is Astiza of Alexandria, priestess of Isis and Athena, devotee of the white Madonna and the black, seeker of Astarte, Artemis, Cybele, Ishtar, Mary, Sophia, and Freya. My husband is Pan and Vulcan, Mercury and Mars, as dissatisfied as Siddhartha and as redeemable as Augustine. I despair for his soul and yet miss him desperately. I'm the white rose, he the red. All these deities are but a hundred shades of the One Truth. I believe I exist to seek, but which revelation? Ambition, vanity, and curiosity are the curses visited upon our family, and lost secrets are fuel to our fire. Wisdom, wisdom! How I wish I could truly achieve it.

A monster I nearly loved has imprisoned us in a mine of Bohemia: punishment for my desires. I've sought foreknowledge and dangerous companionship, and now I pay the price.

Because I've promised my captors alchemical magic to spare my son, I have magic books in abundance. In the margins of the *Picatrix*, the *Lemegeton*, the *Key of Solomon*, and the *Dragon Rouge*, I retain my sanity by writing this account of how I came to be here. In remembering my husband, perhaps I can conjure him like the necromancer I'm supposed to be. He strides to save us, knight in armor! This is my fantasy. The reality is that he may be oceans away, or have no idea where we are, or have been seduced. He's a good man, but imperfect. Like me.

I'm convinced Ethan lives. I'd know in my heart if he died. But I no longer know if he seeks us. I shouldn't doubt him, but he has an eye for other women. I think about this because I've strayed with my soul.

What really torments us is our own conscience.

Ethan and I were separated when my son and I fled the treachery of the Comtesse Catherine Marceau, who had shared our apartment in Paris. My husband had just promised us not to part, but then Talleyrand wanted consultation, and Catherine promised Ethan would quickly return, and the brute policeman Pasques towered like Goliath. Instead of trusting my instincts, I was foolish enough to agree. Time dragged on. Harry and I were pulled deeper into the shadows of the cathedral. More police materialized. As the crowd murmured like a heaving sea at the appearance of Napoleon and Joséphine, I realized we'd been betrayed and my husband was about to be arrested. I decided to flee east, which French authorities would least expect, and count on Ethan to make his own escape.

We'd learned that the scholar Albertus Magnus had built a mechanical man, or "android," in the thirteenth century to foretell the future. In desperation I decided I'd find this machine by myself and use its power to protect my family. Or at least use its value to bargain! Hubris.

I remember the smoke of censers rising in the winter sunbeams in Notre Dame, and the thud of celebratory cannon, when I finally realized that while we thought Catherine was an English spy, she was actually a French one. She had fooled us from the beginning, helping to betray royalist conspiracies to Napoleon, and wanting my husband for herself. Ethan, and the Brazen Head.

So while Catherine moved forward to watch Ethan's arrest, I silently took Harry's hand and backed into the alcove chapel of St. Michael at Notre Dame, having learned in my studies that a secret spiral stair behind its altar led to a crypt below. There's no exit from this room of tombs, but our disappearance caused momentary confusion. When men scattered to find us, we managed to creep up, battle past Pasques, slip out a rearward door, climb the wall of the archbishop's garden, cross the pont, dash to the eastern end of the Île Saint-Louis, and drop unseen onto a barge laboring up the Seine. At midnight, using light snow as a cloak, we slipped ashore at Neuilly-sur-Marne and hid, shivering, in a convent graveyard.

For the next three days Harry and I walked east, watchful for patrols. We finally had the opportunity to join a traveling circus of acrobats and clowns, a migratory example of the ring shows that Philip Astley had organized across Europe. We could hide amid its peculiar circle of characters and animals. I told its leaders that I was a sorceress who could cast fortunes, and because I was pretty, starving, and Egyptian—since Napoleon's expedition, the world is mad for all things Egyptian—they took me on. We played Christmas carnivals at Strasbourg and then, on the third day of January 1805, slipped across the Rhine.

What had become of Ethan, I'd no idea.

I feel the need in this crabbed journal to explain my affection for my husband. Ethan Gage is a man of action, a traveler, dreamer, and, in his own words, a climber, drawn to people of power or notoriety. He has the restlessness of men. I am reclusive, scholarly, and judicious, with a mother's caution and a woman's need for home. I also know, in ways he does not, how alike we are.

My husband resolves to find rest for us, but that's not really what we seek. I, too, enjoy new places. The only difference is that I savor the journey as much as the destination, while he imagines an ending. There are no endings, only steps.

Both of us are curious. He was my liberator in Egypt, and the first and only man I truly loved. Ethan can be rash and shallow, but also greathearted and thrilling, even dangerous, a frightening hero when unleashed. His strong hands make me shiver, and his odd insights make me laugh. We're the light and the dark of the moon, two sides of the same coin, Jupiter and Venus. I reform him; he inspires me.

Harry and I left the circus in February. My inquiries in Germany took me to castles, crypts, town hall records, and the scriptoriums of monasteries. I studied books such as Comenius's *Labyrinth of the World*. As I journeyed east, I felt I was falling back in time and deeper into mystery. The turreted castles became craggier and ill repaired, blank windows looking over a wintry landscape with blind eyes. Broken towers reached like scrabbling fingers. The season was dim, night early, shadows long, snow spotting the fields, and the rush-and-tallow lights of rude cottages were faint as misted stars. Bohemia seemed older yet, a land of forest magic and cave revelations, its rude carts creaking ominously as they crept on miserable tracks. Ravens wintered on the branches. Wolves bayed in the woods. Harry clung to me like an infant. He misses his father. He needs a father.

The stem that I followed was the rose. A dried rose led me to our informant Palatine in Paris, rose windows dominate Notre Dame, the spy Rose befriended Ethan, and the sacred symbology of the rose guided the mystic Christian Rosenkreutz. At the Bohemian town of Český Krumlov, looped by a river and protected by a castle growing out of a cliff, the symbol of the ruling families is the five-petal rose. This is the symbol of the five wounds of Christ and the five elements that make up the universe: earth, air, fire, water, and the fifth element, the life force itself. In geometric terms it is synonymous with the five-sided pentagram. The flower was everywhere embossed on walls and ceilings.

I took this as a sign.

In a world in which many cannot read and write, symbols are how scholars communicate with the illiterate. Every church is a picture book, its story told with stained glass windows, saintly sculptures, and paintings. Every coat of arms tells a patriotic story. Addresses in Bohemia are pictures, so one resides at the House of the Boar or the House of the Golden Stag or the House of the Three Hearts, its sign painted over the door. No symbol is more potent than the rose.

A rosebush sprang from the blood of Adonis, and another from the drip of blood from Jesus' wounds. In the unfolding petals is the expanding cosmos. The six-petal rose stands for love, seven for inclusion and perfection, and eight for rebirth. The thorns are life's obstacles on the way to grace. Every culture reveres this flower, and every lover presents it as adoration. Rose is the first name of the French empress, although Napoleon prefers Joséphine. Cleopatra carpeted her bedchamber ankle-deep with petals for the Roman conqueror Antony. The flower's quick withering is symbolic of the fleetness of time, and so the Roman Rosalia was a feast of the dead. The labyrinth of petals was a sign of secrecy, so a confidential Roman meeting was marked by a rose over the door, the confidences said to be sub-rosa.

Christian Rosenkreutz combined the rose with the cross, meaning he combined knowledge with faith, and beauty with the inevitability of decay. In Paris we stole the crown of thorns, and now I seek an alchemical marriage in my prison. Chemists believe that uniting light and dark, thorn and flower, will bring unity and perfection. So I felt that the carved rosettes set in the castle at Český Krumlov, coat of arms of the House of Vitek, were a sign of Rosenkreutz.

The Viteks, who built Krumlov Castle, were succeeded by the Rosenberg family in the sixteenth century, their name meaning "Mountain of Roses." Surely this was no coincidence. Now the rambling edifice is inhabited by the Schwarzenbergs, and they had heard of my fortune-telling in Germany and sent an invitation. I presented myself as a seer and expert on the tarot, suspecting that, like many aristocrats, the Schwarzenbergs are bored and seek distraction. I made my way with Harry up the cobbled town street to the rambling castle, courtyard succeeding courtyard. Duke and Duchess Josef and Paulina Schwarzenberg are patrons of the arts, alarmed but intrigued by the rise of Napoleon, and fascinated by modern reports of new inventions and curiosities.

They waited for me to tell them what I wanted to know myself. The future.

CHAPTER 5

It was just as well Astiza wasn't in Venice, given my need to sneak into bedchambers, make arrangements at brothels, and resort to aggrieved theft. In fact, considering my wife's prolonged absence, I'd have preferred to spend more time admiring the Countess Nahir, since I'd been celibate for nearly a year and was addled as a stag in autumn. Not that I could justify a liaison, particularly one with a lover of my new enemy, though on the other hand my wife would never know, but still, I'd taken vows, however, a man can't be blamed for looking, yet it was foolish to risk my marriage when I was about to save it, though it had been a bit of a slapdash ceremony on the deck of an American naval vessel and my, how the light silhouetted Nahir's form . . .

The baron's steady aim cut short my moral debate. As he cocked the hammer, I did the only thing that occurred and charged the four-poster, breaking the frame and bringing the silk canopy down on the interrupted lovers.

The pistol went off, but missed.

I went back to scooping up my money, listening to the shouts of Richter's agents hurrying from below. I'd half-finished reassembling my fortune when a rapier—did the baron keep an arsenal under his pillow?—slit the canopy fabric. The hideously scarred man struggled upright, waving his blade with one hand and hauling up his breeches with the other. He was a terrible sight, in more ways than one. Half-naked Nahir was shrieking like a ninny but had the wits to purposely crawl out from under the other side, making for the door to the boudoir and sitting room.

Someday I'm going to find a quieter way to make a living.

"It's no good, American," the baron said. "We knew that spymaster and scoundrel Ethan Gage, the most hated man in Europe, would come this way to get to his family. And that his own groveling greed would snare him."

Richter's men began hammering on the apartment door.

"The name is Franklin," I insisted. I abandoned the purse and wrenched at one of the toppled posts of the bed, ripping it free of fabric and turning it into a crude lance. "You've obviously got me confused with someone else, because I'm quite popular everywhere I go."

"No, you're the sharpshooter and electrician Ethan Gage. We've been expecting you in Venice, and we are going to appropriate the broken sword hilt you stole from the grand chamberlain of France." He nodded at the relic resting on the table. So Talleyrand's antique rubbish was actually somehow valuable. Interesting. I'd been using it like a shop tool.

Richter gave a leap from the tangle, landed like a cat, fastened a strategic button, turned sideways, and lifted the rapier: en garde. The poise was impressively athletic, but what the devil had happened to his face? His jaw was a wretched pudding.

"The hilt was given, not stolen," I corrected. "Not that I have any idea what you're talking about." I raised the bedpost like a quarterstaff. En garde yourself.

"Talleyrand told his agents the hilt would identify you, and one of his agents was persuaded to tell us."

He lunged, and I parried with the post. We circled the table where the gold waited, the baron on one side and me on the other. At least he'd called me spymaster and electrician, which was better than dawdler and mercenary. And I had been a spy, if not a particularly effective one. But spies are required to deny their profession; it's part of the job. So I gave it a try. "I bought a piece of junked weaponry from a rogue in Batavia. Or was it Brussels? His name was Gage, now that I recall."

Richter thrust, and his blade tipped the table and threw purse, hilt, and gold onto the carpet. He grinned, or tried to. Parts of his lips were burnt through, and the injury had settled into a permanent grimace. I slashed at him with the bedpost and he hopped back.

"What the devil happened to you?" I asked.

"When you learn that, you'll understand your doom." Another advance, my parry, and then a sharp thrust of wood toward his shoulder to make him spring back yet again.

"The injury has addled you. I'm Franklin, I say."

His sword tip cut back and forth like a darting hummingbird. Elegant as a dancer, despite his disfigurement. "Monsieur Gage, you left entirely too many clues at the gaming table with your prattle and your play. I'm impressed you somehow got to Venice from Cadiz, but mystified that Talleyrand ever trusted you at all."

"Never met the man. Well above my station."

We clashed again, steel against wood. He got past my guard to flick at my chin and it was my turn to jump back, but then I swung, driving the point of the rapier into the carpet and pressing until it snapped.

He cursed, backed to the fireplace, and snatched up a poker. Then he circled like a tiger. "You're supposed to be serving as Napoleon's envoy with the Combined Fleet at Cadiz but somehow deserted to Venice. Or can you be two places at once, monsieur?"

"But that proves I'm Hieronymus Franklin, does it not?" The charge of desertion was unfair, since my French ship had been shot out from under me. I did try to get Captain Lucas to sail for Gibraltar and abandon the rest of the French to the late and ferocious Admiral Nelson, but the officer had too much pride to listen to my realism. Now he was a British prisoner, his ship was at the bottom of the Atlantic, and I was dueling with a half-melted madman.

"Your quick arrival only proves you're slippery as an eel."

"I've heard of this Gage," I tried, "and he's a rascal and a sycophant. Not a man of character at all. By reputation he hardly manages to be at even one place, given his wandering attention, so I can't imagine how he'd conspire to be in two. No, I'm the affable Phineas Franklin, relative of the famed . . ."

"I thought you said it was Hieronymus Franklin," Nahir spoke up. The object of my momentary infatuation had come back into the bedchamber wearing a robe and armed with a blunderbuss.

I backed from both of them. "It's hard to remember in all the excitement. Please put that weapon down, my dear. I've seen those guns at work, and they're not very discriminatory."

She raised it instead. "You should have knocked."

I eyed the purse on the floor. "If the pair of you aren't working for Talleyrand, who are you?" I stalled.

"Scholars of the rose," Richter said. "Like your wife."

He knew of Astiza, too? Could this card cheat know her whereabouts? I felt panic and hope. "Not the same, surely." I had to anger them into mistakes. The men outside were thundering on the latched and barricaded door and calling for a beam to batter it down. "You're considerably deformed, Baron, and it's easier to kiss a man who still has lips, my lady."

She flushed, and aimed.

I charged Richter, holding the bedpost like a lance. He dodged my joust but tripped, knocking one of the candles into the wreckage of the bed, which caught fire. From his knees, the baron swept the poker upward. My bedpost was whacked from my hands, striking a mirror and shattering it into shards. A decanter exploded, spattering the wallpaper with wine.

"Stand still!" Nahir cried in frustration, the muzzle of her gun rotating.

I scrambled for the sword hilt and the purse.

The apartment door smashed open, men charging, so I hurled the little table in their direction, making Nahir duck. It banged into a knot of sentries, who fell into a tangle, cursing.

"That sword hilt is useless to a man as shallow and ignorant as you, Ethan Gage," Richter seethed, coming up behind to brain me with the poker.

Fortunately, Nahir had struggled back to her feet. "Surrender or I shoot!" She was inadvertently aiming at both of us. I dropped to the carpet, Richter rolled toward the burning bed, and the shotgun went off with a roar, its pellets kicking up a flurry of silk wallpaper and plaster dust.

The room was filling with smoke, and now shots came from Richter's guards crouched in the boudoir, punching holes through the fog to drill the room's paintings. The volley forced Nahir to fall to the floor as well, all three of us scrabbling like worms. So much for dignity.

"Stop shooting, you fools!" Richter cried. "Seize him!"

It was time to leave.

The sword hilt and the purse were within reach. I grabbed, jumped up, ran, and dove.

I smashed through glass and fell into blackness toward the Grand Canal, the risk of drowning superior to staying with lunatics. Shouts and shrieks followed my exit. I fell for what seemed endless seconds and hit cold, dirty, and brackish water, making a spectacular splash. I sank to the muddy bottom, pushed off, and surfaced gasping.

I looked up. The baron's form was silhouetted in the illuminated window high above, flames behind him. I glanced about. Could I find a boat?

"There!" Richter shouted, pointing. "Bring him to me!"

I turned, treading water. Gondolas were bearing down from either end of the Grand Canal. In the bow of each was a caped poltroon with a lantern that illuminated their guns, swords, and pikes.

I quickly struck out as planned for the Palazzo Grassi, across the canal from Rezzonico, a little heavy in the pockets from purse and broken hilt. The guns on the gondolas went off, bullets slapping water. My strokes accelerated.

I came to a palazzo foundation slimy with weed and surged onto its stone quay like an otter. Someone took another shot at me from Ca' Rezzonico, a bullet chipping a cherub. A skiff was moored at the palace's dock, but the pursuing gondolas were converging, preventing escape by water, and there were no walkways along the canals. With foresight, I had scouted my escape before sunset and now scaled a palace pillar as if it were a tree trunk, using memorized sculptures, balconies, and pediments for hand- and footholds. Gunfire supplied boldness.

I dragged myself onto a steep tile roof, scrambled to its ridge, and stood, swaying. Below I could hear shouts as the gondolas banged against the quay and pursuers leaped ashore. More boats were converging.

I waited like a fox to lead the posse on a merry chase. Richter said they were scholars of the rose. Were my pursuers Rosicrucians? Or had I run afoul of some new secret society I'd never heard of?

I heard shouts, pounding on doors, shutters opening, a bell

clanging, and then the rat-a-tat tramp of boots racing up stairways. Richter's allies were ascending like an army of ants.

Ahead was a jumbled sea of roofs, with the bell tower of the church of Santa Maria del Giglio half a mile distant. Another shot, this one whining past as the shooter aimed at my silhouette against the sky. I took off running on the ridge crests and didn't gauge the leap required by the first alley so much as stumble onto its yawning cavity, lunging across from sheer momentum. I crashed onto tiles on the other side, lurched up, and looked back.

Two dozen caped figures had heaved themselves over the eave of the palazzo's roof and were fanning out to pursue and surround me. Yes, this was about more than a card game.

I scampered along roof crests like a cat, pistols banging behind me. The sizzle of the shots got the blood up. I became reckless, vaulting from housing block to block like a madman. I learned to leap the canal canyons at full tilt, legs and arms pumping as I churned into space. I'd slam onto the other side, slide perilously down the clay tiles, grab desperately to arrest my fall, kick with my legs, and be off again. I could hear the crashes and grunts of agile men making the same jumps.

They were bunching into a pack, as I'd intended.

I wove in and out of narrow chimneys, feeling their heat, and made for the clothesline I'd earlier stretched between two of them. I hopped across the taut rope and kept running, my pursuers bounding like bats, with capes flaunted behind. When I paused and shouted to taunt, I drew more shots. The excitement helped them come on heedlessly.

"He's slowing! We've got him!"

They vaulted a roof ridge, came down charging, and ran full tilt into my tripwire. It snapped, breaking the clay tube of a chimney, but not before half a dozen gave a snarling shout of surprise and went tumbling over the edge, hitting a canal below with cannonball splashes.

The rest had to slow, wary of more mischief.

I spied the brothel I had earlier scouted. There was an attic dormer window hung with translucent red linen and illuminated by a candle. I eased myself in, gave a somewhat damp salute to a couple's buttocks arrested in mid-coitus, and descended narrow stairs to the salon below. It's best to be bold when striding into a place you don't belong, especially when dripping from a canal. I strutted like a rooster, complimented the madam that "the clothed bath" was as invigorating as her strumpet had promised, tossed a coin from my recovered purse, slipped out a balcony door, and scrambled across another roof to where I could clamber through the bell windows of the adjacent church tower. Ladders led down to Santa Maria del Giglio.

I was in a marble side chapel with baptismal font. I looked about, panting. A few candles illuminated a baroque facade of winged angels, fat cherubs, and draped saints. There was a brass organ mammoth enough to herald the Second Coming, and paintings the size of mainsails that showed pious people doing virtuous things. More to the point was a line of rough-hewn wood coffins to transport Venice's dead to a burial place outside the city.

The church was a way station, I'd learned, where the deceased were gathered for transfer to a cemetery island.

This, like so many things, had been Napoleon's idea. One reason perfume is so popular in Venice is the city's stink, and the odor of the insufficient lagoon circulation was made worse by the Venetian practice of disposing of corpses. There's no ground, the city being built on pilings in a marshy lagoon, and the age-old habit of interring relatives in watery cellars meant that their decay added to the rankness. The French emperor has a nose offended by anything but a battlefield, and when in Venice he ordered that cadavers be buried on the nearby island of San Michele, occupied by a monastery of the Camaldolese Order. Funeral gondolas exiled the bodies in the same way that

Parisians are reburying millions of skeletons in limestone quarries under their city.

It's modern to tuck the dead away, out of sight and out of mind.

Expediency makes strange bedfellows. I lifted the end of each coffin to gauge its weight, located the slimmest cadaver, and used Talleyrand's broken sword to pry up the lid. The young woman inside had a broken neck, her head rocking back and forth like a doll's.

"I apologize for the intimacy, signora," I whispered, "but this is for love and rescue of my family."

I climbed in beside her, not completely horrified. I've had experience with battlefield dead and catacomb bones, and have come to regard corpses as not much more remarkable, or grisly, than a side of beef. I needed escape, and this unfortunate woman, who had probably died in a fall, could provide one. I pulled down the lid as tight as I could, nestled next to my uncomplaining companion, and waited.

Whether my pursuers followed me through the brothel I know not, but a half hour later I heard surly commands, complaints from roused priests, the clank and screech of unlocking doors, and the tramp of boots. Richter's henchmen were searching the church like a herd of buffalo. Why did a Bohemian baron care so much about me and my broken sword?

Was he pursuing the Brazen Head as well?

What had burned his face?

Had lovely Nahir known my identity when she invited me to the brelan game? Yet how could I have been expected to appear in Venice?

And how had he heard of Astiza?

None of the rose scholars lingered near the coffins, feeling like most people that they'd get to one soon enough.

Eventually, they left entirely.

I actually dozed as morning came, since it had been a wearying night. Then I woke to morning Mass, the buzz and shuffle of worshippers, a funeral for one of the dearly departed, and finally the clump of cemetery workmen arriving for the day's cargo of caskets.

"Jesus Lord in Heaven, here's a fat one," they remarked as they hoisted my container. "Ate enough for two, this one did."

"He'll sink into the mud that much faster," said his companion, "and if the sinner is meant for Satan, his gluttony will hurry him on his way."

"Lid's not even tight." They hammered it down, which would have been disquieting except that I'd left the stub of sword in the joint to ensure air and a slight crack.

I was carried, swaying against my sad companion, then carted, and then floated aboard the funeral boat. Once I sensed we were seaborne, I used the broken sword to pry against my board ceiling and make escape quicker. I had to be able to resurrect faster than they could shovel.

It was winter's dusk by the time the young woman and I were lowered into her island grave. I heard the first rattle of dirt thrown on top. That was when I pried for dear life, shouting, "Wait, wait, I've come back to warn you!"

Cries of terror.

I kicked, pushed, and finally burst through the boards, standing upright in the wreckage. I peered over the lip of the grave. The cemetery was empty, the burial tools abandoned. The workers had fled.

They'd come back to find a woman, not a man, quite dead after all. And new stories would be told about the ghosts of San Michele.

Night was already falling again after this brief winter day. I hurried to the shore, stole a funeral gondola, oriented myself by Venice's lamps and the North Star, and sculled to find a trade ship to buy passage to Trieste, planning to travel by coach from there. I was damp, mud-smeared, and musty, but newly risen. It was time to rejuvenate myself as Ethan Gage and hurry on to Vienna.

A man is not completely born until he is dead, my mentor Franklin had said.

Somewhere my wife and son were in peril.

Richter's agents were in a boil behind me.

And it was past time for answers from the prophetic Brazen Head.

CHAPTER 6

Astiza

As with all grand and venerable castles, the agglomeration of architecture at Český Krumlov is haunted. Naiads guard treasure in the lake of the castle gardens. A spectral White Lady, cursed by her father for not forgiving his cruelty, wanders the halls with white gloves at cheerful events and black gloves when death nears. On the floorboards of the castle theater are bloodstains from the virgin Evelyn, an actress with unrequited love who stabbed herself to death onstage. Decades of scrubbing have yet to rinse her rose stain away.

The castle bell tower has a golden flagstaff, green copper roof, and rose-colored paint bright as a stick of candy. The rest of the castle is grayer, the centuries having produced a rambling warren perfect for aristocrats and mice. Its pride and penury are evident in the bears kept captive in its dry moat. The castle's Czech families have claimed relation to the prestigious Ursini family of Italy, *ursus* is the Latin word for "bear," and the beasts are imprisoned to bolster the pretense. They pace, more forlorn than fierce, while bored sentries pelt them with vegetables. Harry was fascinated, and leaned too far over the moat parapet before I pulled him back.

The moat bridge leads to a gate and courtyard with barracks, mint, and buttery. Then another gate, and a tunnel up the hill that twists so the way is blind to invading troops, who can be met with grapeshot ricocheting down the passageway. The castle is no longer a practical fortification, however. There are still stone dungeons and kitchens below, but the top is Renaissance and baroque rooms with leaded glass windows, ceramic stoves, and Flemish tapestries. We passed through the chapel, hall of mirrors, and Chinese salon. Most charming was the masquerade hall, where the artist Lederer decorated every inch of the walls with life-size frescoes of ballroom attendees in carnival costumes, posed as if viewing the dance.

"The people are dressed like clowns!" Harry exclaimed. I loved the whimsy.

A chamberlain led us across the enclosed Na Plášti Bridge to the "Princes' Box," in the huge castle theater, the last building before the castle gardens. It was in their theater that Josef and Paulina Schwarzenberg could live for a few hours in worlds more controllable than the violent one of Napoleon. That is where they chose to receive me. Fortune-tellers are entertainment.

"Ah! The gypsy seer!" Paulina greeted. "How propitious that you've arrived at a time I'm trying to talk sense into my husband."

"Destinies entwine," I recited. "Signs from heaven."

"I wish God saw fit to correspond with me," grumbled Josef. "His whispers seem audible only to the fairer sex."

"Audible to those who listen," I said.

Paulina laughed and clapped her hands.

"Hmph. You are Astiza?" He looked at me skeptically. "Curious name."

I curtsied. "A priestess from Egypt, by way of Paris, the French city founded on a temple of Isis at the place where Notre Dame stands today." Soothsayers from the East fascinate Europeans. I bought clothing to dress the part, and wore a peaked felt cap, black cloak, pointed boots, and a dress spangled with stars. An ankh and the Eye of Horus dangle at my throat. My fingers have rings with hieroglyphic symbols, and my waist belt is embossed with the signs of the zodiac. My dark hair falls, deliberately wild, to the small of my back. I carry a white-handled dagger for magical spells, a wand of ash, and a satchel with pens, ink, parchment, incense, candles, and metal pentacles of the five-pointed star. "This is my son, Horus, named for the falcon god."

Paulina smiled. "More sparrow at his age."

"A sparrow hawk!" Harry said.

"Can we really know the future, priestess?" Josef asked.

"It depends on interpretation," I replied. "The Roman emperor Valens, when he wished to know the name of his successor, used a chicken for divination by assigning letters to grains of wheat and watching which ones the bird pecked. The feathered diviner spelled out T-H-E-O-D. When the emperor learned this, he assumed it referred to his high official Theodotus and had the poor man killed to extend his own reign. Shortly afterward, Valens lost his life in a battle with the Goths. His successor was a man named Theodosius."

"Such stories chill, do they not?" Paulina said. "Josef, our visitor has more wisdom than the crones who sell predictions for a pfennig in the market square."

"And she has a clever helpmate." Josef patted Harry like a dog. "But then, you expect more than a pfennig, don't you?"

"The quality of a reading is reflected in what one pays," I said. "I contribute learning to my interpretations. Antoine Court de Gébelin believed the tarot is an abbreviation of the Book of Thoth, a long-lost scroll of ancient wisdom." I didn't mention that my husband had found that book and that we'd watched it burn. "I've had instruction from the famed Marie Anne Lenormand in Paris." Lenormand was a celebrity in Napoleon's court, made rich enough by her prophecies to buy a house. I've been paying for my own journey through life by casting fortunes, mixing herbal remedies, serving as midwife, and selling songs. I'd practiced the harp while a prisoner of Leon Martel, and the flute while living in Paris. My habit was to practice when Ethan was absent, since he was tempted to lend his voice and is a terrible singer. In any event, the money I earn is not enough to afford books, let alone a house, but then, I can't carry a magical repository with us anyway. I prowl the libraries we pass, looking for clues to the Brazen Head. My readings suggest Rosenkreutz came this way.

So I flee, even as I seek. It troubles me that the French police did not make more effort to chase us after our escape from the coronation. Did they let us go to follow us now? Sometimes I feel we're being watched as closely in Bohemia as we were in Paris.

Josef would not be part of such a cabal, I assume. He's a noble who retains the enthusiasms of a child. "We're debating whether I can safely fly Apollo's chariot at our audience during a performance," the duke explained. "I want to descend like a god, but the theater rigging is old. My wife wants you to forecast my chances."

"Perhaps I should inspect the ropes and pulleys."

He laughed. "Our gypsy is sly!"

"I'm not a gypsy. I'm a scholar, seeking knowledge."

"But an Egyptian, no?"

"Yes." I knew the gypsies are reputed to have originated from my nation, hence the name. Others say they are the Rom, from

Slavic lands. "The wise say that, of the ancient magicians, Egypt had nine-tenths."

"Then come, priestess! Comfort my wife by inspecting my winged chariot."

He led us up a spiral stairway to the attic above the theater. A wooden footbridge crossed rafters to give peeks of seats and stage below. We glimpsed brightly painted balconies, candles mirrored by brass reflectors, and hard benches like pews. The loft itself was gloomy timbers and branching catwalks, a cavity to enchant my son. I looked up. A few bats slept. Below, painted scenery hung from pulleys. Drums of rope could be turned like an anchor capstan to raise and lower clouds, castles, or storms. Suspended in midair was a full-size chariot with golden car and scarlet wheels.

"I perform in my own dramas," Josef said. "I want to sweep down to capture Aphrodite, but my practical wife fears I'll crush her instead."

"We're too old for this foolery anyway," said Paulina. "Why can't you just fall off your horse while hunting, like ordinary men?"

"Because I am extraordinary, madame. And a good horseman."

"Let's see what the cards say."

"You want the tarot here in this loft?" I asked Paulina.

"Does it matter where you spread them?"

"Truth pervades even an attic." One learns to play the role.

"And what is your fee to cast a fortune?" Josef said. "Like so many nobles these days, I have more castle than money."

"Then you'll be pleased to learn I want only ten talers. And an answer to a question."

"Ha! Do you know how much value my wife puts on my answers?"

I smiled. He's playful. Outside these walls the emperors Francis, Alexander, and Bonaparte upend whole kingdoms. Inside his theater, Josef can pretend. "Then I offer you a bargain."

There was a plank nailed to the timbered wall where servants rested beer and bread while working. I brushed their crumbs aside and spread the deck. I've learned from my husband how to mark cards by roughing the edges or spotting the back, and so can turn what seems appropriate to the situation. I peeked at the rigging and noticed a cracked drum handle, frayed hemp, and knotted repairs. Like all occupations, the tarot benefits from close observation and critical thinking.

Josef chuckled as I turn over the Chariot card, and Paulina took a breath at the Lovers. I revealed the Sun, the Hanged Man, and the Fool, which made my own heart lurch. The Fool is my Ethan.

"It's not propitious," I forecast, selling them common sense. "Here's the Sun, Apollo, and his Chariot, but the Hanged Man suggests a mishap." He dangled by one foot. "You'd be wise, sire, to refrain from attempting flight."

"I told you so," Paulina said. Always enlist the wife.

But Josef regards this risk as challenge. "I cannot tell if your prophecy is correct unless I fly across my painted sky, no?"

"It's a fall that will make it correct. I might not collect my fee if you're dead."

Josef had a knight's reckless grin, and indeed I turned over a knight as well. "Then ten talers now." A servant counted it out.

"This card forecasts boldness," I admitted, pointing to the knight.

"Now I'll demonstrate why the tarot is superstition," Josef said. In great good humor, enjoying his wife's fret, he donned painted wooden armor, put Apollo's crested helmet on his brow, and mounted his suspended chariot. I could feel what would happen—I have the Sense, even without the Brazen Head—but judged that the fall would hurt little but his pride. Harry was goggle-eyed at the man's costume, and in awe of the magic his mother commands. This will diminish as he grows, but it flatters me now. Do we have children to be admired, if only briefly?

I had prayed to Isis-Mary, and she promised I'd learn something useful in this palace of roses. The duke's servants swung the chariot free, Josef flew like the gods, and drums and pulleys cranked him down to where an audience could gasp.

The ropes creaked and twisted.

Josef swooped, the servants grunted to control his flight, line unreeled . . . and the winch handle snapped off at its base.

As Paulina shrieked and Harry yelled, the drum spun out of control, hemp particles puffing like a cloud. The golden chariot with its golden god smashed onto the stage, Josef swearing as he bounced off the boards in his pretend armor. We thundered along the footbridge, descended the spiral stairs, and rushed up the theater aisle.

Our shaken Apollo rose, bruised but intact. His chariot lay in three pieces, his helmet amid the ruins.

Josef looked at me warily. "Madame, you are indeed a sorceress."

"A priestess. I hope you're not seriously hurt."

He tentatively shook his limbs and then stood tall. He is, after all, a duke. "No more than a knight thrown at a joust. But your tarot . . . Emil, what happened?"

"A handle, sire. The rigging needs replacement."

"Which I can scarce afford. Well." He looked up to the rafters. I looked down and noticed the dark stain where the virgin Evelyn had killed herself. "Ten talers is cheap for good advice."

"And costly when ignored," Paulina said. She turned to me. "I'm impressed. Will you read my fortune for another ten?"

I hadn't asked my question yet. "As you wish. Would you prefer your own chambers?"

"No, here. Now." She was excited by my success. I glanced at the stain again and she followed my eye. This couple liked to dare fate.

I hoped for a happy fortune but dealt apprehensively on the

lip of the stage. Despite my markings, sometimes the cards have a will of their own. I turned the first.

"A Three of Cups," I said with relief. "It suggests merriment. A dance, perhaps, in your painted ballroom."

She clapped her hands again. "I so love a party."

Then I turned over the second. The Devil, meaning my fingers betrayed me. I frowned. "This suggests a dangerous and powerful being. The host?"

"Witch, you strain our hospitality," Josef said, only half in jest.

I hurried to correct my suggestion. "Perhaps, madame, you will dance as a guest in another capital, with a powerful but dangerous ruler."

"Paris!" She laughed. "And Bonaparte!"

The words gave me a strange premonition. I turned another card. Death. The skeleton. The number thirteen. The duchess blanched.

"What evil is this?" Josef didn't like my tarot.

And another. The Nine of Swords: grief, or the nightmare. It's the most dreaded card, forecasting disaster. Usually the tarot can be read to satisfy a customer, but this hand confounded me.

"What does it mean?" Paulina asked, her voice small.

The cards lay across the bloodstain of the suicidal Evelyn. Understand that the world is not neutral. Places have spirit, both good and bad, and this was a poor choice for my work. "Are you attending a ball, duchess?"

"None is planned."

"Good." I turned again and the card showed Six of Swords, the boatman, sign of a dangerous journey. "Nor must you go if invited. There's danger for you. A fire, perhaps. Avoid powerful men. Avoid Paris." I had a dark image of her in flames.

Paulina looked worried. "Yours is a dark art."

"I'm sorry, duchess. I'm as surprised and puzzled as you by this hand."

Josef kicked at a fragment of chariot. "First a winch handle snaps and then you frighten my wife. What's your real purpose, sorceress?"

I drew Harry close. "The cards don't always say what we want to hear."

"This theater is a place of joy." He eyed me as if I crept on my belly like the demon Ialdabaoth, a monster from suppressed religions.

"If I've not amused you, I'll take my fee for your wife's prophecy, ask my question, and go."

"No more talers. Not for that."

I took a breath. "I'm not a witch, sire, I'm a scholar. Cheat me of payment if you must, but I pray to search your library for clues to a quest."

"No. You bring ill tidings. I don't want you under my roof."

Persistence is courage when the host could call soldiers. "You promised to answer a question."

"I've changed my mind."

"Don't tempt fate by cheating the tarot, sire."

"Josef, please," Paulina said.

He didn't fear me, but he feared bad luck. He scowled. "Ask your damned question, and then take your pup out of here."

I couldn't betray fear. If one wants to be a seer to the noble and wealthy, self-confidence is imperative. We're actors. "I've learned from my studies that the mystic Christian Rosenkreutz, seeker of the secrets of the rose, may have sought shelter in this castle, and possibly hid an object he was protecting from Catholic inquisitors. Do you know anything of this episode, or where Rosenkreutz went? It's his path I seek."

"The founder of the Rosicrucians? You think that's why the House of Rožmberk, builders of this castle, adopted the rose as their coat of arms?"

"Your chapel ceiling has the golden triangle with the all-seeing eye. There were mystics here, my lord."

"There are mystics everywhere in this land of caves and forest." Now the duke looked intrigued. He knew something. And I was confirming that the legends he'd learned as a boy might have a grain of truth. Had he seen the ghost of the White Lady on moonlit evenings and realized there's more to reality than we admit?

"The tale is that an odd mystic named Rosenkreutz did come with a wooden coffin. Inside was a being variously described as a corpse, a mummy, or . . ."

"An automaton," I finished. "A mechanical man. The word *android* was coined for it a century ago, from the Greek meaning 'in the shape of a man.'"

"A golem, some say. The Jewish mud men who come alive and roam the night." He shuddered. "They tear Christians limb from limb."

"Only those who harass the ghetto."

"The Rožmberks welcomed this strange Rosenkreutz as a scholar and diversion, a prophet like you, and then came to distrust him, as I distrust you. Was he a seeker of truth or an agent of Satan? They shut him in the dungeon, telling him to buy his way out by turning lead into gold. He ordered furnaces, crucibles, and chemicals. Then he burst through the castle wall."

"Broke through solid stone?"

"By magic. There was an explosion, but he had no gunpowder. He lowered his mysterious cargo to a waiting boat on the Vltava River and set out rowing for Prague. There he disappeared among magicians, astrologers, and numerologists."

"But where was he going?"

"His motto was 'As above, so below.' From the depth of our dungeons, he wanted to climb the Astronomical Tower in Prague's Klementinum."

"And?"

"Legend swallowed him up. Whatever it was he dragged in that coffin, it disappeared." He looked sourly at me. "It's said he vanished into a hidden tomb in a ruined castle. Be careful, fortune-teller."

"Josef, the cards aren't her fault," Paulina said.

"Go to the Klementinum, priestess. I'm told there's a wandering bishop there making the same kind of inquiries." He looked at me slyly, and I wondered if this duke was as simple as he pretended. "His name is Primus Fulcanelli, and perhaps you can tell *his* fortune."

"And where would this ruined castle be?" I persisted.

"If anyone knew that, it would have turned from castle to pit from treasure hunters digging there."

"So Rosenkreutz was at least here. Can you show me his cell?"

"Superstition and old wives' tales, all of it. But I'll give you a peek at the dungeons so you won't be tempted to come back."

The descent was to earlier and grimmer architecture. Sunlit baroque rooms gave way to medieval apartments below, and then stone cellars and cells. Here one could see the bony rock that the castle clung to. Color disappeared. Windows were arrow slits. Our lanterns seemed to dim.

My boy jumped at the squeal when a heavy wooden door with a small grilled window was hauled open. It had been ages, I guessed, since any prisoner had been housed here. The cell was empty, barren, and cold.

"No window?"

"Masons filled it in after the explosion."

The repair, of different-colored stone, was about six feet in diameter.

"And Rosenkreutz left nothing behind?"

"He took his coffin with him."

I tingled at his presence. Yes, centuries had passed, but wisdom had resided in this room. As if by an invisible spirit, my head was turned to gaze upon the opposite wall. "Swing the open door away from the stone there," I commanded.

Josef hesitated, then nodded, and a servant complied.

I took a lantern and studied the wall. There were scratches, so grimed that a quick inspection would miss them. One was a crude drawing of a rose, worked on the stone by a rusty nail or spoon. Below were letters in Latin:

SICUT IN CAELO ET IN TERRA.

"It's a church phrase," I said. "'As in heaven, so on earth.'" An abbreviated version of the Hermetic wisdom, 'That which is below is as that which is above, and that which is above is as that which is below.'"

"What does that mean?" Josef asked.

"Unity. Our lives are mirrored in the heavens, because in the end heaven and earth are one. We look to the sky for the chart of our hearts."

"That's lovely," Paulina said.

"Pretentious," said Josef.

"There's another mark here. Look." Above the rose was a single scratched line. It could be described as a very broad *U*, or a *C* laid on its side, or a bowl, or a valley. Yet the angle where the base turned upright was angular, not curved. I shivered. "Does this mean anything to you?"

"Prisoners make all kinds of marks," Josef said. "Most are obscene. Rosenkreutz was simply mad."

"But he left signs like bread crumbs in a forest."

"If that's a sign, Madame Witch, you are welcome to it."

"The written word has power. Letters have power. Hieroglyphs have power. In ancient Egypt, this hieroglyph symbolized *ka*, the eternal soul. This could have been a mark of Christian's union with God, or his expectation of life after death."

"Or the fact he expected to die in here."

"And yet he didn't. How far down to the river?"

"A hundred feet, but one could work down the steep cliffs. How he lowered his mysterious box I've no idea."

I turned to Paulina. "The Goddess meant for us to meet this day, duchess, to teach your husband a lesson and give you warning. Don't forget it! The world of your theater is a plaything. The world beyond grows dangerous. War is coming, and I and my son must hurry before it arrives."

CHAPTER 7

My freedom lasted the one exhausting week it took me to flee by coach through the Carinthian Alps to Vienna. It was nearly a year since I had been separated from my wife and son at Notre Dame, and nearly two months since Catherine Marceau had written to warn that they were captive in Bohemia. Each day that dragged as we traveled increased my dread that I would be too late. I didn't know what had happened to Astiza, and I didn't know if Baron Richter had any connection to it, but I did know, in my soul, that she and Harry were in grave danger.

As usual, it was a miserable trip. The autumn disrepair of the roads left my ribs sore, my digestion in turmoil, and my sleep fragmented. Passengers were conscripted eight times to help push the vehicle through mud and snow. My pantaloons were spattered to my waist, my stockings were clotted, and between exertions

I had to wrap a scarf around my ears to keep warm. Six men crowded our cab, and I became dizzy from pipe smoke and their breath of salt fish, sausage, and garlic. When they bought spirits to ward off the cold, the jouncing coach always reduced at least one of them to vomiting.

The narrow spires of Vienna finally poked above the horizon like salvation. Surely Bohemia, Prague, and my wife and son could not be far beyond! Yet the vast Schonbrunn Palace, outside the city—Versailles of the Austrian empire—was curiously quiet when we went by. We clopped past empty grass drilling grounds outside Vienna's walls, and passengers peering from the windows muttered that the Schotten Gate had no Austrian guards.

A French tricolor flew instead.

We were allowed to pass into the city as if swimming into a net. Vienna was as intricate as its pastries, a toy land of Germanic architecture sliced like a pie by grand avenues that led to great squares. It was subdued this gray dawn of Wednesday, November 13, 1805. Shops were shuttered, market stalls empty, and pedestrians few. A banner advertising a new Beethoven opera, *Leonore/ Fidelio*, was being taken down before its premiere performance.

Invasion had closed the Opera House doors. The French had arrived before me. This was wretched luck.

I knew nothing of marching armies but could shed light on music. "Napoleon no longer cares for Beethoven," I told my fellow travelers. "The composer was going to dedicate a symphony to the First Consul and then changed the name to Eroica to protest the shooting of the Duc d'Enghien. Be careful what you hum."

We alighted from the coach to learn that all my calculations had been overturned. When I last saw Napoleon, at the end of August, he was on the English Channel, just starting to march east. Armies move ponderously, and I'd assumed there was plenty of time to make a run around his empire by sea and get to my wife. Yet here in early November, the French had already seized the enemy capital, searing across Europe like a comet. While Nelson was winning at Trafalgar, Austrian general Mack was surrendering to Napoleon at Ulm. Emperor Francis's Russian allies had been outflanked and sent fleeing. In less than three brilliant months, the French army had killed, wounded, or captured a hundred thousand enemy troops.

French cavalry were clattering aimlessly this way and that, as if not sure how to actually possess what they'd captured. Most Viennese had disappeared indoors. Women were completely invisible, although the streetwalkers would venture out soon enough. I began hiking toward the Danube River, noticing the scrubbed cobbles and polished windows. The Austrian capital is half the size of Paris, twice as clean, and smells three times sweeter than Venice.

For a quarter-mile I congratulated myself on passing unchallenged. However the curiously scarred Baron Richter had learned my true identity, surely no one else would! But then there was a thunder of hooves, I moved to one side to let the French pass, and a Napoleonic prince riding a black charger suddenly reined up to turn and stare at me with astonished recognition. I gaped back, since his mount was worthy of a circus. The stallion had a tiger-skin saddlecloth, with the tiger's head bouncing above the steed's tail. The four paws and tail drooped to the horse's belly. There was a golden bit, embroidered reins, and silver spurs.

"By the Blessed Mother of Christ, it's Ethan Gage!" the rider cried. "Is fortune finally smiling?"

With dismay, I recognized Marshal Joachim Murat, a hard-charging cavalry general who'd played a key role in Napoleon's self-crowning. "Hello, Joachim," I said warily. We'd known each other slightly in Egypt.

By reputation, Murat's dimness as a strategist was rivaled only by his courage as a warrior. As vain as he was handsome, he was born to model for dramatic portraits, with a powerful torso, a riot of black curls that fell to his shoulders, muttonchop whiskers that clamped a manly cleft chin, and lips locked in a jaunty duelist's grin. Even in the middle of a lightning campaign in foul November weather, the general was a peacock. He wore a shako hat with ostrich plumes, a pelisse of wolverine fur on one shoulder to ward off sword blows, a tunic stiff as a breastplate from its excess of braid, a diamond-hilted saber, and red Moroccan boots. Skintight cavalry breeches showed off his muscled legs, and epaulets exaggerated the width of his shoulders. *It is the eye of other people that ruins us*, Franklin said. *If I were blind I would want neither fine clothes, fine houses, or fine furniture.*

Murat carried a black riding crop in his white-gloved left fist and maneuvered his gigantic horse to block my way. What truly arrested me, however, was not Murat's size but his expression. The habitual swagger was spoiled by desperation. His eyes betrayed worry and, at the sight of me, hope.

Which is the last thing I wanted.

He turned to staff officers reining up around us. "Look! This man has been a spy for Napoleon; I knew him at Abukir. If the American electrician has been sent by our emperor to lend wizardry, maybe this day isn't as confounding as I feared."

Confounding? Despite myself, I was curious. "You just conquered the Austrian capital, did you not?"

He leaned down to whisper. "And been scolded by Bonaparte for doing so. I swear he hectors me more as brother-in-law than he did as general."

"It's hard to stay on Napoleon's good side," I commiserated. Powerful generals are more tractable if you can address them as equal. "But I hear you're doing well. I'd chat, but I'm in something of a hurry."

I'd first met Murat when he campaigned with Napoleon in Egypt and the Holy Land seven years before. He'd taken a bullet through his cheeks at Abukir while sabering off the fingers of a pasha, and grew his whiskers to hide the scar. His mouth had been open and shouting at the time—Murat had a reputation for seldom shutting up, especially about himself—and the ball had passed through without clipping either teeth or tongue.

"It's the first time he opened it to good purpose," Napoleon quipped. The emperor thought his marshal had the force, and intelligence, of a cannonball.

The twin pockmark scars, just barely visible, only added to Murat's dangerous allure. He had acrobat muscles, bedchamber eyes, and a prodigious sexual appetite requiring satisfaction every time he camped. He'd probably sired a dozen illegitimate offspring during this campaign alone. This roguish reputation had only intrigued Napoleon's sister Caroline, who'd fallen in love with a man fifteen years her senior when she was still a child. When it had come time to marry, she passed over the general Bonaparte preferred—the quietly competent Jean Lannes—and chose the flamboyant Murat, whose fierce ambition matched her own. The emperor's brother-in-law earned the nicknames "Golden Eagle," from his men, and "Don Quixote," from Napoleon.

"Doing well?" he replied to me now. "I'm a grand admiral!" He laughed at his own absurd fortune. Murat wouldn't know an anchor from a rudderpost and had been miserably seasick on the voyage to Egypt. The title was bestowed as another excuse to shower the royal couple with money. Napoleon spoiled while lecturing, hoping to buy love at the same time he tried to shame into respect. His sister and brother-in-law responded with manipulation. The rumor was that Murat and his wife believed they'd be a better emperor and empress than Napoleon and Joséphine, or at least handsomer ones. Caroline pouted and wept until her brother proclaimed her a princess. This made Murat not just a marshal in charge of a cavalry corps but a prince.

By contrast, Bonaparte had done little but make me a fugitive. I know life isn't fair, but it's irritating to be reminded of it by the master of a prancing horse with bouncing tiger head—dressed in a uniform costing more than I'd earned in years of service—while simply trying to cross the street.

"Excuse my interruption," I said, trying to step around. "I'm sure you're busy." A bugler mounted on a white mare blocked my way. The street had filled with cavalry, putting me in a ring of intimidating horsemen. Some had bearskin hats that rose like shaggy towers, and their sabers banged and rang like chimes. Sashes held pistol butts, and pennants were topped with lance heads.

"You've an odd way of turning up, Gage," Murat said, and addressed the others. "This American was at the pyramids and Marengo, but I've also seen him at Boulogne, the Invalides, and Mortefontaine. He's like a cat hurled into a pond that finds its way home. It amuses the emperor." He turned back to me. "Are you on a mission?"

"To Prague. Secret, hurried, vital. I have to cross the Danube."

"Then fortune has indeed united us! There's no crossing to be had. The enemy holds Tabor Bridge, and they'll shoot if you come from our lines."

"I wasn't planning on there being any French lines."

"Neither did Emperor Francis! We're pushing him to his own frontier!" Murat leaned down again, treating me like a confidant. Men always want to either shoot me or trust me, neither course warranted by the facts. "Truth be told, we've ridden ahead of Napoleon's orders. Vienna was a fruit begging to be picked."

And its capture would assure Murat fame. "Then I'll search for a boat," I tried. "I need to get to Bohemia."

"But you're Talleyrand's man, are you not? Like me?" The patronage of the grand chamberlain was typical of the interwoven strands of Napoleon's new aristocracy, a gang as tight and treacherous as Corsican bandits. Twenty years before, Talleyrand had been a churchman who didn't believe, and Murat a boy bored by studying for a priesthood. The two had allied and risen together.

"Perhaps." I stalled. I'd been recruited to work for the foreign minister at the coronation but agreed only out of expediency, and escaped after stealing Talleyrand's cloak and taking the broken sword. I'd cut my puppet strings.

"Good news, Gage. I've seen the grand chamberlain's other agents here, your comtesse and policeman. You'll be joining together?"

I tried not to choke. Catherine Marceau and Pasques, my two enemies from my adventures before Trafalgar, were in the Austrian capital? Catherine had pretended to be a comtesse while betraying us, and Pasques was a policeman the size of a bull who'd plagued me since I met him. I'd escaped from Richter in Venice, only to stumble across another nest of plotters in Vienna?

All looking for the Brazen Head, I guessed.

I couldn't risk having them see me, lest they cry "English spy" and have me arrested, tortured, seduced, or lectured. I feared they were looking for Astiza and that my presence would convince them that they were getting close.

"Certainly not, Marshal," I said. "My orders are to remain alone and anonymous." I had no orders, of course. "You've put me at hazard by calling my name and surrounding me with cavalry. You must let me slip anonymously by."

"The marshal prefers to be called Your Serene Highness," the bugler interrupted.

"I'm afraid I must borrow you, Gage," Murat said. "I'm in trouble with the emperor because of my own initiative. I'm winning the war yet being blamed for losing it. I've galloped ahead and been told to fall behind. It's all jealousy, posturing, and politics. You've a reputation for being sly. Swing up behind my bugler there and come to my headquarters. Maybe we can help each other across the river."

This was tempting. "It's imperative I not be seen by Talleyrand's other agents. Imperial secrecy."

Murat addressed the bugler. "Give Gage a cuirassier helmet. The horsehair plume and cheekpieces will hide him." He turned to his cavalrymen. "The American is a rogue and a scamp, but a master of intrigue. Remember, you've never seen him. He will disappear like the Invisible College."

That name gave me a start, reminding me of Richter's oddly invisible agents. We set off at a brisk trot, the muscular cavalry column filling the street. I leaned in close to Murat. "What's the Invisible College?"

"Mystics. Talleyrand told me to keep watch for them; I don't know why. There always seems to be secret societies here and there, mucking about."

At Stephansplatz, an entire regiment had paused to await orders in the chill air, drinking from the fountain and ordering stableboys to fetch hay for the horses. There was an inn in the shadow of the great cathedral, and here Murat had established his command post. We dismounted and he beckoned me inside.

The interior was warm, dark, and smoky. "Privacy!" Murat demanded.

"A room in the back, general?" the frightened innkeeper inquired.

"Your Serene Highness," the bugler corrected again.

Murat's boots clomped, spurs jangling, and his scabbard swung like his tiger's tail as he led me deeper into the building. There was no obvious escape. How could I turn this conscription to my advantage?

"I imagine you enjoy being at the center of things again," Murat said as he plopped onto one wooden chair and put his red boots on another. The place smelled of beer. Despite the early hour, I wished I had one in hand.

"Being useful is a mixed blessing." I looked for another chair, but there was only a stool to balance on. A hussar slammed shut the door.

"But fame attracts ladies, no?" Murat went on companionably. "I remember you flirting at Mortefontaine and rutting the emperor's sister."

"I do recall meeting Pauline," I conceded, grateful I'd never flirted with Caroline. "Whatever happened was her idea. And I'm married now."

"I've tasted that peach myself, as have half the men of Paris. Pretty Paulette is insatiable. My wife is, too, but more judicious."

"She chose you, Marshal."

"Not that Caroline is saintly. We've both had opportunities to stray. We have the same birthday, you know, and are much alike. Napoleon says I need women the way other soldiers need food."

This kind of talk offered nothing but peril. "My wife is faithful."

"You hope." He laughed. "Where is she?"

"I'm not quite sure." It sounded rather hapless.

"You've misplaced her! You're no saint, either."

I was annoyed. "Nor have you struck me as a serene highness."

He waved his hand. "Men compliment me with titles I can't keep straight. But I'm a knight, not a butcher. Do you know why I charge with riding crop?"

"To lash your horse to the front of a charge?"

"I don't want to kill anyone."

I blinked.

"Yes, the terrible Marshal Murat, winner of a dozen victories, cut by a saber, hit by a ball, cavalier extraordinaire, prefers the slaying be left to others. This is my secret, Gage, but rogues like us are practiced at keeping secrets. I did study for the priesthood, I remind you. I remember the Commandments."

"You keep taking me by surprise, Serene Highness."

"I've yet to kill, and I sleep better for it. I sleep serenely."

"Is that a boast or a confession?"

He laughed. "And now you magically appear in Vienna, again the hanger-on."

It was time to be honest, lest I find myself harnessed to this glorious fool. "On the contrary, there's been some confusion. I'm not working for Napoleon, Talleyrand, or anyone else. I've become a neutral and independent scholar. Our meeting was odd coincidence. My only mission is to reunite with my family. We were separated during my earlier work for the emperor, and duty has kept us apart."

"What duty?"

"Scholarly. Historical." Talleyrand's sword hilt dug at my back.

He shook his head. "Gage, I've watched you since the war in Egypt. 'There goes a clever man of vast longings, negligible ambition, and no understanding of the realities of life,' I said to myself. 'The fellow who tries everything, and accumulates nothing.'" He sat back, feigning disappointment. "I'm dismayed you're not working for our foreign minister. It would be an easy way to get rich. You've a chance to tie your fortunes to the glory of France, and yet you never admit your need for a patron and mentor."

"I just don't want to be kept."

Murat thumped his boots down on the plank floor and leaned forward. I could smell his cologne. "In truth, you've betrayed Bonaparte as well as helped him. Am I not right, scoundrel? Did you not oppose us on the ramparts at Acre?"

What was this interview really about? "Only after your commander tried to execute me at Jaffa." The memory still rankled.

"Look at me, Gage. An innkeeper's son, a failed priest, not a prospect to my name, and now I'm a prince of France. Do you know how much money my wife and I will earn this year, beyond whatever I steal on this campaign?"

"More than you need, I'm guessing."

"A million francs! Maybe two! When a laborer makes a few hundred! Why? Because I'm brave, yes. Handsome enough for the emperor's sister. But more than that, because I ally with Napoleon and stay loyal to his cause."

This was true. The cavalryman had fetched the cannon the young Napoleon needed to crush a revolutionary mob in Paris, starting Bonaparte's meteoric rise. Murat had then attached himself to Napoleon's staff, fought in three major campaigns, and courted Caroline. He was a very astute fool.

"While your allegiance is to yourself, mine is to my country. As a result, I have a quarter-million men marching behind me. You have nothing. You're like a man strolling between two volleying armies, expecting not to be hit. So listen to my advice, wandering American. It's not too late to make something of yourself! You can ride with me into history, and when we crush the emperors Francis and Alexander, you can search for your family as a conqueror instead of as a supplicant. How does that sound?"

Dangerous. I'd had my fill of armies. Conqueror or not, a soldier was still subject to orders, gunfire, and the disastrous whims of officers and fate. The last place I wanted to be was at a final showdown between three warring emperors.

But how to get away when French troops galloped on the south bank of the Danube, and Austrian and Russian troops guarded the north?

"I've no cavalry training," I said, stalling. "It takes years to make a good one."

"But you have a diabolic mind. Don't deny it! You studied with the wizard Franklin and chased ancient secrets. Your skill is improvisation, imposture, and scientific trickery."

"What is it you want, Joachim?" I desperately used his first name again, because I was entirely in his power.

Now his face fell and he looked embarrassed as a schoolboy. "My brother-in-law has insulted me." The transformation from boastful warrior to worried subordinate was astonishing. "Here, look at what he sent me upon word of my capture of Vienna." He pulled out military correspondence and shoved it at me.

I recognized the seal and signature of Napoleon. "My cousin," it began, the salutation Bonaparte used with all eighteen of his marshals. "I cannot approve of your way of proceeding. You go right on in an empty-headed way without weighing the orders I have sent to you. You have thought only of the trifling glory of entering Vienna. There is no glory where there is no danger, and there is none in entering a capital which is undefended."

This did seem rather irritable, and ungrateful to boot. "What were you supposed to do instead?" I asked, trying to sound sympathetic.

"Harry the Austrian army. But ignore Vienna? Ridiculous. Nonetheless, I have to prove myself to him again, as I have countless times before. I am his faithful squire. There's just one small problem, and this is the problem you will solve for me."

"What problem is that?"

"The enemy holds Tabor Bridge, which we both want to cross, preventing you from looking for your wife and me from chasing the Austrian army."

"Tabor! Napoleon fought near a mountain of that name in the Holy Land. Sent the Turks running, he did."

"Well, the Austrians have mined this Tabor with gunpowder."

"Because you wasted time taking this city. Because you didn't cross the Danube when you had the chance to flank the enemy." Yes, I piled on. It's more fun to fault others than yourself.

"Because I recognized opportunity!" He slapped his thigh. "History will remember me as the liberator of Vienna. But that was yesterday, and today we need the Tabor Bridge." He leveled his finger. "It is guarded by cannon, a thousand muskets, and fused with enough explosives to blow us all to hell. So you, Ethan Gage, are going to capture it."

I blanched. "Me? How?"

"That is what you must think up." He took out a pocket watch. "The emperor is in a hurry. Succeed, or I will shoot you."

CHAPTER 8

Napoleon allowed his marshals much discretion, but little error. If Murat had done what he was supposed to do, his cavalry would be harassing the emperors of Austria and Russia. Instead he'd stayed on the south side of the Danube River for the glory of entering Vienna. Now the Austrians had turned the long wooden Tabor Bridge, which crossed the river across marshy islands, into a gigantic bomb.

My lies would defuse it, or at least that was the plan. "You've had more practice, given that you are a professional man of guile," Murat reasoned. I'm actually honest to a fault, but strode down the wooden planking with deception rehearsed, using a cavalry lance to carry a white flag. I've found the occasional lie a useful social lubricant, along with the harmless compliment or the well-rehearsed joke. Given that most conversation is tedious and predictable, we should all practice adding spice by lying.

Murat initially judged my idea as dishonorable and then, when I explained that subterfuge was the only easy way to get across the river, brilliant. He added trickery of his own. The floodplain of the Danube is thick with trees; so, while my boots thumped the planking, French soldiers threaded into the brown foliage behind me, ready to rush. Accordingly, there was a line of Austrian muskets and cannon ahead, the French behind, and beneath me a hundred kegs of gunpowder. If things went poorly and shooting began, my plan was to hurl myself into the river. The last autumn leaves rafted its current, and daylight was so brief, it seemed on loan. If I weren't blown to atoms, I'd likely freeze and drown.

Still, one of the attractions of war is how natty it all is, giving men a chance to preen. I'm a poor leader—too much responsibility—and a worse follower, shying from all uniforms and flags if it means I have to take orders. My cause is my family and me, which usually implies careful neutrality and staying out of battle. If everyone were as incorrigible as me, wars would snuff out from lack of fuel. Still, to take my mind off the fused gunpowder, I studied the fashion of the opposing army. The French use blue or green coats, go mostly clean-shaven, and are ordinary-size men fond of song and wit. The Austrian grenadiers, by contrast, were strapping, big-booted, flamboyantly mustached, and stern-faced farm boys in white uniforms with yellow facings, their black leggings buttoned to mid-thigh. They leaned on their muskets to study me with narrowed eyes, puffing on clay pipes. The officers wore white, too, with tricorne hats, red and blue sashes, gilded scabbards, and gray capes.

White isn't as impractical as it appears. It is bright in battle, cheaper than colored cloth, hasn't been weakened by harsh dyes, and can be dressed for parade with chalk or pipe clay.

The Austrians watched my approach, in brown civilian clothes, with disbelief.

"This bridge is about to be blown!" one called out in French. "Are you a simpleton? Get back to town!"

"An emissary! A word, please, as sweet to your ears as mine!" I hoisted high a bottle of champagne. "A French gift to celebrate with, my new friends!"

Much of war consists of waiting, and because I provided relief from boredom, I knew they wouldn't immediately kill me. An officer's hunting dog was loosed to race, bark, and sniff, but I didn't flinch or break stride. Bravado is necessary during a ruse. "Call off the hounds—I'm not a boar!"

This earned a rough laugh.

There were three regimental battle flags at the northern end of the bridge, sporting the Austrian double-headed black eagle. A cavalry colonel trotted forward to confront me. I quickened to get past the mouths of their cannons, which always look gigantic from the front end. Then he stopped me.

"Halt! What are you doing here?"

I raised the champagne higher. "Drinking to the miracle of your health, as your good wife will as well, once she learns you survived the war." I made my voice carry to the ranks.

"I have no wife. Who in Hades are you?"

"A neutral emissary from the celebrating French. It's been a wearying campaign. But now the fighting is done!" I shouted this last, throwing my arms wide, and soldiers straightened in consternation and hope.

"My name is Ethan Gage," I continued, "protégé of the late Benjamin Franklin and confidant of Jefferson and Bonaparte. I am a friend of all nations, and a lackey of none. My studies brought me to Vienna, and French acquaintances enlisted me for this pleasurable duty."

"Acquaintances?"

"I was an adviser at the pyramids and Marengo. Murat and his fellow marshals asked that I, as an American neutral, share the good news so we can begin negotiations."

"What the devil are you talking about?"

"The war is over!" I shouted this as loud as I could, since a lie needs emphasis. There was a murmur as my rumor rippled up and down the riverbank. Men stirred like trees in a wind. The colonel looked at me suspiciously.

"What do you mean 'over'?"

"An armistice has been signed. And your name, sir?"

"Franz Geringer."

"Marshals Lannes and Murat would like to confer with you. Can you guarantee their safety if they cross the bridge?"

"I've heard nothing of an armistice."

"Which is why I'm telling you. I'm a skilled diplomat, having negotiated the Treaty of Mortefontaine, the sale of Louisiana, and the surrender of Cap-François." This was a slight exaggeration, but *Half a truth is often a great lie*, Franklin told me, and thus useful, in my experience. "Your general Mack has surrendered, your capital has fallen, and your Russian allies are retreating to their own country. Surely you can understand why the wise emperor Francis has agreed to end hostilities. To friendship!"

It's a wonder that any officer would swallow such nonsense, but history books confirm that the Austrian did. We believe what we want to hear, and I'd tempted him with survival. I could see the mental debate on his face.

"What harm to listen to what the French have to say?" I coaxed.

"Because you're roughly dressed and have no retinue or credentials. You look like a rascal, a knave, a rogue, and a trickster."

"But completely unarmed." I opened my coat. Talleyrand's broken antique sword was still in the small of my back, since I dared not show it to Murat or his men, but I had no real weapons. "The French generals will be at the mercy of your cannon. They ask only that you share their good news."

Geringer hesitated an agonizing minute longer and finally gave a reluctant nod. "I guarantee their safety."

I turned and waved the white flag and walked back to meet

my conspirators at mid-span, Murat cocky and Lannes smooth. Lannes had also been with Napoleon in Egypt, a bullet wound at Acre giving him a permanent crick in his neck. I'd been on the other side, but soldiers don't hold such things against each other. We were comrades for having been tormented by the same heat and flies.

Accompanying the two marshals were Murat's chief of staff, General Auguste Belliard, and several aides. Lannes and Murat chatted, Belliard had his arms clasped behind his back, and the entire group gave a holiday air. I peeked down. There were gaps in the planking, and I could see French sappers crawling on the timbers beneath, making for Austrian explosives.

The French paraded with me back past enemy barricades, crowded the artillerymen away from their guns, and smiled upward at the still-mounted Geringer, whose horse backed a nervous pace. The dog growled.

"The American has given you the good news?" Lannes asked.

"He said an armistice has been signed."

"Negotiations are proceeding for a complete end to the war," the boyish-looking marshal bamboozled. "There will be no more slaughter."

"How do I know you're telling the truth?"

"Would we put ourselves at the mercy of your guns if we weren't? Go get your general. Maybe he's received a dispatch." Any delay was in our favor, since we needed to defuse the gunpowder. I decided it might help to uncork the champagne.

"A celebratory drink," I offered as it popped and foamed. "For your mistress, if you don't have a wife." His officers looked at my bottle greedily and, at my urging, began passing it around.

"Fetch General Auersperg," Geringer said.

The French marshals were as skilled as the actors in the Comédie-Française. Their relaxed friendliness spread like contagion among the Austrians, who, after all, had been badly beaten to this point. Without being told to, some of the infantry began to stack arms, jabbering in German. Lannes suggested that it violated the spirit of the occasion to have cannons menacingly pointed. The Austrian colonel, who had taken three swigs from my bottle, agreeably ordered them turned around to point toward his own lines.

Karl Josef Franz Graf von Auersperg, the Austrian corps commander, came galloping up. Their general was suspicious, but also confused. "Why are you drinking with the French? And why are those soldiers on my bridge?"

Murat bowed, sweeping off his plumed cap. "Marshal Joachim Murat at your service, General Auersperg. Greetings from the emperor of the French. The war is over. We are celebrating."

"That doesn't mean your men can just walk across!"

"They are stretching their legs to seek new friends. If hostilities are at an end, it might be more convenient to have us out of Vienna and camped on the north bank. Your citizens are anxious to reopen their shops. If your regiments could make room?"

"The French infantry hope to exchange souvenirs of the campaign with your own men," I put in. "Perhaps soldiers on both sides can make money. All should profit from recent hardships." Always appeal to greed. "Care for champagne?"

Auersperg turned to his colonel. "How do you know there's an armistice?"

He pointed at me. "This civilian said so."

"And who is he?"

"Ethan Gage, the famed American diplomat," I said.

"It's true, general," Lannes smoothly insisted. "This Gage has the ear of our emperor and his own president, the esteemed Thomas Jefferson. A toast to peace."

"American? He's on the wrong side of the ocean!"

"I was pressed into service while on my way to be reunited with my family," I explained. "My heart soared when you opened this bridge."

"Where are the documents attesting to this armistice?"

"On their way, surely. It takes time to write them up."

The general's head swiveled like an owl's as he took in his troops busily disarming themselves, the French two-thirds across, the swollen river, the spires of the capital. "This is a trick, damn it!" he suddenly roared. "Colonel, arm your men!"

It was too late. Even as he shouted, the French aides seized Geringer and hauled him from his saddle, muffling him. Murat seized the general's bridle. "Don't shoot, don't shoot, there's a misunderstanding!" the French officers cried out in French and German. Some Austrians snatched up their guns and tentatively pointed them at our tangled group while others hung back, confused by the tumult. There was no clear line of fire. French artillerymen ran forward to man the Austrian cannon that had been turned.

"Don't shoot, don't shoot!" Both sides were crying it.

Geringer bit the hand held over his mouth, a Frenchman howling. "Light the fuses!" he cried. "Blow the bridge! Kill the damned American!"

Prudence suggested I absent myself. I shoved through the churning crowd to the bridge railing and swung over to drop to the beams below, leaving the two forces to their tangle. I looked back toward the Vienna side of the river. The French sappers had reached the first explosives, methodically cutting fuses and disarming the kegs of powder. Yet most still remained, and the French above could still be killed in an eruption of fire and splinters.

I found a fuse and grabbed it like a vine, taking out Talleyrand's stub of sword to cut it.

Then someone gave me a great clout in the back of my neck and I fell toward the river, gasping in surprise.

One of my arms managed to grasp a beam before I fell in. My feet splashed the surface of the water, I hung on desperately, and then a boot stomped on my forearm, trying to make me drop. I yelled, fell further, and grabbed a lower timber, cold water surging around my waist.

An Austrian sergeant loomed over me, glowering. He aimed a pistol.

I threw water at him as he pulled, the spray making him jerk enough that the bullet went into the river, leaving his pistol empty.

My assailant grunted in frustration and reached up to the fuse I'd just grasped. Taking a smoldering match from a cartridge box, he lit it. The cord puffed and sizzled as merrily as frying bacon.

I leaped for his boot, grabbed, and yanked. He lost his balance and fell with me. We landed hard on a lower beam, wrestling, the current swirling inches below. He clawed for my throat while I punched him in the eye.

"Help, he's trying to blow it!" I shouted. The cry was lost in the rush of the river and the clamor above. The burning fuse was nearing the nearest keg.

The bastard's hand closed on my throat. He was a damned hero, I realized, determined to take himself, me, his general, and a hundred Frenchmen to hell in one great fiery explosion.

So I used the palm of my hand to ram the underside of his nose. The Austrian's head snapped back, eyes crossing and blood spurting, and then I heaved up and let a knee come down on his hand.

He howled, and his balance was gone with his grip. He hit the river with a splash and was gone.

The fuse was spitting and smoking toward the keg. The nearest sappers were shouting warning. I bounded like a squirrel, reached the keg of gunpowder, and hacked with Talleyrand's broken sword.

The fuse sputtered out, sparks falling into the water.

Shaking from relief and exertion, I made my way to the gunpowder kegs on the other side of the bridge and cut that fuse, too.

The sappers cheered.

I worked my way to the Austrian side of the river, dropped to the muddy bank, and clambered to the road above. To my relief, Murat and Lannes had the situation under control. French troops had reached the northern shore, the Austrians had lost their advantageous position, and French cavalry were clearing a wedge on the banks. The Austrians were too confused, and unready to resist. My stratagem had succeeded. We had the bridge, and the enemy was falling back.

General Auersperg, boxed in by French troops, was furious. He pointed at me. "There's the one! That's the one who lied and tricked!"

"The English poet John Lyly said all is fair in love and war," Murat replied. "I give you leave to rejoin your men, general, on the condition that you withdraw north to join your emperor. You can thank us that we haven't kept you captive."

"What benefit is that? Francis will imprison me for losing this bridge." The horror of what had happened was beginning to dawn on him.

"Then be careful of Americans. They are a sly and wily people, violent and greedy, a nation of rebels, opportunists, and sharp traders."

This assessment seemed unfair, but before I could protest, the Austrian spoke up. "If I see that one again, I'll shoot him." Then Auersperg, flushed from humiliation, wheeled his horse and made for his own lines, calling his troops to fall in behind him. The French continued to pour across in a tide of blue and green.

Murat turned to me. "*Mon Dieu*, have you been in a sty?" He was still a peacock, his uniform spotless. I was half-soaked and muddy as a pig.

"An Austrian sergeant did his best to blow you up, and I had to stop him," I replied. "I'm cold, sore, and frightened. Could I have some champagne?"

"It's gone. But admirable pluck, American. And all's well that ends well, Shakespeare said."

"I didn't realize you were a student of English literature."

"I don't care for books, but I like epigrams. They're short."

"This ends well if the capture of the Tabor Bridge gives me permission to go find my wife and son," I pressed.

"Absolutely," the marshal promised. "Once we've achieved final victory and there's no danger of you doing the same kind of trick for the enemy, I'll send you on your way."

"Final victory!"

"You're too valuable to wander about, Gage. Besides, the Austrians would simply kill you. You're safest with us."

"I would be first in line to shoot him," the humiliated and captive Colonel Geringer said.

"I believe first in line would be General Auersperg," I corrected, just to keep my enemies straight.

"I don't blame you," Murat said to Geringer. "Gage is as empty of conviction as a lawyer, as pitiless as a doctor, and as greedy as a moneylender. In other words, a man of great use."

"My loyalty is to common sense," I protested. "I'm just trying to get to Prague. I seek reunion with my family." And I wanted to stay several leagues in front of seductive and treacherous Catherine Marceau.

"Napoleon seeks reunion with you. You've been conscripted, Ethan Gage. You have proven entirely too useful."

CHAPTER 9

Astiza

Prague is no longer the capital of the Holy Roman Empire, as it was under eccentric emperor Rudolf II two hundred years ago, but it remains the capital of mystery and magic. The city lies in a bowl that legend says was hammered by a rock from the sky. Its gates are dark as charcoal, and bulbous black towers, tipped with gold, sprout spires like pitchforks. Church steeples look like wizard hats. Lanes are a labyrinth. Alchemists, magicians, dwarfs, soothsayers, necromancers, numerologists, and astronomers live here, communing with God and the Devil. It's the city of Paracelsus, Sendivogius, Setonius, Mamugna, Geronimo Scotta, Tadeáš Hájek, and the seductive witch Gelchossa, daughter of wizard John Dee. Prague alchemist Edward Kelly had no ears, having had them cut off as punishment for forgery. Prague astronomer Tycho Brahe had no nose, or rather had a brass one to replace the flesh lost in a duel. Johannes Kepler taught that God's path for the planets is not the circle but the ellipse, confounding belief in divine perfection. Here Faust made his fatal pact with the Devil, and Rabbi Loew made a mud monster called a golem to protect the black-clad Jews. Ghosts haunt the monasteries, and succubi the palaces. Ask anyone who lives there: Prague is a city of talking cats, bells that refuse to ring, prophetic ravens, poisoned moonbeams, and comets that foretell war.

In the imperial palace that looms on the other side of the Vltava River, mad king Rudolf built a great hall to house his collection of curiosities. In the gloom of the Czech winters, gray light filtering through high palace windows, he walked alone to finger a six-foot-long unicorn horn, the agate bowl he believed might be the Holy Grail, prehistoric spearheads, nails from Noah's Ark, a desiccated dragon, and a chalice made of rhinoceros horn. He had a bell to call the dead. There were ticking clocks, crystal balls, telescopes, astrolabes, and an iron chair that clasped its occupant.

Ambassadors gave Rudolf tiny demons imprisoned in gems of amber.

I came to Prague with Horus because this city is a magnet for mysticism and science. It's the crossroads of East and West, where the rationalism of the North marries the passions of the South. It's a place to suspect time is an illusion, and reality a veil. When valley fogs roll and lamps glow like orange moons, when monsters sleep in attics and ravens hop across headstones, when red light burns in alchemist cellars and sulfur issues from clay chimneys, then all mysteries thrive, and any answer seems possible.

I timed my arrival to the Mansions of the Moon, the twenty-eight stations that Luna progresses as it waxes and wanes each month. My entry was the gate beneath the Powder Tower, the city armory. I found quick and temporary employment as a healer and fortune-teller in a herbarium near Old Town Square, earning enough for a garret while searching for the Brazen Head. The question I will ask it: When will my husband return?

The Klementinum of the Jesuits has become Prague University since the Catholic sect's suppression by Empress Maria Theresa. Its library's merger with Rudolf's alchemical collection means there might be clues about Rosenkreutz, who rowed his boat and its coffin-shaped cargo to the water gate at the Klementinum's base. How could the Rosicrucian dissolve castle walls? I must learn this.

My first problem was gaining admittance. Temples of learning typically refuse admission to my gender, so I dressed in my sorceress robes and presented my travel-stained endorsements from Talleyrand. Nonetheless, an officious librarian barred my entry. "The scriptorium is for scholars only," he told me. He peered at my son with distaste. "Women, children, dogs, and Jews are prohibited."

I was ready for this. I gave a nudge, and Harry darted past the man's folded arms and into the barrel-vaulted repository beyond. I'd told Horus that a "wandering bishop" in a wine-colored cassock kept a mechanical parrot on his shoulder that could sing in French and English. This scholar was Primus Fulcanelli, the student of the occult that Duke Josef Schwarzenberg had suggested I seek.

"My child!" I cried on cue, looking accusingly at the librarian as if it were his fault Harry had dashed past. A man will defer to women when it comes to a four-year-old. The confused clerk hesitated just long enough for me to push past, his hand scraping my cloak in a futile attempt to stop me.

I trotted until arrested by the library's beauty. It's a baroque hymn to the human mind, as stately as a shrine. There are two dozen black pillars, their tops wrapped with gold, twisted in the

Solomon design that originated in the Holy Temple of Jerusalem. Ceiling murals celebrate the history of learning. Oriental rugs muffle sound, and heavy oak tables are heaped with opened books. On stands between are globes, clocks, and models of the seven astrological planets: the sun, the moon, Mercury, Venus, Mars, Jupiter, and Saturn. There are also seven hells and seven heavens, seven sacraments in the Catholic Church, seven gifts as defined by Saint Thomas Aquinas, seven deadly sins, and seven days in the week.

Truth is revealed by numbers.

Harry cornered a scarlet-robed scholar. "Do you have a parrot?"

Far from being offended, the surprised bishop seemed charmed by my son's French. "If I did, wouldn't I be a pirate?" he said in the same tongue.

"I wanted to hear it sing!"

"And what crevice did you escape from, little mouse?" I hurried to catch up, my spangled skirt kicking up loose papers as it swirled.

"I'm not a mouse."

The man bent. "Really? You are very small."

"I'm a boy!"

"Harry, leave that man alone."

"No! I want to hear his parrot sing."

The bishop straightened. "This is your son?"

"Apologies, Monsieur . . ."

"Fulcanelli. Primus Fulcanelli, a Latin scholar from Rome." He turned to Harry. "I'm afraid I don't have a parrot, but I wish I did."

"Harry, Mama was mistaken."

My boy was disappointed. "I saw a parrot in a circus."

"Look, there's a model of the planets. See how the balls go round and round? Take a look while I apologize to this man." I turned to Fulcanelli, balancing between being demure and being bold. "He's very fond of novelties, a trait of his mother's. You are a Jesuit, Monsignor?"

He was intrigued by my intrusion. "That aggressive order was banned from Prague a generation ago. I'm a Catholic bishop without a diocese, and so am called 'wandering.' My kind finds other usefulness, often in scholarship, while keeping our connections to Rome."

" 'I'm embarrassed to have interrupted you, and yet you may be the answer to my prayers. I need this library for my alchemical studies."

"Do you? My own intellectual quest has brought me to Prague. And you are?"

"Astiza of Alexandria. I'm a scholar of mechanical contraptions. I told Harry there might be a parrot automaton here."

"You said it was a bird!"

"Harry, hush." Fulcanelli and I studied each other. He was a remarkably handsome churchman, his manner recalling the poise of the swordsman more than the piety of the clergy. And he looked appreciatively at me. I turn heads when I wish, using it as a tool when needed. Bishops have the rank to appreciate beauty without accusation of moral failing. So: he is a prelate, he is a scholar, he is a man. "I'm afraid my boy embodies the last of the Five Processes," I said. This is energy, my host would know. The others are essence, sense, vitality, and spirit.

The librarian I'd pushed past hurried up to us, flushed with consternation. "I am sorry, holiness!"

Fulcanelli gave a dismissive wave. "On the contrary, Havek, I suspect this lady is precisely the kind of scholar I was hoping to meet."

"But she is a woman!"

"I see that."

"And not even Czech or German!"

"Eastern, I'm guessing. Greek?"

I gave a slight curtsy. "Greek and Egyptian, Monsignor."

"The nations of philosophy and magic. And you have no husband?"

"I do, but we're traveling separately."

He puzzled over this but didn't press. "And I'm guessing you came here to seek me out. Few meetings are accidental."

"Your scholarship was commended by Duke Josef Schwarzenberg, of Český Krumlov Castle."

His eyebrow elevated. "You have impressive friends." He turned to Havek. "You may leave us."

"But she has a child!"

"Whom I've decided to educate. You've done your duty, now go, go." The poor man retreated and Fulcanelli turned back to me. "You're a student of esoteric thought? That discipline is a maze of speculation."

"Dangerous as well," I said. "*The Sacred Magic of Abramelin the Mage* is reputed to bring fatal accidents to anyone who reads it."

He cocked his head. "And have you read it?"

"I am alive," I replied evasively but with a flirtatious glance. I can be shameless when I have a reason to be. It's another way my husband and I are alike. "I'm a student of transformation, Bishop, believing the age-old creed of 'As within, so without.' I search for my divine spark in the wisdom of others." I gestured to the books. "I've studied texts in Egypt, Tripoli, Martinique, Paris, and Heidelberg."

"And you bring your child into shrines of learning?"

"We have no regular home, or nanny. He can already read."

"Remarkable."

"I keep him quiet with practice of his letters."

"And promises of mechanical parrots."

I smiled apologetically and looked at the banks of books, the arched windows giving shafts of light between. The library was two stories high, with a gilded balcony giving access to the uppermost shelves. Many of the leather bindings had cracked with age. My heart raced at what I might learn.

"Where is your husband traveling, madame?"

"I'm afraid I don't know. We were separated." I shrugged, hoping to suggest it was a tiresome story yet making clear that I was legitimately partnered.

"And you seek the divine spark?"

"As you know, alchemical seekers believe the God Without is also Within. We search to purify lead into gold and the soul into salvation. We believe we can pierce the veil and achieve reunification with God by our efforts."

His look was amused, not censorious. "Such alchemy is heresy to the Church."

"Such alchemy is religious inquiry. You and I share the same interests, Bishop."

"Yours is not a quest for busy mothers."

"It's partly a quest to find my son's father. He may be in danger."

"Papa disappeared," Harry piped up, "but before that we hunted for candy!"

I'd made Fulcanelli curious. I practice intrigue, which makes it hard for men to ignore me. I'm intelligent, which makes them wary. I'm purposeful, which makes them threatened. I pay attention, which flatters. I dress in costume. In a world in which men have strength, power, and desire, women must have wits.

"Why in danger?" he asked.

"Powerful people seek what we seek. The alchemist Robert Grosseteste, chancellor of Oxford and bishop of London, is one of many who wrote of a bronze automaton made by Albertus Magnus five or more centuries ago."

"The Great Albert. Also called Doctor Universalis."

"Yes, Bishop. I'm hoping to find more of Grosseteste's writings."

"Why? It's an old tale. Saint Thomas Aquinas destroyed the machine."

"Some think not. My own search suggests that the machine passed through Prague, or still resides here somewhere."

"Do you really think so?" To the bishop it was a fairy tale. "Like the legendary golem of three hundred years ago, created by Rabbi Loew to project the Jews and now supposedly tucked away in a synagogue attic?" This was a history well known to Europe's religious scholars.

"I'm following the petals of the rose as clues, seeking signs in the stars. You're a Catholic welcomed into a city with a history of hostility toward your creed, Primus." I used his first name deliberately, as an offer of friendship. "I similarly ask for help from this institution, despite its hostility to my sex."

"Not hostility. Just . . . exclusivity."

"I ask only to read. None need talk to me or look at me."

He laughed. "Too many will be tempted! And surely you've found the texts you need in other libraries."

"Far from it. I hope you have the *Monas Hieroglyphica* of John Dee, *The Arbatel of Magic*, *The Book of Secrets* by Albertus Magnus, the *Corpus Hermeticum* of Marsilio Ficino, *The Ordinal of Alchemy*, and works by Michael Maier, the Comte de Saint-Germain, Maria the Jewess, and Grand Professor Martines de Pasqually."

"An impressive list."

"We live in an age of books. I believe that with enough study, we learn the truth."

"If only facts, speculation, and truth were the same thing." He considered me, his eye straying to Harry.

"What is *your* quest, Bishop?"

"Magic, I'm afraid, or rather the disproof of it. The Church doesn't want saintly miracle confused with parlor tricks and hopes to get at the truth of what medieval magicians and alchemists claimed. If you're inclined to believe, I'm required to be skeptical."

"Perhaps we would make a good team."

"Perhaps." He considered. "I think your odyssey is for an object that no longer exists, madame, if it ever did. But you show every sign of being a serious scholar, and this city has welcomed thinkers from all over Europe for five hundred years."

"It's true my quest may be futile," I admitted. "But how interesting if I succeed! In medieval times, the Brazen Head might have been feared as evil, but savants and clergy have the chance to study it in our scientific age. How did it work? What could it foretell?"

Fulcanelli came to his decision. "I'm moved by intellect, persistence, and"—he looked down at Harry—"boldness. So as a senior scholar of this exquisite library, I grant guest privileges and offer partnership." He smiled and my heart jumped unexpectedly. "Will you start in Philosophy?"

"History. I'm looking for mention of Christian Rosenkreutz."

"The Rosicrucian founder? We regard his teachings as heretical as well."

"And you'd regard me as a pagan, but an ecumenical one. In Český Krumlov, I was told Rosenkreutz might have come here to Prague as a fugitive from a dungeon, rowing a boat with the Albertus automaton stored like a corpse."

"So what became of it?"

"That's what I'm trying to find out."

"Perhaps it *was* evil, and Rosenkreutz was the one who destroyed it."

"Perhaps. Or maybe it was so powerful it was hidden away. Is the Brazen Head the kind of curiosity that Rudolf II would have coveted?"

"Yes. And what will you do if you find it?"

"Use it to help find my husband, and for that I need your friendship."

I long for a friend. Among my stops had been the castle of Germelshausen, in Germany's Thuringia. It's a desolate ruin miles from any village or farm, surrounded by black pine and mossy crags. The walls are as dark as the trees, scorched from fire when the Dominican fanatic Tors sacked it, and the keep has a shattered top like a broken tooth. It was snowing when Harry and I came, and utterly deserted. The little fire we built in a corner of the roofless great hall barely staved off the cold, and we heard the baying of wolves. A statue of the Goddess was toppled in a courtyard overrun with dead brambles. The statue's head had broken off and was missing.

That was the night I felt most alone these past months.

According to the legend we'd heard in France, Rosenkreutz had been only five, little more than Harry's age, when Count Conrad and Tors attacked his family home because of their reputation as a nest of pagans. The child was smuggled out a tunnel by a freethinking monk and raised by the Albigensian sect of Christian heretics in France. As an adult, he wandered from Damascus to Madrid, absorbing knowledge. He took the German name for "rosy cross," Rosenkreutz. He believed scholars should dedicate their research to the betterment of mankind, and that alchemy could lead to the divine spark within us. Now the Rosicrucians have taken his name, and that order and other questers after truth are known collectively as the Invisible College. I should tell Ethan, because he's intrigued with secret societies.

"If you find this Brazen Head, what else will you ask it?" Fulcanelli inquired.

I was deliberately evasive. "How to conduct our lives, I suppose."

"The Church answers that question."

"Then life's meaning."

"The Church again."

"How to respond to great events, the march of armies and the claiming of thrones."

"The Church once more. Perhaps, madame, Thomas Aquinas regarded this Brazen Head not as evil but simply redundant."

"Or maybe he didn't like that the answers of the Brazen Head were different from the answers of the Church."

"Ha! Very good. You'll fit well in Bohemia. You have intellectual impudence. Prague is a city of dangerous speculation."

"In America, the home of my husband, it is called curiosity."

"American? You *are* an odd family." Yet I was succeeding in seducing his own curiosity, and had to take care that he didn't mistake my partnership for something else, bishop or no. "Here, under ceilings painted with philosophers," he said grandly, "I give you leave to study. Heresy is wicked, and the devil can lead us astray, but truth is never dangerous, because it always leads to the same place."

"Your church?"

"To that which we are seeking. And what destiny tells us we must find."

Chapter 10

It's never wise to be the bearer of bad news, particularly when the recipient is Napoleon Bonaparte. He was difficult enough when we started our relationship in Egypt, and he has since become more irritable from the misery of power. The higher Napoleon rose, the further he could fall. The more he commanded, the more people demanded. The more trappings of royalty he took on as emperor, the more Europe's aristocracy called him impostor and usurper. He greeted me, after two months' campaigning, with too little sleep and too much impatience.

"Gage in Bohemia? I thought I sent you across the English Channel." His voice was brusque.

"I did as you asked and conducted naval diplomacy with both sides," I said. "It ended badly, through no fault of my own." I refused to make meek excuses, even though it was intimidating to thread through his ring of imperial guardsmen, Mameluke bodyguards, unctuous aides-de-camp, and hovering colonels. I'd be more than happy to be dismissed from this consumptive army that ate its way across Austria.

Murat had escorted me to Napoleon's tent in a field camp near Wolkersdorf. The French were marching toward the city of Brunn, twelve miles short of where the retreating Austrians and Russians had turned to rally, and a great battle was brewing. As I reluctantly rode with French cavalry to report to the emperor, we followed the telltale trail of war. The half-frozen roads were mush churned by hooves, boots, and wheels. Columns of smoke marked where marauding cavalry, looting infantry, or opportunistic bandits had set fires. Peasants mournfully watched the army pass, the refugees bent under their belongings and so thickly wrapped that they looked like walking tubs of laundry. I shared bread with some of them. The Russians were the most brutal, they assessed, the Austrians the most hungry, and the French the greediest. Did I know which way they should flee?

I did not. The smell of dung, corruption, and ashes was everywhere.

We passed a train of whores, peddlers, moneylenders, thieves, beggars, madmen, and shirkers, the types that stick to every army like burrs on a tail. Calloused and weathered vivandières, long hair tucked into their woolen scarves and voices hoarse from calling, slogged in their secondhand hussar jackets and filthy skirts to offer *tonnelet* kegs of brandy painted a patriotic red, white, and blue. The price was a franc per ounce, and fatalistic infantry paid this absurdity. They might die tomorrow, so what value was money? And did mademoiselle wish to sell something more as well?

We also passed corpses hanging from bare trees, the bodies presumably those of spies, partisans, or bandits. Crows pecked at the frozen flesh, and the land was gloomy. The fields and copses of wood were flecked with patches of old snow. The soldiers were tired. They'd already marched a thousand miles, fighting a dozen small engagements. The farther they advanced, the more the odds mounted against them. Napoleon needed a decisive victory to finish this war.

Everyone was cold and wet. Officers claimed billets in houses, paid for with letters of credit, and the generals had field tents. Wagoners could sleep in, or under, their vehicles. The rest had only their greatcoats, called capotes in French, and slept in the open when they couldn't commandeer a shed or barn. Their pack was their pillow, and tied rags their nightcap. Most hadn't changed clothes for three months. Wash water had a skin of ice each morning, and the army moved too fast to dig proper latrines. Napoleon might disdain Venetian corpses, but he was never fastidious about the stink of his own regiments, which you could smell before you could see. Now he frowned at me.

"What do you mean, 'It ended badly'?" he demanded.

Could he not know of the battle off Cape Trafalgar? "When Admiral Villeneuve learned he might be relieved of command at Cadiz, he decided to sail and fight."

Napoleon's sigh steamed in the cold, the air chilly even in a square tent crowded with officers. Outside, sleet skittered. The general gave me a cutting look. To avoid those gray eyes, I inventoried how emperors campaigned. A checkered canvas tarp made a floor, a folding camp chair served as throne, and his bed was a thin mattress on a folding iron frame. Accoutrements included a sword, pistols, and a toilet kit that held toothbrush, tweezers, tongue scraper, scissors, ear picker, and corkscrew. There was a jar of licorice, a small looking glass, and a gilded bottle of cologne.

The emperor was dressed in his habitually modest green uniform coat of the chasseurs, wearing a colonel's epaulets. He'd lost weight on campaign.

"Gage helped with the ruse at the Tabor Bridge," Murat put in. "Under my command."

The cavalry commander was still smarting from a second rebuke by his emperor brother-in-law. Having been scolded for wasting time taking Vienna, Murat had briefly redeemed himself with my cheerful lies at Tabor Bridge. But then the idiot had fallen for the same trick three days later! Russian prince Peter Bagration delayed French attacks by claiming another armistice, and Murat was confused enough to allow the enemy to escape. Napoleon's reaction was volcanic. Now Murat, splendiferous and moody, was trying, like a happy but chastened hound, to get back in the emperor's good graces. Bonaparte's suspicious scowl swung from me to Murat and back again.

"Villeneuve risked battle? Gage, I ordered you to negotiate peace with Admiral Nelson to preserve my fleet! A naval show-down does me no good when my army is preoccupied with Austria and Russia. The navy was to wait until I returned to invade England!"

I tried to look dignified and opaque, like Foreign Minister Talleyrand. People rise by learning to talk at great length about as little as possible. "I counseled both Nelson and Admiral Villeneuve to accept a mutual truce, and enlisted Emma Hamilton to make Horatio see reason. But I couldn't prevent battle."

Napoleon scowled. "Give me your report."

"You haven't heard?"

His tone was flat. "This is my first word of it."

The naval disaster had been fought four weeks before, and it was left to me to bring the bad news? What monstrous luck! I glanced at the marshals around me, hoping for support, and they all looked away. I cleared my throat. "I'm afraid Villeneuve was defeated."

There was a groan from the entire assembly. Napoleon's valet, Constant Wairy, made a fastidious note from his seat at a field desk. The bastard was probably already planning his memoirs, I thought darkly, and no doubt would paint woeful messengers in a bad light when making his own brilliance shine brighter. As much as I was unhappy with my recruitment into yet another Napoleonic adventure, I was also jealous of any climber more toadying and successful than me.

Napoleon interrupted my jealous reverie, face clenched tight as a pack strap. "How badly?"

"Both your fleet and the Spanish put up a brave fight, but the English are rather expert. I had to leave before the incoming storm fully hit, but your sea power suffered a substantial subtraction."

"Don't talk like a damned courtier. What's the sum?"

"Almost every ship in the Combined Fleet was either captured or sunk."

Now curses from the officers.

"Storm?"

"There was a hurricane after the battle, half the ships already dismasted and drifting. I was already hurrying to give you news, so didn't see the sinking, but I suspect the weather made things go from bad to worse."

"Disaster!" hissed Marshal Lannes.

"The Combined Fleet is gone?" Bonaparte's tone was near disbelief.

"I'm afraid so, *mon empereur.*" It never hurts to use a flattering title. I pondered on a way to soften the blow. "Nelson was wounded and almost certainly dying. It was fearsome havoc on both sides. I barely survived."

He looked at me with disgust. "Yet here you are, fifteen hundred miles away, without a scratch."

"My bruises are healing. I'm hurrying to save my family. I am told my wife might be imprisoned in Bohemia."

"Family!" He jumped from his camp chair and pounced like a tiger, grabbing my ear to inflict a torture he'd learned from his

Corsican mother, Letizia. He twisted my lobe with relish as I yelped in surprise. I bent my head and then turned my entire body to try to lessen the corkscrew of pain, but he squeezed like a vise. I'd have punched the bastard, but then I'd be shot.

"Your Majesty!" I gasped, as humiliated as a schoolboy. He used this torture on almost everyone, including women. A light pinch was a mark of favor, while a sadistic clamp made displeasure plain.

"You deserted my fleet to look for your family?" he roared.

"I didn't desert! The *Redoutable* sunk out from under me!"

"How could you get here ahead of everyone else?'

I was grimacing. "Habitual brilliance. I'm an experienced traveler, as you know. My family is near, and I've been in a lather to find them. And you. I thought you'd find my intelligence useful." Yes, now that I was Ethan Gage again instead of Hieronymus Franklin, I'd pretend to be the long-lost agent until I could escape again. What wretched fortune to survive a naval catastrophe, only to fall in with a marching army! Bonaparte moved too fast.

He finally released his grip and I staggered back, eyes watering. His hands were small, fine, and strong. His face was flushed, eyes darting to his maps, his mind calculating. "Did Villeneuve die?"

"I don't know. His ship surrendered."

"That fool has ruined everything."

Best to move on, I thought. "The good news is that Marshal Murat put me to use in Vienna. I think I've done my share."

"I conscripted him!" Murat shouted. The officers laughed.

I waited. Napoleon knew that I'd spied and fought for both the French and British sides—he had used that to his own advantage—and that my country was across an ocean, and my loyalties focused mainly on my family. I never entirely belonged anywhere, and yet was of service because of it.

Bonaparte sat heavily in the tent's only chair. His fleet destroyed! For three years he'd dreamed of invading England. Now, even if he won here, invasion was impossible. World domination required destroying Britain, not Austria, and destroying Britain required destroying British ships. Not a single English vessel had surrendered to the French.

"Gage, you materialize like an omen. Like the Little Red Man." There was a murmur at mention of this prophetic gnome; it made his marshals uneasy. "One moment you're helping France, and the next you're consorting with the English spymaster Sidney Smith. You swing like a weathercock."

"I'm an American neutral. I just want my family."

"What happened to that rifle I gave you? It was worth a small fortune."

"The British have it."

He closed his eyes, summoning control. "Always the damned English." Then he opened them, their gray cold and commanding. "Your news makes our campaign more important than ever."

"You've never had luck with the ocean."

"Well." The emperor collected himself. "If we are defeated at sea, we must smash Alexander's Russians and Francis's Austrians on land. They have foolishly become England's lackeys and must be destroyed because of it." He took a breath and stood again. "Which we will do. You've brought clarity, Gage, like a dousing from a bucket of ice water."

"Thank you, Your Majesty."

His eyes swept all of us. "We've had a month of astounding victories. We've conquered General Mack, taken the enemy capital, and seized his military stores for ourselves. But a final victory is assured only if I can get my enemies to engage before they fully gather their forces. I need them overconfident, I need them hurried, and I need them confused."

"If they're confident, they're fools," said Murat. "We've chased them from the Black Forest to Moravia."

"And yet our supply lines are stretched, our armies scattered, and the English naval victory will give them encouragement." Napoleon moved to a map, lips pursed. "Constant, how far away is the 4th Dragoon Division?" The question was a bark.

"We've had dispatches, *mon empereur*." The secretary jumped to another table and began sifting through messages. "I recall seeing it, and if you will give me five minutes . . ."

"The 18th regiment of the 2nd Brigade is commanded by Lefebvre-Desnouettes and is at Stockerau with orders to take Znaym, three hundred men," Napoleon recited without waiting. "The 19th is at Pressburg and ordered to Holitsch, four hundred men. The 17th, 15th, and 27th will hold at Gundersdorf for further orders, which will bring up Laplache's brigade of one thousand." It was a brilliant display of memory, and I'd no doubt Bonaparte could repeat the entire army list. His power of recall was dazzling. He didn't curse luck; he made it. "You're a gambler, American. Would you bet on my cards?"

"In brelan, the cards are secondary to the bluff," I said, relieved that anger had turned to solutions. My ear still smarted. "You can take any pot with strong cards, but the art is winning when your hand is weak."

Now his look was appreciative. "See? This is why I retain Gage. He's a rogue, but not a stupid rogue. Find the utility of every man."

"Wise counsel," Murat said, in order to remind us again that he'd found me.

I straightened. Not my choice of compliment, but better than I usually get. Some officers regarded me jealously, and I realized I could make too many enemies by making Napoleon too much of a friend. Careful, Ethan.

"The Allied strategy is to draw me on," the emperor continued, taking on the tone of a lecturer. "I have fifty thousand men here in Bohemia, but Francis and Alexander have gathered eighty thousand at Olmütz. There will be a hundred thousand if we give enough time for Constantine and Essen to come up. We are using another fifty thousand guarding Vienna and my supply lines to France, but Austrian archdukes Charles and John are bringing eighty thousand in forced march from Italy. Ferdinand has ten thousand to the west to fall on our rear. Masséna is too far away to come to our aid. The British and Swedes threaten the Low Countries, and the Italians and British make mischief in southern Italy. Gage, you're a student of Hannibal and the casino. What kind of hand am I holding?"

The only reason he tolerated me was honesty. "A dangerous one. If you give the enemy time to act in concert, the odds are hopeless." Another murmur. "You could take your winnings, the capture of Mack's army, and negotiate for the best peace you can get." I turned to the others. "Or you can go all in."

Napoleon smiled. "Indeed. I've put my head in the noose to pursue my enemies, and my only course now is to make them even more reckless than I am. What strategy would you adopt in brelan, Gage?"

"I'd bluff. But in this case the cards are exposed, since both sides have scouts who can count. The Allies know they outnumber you, and the longer they wait, the greater their advantage."

"Exactly. My spies tell me Russian general Kutuzov has counseled exactly such patience, but younger and more eager Russian princes are anxious to fight. There's no glory in delay and maneuver. Kutuzov is a commoner, and they despise him for it. Emperor Alexander is torn between common sense and the aristocracy he must placate to consolidate his power. I, meanwhile, need a decisive battle while I can still even the odds. I need Alexander to attack, but only when and where I want him to. How do you draw an opponent out, American gambler?"

"By feigning weakness."

He turned to the others. "And what would look weaker than

sending a foreign hanger-on like Ethan Gage to beg for time from an enemy?" The officers laughed.

This new diplomatic duty was alarming. I was searching for my wife.

"Gage does exude a certain craven cleverness," Marshal Lannes judged.

"The kind of duplicitous diplomat who negotiates to save himself," Murat added. "Royals will remember his treachery at Tabor Bridge and view our use of him as cynical and desperate."

"The American is obsessed with his own family when the world is on a knife-edge," Constant chimed in.

"The world is always on a knife-edge," I said, but no one was listening.

"Gage is as feeble as a hare in a snare, with Alexander the watching Russian wolf," added Napoleon's aide-de-camp General Anne-Jean-Marie-René Savary. "Using an American will confuse them." This guileful officer had won the emperor's favor by commanding his bodyguard, crushing French rebels, and overseeing the illegal execution of the Duc d'Enghien. Any sensible man was wary of him, including me.

"Exactly," Napoleon replied. "We're going to choose our place to fight, cousins. And we're going to use the American to bait the trap." He turned to me. "Gage, I'm sending you with Savary to offer a truce. The more the enemy holds you in contempt, the more likely you are to succeed."

"I know nothing about Russians."

"I don't want you to study them. I want you to draw them to where I can kill them. We have a week at most to destroy them before they become so strong that they destroy me."

"Lure them where?"

"Exactly." Once more he addressed the others. "The Allies have three choices. They can march into the forested hills of Bohemia, to my far left, between Brunn and Prague, and hurry westward to cut my supply lines and retreat. But that puts their army columns on hilly forest roads, out of touch with each other."

"We could crush each column as it emerges from the woods," Lannes said.

"Second, they can march directly from Olmütz toward Brunn and attack me head-on. But I have a choice of several heights to make a stand on, and if I lose I simply fall back on my supply routes. Even an Allied victory could result in stalemate."

"The last thing Czar Alexander wants," said Savary. "He fancies himself Alexander the Great. Emperor Francis wants to be Charlemagne."

"Third, they can swing south, around my right. If successful, this puts them between our forces and Vienna, and closer to the Austrian dukes coming from Italy. They would retake their capital, unite their forces, and force me into a precipitous retreat. A combined army could chase us all the way to Paris."

"You think they'll try that," I summed up.

"I prepare for every contingency. But that would be my choice, were I Alexander or Francis. So: a thousand miles from home, winter coming on, enemy reinforcements marching from all directions, our supplies thin and troops tired. What is our task, cousins?"

"To have them try to turn our right flank in a place of our choosing," Murat said. He had the eagerness of a schoolboy and recited the answer the teacher wanted. "And then strike a devastating counterblow."

"You are learning at last. Yes, to turn their own confidence against them. I have ground in mind. We're too weak, and too extended, to attack the enemy at Olmütz. We must convince them to hurry to us by pleading for time."

"The more you beg, the less you get," I offered. "That's been my experience, anyway." I take lessons from my failures.

"I'm gambling like brelan, Gage, and I'm gambling that the

Austrians will recognize you and trust nothing you tell them. Promise me that you can still lie and dissemble, trick and deceive, mislead and divert."

"I'm actually honest to a fault. And even if they think the worst of me, won't they be tempted to just shoot or hang me?"

He smiled. "That's a risk I'm prepared to take." The joke, if it was one, got a hearty laugh. "No, they'll send you back with a counteroffer to conceal their movements, in time for glorious battle to embroil us all."

CHAPTER II

I will not exaggerate my importance as bait. Alexander I of Russia was a czar at twenty-seven, thrilled to be at war, and an egotist who hardly needed to be egged on by me. The man was convinced it was God's will that the Russians give the godless French a good thrashing. (Never mind that Napoleon had invited the Catholic Church back after declaring the Revolution over and that his regiments shouted, "By the sacred name of God, forward!" when advancing.) By the time Savary and I reached the Allied emperors, their armies had swung from the defensive to the offensive, and on November 28 they drove a French screening force from the Moravian town of Wischau, halfway between Olmütz and Brunn. The ease with which Napoleon's outposts were driven back had astonished and excited the Allied high command. The French were not invincible after all!

Bonaparte had meanwhile found his preferred battlefield, a farmed hill called Pratzen, with broad, gently sloping shoulders. It was west of the château of Austerlitz and just south of the Brunn–Olmütz Road. From its heights he had a panoramic view of enemy maneuvers. The French right flank that Bonaparte expected the Allies would try to turn fortified itself in a lowland south of the Pratzen Heights, protected by frozen ponds, a stream, woods, and the tiny villages of Tellnitz, Sokolnitz, and Kobelnitz. Cannons crouched behind stone walls, and loopholes were knocked in the walls of farmhouses.

Napoleon's left flank thus straddled the road, his center was atop the hill, and his right waited in the foggy valley. Clearly outnumbered, he had ordered Marshal Louis-Nicolas Davout to bring his corps by forced march from Vienna.

The question now was whether the Austrians and Russians would attack, as desired, and if they would do so carefully, as feared. The emperor risked Savary and me to help ensure the former and prevent the latter. Timing was critical. If we could stretch out diplomatic palaver long enough, we'd give the French time to almost equal the Allies in number. If we conveyed weakness, the Allies would turn reckless. My presence was to encourage attack, and Savary's job was to delay it until the right moment.

So once more I found myself in the last place I like to be: between two armies, in a fight I had no stake in, with not even a pistol in my belt. I was desperate to resume my hunt for Astiza and Harry. But I was boxed in by a retinue of Savary's aides and had no alternative until I could contrive to slip away. We rode under flag of truce into the aftermath of the early skirmish, trotting gingerly up the Olmütz Road past a scattering of dead men and horses, abandoned equipment, and broken wagons. Russian dragoons had stampeded the French cavalry, and then the Arkhangel Musketeers had stormed the village of Rausnitz. In the dark following the action, we passed a huddle of more than a hundred

French prisoners, seated miserably in a field with no fire and no food. The Russians guarding them were big, solemn, brutish-looking peasants in coats that reached to their knees. Many had crosses around their necks of a size usually hung on walls. Mounted Cossacks, as lithe as Mongols, roamed the periphery on ponies as shaggy as their fur hats. Light snow fell and melted, the war cast in gray.

Imperial Russian scouts galloped up to meet us, clods flying, the officers excited as hounds by the French retreat. It was the start of great glories to come, they believed. They wheeled to box us in, the nostrils of their horses blowing steam, their own faces red and shiny.

"A message to your emperors from ours," Savary said. "We need to talk."

"It appears you do," a self-satisfied Russian major replied, gesturing to corpses lying near the road. Snow had powdered them like pastry. "The east is becoming less to French liking, I think. Who is that one?" He pointed at my civilian clothes.

"A neutral diplomat," I said. "Ethan Gage, at your service." As is customary, we all spoke French. "American by birth and negotiator by profession. Napoleon uses me for delicate missions."

"Surrender is not delicate, monsieur, and the French must accede to it if they wish to leave Bohemia alive. But you can repeat Bonaparte's honeyed lies to my masters, and bring back truth to the tyrant. This way—we ride through the night."

We galloped past regiment after Allied regiment, their campfires constellations of stars turned upside down. I'd been with Napoleon in Egypt and Marengo and seen the huge scale of war. Yet this campaign had more than twice that dimension. If Napoleon's reinforcements arrived, approximately seventy-five thousand French would face eighty-one thousand Russians and Austrians. These were unprecedented numbers to control, feed, and arm. Conflict was swelling like a tumor, and the challenge was to control its cancer. Bonaparte was Prometheus, bringing not fire but firepower to the world.

The Russian czar had a reputation as a reformer, but his nation remained an autocracy opposed to all that French or American revolutionaries represented. It was an empire reliant on size and serfdom. When enlisted Russians approached their officers with a question, they fell to their knees to ask. These men were beaten like mules, shouted at like the deaf, and shuffled like slaves. They looked like shambling bears.

In battle, however, the Russians were fiercely patriotic and had the reputation of being almost impossible to capture alive. They would die fighting.

We found the two enemy emperors in a manor in the captured town of Wischau. We were ushered into an overheated salon through the usual ring of sentries and functionaries, the inner circle sparkling with braid, medals, buttons, and boot polish.

I decided the Russian looked more the emperor than the Austrian. For one thing, Alexander was ruthless. The czar had boyish good looks and Western tutors, but he'd also acceded upon the assassination of his father, Paul, whose governing was erratic to the point of lunacy. Four years ago, the czar's generals had dragged Paul out from behind the dressing stand where he was hiding and sabered, strangled, and stomped him to death. Then they'd gone to find his weeping son. "Time to grow up," General Nicholas Zubov had told Alexander. "Go and rule!"

And so he did, with typical Russian grit and lack of sentimentality. He brought in a cabal of young reformers, tried to overhaul the sclerotic bureaucracy, and started reforms of his brave but clumsy army. Word was that Alexander had founded a new port on the Black Sea, called Odessa, that was already a success, and was gobbling up other Ottoman lands. He'd also reassured the nobility by putting a stop to any nonsense about freeing serfs. Now he was in the prime of his life: erect, athletic, confident, virile—he went through mistresses like a post rider goes through horses—and resplendent in a black uniform with blue slash. He was a clean-shaven and ruddy-cheeked man with high forehead and curly, sand-colored hair. His boots were bright as obsidian, his spurs golden. He was a Murat with better taste, I decided, and clearly relished the opportunity to save Europe from Napoleon.

Now I'd been drafted to help save Napoleon from him. I felt squeezed between their egos.

Austria's Francis II, by contrast, was thirty-seven, slight, and more timorous, since his armies had been bested by Bonaparte several times. Because he had lost so many men from the surrender of General Mack, his soldiers were now the minority of the Allied army. Still, his officers were trying to graft Austrian organization onto Russian boldness, devising a complex battle plan. Francis was the prissier of the two emperors, in white and gold too pretty for battle, but he didn't pretend to be martial. Alexander had energy, accomplishment, and ambition, while Francis was earnest and plodding, a balding monarch still stunned by French successes.

Savary and I sensed power in the room—it was as intimidating to enter enemy headquarters as it is to walk into a bear den—but not unity. The chamber was crowded with generals of two nations, each as proud as a cock. Russia's Prince Bagration had the beak and jaws of a nutcracker: lean, thin-lipped, and predatory. Napoleon thought him the best warrior of the bunch. General Kutuzov, aged sixty, was considered the wiliest, but he appeared to have been ignored, leaning in a chair against a wall in the rear of the room. He was fat, drunk, and old, his eyelids heavy, yet I saw him watching everyone.

It was Savary who presented Napoleon's proposal. "The French emperor requests a cessation of hostilities for twenty-four hours," the aide-de-camp said, "time enough for both of us to exchange our wounded and consider our positions."

"What wounded have you captured to exchange?" Emperor Alexander replied. He was proud of the skirmish he'd won.

"We're talking about mercy, Your Excellency." I didn't trust Savary, but he was the right man for this job. He could lie like a horse trader.

"And who is this?" the Russian said, turning to study me with distaste.

"An American negotiator of peace," I said, speaking up. "I've supped with President Jefferson and can tell you he admires your reforms, Your Highness." This was true. When you come from a chain of tyrants, any improvement looks good.

"I'm glad to hear it. I wrote your leader in August about the workings of federalism, and he sent me some books. We both have large empires. Yours has expanded with Louisiana."

"I had a hand in the sale of that French territory. My president admires France, too, Your Excellency. I'm sure he'd counsel peace."

"Yet he has doubled his nation and started his own war with the Barbary pirates. Are you representing America here?"

"No. Fortune has made me peacemaker to the French army, and I'm trying to prevent needless bloodshed. Each side has won honors. Twenty-four hours will give you time to begin a mutual retreat, saving countless lives." Everyone present knew there wasn't a whit of a chance of this. When you march thousands of men hundreds of miles, you're damn well going to use them; it was just a question of when. So I was consciously trying to play the fool.

"What if my intention is to sleep in Paris?" It was a jaunty taunt.

"Paris is a long way. I, for one, am half-frozen, and there's time for hostilities to be suspended for Christmas. A truce would be a first step toward an armistice and treaty."

Napoleon intended nothing of the sort, of course, and had explained our roles as actors before we set out. "If Alexander and Francis accept my proposal," he had instructed, "it will suggest they are still too disorganized for a general assault. I will accordingly smash them with an attack of my own. Should they refuse, it will tell us that their own attack is imminent and we must maneuver to meet it. Both of you must watch their eyes as well as their tongues."

"You'd make a fine brelan player," I'd told Napoleon. "And you're clever enough to put my head in the lion's mouth, not yours."

"Yes. Your execution would be another sign of their eagerness for battle."

Now someone shouted in the hot and crowded room. "That insect is the lying scoundrel from Tabor Bridge!"

With dismay I recognized the voice of the Austrian general Auersperg. Hadn't he been cashiered or imprisoned yet? He pushed forward through a crowd of Russian and Austrian staff officers and pointed at me like a biblical prophet. "Do not believe a word this man says. He slithers like a serpent! He's a despicable rascal, a fraud, an impostor, a saboteur, and a reptile." He fumbled for his sword, face mottled with frustration and rage. "He hid in the mud of the Danube riverbank before I could kill him, but I'll run him through now!"

I tried to step back but was hemmed in. "I've no weapon and am under flag of truce, General. This is rather unseemly."

"He claimed armistice before!"

"And you drank champagne to it, if I recall."

Alexander put his hand up, even though Auersperg was an Austrian general, not a Russian one. "No one is running anyone through. This is a negotiation. Put your sword away; you've disgraced yourself enough." Such a public rebuke was devastating, and Emperor Francis colored at this reminder of his nation's embarrassment. Auersperg stepped back, humiliated once more.

I gave him a bright smile, dismissing his criticism. As Franklin said, *Whether you're an honest man, or whether you're a thief, depends on whose solicitor has given me my brief.*

"Why does Bonaparte send an American minion to deliver a message requiring trust?" Austria's Francis demanded, annoyed at my presence and apparently not as philosophical as old Ben.

Savary spoke up. I found Napoleon's aide conceited; he found me flippant. "I didn't know he was at the Tabor, and I'm sure his role is being exaggerated," the Frenchman lied. "The American is nothing; pay no attention to him. He is Napoleon's pet, given to me as much as a servant as anything else."

"The use of a neutral American to propose terms is a deliberate insult to Allied arms," a prince spoke up. This was Peter Petrovich Dolgoruki, a noble so full of himself that he seemed about to inflate and burst. "The contempt of the Corsican usurper is clear. America has no role here. Napoleon has sent a jester."

"You don't think we need his armistice, Dolgoruki?" Alexander asked mildly.

"Not when the enemy has run in terror before us for two days."

I could have pointed out that the Allies had run the other way for two months, but Dolgoruki's pride was exactly what Napoleon was hoping for.

"Here's a letter from my emperor," Savary said. "It is offered in respect."

"Francis?" Alexander asked.

"We will consider it in private," the Austrian emperor said. "Wait here." The two rulers withdrew to another room to read the document, everyone but Savary and me bowing, saluting, or snapping to attention when they did so.

We waited, without chairs or refreshment, for a good half hour. Dolgoruki and Auersperg stared daggers. The rest boasted to one another about their derring-do. Russian majors sipped from flasks of vodka and told ribald stories, and Austrian staff officers studied maps.

"The French are exhausted," I overheard Dolgoruki say. "We outnumber them by thirty thousand men, they've outmarched their supplies, and the time to strike is now. By sending this American, Bonaparte is proposing a truce that can't be trusted."

"Perhaps he thinks a neutral can bargain a better deal."

"And this Gage looks harmless," said a third. "Maybe there's message in his demeanor. Like showing weaponless hands before a parley."

"No, I've heard of this rascal. He was a spy at Marengo, a scoundrel in the Caribbean, and a conspirator in Paris."

It's flattering to have a reputation. I puffed a bit.

At length the emperors emerged, and Alexander called to Prince Dolgoruki. "Deliver this back to Napoleon." He handed him a letter with his own seal. "And take those two back as well. I don't like Gage's Tabor Bridge trick, but he isn't worth a bullet."

For once I agreed.

"Monsieur Savary, my compliments to your master, even while I question the characters he associates with."

Savary bowed. "The French emperor believes every man has utility."

"Not always apparent, is it?" Alexander looked at me.

Then he spoke to his prince in lower tones. Dolgoruki was being given his own misleading mission.

CHAPTER 12

At length the prince saluted and we swung up onto our horses and started back for our own lines, this time escorted by a troop of Russian orderlies. A French lieutenant galloped ahead to find Bonaparte. By now it was morning. I was exhausted from a sleepless night and relieved that this mission hadn't resulted in my being run through by an Austrian madman.

Empty countryside separated the two armies, the coming battlefield exhibiting the stillness of winter.

Entering a deployed army is like sinking into thicker and thicker atmosphere. The first French pickets and skirmishers gave challenge from trees and ditches. Then outlying screens of cavalry were spied, waiting to dash and give warning. Next came light infantry, thick as wasps, and finally the heavy line infantry and artillery beyond, cannons parked and campfires smoking. The Russian prince, who had spent several miles detailing for us the superiority of St. Petersburg over Paris and London—although he had been to neither—absorbed every detail with a soldier's eye. Napoleon was allowing him to observe what he wanted the prince to see.

We came to Rausnitz Brook. Across it, drawn up on the Pratzen Heights, were the two corps of Lannes and Soult. Twenty thousand men stood as if on parade, three hundred feet above the surrounding plains. Winter sun stage-lit the demonstration, the sky pale blue and the rolling farmland brown and yellow. Bugles sounded, drums rolled, and the regiments expertly formed into thirty alternating infantry squares, like a toy-soldier chessboard of blue and white. It stretched for two miles. Bayonets glinted, bands played, and a hundred battle flags lofted in a light breeze. War is pretty, at the start. And then the formations wheeled and the French abandoned a commanding geographic position and retreated west, sinking from sight on the far side of the hill.

Was Napoleon taking the first steps back to Paris?

I glanced at Dolgoruki. He kept a gambler's face, but his eyes betrayed a gleam. That the French were abandoning a commanding position like the Pratzen Heights had to mean that they were weak, uncertain, outnumbered, exhausted, and trying to withdraw. The tide had turned. The Russian bear and the Austrian eagle must charge and swoop to claw before the French got away. I could sense his anxiousness to relay this news.

It was brelan all over again. Napoleon was showing false cards. He would hide some of his soldiers until it was time to spring his trap.

The Russian, convinced that French morale was collapsing, did not suspect this. "Have your commanders lost their compass, Savary?" Dolgoruki gibed.

The aide was almost as good an actor as me. "I don't know what the devil we're doing. I'm only a messenger, Prince, saddled with a petition for truce and an American imbecile as an aide."

"It's probably cold up on that hill," I suggested aimlessly, to reinforce my apparently notorious stupidity. "Marching to get warm, I'd guess."

"We know we outnumber you," the prince pressed. "We know you're stretched thin." It was a boast, but also a clumsy attempt to get information. "We know you hope to fall back on Vienna." He wanted to provoke us into betraying something useful.

"I've seen the French at war in Italy and Egypt," I told Dolgoruki with perfect honesty. "They're demon fighters. Bonaparte can be a lion. As a man who has watched too many wars from all sides, permit me to say that a truce is a chance to save everyone. Just to give friendly warning."

"Now you're a strategist, American?"

"A Franklin man. An electrician. Do you know I broke a French attack once with a jolt from electrical batteries? Franklin learned how to store energy in jars like pickles. It's the damnedest thing."

"He exaggerates," said Savary, who had no idea what I was talking about.

"I'm just saying this is your last chance to parley."

Yes, we were quite the dissemblers, Savary and I. The French army seemingly going backward, Napoleon begging for twenty-four hours, and the full might of Russia finally assembled. I'd have been eager to attack, too.

"Let's hear what your emperor replies," the Russian said. He stretched in his stirrups, obviously excited and impatient to report back.

Napoleon deliberately kept us waiting, and as the three armies shuffled, I had the common sense to take a nap. Soldiers and diplomats learn to snooze when they can. Finally, well after dark, Bonaparte galloped up with an entourage of fifty officers, ready to receive the written reply of Francis and Alexander. He opened the letter, read by lantern light, frowned—pretending again—and walked apart from us to confer with Prince Dolgoruki alone.

We couldn't hear what was said, but their voices rose higher. After fifteen minutes, too brief for any real negotiation, the French emperor waved his hand dismissively and the prince bowed and strode back, stiff as a stick. He mounted his horse and called his orderlies.

"The Russian and Austrian emperors have not agreed to a truce, and yours insists he is not retreating," the prince said. "It seems you are bent for war."

"As are you," Savary replied.

"We will meet battle like brave men."

"Courage on all sides, I suspect."

"Those who have to fight." The Russian glanced at me, and I shrugged. Then he yanked his reins tall, proud, and eager, and galloped. Good riddance.

Napoleon mounted his own white mare, a splendid Arabian named Marengo, and trotted over. The Mameluke bodyguard Roustan hovered protectively behind.

"You provoked them as I hoped, Ethan," he said with easy familiarity.

"I'm happy to help, Your Majesty," I said diplomatically. "I will now leave your service to proceed to Prague. Best of luck, mission accomplished, give my regards to the empress."

"Have a silver snuff box." It was the emperor's standard gift. "I'm pleased with your duplicity. I think Dolgoruki will urge his army to plunge into our plan."

I don't sniff tobacco, but a box to hold it was worth hocking. "Thank you. I'm actually the most honest of men, which is why no one believes me."

"Come," Napoleon said. "Just one more inquiry before you go." Our assembly rode back west on the road toward Brunn, passed the Pratzen Heights in the dark, to our left, and came to the main army, hidden behind the hill. Generals fell in with his entourage as if joining a posse, their bicornes and bouncing plumes reminding me of the soldiers' nickname, "the Big Hats."

We slowed to a walk when we entered the camp of the emperor's guard, tall men with proven battlefield courage who boasted the privilege of growing mustaches. Napoleon called them his grognards, the veteran grumblers. Fires flickered ahead, illuminating the emperor's tent. Napoleon spoke in a low voice. "I want to show you a bauble, Gage. You know how I believe in signs and portents."

"I know you believe in destiny."

"The day after tomorrow is the first anniversary of my crowning as emperor. An interesting opportunity, no? I want to fight on a lucky day."

"Some of my savant friends say fortune is just coincidence."

"Yet I am emperor, and they are not. How else but destiny to explain where I am? Remember landing on the beach with me at Alexandria and finding the woman who became your wife? How else can we explain my rise, and your survival?"

"We're both clever opportunists, *mon empereur*. You more than me."

"And both fascinated by powers beyond the material world. I remember the power of the Great Pyramid, and your quest for mystical objects. Come, inside my tent."

We entered alone, a sign of favor that startled Napoleon's officers and guards. Roustan and Constant tried to follow, but Napoleon waved them off. "Gage is a rogue, but a rogue I trust."

I suppose I could have stabbed the man, but the opportunity didn't even occur to me. Despite my impatience, I felt proud at consorting with emperors. They're dangerous as adders, but seductive as succubi.

He went to a jewelry box inlaid with mother-of-pearl. "I don't really trust you," he said to me alone, "just as I trust no man completely. Trust is for fools. A few men would die for me, like

Roustan and Mustapha, but that doesn't make them friends, and certainly not advisers. I control men with honors, power, money, fear, and praise. You're more honest than most in admitting self-interest, and it's your self-interest I trust."

"I suppose I'm flattered, but I really must be on my way."

"Yes, yes. Here is my charm." He withdrew a curious object slightly shorter than my forefinger. A crystal lion with a human head reposed on a brightly jeweled silver base dotted with rubies and emeralds. The talisman had two jeweled arms curving down like the inverted beak of a long ship, so that if you flipped the object upside down, the base could look something like a boat. Hinged shields hung on either side. I estimated the knickknack was worth more than I'd ever earned or stolen.

"It's beautiful, Your Majesty. Odd. Impractical. Costly."

"It's the Sphinx, but the Sphinx with the face of Joséphine. Don't you see? Canova carved it from rock crystal, a magical substance between the visible and invisible worlds, life and the afterlife. Seers use such crystal."

"My wife would be impressed. A hundred gems, I reckon."

"Precisely 114. They're arranged in a pattern that encodes important dates in my life. In these places"—he pointed to the ruby flaps—"there are twenty-one, corresponding to the twenty-one cards of the tarot. The emeralds are Corsican green. Red rubies represent rose, the name my wife used before I married her. The rose is mystical, Gage."

"So Astiza tells me."

"The artistry is inspired by the mysteries we learned in Egypt. The Sphinx has a lion's body, and Leo is my astrological symbol. Its breasts symbolize my hope that my wife will suckle an heir. The silver cone on the base holds a lock of her hair."

"You're a romantic, general." His marriage was actually turbulent. I'd been present when he almost divorced Joséphine because of her unfaithfulness, and he'd used her infidelity to justify a string of mistresses. Yet, since he crowned her empress, his anxious fondness had grown. He desperately wanted a son.

Napoleon watched me with that intensity that makes every courtier uncomfortable, and every soldier brave. His fingers worked the piece. "This is what I want you to see."

He flipped the ruby flaps upward and held the object so I was looking down on it. "What pattern?"

I thought a moment. "A cross."

"Exactly. The rosy cross of the Rosicrucians, that mystic sect in search of ancient knowledge. I think that order had the power to foretell the future. So my question to you is: Where is the Brazen Head?"

I was startled he'd remember to bring this old quest up on the eve of a great battle, but then, Napoleon forgot nothing. He'd set Astiza and me on our mission to find the mechanical oracle, and could open and close the memories of his brain like drawers in a cabinet. "I presume my wife is looking for it."

"You remember the Little Red Man."

I felt chilled. I didn't want that devilish imp appearing here. "Yes. The gnome serves as your fortune-teller." By legend the creature had appeared to French kings and queens for generations, and lived in the attics of palaces.

"At his convenience, not mine. The creature gives enigmatic hints, but never the full answers I plead for. I need a prophet I can control, Ethan. I need one as reliable as a clock. I need the Brazen Head."

Here was an opportunity. "Which is precisely why I'm hurrying to find Astiza, *mon empereur.* Your diplomatic mission sending me to Lord Nelson delayed our reunion, but I'm desperate to get on with the hunt. You and I are in complete agreement. Send me to Prague. With a stipend for expenses, and maybe a medal for my services." It never hurts to ask.

"And you'll report only to me, not my ministers?"

He must mean Talleyrand. Why everybody was in such a bother to learn the future baffled me, since news is usually bad and death inevitable, but I had to be careful not to be caught between the powerful. "Of course." It wasn't much of a lie, since I didn't believe this "android" really existed. "You can trust Ethan Gage."

"I already told you I trust only your self-interest. So yes, I'll send you to Prague, but in the company of your old cabal of conspirators. They're instructed to keep the closest possible eye on you and, if you find her, Astiza."

"Cabal?" I'd none that I knew of.

"A woman."

"Here? In an army camp?"

"Your former governess, Catherine Marceau. A beauty, as you know, and a spy of unusual drive and persistence. She was a great help at my coronation." He looked at me sternly. "As were you."

My attempt to sabotage his ceremony had been turned into a self-crowning triumph that made Napoleon the talk of Europe—and me overlord of a fiasco. Catherine was a spider who patrolled his webs. Now she'd followed me from Vienna? Catherine was as trustworthy as Delilah with scissors, and I regarded her like the plague. How to put it nicely? "Her combination with my wife would make our mission awkward," I said. "Too much beauty all around."

"The policeman Pasques is here to keep peace between all of you."

I had to clear my throat. "The devil you say. Pasques has come, too?"

"You will find this fabulous automaton, Ethan, and bring it to me. You will be loyal to me and me alone. Is that understood?"

So Baron Richter was looking for the Brazen Head with some kind of Invisible College, Talleyrand yearned for it as well, and Catherine Marceau was employed directly by Napoleon. Working for any one of them was like jumping into a dog pit. I was sweating in the cold. "Of course, *mon empereur*."

"Marceau said she's looking forward to reunion. She's lovely enough to test your wedding vows. I'd like to tup her myself. Look, there she is." He lifted the tent flap and pointed.

A woman with a great mane of golden hair sat fifty yards away by a campfire, facing away, knees pressed primly together, a riding cloak pulled tight against the cold, her slim hands holding a parasol. Next to her was a man as big as a bear. Pasques was leaning close and murmuring something. She was looking into the fire. "She does catch the eye," I managed.

"The pair is thrilled that fate brought you to my headquarters."

"I suppose they are." I'd kicked and shot at Pasques, sabotaged Catherine's pistol, and shoved her across an altar, but not before I'd seen her in the bath.

Napoleon smiled wolfishly. "Always you find attractive companions. You're as bad as Murat. Shall I summon her?"

I had to think quickly. "I ate unwisely." My face had conveniently turned gray at his news, but now I could use that to my advantage. "Before I say hello to a pretty lady, I'm afraid I must visit the latrine." Not the most dignified of escapes, but the only one I could think of.

"Now?"

"Unless you'd lend your chamber pot."

"I think not." His tone was dry.

"Can your guards point the way? I remember at Boulogne you said how hard it was to hold your piss during ceremonies."

He tapped his foot and gestured with his head. "In the ravine behind. Leave by the back of my tent, but be quick. Catherine Marceau is impatient, and I am busy."

"I will run."

And I did.

CHAPTER 13

Astiza

Alchemy comes from the Arab name for Egypt, *al-Khemia*, and embodies mankind's oldest quest, the desire for transformation. The Egyptians mummified for their journey to the afterworld. The Norse believed the rainbow was a bridge to the gods. The Babylonians and Persians speculated about angels, or feathered men who pass through star gates from one realm to the other. Francis of Sicily had a criminal locked in a box to watch him die, hoping to see the man's soul emerge.

No such sight was recorded.

Prophets have foretold the future. Mediums have communed with the dead. Astronomers have mapped the sky. Pythagoras

believed that geometry reflected divine wisdom. Gothic architects put such wisdom into stone. The Neoplatonists believed
numbers were the key to the cosmos, while the Cabalists de-
ciphered sacred texts, believing that one revealed word actually means another. Artists portray hell far more vividly than
heaven. Shamans speak to nature. Scientists weigh and measure.

I believe history is deeper than we remember. A great embry-
onic civilization flourished and failed ten thousand years ago,
leaving our imperfect remnant. In ancient ruins are enigmatic
clues to what we lost. The clothing of First Beings shone, legends
say. They soared through the air. They walked through walls.

As I read in the Klementinum library, I took painstaking notes.
Sometimes Primus Fulcanelli looked over my shoulder like an in-
dulgent father or husband. He stood closer than necessary, and
I failed to push him away. He's a strangely compelling man, his
mind as handsome as his body. I remain faithful, but he disturbs
me in ways that shame. He's an intellectual partner very different
from my irreverent husband.

It's my blessing and my curse to wonder. If you're a woman,
simply asking questions means being called a witch, a sorceress,
or a heretic. I don't care. The furnaces of new factories make ever
more intricate instruments to take ever more precise measure-
ments, in the faith that truth can be calibrated instead of grasped
like a hot coal. I believe truth looks like magic. I believe reality
looks like dreams. I believe the stars scribe our lives. I believe that
prayer talks to one's self, but that the self is eternal and sacred;
that God is within as well as without. I believe that life has purpose, but it is hidden from all but the purest.

So I climbed the creaking, ladder-steep wooden stairs of the
Astronomical Tower, deep in the heart of the Klementinum. I was
persuaded to leave Harry in the care of a nun and followed Fulcanelli's black boots and wine-colored robe upward, floor after
floor, the walls plaster and the beams dark and cracked.

"Are the answers in the stars or in our soul, priestess?" my host called down genially as we climbed. "I'd hate to pant this hard for nothing."

"As above, so below," I recited. "As within, so without. All is one, and one is all. We study the sky to discern events on earth. We search the cosmos to understand ourselves."

"So the view from this cold tower becomes a mirror?"

"The stars burn within us. Day needs night, and sun casts shadow. Understanding will come when we comprehend it whole and see the essential unity behind all things. Death is but a door to understanding, I hope. But I want to comprehend while still alive."

"The Church says the Bible contains all you need to know."

"Yet I understand that the library of the Vatican is greater than any on earth."

He looked down with a smile, and my heart skipped a beat. "Beware, Astiza. You are Icarus, flying close to the sun." He thought me a falcon on his wrist, controllable yet able to fly where he could not.

"I'm a wanderer in the desert, Primus, in the spirit of Abraham, Moses, Jesus, and Mohammed. Knowledge is my water."

"Forbidden fruit."

We climbed past brass instruments that precisely measure the angles to the planets, because astronomers use parallax to calculate their distance. The tower has astrolabes, quadrants, a pendulum, clocks, and telescopes mounted so high that wooden ladders are used to bring the astronomer to the eyepiece. Fulcanelli told me that savants stand there eight hours at a time, freezing or sweating, to measure the position of stars.

To find order, we look for cycles. There's an astronomical clock on Prague's city hall that is four centuries old. It measures time, the phases of the moon, the calendar, and the zodiac. Mechanical figures appear on the hour, representing vanity, miserliness, death, and pleasure. Harry has made us wait three times already for the figures to rotate into view. He's frightened by the skeleton but fascinated, too.

The Astronomical Tower of the Klementinum is less whimsical, illustrating how the world has turned from mystery and astrology to calculation and fact. Ethan's savant friends swear by the new methods, but I fear that the more we measure, the less we understand. Facts obscure comprehension.

After 172 steps—I had been warned how many—we came at last to a balcony that circles the tower, both of us breathing heavily. On the cupola above, Atlas held a globe topped by a weathervane. From the observation deck I could count the city's hundred towers, punctuating a folded range of red tile roofs. The fading winter light was yellow on the western horizon, lanterns lighting and stars popping out. They appeared from nothing, like a code. Why is a star in this place, and not that one?

"This is God made manifest, is it not?" asked Primus.

"And us made small," I replied. "How far are the stars, my wandering bishop?"

"No one knows for certain. Huygens calculated trillions of miles, and some have suggested that the universe is infinite. If God is infinite, why not?"

"How God must laugh at our strivings."

"I don't think so. He wants us to understand."

"*She* wants us."

He laughed, indulging me. "Blasphemy again, if one believes in the Trinity. But you believe in a pantheon, don't you, pretty pagan? How you flirt with heresy even in our liberal age. How you test our partnership!"

I smiled at this mutual teasing. "Yes, I have my own pantheon of goddesses, but each godly being is but a manifestation of the One. We're not far apart, you and me. Or the pope and me. And Bishop Fulcanelli would be uncomfortable indeed in any church council, I suspect. You have your own goals and, I deduce, your own creed."

He shrugged. "I speculate. Creation has produced marvelous books, momentous clues, and inquiring minds. We simply have to pay attention. I want to know what everything means. So, yes, we're alike, Astiza. Doomed by curiosity. Fate has brought us together."

It was a compliment to my mind, but I knew he meant more than that, despite his vows. Men and women can't have simple partnerships. His was the kind of comment I dared not answer if I was to remain faithful. Yet how I was tempted! I looked skyward instead. "I like nights when the stars seem close enough to touch. I want to believe that all of them would fit inside our hearts, and that all the eons of history are but a moment. If we had perfect insight, we'd understand that everything there is here, and everything past and future is now."

"Unity!" It was so dark that Fulcanelli wasn't embarrassed to stare at me. "It is what lovers seek." His face was a mask of shadow, but I could feel his intensity like a stove and took a proper half step away. But only a half step. I was using him while remaining confused about my motives. My desire.

"Friends seek unity, too," he amended. He shifted closer, and this time I let him.

Surely I could trust his pledge of celibacy. But he was a man, as wayward priests have proven again and again. I told myself: I must enlist him but be careful; I need an ally but must be faithful. I am lonely, but I dare not trust too much. I am a woman, with a woman's vulnerability and calculation, and must pretend to be only a seer. "Christian Rosenkreutz described an allegorical wedding that joined the sun and moon, symbols for sulfur and mercury. A royal couple are ritually killed, and then brought back to life by the blood of the phoenix."

"Centuries-old superstition," Primus said.

"Tales of death and resurrection are as old as Egypt. Older. Magic is older than Christianity, and in fact the Romans accused the first Christians of being magicians. They persecuted them because they feared them, as some people fear alchemy today. The alchemists promise power. Science responds with doubt. Yet the gold of alchemical tales is not just bright metal; it's the gold of spiritual understanding. It's the promise that with enough study, and enough steps, one can learn the reason of all existence and purify not lead but our own souls."

"We do that by answering for our deeds."

I ignored this Christian platitude. "Tell me, Bishop: Astronomers can chart the sky and predict the movement of planets. Do you think medieval man made a machine to chart the human character and predict the movement of people? Do you think the Brazen Head really exists?"

"Astronomers prove prediction is possible. Perhaps perfect knowledge allows perfect foreknowledge. Yet I tremble if such a thing is true. I think it would bring great evil."

"But what if we knew of future tragedies and could avoid them?"

"Yes," he conceded, "this automaton could be a mercy as well as a curse. But I don't think you'll find it in the clarity of a winter night, madame."

"I'm trying to imagine where Rosenkreutz might hide it."

"I think your real hope is a necromancer's old manuscript."

"An alchemist. Or astrologer."

"It sounds like you're an alchemist yourself."

"I've studied the theory," I told him. "Teachings about the unity of matter go back to Greece and Egypt. Paracelsus taught that salt, sulfur, and mercury could change one element to another. The alchemist Basilius Valentinus wrote how lead antimony could become a chariot of fire. Hugo Alverda and the Comte de Saint-Germain were said to be hundreds of years old, having achieved purities that allowed immortality. These are the kinds of men Rosenkreutz would have confided in."

"You're mad, priestess, like Joan of Arc. Could you conduct alchemical experiments?"

"If I had to. It's dirty, dangerous work." The sky was bright with stars now. "Read the sky, Primus. To the untutored eye it has no pattern, and yet to an astronomer or shepherd it tells stories like a book." I turned to him, his smell like wood, his shoulders broad. I did not forget Ethan, but he felt very far away. "We were brought together for a purpose, you and me. You're as curious as I am. What question would you put to the android?"

He laughed. "How to build another like him!"

"I would ask how to achieve unity." I was being shameless. Or did I simply yearn for human comfort? How dashing was this churchman!

Fulcanelli cleared his throat. He knew he was being used. He wanted to use me, in as many ways as he could. "In the precincts of the castle are wizards who live on the Golden Lane, an alley where goldsmiths gild and chemists heat cinnabar to make mercury, hoping it will dance its way to gold. Perhaps they know something of the Brazen Head and the mystery you pursue. Are you brave enough to let me take you there? It's a strange, heretical place."

"Discovery requires journeys. Tell me who to seek, Primus."

Now he moved very close, both of us so cold this winter evening that I could feel his heat. "There's one peculiar craftsman, a dwarfish warlock named Auric Nachash. He's studied the *Book of Secrets* of Albertus Magnus. I don't know how much to believe or trust him, but he claims to know fantastic tales of power and sorcery. He might have heard something. He might point you to Rosenkreutz. And he likes children."

I clasped the bishop's arm. A thrill went through us both. I could talk to this man so easily. "Then take me to him. I can master my fears."

"Of him, or me?"

"Why would I be afraid of you?"

In answer he kissed me, and I let him, and then broke free. "Please don't."

He didn't try again. Our arms had dropped away. But I could feel his intensity in the dark and was encouraged, not defeated. "I'll take you on one condition," he said.

"What's that?"

"That you take me with you when you go to find the Brazen Head."

CHAPTER 14

Trying to thread through Napoleon's army in civilian clothes, with no papers and French agents in pursuit, invited execution. So I decided to desert Napoleon's headquarters by joining Napoleon's army. If this seems nonsensical, consider that Catherine Marceau was the last woman I wanted to see, and her ally Pasques was the size and weight of a bulky armoire. Whether they denounced me or joined me in the search for Astiza and the Brazen Head, it would be disaster. Better to find refuge in the anonymity of the ranks and creep away when battle provided confusion.

After fleeing Napoleon's tent, I followed my nose, leaped the stinking trench of the headquarters latrine, and felt my way through the night woods until I came out on a lane a safe distance from the nucleus of command. Then I strode like a Big Hat, my erect posture discouraging challenge. I'd heard a headquarters rumor that Marshal Nicolas Soult might be held in reserve, so his corps sounded like the safest place to be: closest to the rear and convenient for desertion. I'm no coward, but I'm too clever by half to stand in line under fire for a fight that isn't mine.

Or so I thought.

Coming upon the 88th Line Regiment, I asked for directions to the medical tent by saying I had an urgent message. Two wagons were parked outside the field hospital, their teams picketed for the night. Napoleon's surgeon had come up with the novel idea of "flying ambulances" to evacuate the wounded. The hope of getting help when shot had done wonders for French morale. This genius glued soldiers to Napoleon's leadership and made men braver.

A battle casualty was not yet available, but I'd seen French troops contract plague in the Holy Land and yellow fever in Saint-Domingue. Sickness always fells more men than bullets. There is no shortage of corpses, even before the shooting starts. Those who succumb are mourned, or at least regretted, or at the minimum noted in ledger books, but armies are expert at closing ranks and picking over the effects of the dead.

Two women were boiling the uniforms of victims to rid them of lice so they could be reissued or cut up as patches. A new infantry uniform costs 250 francs, is issued once, and is mended to last a campaign; thus, empty clothes are prized. The length of any war can be judged by the raggedness and filth of uniforms. Additionally, everyone stole civilian blankets, cloaks, and scarves to supplement official garb.

The laundresses were members of that small legion of female camp followers that had trailed the Grand Army all the way from the Channel coast. The wives, cooks, prostitutes, and washerwomen were prized, for they sustained morale, cared for the sick, bound the wounded, and did camp chores. Most were tough as mules and sensible as mothers. In battle, many formed an irregular rear rank to fetch ammunition and shout encouragement, dragging wounded lovers to safety, while the pregnant ones looked after the babes that tended to appear during a march, slung on backs like haversacks.

The hospital washing was hurled onto bushes to steam in the dark, making it easy for me to creep and liberate a uniform. The army tagged the clothes in case friends wanted to make first claim, and so I learned I was about to temporarily become the unfortunate Francois Digeon of the 88th Line, Colonel Curial commanding. Digeon had succumbed to influenza.

I'd find a unit far from Digeon's friends.

Digeon apparently came near to my own five feet eleven. The uniform was clammy, but I'd already crawled into a casket, so putting on a dead man's clothes seemed a minor expediency. I took linen shirt, woolen waistcoat, socks, blue coat, woolen capote, and bicorne hat—Digeon didn't have the newer shako—while keeping my civilian boots, since they were far superior to infantry issue. I'd sleep with them either on my feet or under my knapsack pillow, to prevent their being stolen.

I pulled on the dead man's pants. By the grace of Isis, his unit had converted from the constricting knee breeches and stockings of the last century to the trousers of modern times. Most men look better without their legs on display, and pants are far more comfortable than breeches, even with gaiters to keep rocks out of shoes.

Digeon's crossbelts were made of bull hide that was clayed white, one supporting his cartridge belt and the other a sheathed bayonet. There was no musket or pack deposited with his clothes, so I crept through nearby companies to pilfer a gun, the standard cartridge box, a cowhide knapsack, and a leather canteen. My civilian clothes I stuffed into my newly stolen haversack with my mess tin and cup. I'd draw rations and cartridges from my new company.

I also stole a tonnelet of brandy from one of the snoring sutler women. It would work better than money to buy me new friends.

My uniform made me safely anonymous in the vast hive of the army. Should Catherine come looking, I'd be one of thousands of infantrymen. She and I would have our reunion someday, but on my schedule and my terms.

Or so I thought.

I learned immediately that it's uncomfortable being an infantryman. The cloth is rough and the equipment heavy, the gun alone a cumbersome ten pounds. I wandered a good two miles in the dark to seek the safest refuge, finally sneaking into the bivouac of the 14th Line, Colonel Jacques Mazas commanding.

It was midnight when I picked a likely campfire, its *ordinaire* of eight men lying in their greatcoats around it like spokes on a wheel, some asleep and others smoking and quietly talking. This was the basic French infantry squad that had occupied each hut at the vast military camp at Boulogne, where soldiers were paired two to a bed for warmth and economy.

There's a mood to armies, from exhalation to defeatism. Napoleon's Grand Army had quiet confidence. It had trained in the Channel camps for three years. It had overrun half the Austrian empire. Casualties had been light. Now this rugged professionalism was overlaid by the subdued seriousness that comes before a major battle. Men were increasingly absorbed by thoughts of mortality or, should fortune favor them, victory, plunder, or a convenient wound to send them home. While the Russians fantasized that Napoleon was on the brink of retreat, his own soldiers knew better. There would be a ferocious fight on a scale not seen for centuries. This they must win.

I'd seen the reverse at sea, with British confidence and French fatalism.

A sergeant challenged me. "Are you lost, Private?"

"And found, I hope." I had to lie persuasively, lest I be asked too many questions. "I'm separated from Davout's corps. I was knocked unconscious in the fighting near Melk and have been trying to catch up ever since. I've been wandering for a week."

"Davout! He's in Vienna. What's your unit?"

"Saint Raymond's 33rd." I'd heard this colonel briefly mentioned.

"You've still got a concussion if you think you're near that regiment. I haven't heard of them for a month. So you're a straggler? Or a deserter?" He gave me a challenging scowl in the firelight, to see if I'd blink or glance away.

I stoutly focused on his eyes. "I'm trying to avoid an accusation of desertion, Sergeant. François Digeon, reporting for duty." Having practiced looking doggedly earnest, I snapped to attention and gave a salute. My interrogator seemed less impressed by my military bearing than by my tonnelet of brandy. Besides, every unit was understrength. "Can I spend the night here? Perhaps I can march back to Vienna in the morning."

"We're about to fight a battle, imbecile. We don't have time for you to stumble about like a postman looking for an address."

I squatted without asking. "The army is spread for miles and miles. It's hardly my fault I can't find the part that is mine."

The sergeant eyed the width of my shoulders like a trader evaluating horseflesh. "You're big enough for the Imperial Guard. Can you shoot?"

"I'll match any man in this company. Not a great cook, but a scrounger." I nudged the brandy keg. "And my wife tells me I don't snore. Much."

"If so, you're the only soldier in the army who doesn't. To hell with the 33rd—welcome to the 14th Line. We've got stragglers of our own, two dozen men sick, and the enemy on our neck. Fight with us until the army sorts itself out after battle. I'll vouch for you if you stand like a man."

"Thanks to Mother Mary that I've found a good sergeant like you. I won't let you down." Until I desert, I silently amended.

"You must carry your share, Digeon. I'll not have shirkers."

"I am the most reliable of men. You are Sergeant . . ."

"Hulot. Martin Hulot." He gestured to the marmite, the campfire's kettle. "You can dip from the pot if there's brandy in that keg of yours. Have some bread and captured chicken. We spitted it on a bayonet."

"I'm starving." I held forth my tonnelet. "To new comrades."

"Ha, here's a soldier!" He took the gaily colored keg.

"A half-frozen one," I said, rummaging for my tin. "Why war in the darkest part of the year? I've considered the matter at great length, Sergeant, and concluded that our generals are as stupid as our commissary is corrupt, our doctors incompetent, and our whores diseased." Complaint is the badge of the enlisted man.

"We haven't gone into winter quarters because the Austrians keep fleeing instead of fighting," Hulot replied. "But the Russians want a battle, I think. They're barbarians, bred to the snow and as brave as they are stupid. We've learned to bayonet the wounded, because they'll shoot you in the back if you don't. Their princes preen like Oriental despots, but their men are slaves. We'll bring the Revolution to them, all right."

I'd no doubt he would, and planned to read about it in the newspapers. So I let myself become a temporary infantryman until battle actually commenced, playing the role, and in that way found an unlikely friend.

The camaraderie of an emperor's battle staff is male and rough, but its manners are genteel compared with the crass society of line soldiers. My new companions were cynical, foulmouthed, and obsessed with food and sex, given that they got too little of the former and almost none of the latter. I was in a fraternity that would remain dirty, cold, and hungry until the campaign ended. They also had fanatical loyalty to company and regiment, and respect for discipline. They hated malingerers, because a man who slacked put their own lives at risk. They slept closer than lovers, scrounged like bandits, and could outmarch a horse in rough country.

But while there was loyalty in the pack, there could also be cruelty. The strong tended to pick on the weak like pups in a litter and were suspicious of anyone too different. So a brutish corporal named Cheval stole a cloak from a private named Dray, and cursed him as a Jew, a moneylender, and a Christ killer when Dray dared protest.

I'm no knight, and know it's best to avoid the quarrels of others. What the devil, for example, was I doing in a war between three emperors? It was all bad luck and capricious fate. But to take a man's cloak on the first of December struck me as more murderous than prankish, and possible only because the corporal was half a head higher and fifty pounds heavier than the man he'd decided to persecute.

Army conscription had swept up some of France's forty thousand Jews, most of whom live either in Bordeaux, where they work as sailors, or in Alsace and Lorraine, near the Rhine, where they are craftsmen and shopkeepers. Until the Revolution, the Jews sustained a government within a government, living by their own laws and customs. But they also paid taxes and were renowned for their skill in provisioning armies. Citizenship was granted in 1791, to end riots against the Jews in Alsace—some three thousand had been injured—and integrate them into the national economy. Suddenly they could migrate, settle in new cities such as Paris, or be drafted.

Napoleon had shocked Europe by throwing open the gates of ghettos he conquered. To him, the problem of Jewry would be solved by assimilation and emigration. He'd contemplated creating a Jewish homeland in Palestine when he campaigned in Syria in 1799. I'd helped put a stop to his Israel plans at the Siege of

Acre, forcing his retreat, but I had no quarrel with the idea of a Jewish state. It seemed likely to eliminate friction all around, creating a permanent island of peace in the heart of the Ottoman Empire.

Napoleon had told me once that Jews were clever and industrious, and thus a resource to be coveted instead of a plague to be quarantined. Within his armies, anti-Semitism was discouraged.

The French army had shed its Catholicism with the Revolution, and little had been done since to restore religion. While the slander that the French were an invasion of atheists was untrue, matters of faith were of considerably less interest in our company than the physical charms of rumored milkmaids (somehow we never encountered these beings in the flesh) or the gold that might be salvaged from a dead Russian count or general.

But tolerance of minorities was grudging. Decrees did not end prejudice. So Gideon Dray found himself without support when he demanded the cloak back.

"Who says it's yours?" Cheval demanded.

"Every man recognizes it as mine, scoundrel."

"Is that so?" Cheval put the question to his comrades, and several laughed. But an older soldier called out, "Give it back, Cheval."

The bully shrugged. "Now I remember. You stole it from a millinery shop on the march in Linz, Dray, and bragged afterward. It's hardly yours, hoarder. You've still got a stolen blanket, greedy Jew, when some of us have nothing."

"That's because you gambled your own blanket away last night," Gideon replied, "and would have done the same with your greatcoat if your friends hadn't stopped you. Now, in addition to being a fool and a drunk, you're a thief of a fellow Frenchman. Give it back."

"Or what? You'll petition the Sanhedrin? You're no more a real Frenchman than a Turk. Eat shit, Jew." It was safe defiance. Several men had formed up behind Cheval.

I was an outsider like Dray. Reluctantly, I stood and moved next to him. "I watched you bet as foolishly as a mark, Corporal," I said, even though I hadn't seen the game at all. I just don't like bullies. "Don't blame a Jew for your own folly."

"Shut your mouth, Digeon—you don't even belong here. Damned deserter, I'm guessing, afraid to show your face to your own regiment."

"I'm not afraid to show it to you."

Now we were in a circle of interested men, shouting support for one side or the other. Cheval tried to keep the focus on Dray. "The Jew boy refuses to eat what normal men eat, pray what normal men pray, and drink what normal men drink."

"You mean he reads instead." I'd seen Gideon with his nose in a book, and he was conspicuous for wearing spectacles, which were rare in the ranks. His family must have had money, which was another point against him. I noticed now that he'd put the spectacles away.

"I mean I won't shiver while a Jew is warm." Cheval spat and turned away, ostentatiously buttoning the stolen cloak around his neck. His companions grinned, waiting to see what we'd do.

"Robber!" Dray howled, and despite the difference in size, he ran to tackle him.

The corporal whirled, the coveted cape lifting like a skirt, and met the charge with a thick fist, knocking Gideon to the mud. The men roared, always ready for tumult to relieve the tedium. Cheval spat in dismissal and turned to leave again, but Gideon grabbed his ankle and yanked, tripping him. The thief went down with a thud and a growl. The Jew clawed on top.

They wrestled, but it was no match. The bigger man rolled the smaller over and began to pummel with obvious relish, his comrades cheering him on. I knew it was better not to call undue attention to myself, but this was unfair. Sergeant Hulot put a warning hand on my arm, but I shook it off, strode forward, and gave the oaf a sharp kick in the ribs, lifting him off his victim and rolling him hard in the mud.

"Damn you as well, Jew lover!" Cheval leaped up, seething. "You're joining our ranks? Let's welcome you properly!"

He came at me with a bull's rush, but I was quicker. I let him charge by as if I were a toreador, booting his backside for good measure, and danced away. Unfortunately, I backed into his crowd, and they briefly held me and then pushed me forward. Cheval charged to squeeze me like a bear.

I'd just a moment to reach the small of my back before he grabbed me. Talleyrand's broken blade went up to Cheval's face so that the jagged edge of its stump was inches from his eyes. "Let me go or I blind you."

His thick arms gave a final constriction and reluctantly dropped. He backed off warily. "You threaten me with a knife, coward?"

"A broken sword will work well enough, if you don't give the cloak back."

"How brave to wave it when I'm unarmed!"

"And how brave of you to beat a Jew with no friends. Keep it up, Cheval, and I'll gut you like a fish. I can outshoot you, out-fence you, and outbox you."

He studied me narrowly. I was unknown, and it was possible what I said was true. I was also a match for him in size, and de-monstrably quicker.

"I should challenge you to a duel," Cheval muttered.

"You'd gamble your life like you gambled your clothes." I spoke to the crowd. "Listen, if the corporal is such a gambler, let him cut cards for ownership. If he gets the high card, he keeps the cloak. If Gideon wins, he gets it back."

The assembly rumbled, debating this.

"Or do you want the three of us to kill each other over a piece of silly cloth on the eve of an important battle? Do you want to explain that to the colonel?"

Sergeant Hulot looked at me with distaste. I'd inserted myself where I didn't belong and was displaying authority I hadn't earned. He was beginning to regret his acceptance of me. But this was a way out of the quarrel. "Who has cards?"

Someone produced a deck, and I shuffled and held it out. Cheval took a stack and showed the bottommost card. "Ten," he said, with truculence.

I turned to Gideon, who had stood and was breathing heavily, face bleeding, looking at the corporal with malevolence and at me in wonder. He made his own cut.

"Jack."

The assembly gasped, a couple of men hooting at Cheval's narrow loss. In fury, the corporal yanked the cloak from his neck and threw it at Dray. "Good riddance."

"Don't worry, Cheval," Sergeant Hulot said. "You'll soon have a battlefield of corpse clothes to choose from."

"Yes." The bully turned to me. "You shouldn't cross new comrades, Digeon. Bullets can come from all sides."

I gave him a look of deliberate contempt. "So you're a murderer as well as a thief? Confessing before the bloody deed?" I raised my voice. "Remember his threat at his court-martial and execution!"

The soldier scowled, threw his cards into the mud, and stalked away.

Gideon gave me his stack of the deck, which I returned to the soldier who had lent it. I left that man to pick up Cheval's share and blame the corporal for their soiling.

"Why did you do that?" Gideon asked as we walked away. "I can fight my own battles."

"Not very well."

"Are you Jewish?"

"Hardly. I like pork, prefer the Sabbath to be on Sunday, and think Moses was an imbecile for not finding the Holy Land for forty years. But I don't like bandits or bullies, and men like Cheval are all bluster." I slipped the sword stub behind me again. "He won't bother us again." Not that I believed that.

"I'm impressed. Surprised. Puzzled. Few Christians would come to my rescue."

"Well, I'm a pagan. Or my wife is, at any rate."

"Someday I'll repay you."

"No need. But no need to wait to do so, either."

"What does that mean?"

"That cloak you liberated is good German wool, and wide as a blanket. I think the clouds threaten snow. I'm bedding with you tonight, Gideon. You need looking after, and I need to keep warm." I also needed someone to watch my back.

He smiled. "Done. At which time you can explain to me how you rigged those cards."

Chapter 15

I'd spent enough time around French army camps to be acquainted with regional stereotypes. Burgundians are the most jovial, which I attribute to their wine. Bretons are the most melancholic, and indeed, they've been in revolt against all sides, from royalist to revolutionary, for almost two decades. Men from Lorraine are infected by German ambition, the Gascons are the most boastful, and Parisians are the most presumptuous. Jews are assumed to be greedy, which was bad, and smart, which was worse, and secretly rich, which was enviable, and steadfast in their faith, which was most annoying of all, because it implied Christians were wrong in theirs. Such was Gideon's problem.

In Paris, the Jewish conundrum had been a topic of salon discussion. Despite prejudice, Jewish society served a vital function. They were prohibited from owning land, and thus were not farmers; segregated from great companies, and thus were not merchants; and barred from the aristocracy, many trades, and universities. Yet they were superb businessmen, working as shopkeepers, tailors, cobblers, and watch repairmen, to name a few. Napoleon wanted to harness their talents, as he wanted to harness all men.

When French revolutionaries granted Jews citizenship in 1791, Gideon told me, a few moved outside the traditional kehilla, or Jewish society in which law and diet are regulated by rabbis. Most Jewish men outside the army's ranks still remained instantly recognizable, however, with long, dark coats, sidelocks, and beard. In uniform, clean-shaven Gideon Dray was as anonymous as I was, but he made no effort to hide his heritage. He was declared odd for admitting what he was, and combative for standing up for himself. Accordingly, I warmed to him. While I'm the most inoffensive and charming of men, I am often thrown into new countries and societies, making me an outsider. Here again, I was the newcomer in our company. As two outcasts, we bonded.

December 1, 1805, was a day of restless maneuvering. For the first time, I experienced this as a private being marched hither and yon, rather than as an American adviser comfortably ensconced at Napoleon's headquarters, watching the display. I didn't like being ordered about, and I kept alert for a chance to slip away.

We were roused at dawn, the camp coming awake with the habitual coughing, spitting, and groaning. A hot breakfast broke the chill, but we felt apprehensive when we were ordered to douse our fire. We assembled and stood impatiently for three hours, waiting for orders. Rumors flew, because none of us knew anything. Gray overcast scudded above our lines toward the Russians and Austrians, an enemy we couldn't see. Snowflakes danced without accumulation, and my personal opinion would have been to wait for better weather, perhaps six months from now. No one asks a private.

We finally marched half a mile, stopped, broke to lunch and optimistically build new fires, were told to douse them, reformed, marched a quarter-mile more, waited two hours, marched back the way we had come, waited, and finally marched a final half-mile before darkness fell. I reckoned we'd finished a fifteen-minute stroll from where we'd started. Gideon and I remained paired, while Cheval cast murderous looks that didn't intimidate either of us. The other men gave the Jew new respect for fighting back, and treated me like a magician. No one accused me of rigging the cut, but they assumed there was some sleight of hand. God wouldn't allow a Jew to simply win.

I'd rounded out my equipment. My leather cartridge box had wooden shelves drilled with holes to hold fifty cartridges. I was issued three flints, a tin of oil, a screwdriver to repair my 1777-model musket, a greasing cloth, a bullet extractor in case my gun jammed, a knife on a lanyard tied to my waist, an oiled scrap of canvas to cover my gunlock against the snow, and a muzzle plug with tassel to keep rainwater out. Particularly important was a sewing kit to mend my uniform and gaiter straps. A rock in a boot can maim a man in minutes, and an officer who doesn't give his regiment time to sew risks hobbling a quarter of his force with blisters.

We were issued two days' rations, making us guess that battle would come the next day. Why waste more on a man who might die? There were four pounds of bread, cooked into rings and slung on a line over one shoulder, these eaten more quickly than hunger demanded because they got soggy in the snow. There was a pound of salt beef, a quarter-pound of dried peas, and two liters of wine in bottles wrapped with straw, as a precaution against breakage. I transferred the contents of one bottle to my leather canteen. A small vial of vinegar helped make stream water safe to drink.

The result was more than sixty pounds of clothes, gun, gear, and food. Veterans carry this as lithely as a deer carries its antlers, but I felt I was swimming in chains. Escaping to the infantry was beginning to seem a bad idea.

Gideon, however, was good company. He didn't complain and didn't pry too deeply into my background.

"You suffered a blow to the head?" he asked when trying to understand where I'd come from.

"Run over by a horse," I invented. "I remember very little, except that it's best not to be run over by horses."

"You have a foreign accent."

"I lived many years in America and Canada. Then Paris. I had some debts, some trouble with women . . ." That was biography enough in any army, and unlikely to be challenged. "And you, a Jew, fight alongside the Christians?"

"I've yet to find a man in the regiment I'd consider a true Christian. They rut, they blaspheme, they loot, and they kill. I make the best I can of military life, and to not fight back is to guarantee being preyed upon. I was conscripted from a village near Châlons. My opportunistic father took it as a sign from God. He trails the army as a moneylender and pawnbroker. Soldiers curse him as avidly as they use him."

"You must have a skeptical view of society."

"A realistic one. My father knows soldiers like to lighten themselves of money and belongings before a battle because they regard too much of either as bad luck. So they pawn their loot, gamble what they've left, and then ask for loans. If I contrive to survive, I might inherit a fortune. After the war we may visit Prague. It has one of the largest ghettos in Europe."

"I wish to visit Prague myself. I'm something of a scholar. A savant, actually, interested in Franklin's precepts of electricity and Cuvier's speculations on the age of the earth. Prague is reputed to be a center of learning."

"Then God has thrown us together for a reason, my new friend."

Our *ordinaire* included six others, including Henri the cheer-ful, Thibault the complainer, Duval the leader, Philippe the shirker, Charles the big one, and Louis the scrounger. Within the company were bullies like Cheval, plus brave veterans, sickly men who once had been clerks, and the useful skills that come from scooping up a range of tradesmen, farmers, shopkeepers, and stu-dents. The officers were the Big Hats, and the Imperial Guard the "Immortals," because they were kept in reserve and thus safer than the rest of us. The "stew cookers" were more valued than virgins. Anyone could fight, but it was the rare chef who could turn army rations into a decent meal. A good cook was worth more than two whores, three officers, or four priests, the calcula-tion went.

The most prestigious and dangerous position in the company was standard-bearer. The flagstaff was heavy, a sail in the wind, and left the holder defenseless. But ah, the glory of carrying a banner that men would die for! It was sublime. It was suicidal. It was brave. I myself wouldn't touch a flagstaff with a flagpole, but then, I'm sensible, which sets me apart from almost everybody.

"Half these men were combat veterans before this campaign even started," Gideon said, to bolster his confidence and mine. "They've been training in the camps of Boulogne for three years, and not just as companies but as brigades, divisions, and corps. The emperor has given us the best equipment in Europe, and steers us with the same assuredness with which Murat's knees steer his horses or his women. We're outnumbered, but nobody is panicked. We've marched the length of Austria, and can march the length of Russia if we have to."

"I admire your militant enthusiasm," I said, "while hoping to live long enough to enjoy our inevitable victory. I've actually been in a coffin, and don't recommend the experience."

"A coffin!"

"Shared it with a young lady with a broken neck. Too complicated to explain now, but the experience is sobering. Especially when they pile the dirt on."

He looked at me as if I were mad. People believe me when I lie, and never trust me when I tell the truth.

"If it will relax you, Digeon, the army has no caskets on hand," he finally said. "The best you can hope for is a hole, probably a mass burial with a dash of quicklime and a cursory benediction from the wrong religion, after men have picked over your belongings."

"I give you leave to pick at my carrion first, my friend. And I'll take a Jewish prayer as well, just to be safe."

"Agreed. Give me a Christian one. Here's some pipe clay to whiten your crossbelts. Try to make a handsome corpse."

"The handsomeness is assured. But dressing well before we die is not unreasonable. A past female acquaintance told me fashion can be more important than wit." This was Catherine Marceau, who was a useful tutor when she wasn't betraying my schemes.

"Certainly we have peacocks among our officers. Our enemies do, too, I expect."

"So let's shoot them instead of being shot," I suggested. "And contrive to serve a few ranks back, so we can tell our grandchildren about our courage."

When to flee? The anticipation of battle had curtailed any foraging expeditions, sentries had been posted in back of the army as well as in front, to discourage desertion, and officers were anxious about fighting at maximum strength. We were bivouacked in a ravine by a stream, keeping me blind to potential escape routes. Cavalry were herding stragglers back, not allowing them out. So I bided my time, as a good gambler should, trusting I'd be held in reserve until battle smoke and confusion gave me cover.

And then came the most extraordinary evening in Napoleon's life.

We were trying to rest as best we could, but anticipation is the enemy of sleep. Fitful snow had blown all day, the stars were hidden, and our only mattress, the frozen ground, was cold as iron. We lay closer than lovers around a final tiny fire, one side cooked and the other icy, turning in unison like spits of meat rotating in a restaurant. Gideon shared the disputed cloak, which was more tangible reward than I usually get. I lay awake wondering if Astiza and Harry were snug in a cozy apartment or trapped in some foul prison. The night was black as pitch. Was this a time to creep away?

Then a curious rumbling of the kind an excited crowd makes penetrated my fitful doze. I realized the men of our *ordinaire* were stirring. "Get up, something's happening!" I stood, muscles stiff, brain groggy, alarmed by the bustle in the dark. There was a glow in the lines to our left, and I wondered for a moment if the enemy had set something on fire. But no, there were no shots or bugles. Then I saw the flames were moving, advancing like a river of fire, and finally I realized that a torch-lit column of men were coming our way, as if on parade.

We seized our muskets, our officers too uncertain to give orders.

Then shouts and whispers ran up and down the line.

"It's the emperor!"

Napoleon was coming to inspect.

Here was challenge! By the luck of Benedict Arnold, the very man I'd crept away from was approaching me. In procession were officers and Imperial Guardsmen, torches lighting plumed bicornes, bearskin hats, and the turbans of Mameluke bodyguards. Strolling in their center, his hat unadorned and his greatcoat plain, was Napoleon, still surprisingly identifiable by posture and silhouette. His head swiveled like a hawk's, seeming to see into the soul of every soldier. At an hour most generals were snug in their tents, husbanding their energies for battle, he was walking the lines in a flurry of snow, greeting this sentry and that corporal, or picking out a past hero or two with his remarkable memory. His presence had an electrifying effect.

"Vive l'empereur!"

The salutation was a roar. A quiet inspection tour had turned into a torch parade. As Napoleon was recognized, infantrymen spontaneously lit brands in their campfires and hoisted them in salute, the flames steadily expanding. "It's the emperor! It's Napoleon!" Their fervor was greater than for an opera star. They wanted to assert their readiness for battle. The soldiers couldn't leave their place in the army's line, and so the general walked along it, each unit in turn hoisting burning tributes. They illuminated his confident smile.

I'd seen his calculated act before. He practiced having presence.

I retreated into the shadows to avoid being seen. Bonaparte's inspection had triggered a snake of fire a mile long now, sparks flying in the winter wind, the serpent of light a calligraphy of adoration.

"Vive l'empereur!"

The great man's gray eyes caught and held the light. He'd occasionally stop to gently pull an ear, clasp a shoulder, or shake a hand. No man was sleeping now—all were up and all were roaring, except for me. Even my Jewish friend was shouting, and looked at me curiously when I did not. I dared not have Napoleon look my way. Once more I felt isolated and alone, far from home and hollow because of it. Something momentous was happening. The world hadn't seen this kind of military fervor before. War had traditionally been a desultory royal affair of small campaigns by professional soldiers for incremental gains. Now it involved whole nations, and oceans of men. Napoleon had not just seized power; he had reinvented power, fusing French ambition with his own. He was not just a general, or even a conqueror, but the conductor of a strange new fervor.

He passed our own *ordinaire*, slapping the arm of Henri with hearty encouragement and seducing every one of us with a sweep of his eyes. Except me, who knew him better than any man here, all his aspects great and terrible, the titan who represented the best and worst of mankind. When he looked toward me, I shrank back even further into the gloom, so that there was no way he could have recognized me in my uniform. I had to stay absent, lest he turn me over to Pasques and Catherine Marceau and ruin the hunt for my family, which I was desperate to resume.

And yet I had the distinct feeling he had. Did he wink?

Then he was past, the next unit cheering, and our own torches slowly snuffed out in the dark. I silently cursed. Any chance to steal away had been ruined by Napoleon's exciting us as if it were Christmas. Every man was alert and feverish now, and all would see me try to leave. I'd be stopped, questioned, and probably shot.

So I must wait for the fog of battle. Gun smoke and chaos would be my friends. I'd scramble at the peak of confusion, and go rescue wife and son.

Napoleon was in the distance now, new torches lighting, old ones burning out, men cheering themselves hoarse. I've no idea what the Austrians and Russians made of it. There were no cheers or torches from their side.

I came back into the firelight. "Digeon, where were you!" cried Henri. "Did you see him touch me? It was magic! It was like being touched by Christ! How I burn to fight for him!"

"He looked like Caesar," said Duval.

"Handsomer than I would have guessed," said Charles. "And taller."

Gideon put his hand on my shoulder. "So we've seen history, eh, my friend? Not a man here high enough to enter a palace, but we're the ones who have seen him in the field. That's the Napoleon people will remember. And since he's here, I'll fight for him cheerfully enough. What do you think will happen tomorrow?"

"Something great and terrible," I predicted. "The other side longs for battle."

I couldn't explain how I knew this, but my newest friend accepted my wisdom. "We'd better get what rest we can, then."

So we bedded down, once more without sleeping, and I remembered again what the next day was.

The one-year anniversary of Napoleon's coronation, the one I'd tried to sabotage and that he had turned into triumph.

CHAPTER 16

Astiza

The grandly named Golden Lane turned out to be a slit of a street squeezed between the walls of Prague Castle and its in-buildings. I was eager and yet apprehensive when we reached the low, arched gate giving access. Prague Castle is vast, the biggest in Europe, and its complexity is intimidating. There are the guarded royal apartments, the vast St. Vitus Cathedral, the high offices of government, army barracks, kitchens, chapels, sub-palaces, and the galleries where Rudolf kept his bizarre collection. Tucked against the fortress wall in a corner near the Black Tower is the Lane, its row of tiny houses inhabited by goldsmiths, moneylenders, alchemists, and, it appeared, men proclaiming to be warlocks. I don't believe in witches of either sex, but I do believe that some creatures seek dark magic and selfish power. King Rudolf allowed this tiny slum to encourage alchemy. Now, I guessed, it drew dreamers, madmen, and frauds.

Fulcanelli smiled reassuringly. "Come, come. Sometimes the oddest people have the deepest insight."

The Lane was like a trench, a blank wall on one side and hovel doors on the other. The sky was a ribbon above, and the cobbles uneven and worn. Wise men, vagabonds, whores, chemists, seers, and astrologers loitered there. Horus shrank against my leg as we pushed through a swarm of the colorful and eccentric, and once more I felt guilty at the life I'd given him. What kind of nomadic existence had I inflicted on my little boy? He squeezed my fingers as if being held over a precipice.

"No worries, Horus," Fulcanelli assured. "Auric likes children."

"I don't like dogs."

"No dogs."

There were gypsies, beggars, cripples, black-clad Jews, strutting mercenaries, lovelorn noblewomen looking for potions, and fat merchants in thick fur robes. I felt like I'd gone back in time. While the West abandoned magic, Prague incorporated it. The bishop nonetheless led us confidently, a hand on a sword, his manner unlike that of any churchman I'd known. "Don't worry, I've been here before." And indeed, the crowd recognized him and parted. He strode like an earl.

We had to stoop to enter Auric's hovel, a low-ceilinged room that was smoky, hot, and sulfurous.

"It stinks, Mama," Horus whispered. I squeezed his hand back. What a brave explorer he was! With the Brazen Head I might learn of my husband, or bargain for him. I might win us peace.

The warlock Auric Nachash was as ugly as Fulcanelli was

handsome, a squat and warty dwarf with bulbous nose and absent chin. "You brought them! Welcome! Welcome!" His look was a gleam and his laugh a cackle, like a nightmare marionette.

"This lady needs your wisdom."

Ethan, Ethan, where are you?

The heat came from a stove with boiling pots. Coiled copper tubing led to bowls iridescent with pools of metallic green, blue, and red, the wafting fumes like a preview of the underworld. It was an alchemical laboratory, and I wondered what Auric's neighbors thought of his experiments. Distillation of exotic compounds was a notorious source of fire. Yet he slept next to his brews like a hausfrau next to her kitchen. Now he bowed to Fulcanelli.

"She's a pretty witch."

"Not a witch, but a scholar," Fulcanelli corrected.

"And a boy as well! How did you find them?"

"She found me. Everything is fated, Auric, as I've told you." He addressed me. "Is that not so, priestess? Were you not meant to be here, at this time, with us?"

I looked about. The door was shut tight, and the single window to the Lane grimy. Glass jars held dead, hairless animals and organs, all of them colored pus white. I guessed they were used for spells. Harry looked at them with the cautious fascination of a child. I prayed to Isis and Mary. "If we find what we seek. Fate is amended by free will, Bishop." I turned warily to the warlock. "Can you help us?"

"Let's try to help each other." His grin had no friendship in it, and in fact he couldn't hold a gaze. His eyes slid away when he talked, to fasten on things that didn't look back. There was something missing in his character. But he would also cast furtive glances. I caught him looking at my son the way a bird looks at a worm, while Harry shuffled closer to the stove.

"Horus, be careful," I said.

"It's hot, Mama."

"Auric is a seer like you," Fulcanelli said.

"Not as pretty, not as pretty," the dwarf sing-sang. He hopped from foot to foot.

"But we constantly amend and improve our partnership," the bishop went on. "Now you're in our fellowship as well. Our triumvirate is meant to find the Philosopher's Stone and the Brazen Head together. Succeed or fail together. Learn together. Wield power together."

I wasn't sure what kind of partnership he really wanted. "I have a husband," I reminded him.

"No doubt a fine fellow, who, unfortunately, has abandoned you," Fulcanelli said. "I admire your fidelity, and hope you accept our friendship, too." He smiled, standing close.

"Not abandoned. He was detained, perhaps." Was I being punished for seeking knowledge instead of waiting for Ethan? Should I have submitted to imprisonment at Notre Dame? No, we had to escape to find the automaton.

"The Brazen Head has the answers," Fulcanelli said. "But we have to find it first."

I looked down at Auric. "I hope your colleague can help." He had tiny, deep-drilled eyes and bad teeth. The cloying gases had spotted him with warts, pustules, and tumors. His scraggly hair was thin, and his hands reddened as if burned. "I'm told you've studied Albertus Magnus's *Book of Secrets*. Some say it's a dangerous text."

"I've read books both praised and forbidden, madame. I've searched for power as resolutely as a knight searching for gold in a dragon's cave. I've summoned angels and demons and faced the great dark eye itself." The creature was proud of his sorcery. "Albertus was a great man, but I've gone beyond him."

"Not for worldly reward," I remarked drily, examining his surroundings. I've found wry observation an effective tactic. The dwarf flushed.

"My eyes hurt, Mama," Harry chimed in. "I don't like it here." He had the instincts of a young animal.

"Just a short visit. We need this man's help."

"All my profits go into my studies," Auric said, annoyed at having to justify his hovel. "I'm Prague's greatest necromancer. Important men seek my counsel." He cast an eye at Fulcanelli. "I am Merlin. I am Faust. So sit, sit, we'll exchange secrets."

He gestured to a blanket atop a plank bed with straw mattress. I suspected fleas but reluctantly sat, since there was nowhere else to do so, pulling Harry to me. Auric turned to rummage on a workbench while Fulcanelli moved near the door, more like a guard than a guide. He smiled again to reassure me, but everything suddenly seemed false. The smile was chilly, and his eyes speculative. Best to get this over quickly.

"We're searching for a mechanical man made by Albert long ago in Paris," I began.

"It's like a toy that can talk," put in Harry, since I'd tried to explain why we were wandering. "We're going to use it to find Papa."

Auric turned to a sloping shelf crammed with books. He took off a heavy one, dusty and stained. "Yes, the Brazen Head. Fabulous legend. An automaton to tell the future! And yet destroyed by Thomas Aquinas, no?"

"Some in Paris thought it might have survived." I could impress or frighten them with names like Napoleon and Talleyrand, and yet those ambitious men were very far away. "I'm trying to follow the trail of Christian Rosenkreutz, because of legends that he took the android."

"Ah, Rosenkreutz. The whereabouts of his tomb is a great mystery. And yet there are tales of a ruined castle in Bohemia or Moravia, and caverns beneath a sacred mountain. No one knows which one, yet treasure is reputed to be buried there. I would like treasure. I would like that very much."

I decided to hold back what I'd guessed at Český Krumlov. Best to keep our ultimate destination to myself.

"As a fellowship, we might find it." The dwarf nodded, more to himself than to us. "Success will make us rich."

"The Brazen Head promises only wisdom."

"When rich enough, men will judge us wise. It's not that the wise always win, but that winners are deemed wise." He cackled again, then grew serious. "Do you know which castle?"

"No." This was only half a lie.

He looked annoyed and glanced at Fulcanelli. "Is she useful?"

The bishop shrugged.

I gestured at his alchemical stews. "Have you made lead into gold?"

"I haven't achieved that purity, no. So what *do* you know, Astiza? How can you aid us on this quest?"

I glanced at Fulcanelli, but the bishop was only watching us expectantly. "I'd expect to find roses on Christian's path."

"Hmph. Do you know alchemy?"

"I studied in Egypt."

"Perhaps we can make gold together."

"I'm not interested in gold. I'm a pilgrim looking for a relic. It's why I came to Bishop Fulcanelli at the library, and why I've come to you."

Now Fulcanelli's look was possessive, and his glance at Auric was a smirk. Something was terribly wrong. When the bishop spoke, his tone was critical. "You walk a thousand miles, scamp in tow, knowing so little? I don't believe you, Astiza. Share your secrets with Auric, and let's get things done."

"Don't call my son a scamp." I held Horus closer. "He's a good boy."

"Very good," said Nachash, and then he shocked me by obscenely running his tongue around his lips. What foulness was this? I stood to go, confused and alarmed. Why had he brought me here? But the bishop blocked the door.

"Primus, please."

Fulcanelli stepped forward and shoved, harder than he had to, so that I sat back down hard on the bed. Harry began to cry.

"What's wrong with you?" I looked furiously at bishop and dwarf. "I'm asking you as a mother and wife for help!"

"You're a widow, not a wife," Fulcanelli said coldly. "Your husband is almost certainly dead."

"You don't know that!"

"I know your betrayal of Minister Talleyrand, your theft of sacred objects, and the fact that your husband has been chained to a French warship that is likely doomed to destruction."

"A warship? What?"

"Gage is in Spain, shackled in chains of his own forging."

"Then he's alive!"

"Soon to be dead, I think. Nelson is coming."

"If he escapes, he'll come here! I know he will!" I thought furiously, picturing maps in my head. "Through Venice, perhaps. By sea!"

"That would be magical indeed."

"Why are you treating me like this?"

"Because you care more for sorcery than love, and I am not a patient man. You care more for a mechanical head than the head of your child."

"Child soup," Nachash said. "Bones and fat, bubbling in a broth. Or we will bake him in the oven, Baron Wolf, and crack his bones for their marrow." His grin was hideous. "Did you know the marrow becomes sweeter in the first roasting, when the little boys scream?" He cackled again and danced a little jig.

I was paralyzed at my own foolishness. What folly to come here, and to trust a man I didn't really know! My head was whirling. Was this a bad dream? "Baron?" I managed. "I thought you were a bishop."

"I am what I say I am," Fulcanelli said.

So was he even Fulcanelli?

"You should kneel," Auric suggested. "Kneel at his belt. He's Baron Wolf Richter, high priest of the Invisible College, and you try my master's patience." The little monster was clearly mad. Was he even human? He was a pustule of a creature, a casting gone wrong.

Fulcanelli's stare was lifelessly cold, as pitiless as a serpent's, and the confiding empathy we'd shared at the Astronomical Tower had vanished like smoke.

"Where is the sword hilt?" he demanded.

"*What* sword hilt?"

"You think us fools? Tell us what you know. What game is your family playing?"

"You're mad. I came here because I didn't know enough!"

"Tell us or we cook your son," Auric said. And he scuttled to put across a beam to bar the door.

"I thought you liked me," I protested weakly. "We were partners."

"We're still partners," Fulcanelli—or this baron—said. "And, oh yes, I like you, I like you very much. Tell me what you really know, Astiza. Why did you go one way and your husband another?"

"We were fleeing!"

"Why does a mother bring her boy here? What have you learned about the Brazen Head that makes you risk everything to find it?"

I closed my eyes. "I want to find it so we'll be left alone."

"Tell me the truth, or by Satan I'll have you now on this crude bed, in front of your whining brat, just before my servant eats him." Fulcanelli's voice—no, it was this Wolf Richter's!—had changed, becoming deeper, more guttural. Or was it I who had gone mad?

Somehow I had to force my way past two men or Harry and I

would be doomed. My meeting with Fulcanelli-Richter had been no accident, I realized; somehow he'd been waiting for me here in Prague. Had Duke Schwarzenberg alerted him from Český Krumlov? The grotesque alchemist was not a wizard of dark arts but a creature of evil tortures. I was without help. My hands scrabbled on the bed, looking for a weapon. All I had was the dirty tick of straw.

I stood again. "Let me go or I'll scream."

Nachash laughed, and so I did scream, or tried to, but this terrible baron hit me with a blow so hard that the room flashed white and roared as it whirled. I spun and fell hard on the mattress, facedown. I could hardly see. I could hardly breathe. I felt nauseated.

"Mama!" Harry was screaming in terror.

"By God, I'll have you now."

"It's better when they resist," the little ogre encouraged.

The baron's powerful hands gripped the top of my gown and tore it down the back. I twisted to claw at his face, so he stopped to slap me and spit.

We're about to be murdered, I thought dimly. We've come to a devil's lane and found a portal to hell. I smelled it when we entered. Why didn't I run?

A hand grasped my necklace, with its ankh and Eye of Horus, and twisted it tight. I couldn't breathe.

And then Richter howled from a shock of his own. "Bastard imp!" He lurched off me and spun as if stung, and Harry flew hard and banged against a wall. I got enough air to shriek with fury. The tumult had knocked Auric aside, too.

"The whelp bit me!"

The dwarf chortled. "You can have a sip of my soup."

"I'll bash the hellion's brain in." He wheezed and bent toward my son. I lurched upward, sick from fumes, breathless from strangulation, my gown in ruin, and reached to grab his arms. The baron was strong as a stag, but I hindered him for just a moment. He tried to shake me off. Auric began banging on me with an iron kettle, baying with merriment at the chaos. The more I resisted, the more he cackled.

Richter shoved again to bounce me on the bed. "Wait your turn," he growled. He turned back to my son.

And screamed. Horus, in wild desperation, and with the courage of a youth three times his age, had grabbed one of the stone bowls holding the metallic distillates and hurled it at the madman's face.

The potion was hot, acidic, and sticky. A sluice of goo slashed across Richter's jaw and cheeks, sizzling, and more hit a candle and flared up like breath from a fire-eater. My assailant howled in shock and surprise.

"You little demon!"

"Harry!"

"I melted him, Mama!"

"May Satan damn you!" the crazed Richter-Fulcanelli roared, clutching at his burning face as he staggered around the room. His flesh was melting like candle wax.

Auric watched in shocked fascination, the other's pain seeming to calm him. "Don't kill her," he cautioned. "Not until we have the other."

Richter found a bucket of water and emptied it over his own smoking head. "Aggghhhh! You bitch of a sorceress!" His flesh steamed.

"We need them all, every one, to control each other," Auric went on. "The mines, master, the mines!"

And then his kettle swung to strike my dizzy head, and that's all I can remember.

CHAPTER 17

The snow stopped during the night, replaced by cold fog. The long dark seemed endless. It was victory when I was finally able to see my outstretched hand, triumph to make out the prone and hunched forms of my companions, and reassurance to spy the trunk of a tree ten paces away. Dawn was sluggish and clammy. Beyond our immediate surroundings, the world was shrouded. I stood, shivering and miserable, to stamp my feet and rub my gums. Wood was added to the fire, we dipped our last soggy bread in the reheated stew, and we looked to our equipment. The campfire smoke added to the miasma.

"A foul day for fighting," Hulot muttered. "I need another tonnelet of brandy."

"Then give me leave to fetch one," I suggested.

"Ha! You wouldn't stop until you reached Paris, Digeon. None of us would. No, I'll keep you for battle."

Escape would not be easy.

From somewhere to our right a rumble began, like distant thunder. Someone was shooting at someone. "Our flank is getting an uncomfortable reveille," Hulot remarked. "It wakes you up, doesn't it?" It did seem to match Napoleon's prediction that the Allies would seek to overrun the French right flank and get into our rear. Yet I'd neither seen nor heard sign that Bonaparte was shifting forces to block such a move. In fact, he'd given up the commanding Pratzen Heights and passively invited attack in this valley. It was foolish and lazy.

I knew him better than that.

Whatever his plan, I was stuck in the middle, hoping that Soult's corps would remain in reserve. If ever there was a war I cared nothing about, it was this one. What cursed luck to have run into Murat in Vienna, chaining me to this madness ever since. The harder I tried to escape, the deeper I seemed to be ensnared.

"Digeon, you'll replace Garat in the front rank," Hulot instructed as we formed. "The imbecile broke his foot by allowing a cannon wheel to run over it and will miss his chance at glory."

"Allowed? Or arranged?"

"He wept when told he couldn't fight."

Good God, the world is full of fools. "I'm rather tall," I tried. "Wouldn't it be wiser to have me behind, where I could shoot over the heads of others?"

"New men go in front to be watched and backed by their fellows. Besides, maybe the enemy will find you intimidating. Rise up on your tiptoes, Goliath, and put them to flight."

"As tempting target."

"Be proud of this opportunity to prove yourself."

I was frustrated, caught in a vast military machine, with no flexibility to exercise my habitual cleverness. The front rank sponged up bullets, and putting a man of my capabilities there was a terrible waste, at least to me. "I'm actually rather expert with a rifle," I tried again. "Perhaps I could serve as a chasseur." These skirmishers moved independently and sought cover.

"Is that a rifle you are carrying, idiot? Did you arrive from a chasseur regiment and dye your coat from green to blue? No, you are line infantry like the rest of us. Shoulder your musket and take your place like a man."

The others hooted. I pretended I was only joking and lamely tried to retrieve a reputation for courage by demonstrating experience. "Do you have any buckshot? I spent time in America, where frontiersmen shoot with both buck and ball. Given a musket's inaccuracy, it might increase our chances of hitting something."

"Ah, you mistake me for an armory? All our buckshot seems to be taken, Digeon. The Big Hats must have gone fowling. But here, idiot, is your bayonet, which is guaranteed to hit something should you get close enough to the enemy to stick them with it. Shall I instruct which end is the front?"

This brought another good laugh. The sergeant was on his own tiptoes to address me, his mustache almost close enough to become my own. I could see flecks of tobacco in the hairs.

"I suspect I can remember."

He rocked back to his heels and clapped me on the shoulder. "If you don't, I will stab you myself." Then he addressed the others. "*Oui!* Our newest replacement is so stupid that he may forget in which direction the enemy resides! Should he charge the wrong way, toward our rear, will the rest of you kindly shoot him?"

"You may rest assured, sergeant," Cheval said. "Put the cardsharp in front of me. I will keep him in step."

"No need to put biting horses in the same harness," Hulot said. "Digeon here will be near the standard so he can't get lost or waste time experimenting with his musket load." He nodded at me. "Fight well, straggler, I have my eye on you. Pray that your card luck carries over to battle."

With this encouragement, I fell in with the fatalism all men feel when marching into combat. One is swept by fate into a torrent. We checked our gear for the hundredth time in the fantasy that something would make a difference. Men entrusted last letters to one another. I had nowhere to write to, and realized Astiza might never hear of my death.

Units began to form in column. We'd wheel into line when at grips with the enemy.

Officers on horseback loomed out of the fog, gesturing with swords, while the thuds from our right grew louder, thumping like tribal drumming. The order came to cease speaking. We obeyed better than schoolboys, in hopes we'd be hidden until the worst was over.

Then began the waiting. I'd experienced this agony at the light winds of Trafalgar while Nelson's fleet closed ponderously with the French and Spanish. Here the anxiety was again. The brain can conjure horrors more terrible than any actual one, and so the tedious standing gave ample time for imagination.

"Let's get on with it," Gideon muttered under his breath.

We stood still as statues so there wouldn't be a rattle of equipment. I could see only fifty paces in the fog and thus spied little beyond the universe of my small company. In theory, Soult's gigantic corps of twenty-six thousand men was poised around me, but it felt as if my fellows and I were waiting by ourselves for the entire Russian and Austrian armies. We'd eaten little, out of the belief that gut wounds were worse on a full stomach, and drunk less, knowing we wouldn't be allowed to fall out to piss. We preferred not to humiliate ourselves by wetting our trousers. By midday we'd be parched, but better dehydration than embarrassment. So we stood, hungry, thirsty, and cold, our breath adding to the fog, without a word of explanation about what we were supposed to do or when we were supposed to do it.

The light grew stronger, and the mist changed from gray to white. It was a sunny winter's day on the Pratzen Heights, I guessed, reminiscent of the sun that had glowed at Napoleon's coronation the year before. Yet in our valley the fog hung and hid, each man damp and alone with his thoughts. Even prayers had to be silent. It was quiet enough to hear the click of rosary beads.

I shifted, swallowed, and experimented with sleeping standing up, without success. Bored, I opened my eyes again. Nothing had changed. Sergeant Hulot stalked in front of us, puffed and frowning, and a cluster of dismounted officers waited ahead of him, their horses twitching. The thunder on the right kept growing. Musket and cannon fire was as continuous as the roar of surf. Still we did nothing.

I allowed myself to hope that the battle was being decided without me. I'd find an excuse to creep off, and then embroider my army experience a decade from now—warm, well fed, and alive.

My hands were numb. So were my feet, I decided. And my nose.

Nothing. Nothing. What was Napoleon doing?

And then suddenly there were bugles and shouts as crisp as the crack of a cannon, relayed up and down the line. A colonel swung up onto his horse, trotted in front of us, and pointed with his sword, which was helpful, since I'd lost all sense of direction. *"Sacré nom de Dieu, forward!"*

A companion looked at a watch. It was ten o'clock. Had my bet failed, and Soult's corps was to engage after all? My luck kept worsening. We stepped off as if one organism, as syncopated as androids, as mindless as golems. Frosted grass at first, and then the crystallized mud of a frozen field. As we marched at the standard pace of seventy-six paces a minute, the land began to rise.

I gloomily guessed our destination. We were marching back to the Pratzen Heights, which Bonaparte has so conspicuously abandoned just two days before. The Austrians and Russians had since occupied them, so now we had to attack uphill? What madness was this? Had the French never heard of Bunker Hill? I couldn't help playing amateur general, and desperately wanted to fall out, rejoin the emperor's command, and point out the error of his ways.

No chance. I was sandwiched by men—Gideon at my left shoulder, the regimental standard to my right, and men behind, Cheval lurking back there somewhere. Company after company, regiment after regiment, division after division. I could no more reverse direction than I could reverse time.

The mist thinned as we slogged uphill, and our army rose from a white sea. The flags, with their bright bronze eagles, emerged first, so looking to one side and the other, I could see for one moment a forest of standards with no soldiers to go with them. Then Soult's corps as a whole climbed out of the mist and into the bright low sun, entire divisions sprouting from where we'd been hidden. Tramp, tramp, tramp, steadily uphill. I thankfully warmed.

Soult and Lannes had four divisions in all. Two battalions of light infantry formed a skirmishing line while we line soldiers followed in column, like parallel battering rams. There was a murmur that rose to an exultant shout as we cleared the fog and spied one another. We were not alone after all! Hundreds of flags, tens of thousands of men, syncopated like a vast machine. Cheers rolled to join the thunder of the battle to our right. Batteries of cannon were firing there, guns flashing in the smoke. The sun itself seemed at Napoleon's command, gleaming to illuminate tens of thousands of bayonets.

Bonaparte weather.

I got my bearings. We were advancing more or less east, into the sun. To our right the land fell away into a tangle of wood, stream, and village, and it was from there that the roar we'd heard for the past two hours continued. The fog in that hollow had been thickened by gun smoke. Flags rocked and pitched as if they were masts in a stormy sea. A desperate struggle was going on as the Allies tried to get around us to roll up our formations.

To our left—the north—there was a broad swale between the Pratzen Heights and the wooded hills miles beyond. Huge numbers of men moved there as well, cavalry swirling in great turgid currents. There was smoke, dust, and tendrils of fog.

We were in the center, marching toward the heart of the enemy. It seemed to me it would be a bloody business, yet not only could I not escape, but I found myself unexpectedly caught in the thrill of it. I, the American skeptic, selfish and opportunistic, actually forgot for a moment about my own safety and felt swept up in a greater story.

There's beauty in a military assault, uniforms bright and brushed, crossbelts chalked, buttons and bayonets gleaming that men polish for luck, legs as coordinated as a centipede's. General Duhesme in Boulogne told me once that I should surrender to military passion, give myself over to discipline and courage, and that the greatest exhilaration in life was belonging to a unit and a cause. My futile attempts at personal independence, he predicted, would lead to nothing but misery. I finally understood what he meant. The air seemed charged with the shared camaraderie of sacrifice and danger. We were fused as fiercely as if we'd joined a messianic religion, and at that moment, in that place, there seemed no higher purpose than to close with the enemy. The weight of my weapons was forgotten, hunger and thirst were forgotten, my heart hammered, and I was drugged by spectacle. My only purpose was to keep my place in line as we strode over plowed clods of earth. My life had come down to one chilly, sunlit moment, and Napoleon understood this. He was the conductor of a vast and fatal game in which we were momentary madmen, joyous participants in his ambition, because he'd given purpose to ordinary lives. Close, fight, win.

So we marched up Pratzen Heights.

Battlefields are big. Ours was eight miles wide as the two huge armies stretched to try to flank each other, and our march up that three-hundred-foot-high hill was a mile in length, a lockstep advance that consumed an eternity, by which I mean half an hour. At any moment I expected a barrage of cannonballs and a volley of musketry, and yet the enemy banners couldn't even be seen.

Where the devil were the Russians and Austrians?

Belatedly, I realized what Napoleon had always expected: the enemy had weakened its center to strengthen its flanks.

Suddenly a cannonball did come, seemingly out of nowhere, skipping across the hard ground like a bowled stone. It hit our column at an angle and knocked aside five men with astonishing violence. They didn't fall; they flew, or rather parts of them did, and sprays of blood flew with them. We gasped, instinctively recoiled, and then accelerated to close up the gap.

"Steady. No faltering there! Dress that rank!"

There are many kinds of courage, from facing a peril alone to defending an unpopular opinion. One of the most daunting is standing in the front rank of an infantry line. The dashing uniform makes a splendid target, its crossbelts the perfect aiming point. One is expected to neither duck, dodge, nor turn, lest too much fidgeting dissolve the cohesion of the company. Upright and face forward is the soldier's task, to stand stout even under the worst bombardment and the most terrifying cavalry charge. This expectation is entirely counter to human nature, and the only way to achieve it is ceaseless drill and discipline.

Stiffening a soldier's resolve is the instinct to avoid shame. Few have any idea what war is about. Yet better to be killed or crippled than to let down your comrades and be branded a coward. Men fight to become men—to save this comrade and avenge that one.

The enemy's transfer of units allowed us to climb the long western slope largely unmolested. Orders rang out when we were halfway up, and we deployed from column to line, now presenting a wide hedge of bayonets. I followed Gideon's lead, shoulder to shoulder, and there were enough stumbles on the uneven ground that my untrained awkwardness drew no particular attention. We aimed for a village near the crest of the hill.

"It looks abandoned," Gideon said with hope.

A battalion of French skirmishers had disappeared over the crest, which seemed promising. But then there was an eruption of gunfire, and smoke swelled at the summit like an ominous thunderhead. We turned slightly to skirt the village, hoping to find a way clear, but a line of Russian musketeers from Novgorod rose as one from a shallow depression before us and fired before we could think.

Our entire line recoiled, as if struck by an enormous whip. The surprise, the flashing ripple of enemy gunfire, and the sizzle of bullets shredding the air were a shock. No amount of training can entirely prepare troops for it, or for the tumble of dead and wounded. The discipline of the 14th temporarily evaporated, and we reeled in retreat. I paused to fire, and many others also shot, but we were too rattled to be very effective. We spilled in confusion back down the slope for a hundred yards, the ascent of units behind finally stopping us. Hulot cursed our whores of mothers for our momentary collapse and hollered at us to reload. This task took about twenty seconds. Rip cartridge, pour powder, drop the ball down the barrel, ram the wadding, prime the lock. The routine steadied us. Then brigade commander Baron Thiébault appeared on his horse, imposing and fearless. The men straightened at his inspection, and when he waved his sword, we roared *"Vive l'empereur"* and started back uphill. I found myself shouting the chant as loudly as anyone, to bolster my courage. I was in it now, and we charged back the way we'd retreated. Our line weaved or jumped over several dead and dying men from our company.

"Remember!" Hulot roared. "At fifty yards aim for the knees, at one hundred the waist, and at two hundred the head!" He was accounting for the tendency of musket balls to fly high at close range and drop at a distance.

The Russians fired too soon this time, most of their balls passing harmlessly. They were nervous, too. Some of our men instinctively ducked, too late to actually make themselves safer, and their comrades laughed and insulted the instinct. Then we halted, Thiébault signaled with his sword, and it was our turn to shoot. The roar clapped my ears, the musket kicked my shoulder like a boxer's punch, and burning powder from the firing pan pitted my cheek. There was so much smoke we couldn't see what effect we'd had, but there was no time to reload.

"Charge!"

We ran through the haze of gun smoke and saw the line of dead and wounded Russians our volley had produced. Behind, in the swale where they'd hidden, the Novgorod survivors were furiously trying to reload. We howled like banshees and were on them before they could level their guns, bayoneting a score while the rest broke and fled. In an instant the 14th Line had redeemed itself.

"Finish the wounded. The Russians will shoot you in the back if you don't."

I left this ruthless task to others, since there were several enthusiasts, Cheval among them. Then we reloaded and stepped off again.

We came over the crest and looked down Pratzen's eastern slope. Before us was a magnificent view toward the château of Austerlitz, several miles away, the intervening miles filled with columns of white-coated Austrians and green-coated Russians. Artillery boomed, cavalry raced, flags flew, and bayonets glinted, all in glorious confusion. Another cannonball came bouncing, a gray blur that hit our line ten men to the right of where I was standing. It threw two soldiers into the air and disemboweled a third before careening into our rear. I was glad I knew few of my fellow soldiers, given how they were falling. The Russians we'd routed had stopped their flight partway down the east side of the hill, turned, and with fresh battalions were now marching bravely back toward us.

"Dress the line! Steady! Aim!"

More cannonballs from the enemy guns, knocking men over like ninepins.

"Fire!"

Our volley shocked them. With our soldiers settling down, we shot to good effect. Pack enough fellows together and a company of muskets works like a gigantic shotgun. Russians pitched, reeled, and toppled.

"Fire at will!"

Now it was a contest of speed and accuracy, and here the long hours of French training paid off. Slam a musket butt-first to the ground, reach for a cartridge, tear, load, ram, prime, up, aim, shoot. I'd regarded my musket with contempt, thinking it heavy and inaccurate compared to my old American long rifle. But in that moment it was my dearest friend.

The smoke choked. My ears rang. My only orientation was our flag, and that fell and then rose again. I assumed the first bearer had been killed.

"Advance!"

We strode forward, slowly this time, as if wading into water, flinching from sheets of bullets. I sensed, more than saw, men falling near me. We followed Hulot as he led us diagonally down the slope of the hill.

"Halt!"

Our commanders arranged us in checkerboard fashion, providing gaps for field guns to be run forward. The French artillery had followed us over the crest of the hill. Now their crews pushed them by hand, dropped the tails of their carriages, and aimed. The Russians were crying out desperately, shouting and pointing to get their men to aim at the cannoneers.

The guns roared first, firing canister and grape. The storm of jagged metal harvested like a scythe. We felt the concussion of the guns and the fan of fragments shaking the air.

They hit the massed Russian formations, and the enemy line collapsed.

"After them!"

We whooped and swept downhill, bayonets leveled. Fleeing Russians collided with fresh Allied units struggling desperately to support. The enemy lines were thrown into chaos. We shouted in triumph. As the enemy reeled, we halted, fired, and received ineffectual fire in response. With a final charge, we scooped up enemy banners and two wounded generals and found ourselves temporary masters of the reverse slope. From here we could wheel right into the enemy rear or turn left to assault his forces on the Brunn–Olmütz road. Our artillery had the high ground. Unless the Allies rallied, they were split.

I caught my breath. My throat was parched, my eyes stung, my shoulder ached, and my bayonet was bloody, although I had no recollection of sticking anyone. Hundreds of men in French blue and Russian green were sprawled on the frozen ground. The screaming of shot horses drowned out begs for help. Eyes, both human and animal, rolled in fear.

I felt exhilarated. To beat death is to savor life. And if the entire enemy army collapsed and we pursued them, there'd be enough chaos for me to escape.

I looked around. Gideon was still standing, too.

Then another cannonball. A major I didn't know, reining his excited horse, was cut in two. The ball sliced him at the waist, torso leaping. His clenching legs, completely detached, sent his mount sprawling.

The poor man came down with an expression of stunned surprise, his chest ending in a tangle of gore.

"Re-form!" the order floated across the field. "They're counterattacking!"

The battle wasn't over yet.

CHAPTER 18

White-coated Austrians marched back up the Pratzen Heights to support the Russians. Realizing their mistake too late, the enemy had allowed Napoleon to seize the crown of the hill, and now needed to retrieve it or face disaster. Commander Thiébault ordered our three six-pound field pieces loaded with round shot. Cannonballs are hideously effective when skipped on hard ground, and the frozen earth of Austerlitz was perfect for murder. I watched the solid French shot drill holes in the Austrian lines as neatly as the bore of an auger. The enemy tramped bravely toward us anyway, closing their gaps, but you could see the formations quiver as they were pounded. The Austrians fired too soon, bullets whapping into the dirt in front of us. Then they gave a great shout from the cloud of smoke they'd conjured—*"Gott in Himmel!"*—and charged like berserkers, emerging from the haze with bayonets leveled. Our front line had been ordered down on one knee, so that my eyes were at the same height as their points. I can't recommend the perspective.

"Steady!" Hulot cautioned. "Hold your fire. Hold. Hold . . ."

The Austrians were red-faced and open-mouthed, taking precious breath to yell as they sprinted up the slope. Their line grew ragged as some outpaced others, and still Hulot ordered us not to shoot. "Wait . . ."

My God, they looked ten feet tall, shoulders as broad as an ox's, knuckles white from gripping their empty muskets, eyes crazed.

"Fire!"

A huge crash of shots enveloped us in smoke. Dimly seen, half the enemy seemed to collapse. We reloaded frantically, which is damned awkward while kneeling. A few of our own were overcome by instinct and stood to flee the Austrian charge. One was accidentally shot dead by a companion aiming from the rank behind.

"Fire at will!"

The shooting rattled like a drum. The battlefield was murky with smoke. Austrians fell, the survivors slowed, then stopped, and then seemed to be weaving like drunken men, some wounded and the others unclear what to do. We lit into them, me included, because once you're in a battle, all you think is to shoot the other fellow before he can shoot you. I tried to aim but had no idea if I hit anyone. It was simply a race of firepower. Bullets sung by my ears and kicked gravel into my face. A supporting regiment was coming up behind the enemy, so the three French cannons went off again, cutting great gory gaps.

"Now—charge!"

We swept through as if they were straw. We'd butchered wounded Russians but made prisoners of the Austrians, who were civilized and worthy of ransom or exchange. We rushed another hundred yards before running into the massed fire of still another unit.

Screams, wet coughs, moans. More French fell around me. They spun, sagged, knelt. Survival was a question of cruel luck. Some looked surprised when shot, some horrified, and some seemed to fall asleep. Hulot's head snapped on his shoulders, bits of skull flew, and he fell over. I looked anxiously for Gideon. Still standing! Our muskets empty and our line in disarray, it was our turn to retreat, this time uphill. My eyes watered from grit. My thirst was ferocious. I was sweating despite the cold. I grasped my canteen and took a swallow of watered wine before sharing it with Gideon. He gulped with a nod, and other hands reached. The canteen came back empty.

I looked about blearily. For miles on my left and my right, great clouds of smoke rose into the winter air. Huge formations of men tramped this way and that. Battle is a minuet turned into a stampede, with officers trying to direct herds of men in the right direction. Distant units crawled like ants, their movement as ponderous as barges. They'd drift close to each other, pause, and erupt in sheets of musket fire. Flags would shudder as if in a stiff wind. One side or the other would crack and give way, but not for long. Then a counterattack, and the slaughter would go on. Bodies entwined like lovers.

We endured three more attacks over the next half hour. By noon, the sun still low in the December sky, a third of the 14th Line was down. Wounded men observed their own blood with horrified curiosity, trying to tie off the leak. They curled in pain, or crawled, or groped. Sometimes friends helped. The dead sprawled in all kinds of improbable poses, dignity irrelevant. The blood was astonishingly bright, seeming to glow.

Enemy dead far outnumbered our own. Each time a Russian or Austrian regiment engaged one of ours in a duel of musketry, French speed and accuracy wrecked their formation. Allied cavalry made a charge at the 10th Line, next to us, and accomplished little but the massacre of their own members. Saddles were swept clear by disciplined infantry fire, then terrified horses thundered between the armies, looking frantically for an exit.

French artillery also gained a steady edge. Allied guns were systematically dismounted, broken, or abandoned. Others were captured and swung around to point the other way. As each minute ticked on, Napoleon's advantage grew.

Men fired at each other point-blank, fenced with the bayonet, and warded off hundreds of galloping horsemen. The contest for Pratzen Heights raged for a good two hours, entire battalions dissolving like spring snow. At times we could pause as observers, gulping breath, loading our muskets and waiting our turn, and minutes later we'd be in the thick of it again. None of us completely understood what was going on—battles are confusion when you're in them—but the enemy kept advancing and backing like the surf of a receding tide, each time leaving more dead and wounded in its wake.

Finally, along a hillside line two miles in extent, the Austrian and Russian lines broke toward the southwest. French cannonballs followed, skipping like stones on water. We watched a retreat become a route. The enemy was dissolving from army to panicked mob.

"Now—after them!" Baron Thiébault cried, his voice hoarse.

We stepped off in exhausted pursuit. We'd won. I'd survived. It was over. I was too weary to be joyous, but I was curiously proud. I stumbled on a clod of earth.

And then an enormous blow hit my shoulder.

I pitched forward into the crystallized ice of the dirt before fully realizing what had happened. My musket went flying, my hat tipped over my eyes, and my knapsack rode onto my neck. For long, anxious seconds I lay facedown, stunned. At first I couldn't draw breath, and then I took in a hesitant, shuddering inhalation, wincing from pain.

I'd been shot.

The shock made me dizzy, and the strength had left my legs. My head was downhill from my feet, and I felt annoyingly helpless. I lifted my head to cry for help and managed a strangled "ack," spitting dirt.

Gideon was standing protectively over me, aiming his musket back uphill in the wrong direction. Had we been surprised from behind? He fired.

I heard a grunt, and a thud.

Then he turned to me. "Are you dead?" My new friend knelt, his face black as an African's from powder burn. He probed my shoulder and I gasped in fear, fury, and outrage.

I gritted my teeth to answer. "I don't think actual death is this painful."

In heroic stories, characters fight through their wounds, excitement giving endless energy. I, alas, felt like I'd been kicked by a mule. A musket ball as wide as a kidney bean and heavy as a gold piece had torn through my body. I had the twin sensation of finding it agonizing even to take breath, on my right side, and shocked numbness on my left.

"Be still, my friend." Gideon took out his briquet, a large camp knife, and cut off my pack straps and empty canteen, casting them aside.

"Please keep my civilian clothes," I had the presence of mind to gasp.

"You're hoping to change?"

"Exactly."

The Jew considered a moment, shrugged, and added my belongings to his own. "Now I have a double load," he said. "Your left shoulder was hit from behind, cracking your shoulder blade. A few inches different and it would have hit your heart and spine. Murderous bastard."

"Behind?" I coughed, some of the spittle bloody. "I was facing forward."

He rolled me onto my right side while I roared. "Our battle is over. Come, can you walk? I see no promised flying ambulance, so let's get you to a field station for vinegar and a bandage. I think the ball went clean through. You're lucky at more than cards."

He had a strange definition of luck.

He got an arm around my torso, braced the butt of his musket for leverage, and heaved me up. I almost blacked out. I swayed, my legs like pudding, and wanted nothing better than to pass out. After all, I'd already practiced being dead.

But Gideon wouldn't let me. "Stay awake, Digeon! Go to sleep and you die! Now *walk*, or you'll kill both of us! Bullets are still flying!"

"I'm not Digeon."

"Don't babble! Save your strength!"

"I'm an American named Ethan Gage." If I died, I wanted him to get word to Astiza. He paid no attention.

So it was with superhuman effort that I took a step, and then another. My legs were indeed unharmed, and as the advisability of getting treatment penetrated my brain, some strength returned. My vision began to clear. Survive, to see your wife and son.

"Don't trip on the shit."

I looked down. It was the bully Cheval, grimacing from being shot dead through the chest. He seemed to be giving us a last evil eye, despite no longer seeing anything. He clutched his musket, ramrod in the barrel—he had been killed while trying frantically to reload. I realized that when I was shot in the back, Cheval had been only a few paces behind.

And that Gideon had then fired in his direction.

These weren't the first acts of revenge committed on a battle-field. Having waited all day for a Russian or Austrian to shoot me, Cheval had finally got to it himself.

We went on. I tried to stick to stoic silence, but every step was a stab of flame, and my mutterings and curses were scalding. Some wounded do better, I suppose.

At the summit was Napoleon. I assumed I remained safely unrecognizable from my smear of powder smoke, blood, and dirt. I was one of hundreds of wounded limping to the rear, my right arm around Gideon's shoulders. But I still shrank while the emperor surveyed like a god, even as some of the maimed shouted in exultation. That's how much you get your blood up in battle.

I was conspicuous in my silence. My shoulder seemed loud enough.

The emperor swept the battlefield with his spyglass, his expression one of grim satisfaction. He was surrounded by half a hundred officers and couriers poised to race off with orders. There was a rumble of hundreds of drums from the far side of the hill, and giant French grenadiers in bearskin hats rocked into view, rank after rank, cresting the bloody battlefield to march on down the eastern side. They were as precise as a chorus line and as unstoppable as a glacier. They stepped over the dead and wounded as primly as if on parade. It was the Imperial Guard, being sent to deliver the coup de grâce to a smashed and demoralized enemy. Gideon and I stopped to catch breath and look back at the carnage, like looking down on a map.

The Allies seemed to have evaporated from the battle's center. French blue stretched toward Austerlitz as far I could see. To the north, Murat's cavalry was pushing back the enemy, and to the south the French were herding the fleeing armies toward a frozen stream and ponds. The ice on the ponds was beginning to shatter from French cannon fire and the weight of refugees, and I could see green-coated Russians disappearing into freezing water. They were drowning.

"The enemy is routed, *mon empereur*," said a general to Napoleon. "No victory has ever been more total. They will run all the way to Hungary."

"Easier to kill them here," Bonaparte replied. "Get the cavalry forward before we lose the light."

Indeed, it would be dark in a few hours. I wondered how many wounded would die of cold.

"Shall we take Olmütz?"

"Francis and Alexander will plead for an armistice before then," Napoleon predicted. "The war is won, cousins." He stood in the stirrups, stretched his frame as his white horse shifted under him, and proudly watched his Imperial Guard file into the smoke below. His face was radiant as a bride's, his posture erect, his bicorne turned to emphasize the width of his shoulders. In a single day, Trafalgar had been avenged. The coalition Britain had assembled to fight Napoleon was shattered. He would redraw the map of Europe like a child with a pencil.

I wondered if England would quit.

"It's a beautiful sun we have this day, is it not?"

"Yes, *mon empereur.*"

Napoleon slowly swept his arm along the view as if freezing it in his mind. He'd risen from nothing, proven unbeatable, and had a thousand plans and strategies. Since the dawn of civilization, governing had been granted through birth, justified by the theory that the leisure of the aristocracy separated the highborn from the muddled motives of lesser men, giving them time to learn and apply wisdom. Churchmen were sheltered for the same reason.

Napoleon had replaced these privileged classes with tradesmen and strivers, elevated by cunning and courage. Europe was turned upside down. The future would be a frenzy of the ambitious and able, the ruthless rising and falling like flames. No man would relax. Any could triumph.

And me? I was wounded, penniless, cut off from my family, a fugitive from all sides, and wary of the French spy Comtesse Marceau. I was a modern man like Napoleon—self-made, but a parody of success.

"It was exactly a year ago that I crowned myself emperor," Napoleon said to his companion. "That was a noble day, though a damned uncomfortable one in those coronation robes." He laughed and turned to his other officers. "But *this* day, cousins, the day of Austerlitz, is the best of my life. The best day, after the best night. Our army is invincible, and these wounded will gladly return to it as soon as they are able." He swept his arm again, taking us all in. "Your wounds are a badge of honor!" he called. "I salute your courage!" For just a moment I felt his gaze stop on me, and I braced for recognition. His eyes narrowed. But then a heartbeat later his eyes moved on, me a tick in his surveillance. He muttered something to one of his aides. Then he nudged his horse forward and passed us. "And now we look to the future."

Did he glance my way once more?

I realized I was wet. I looked down. My torso was soaked from a blot of blood that had browned as it clotted. I'd been shot, I reminded myself, my breathing labored. I felt nauseated. The battlefield began to whirl.

"We must get away from that man," Gideon muttered of Napoleon.

And then all went dark.

CHAPTER 19

Astiza

In medieval times, the silver mines of Kutná Hora made Bohemia one of the richest provinces of the Holy Roman Empire. Sixty miles of tunnels wormed through veins of ore, and thousands of miners with picks and shovels crouched and crawled to their stations like doomed troglodytes. The mines have since played out and been abandoned. The city of Kutná Hora remains, half-forgotten, making it a discreet hideaway for occult alchemical experiments. Horus and I were bound by ropes in Prague and transported by sealed wagon. My muscles cramped and my son was feverish, moaning from burns to his hands. He'd been thrashed, starved, and threatened. I'd been told that only my abject cooperation could save him from worse. I'd fallen in with monsters, and waited to be raped. Yet Fulcanelli—no, Richter—was so mutilated and in such pain that he'd lost any immediate interest in possessing me. Auric painted him with ointment and swathed his lower head with bandages. While the dwarf drove, Richter would open a shutter from the driver's bench and peer at us with dark, sharklike eyes, betraying no feeling at all. He didn't speak on the journey.

We traveled many hours—I lost all sense of time—and after an eternity stopped in the old mining town, none but ghosts awake. There were growling hounds at the wagon wheels to discourage escape, and Harry shrank against me, whimpering. I wept with him, furious at my own folly in trusting a "bishop" who was clearly not. Then we were carried into a tower tied to the old mines below. We were pushed down winding stairs hewn from solid rock. At the bottom we passed cells with iron bars and were shoved into a windowless underground apartment used for magical experiments.

It was dim as a dungeon in our new prison. Richter took a seat on a stool in the alchemical laboratory, caped and bandaged, a rapier at his side. Despite his disfigurement, he posed erect as if sitting for a painting, watching us as we looked around. The primary chamber had stoves, distilleries, bookshelves, flasks, bowls, and crucibles. Beyond was a tiny cave for sleeping, with more books. There was a crude chimney, and the stink of fumes. The baron took some satisfaction from our sense of doom. Unless we escaped or were rescued, my son and I would eventually face far ghastlier pain than he had. The only question was when.

My tongue was thick with thirst—we'd had no food or drink for a full day and night at least—but I managed a croak. "Where are we?"

"The place where you will rejoin your husband."

Like a fool, I actually looked about. Ethan here? Or his body? But that wasn't what Richter meant. Still, the words gave me wild hope. My heart stuttered.

"You've dissolved my face, but not our partnership," Richter said, his teeth clenched from pain. "In fact, your hellion has sealed our alchemical wedding. You've been enlisted in the Invisible College, madame—that mystic fraternity that follows the secrets of the rose. Congratulations, witch."

"But with me as master, and you as a slave," hissed Auric.

"Yes, as our slave, my little friend." He stared hard at me. "You will obey my dwarf in all things. If you don't, your boy will become supper."

My gaze darted. Two candles guttered in a chamber fifteen feet wide and thirty long. The door was made of stout and ancient wood. There were cauldrons, hanging hooks of iron, buckets, and vials. "So you are cannibals." My guilt at trapping my son ground at me like a millstone, and the only thing that assuaged it was fury. How I longed to kill our two tormentors! But I needed a plan, not an impulse.

"I don't share my assistant's peculiar tastes, which are for pleasure, not nutrition."

"I'll do what I must to protect my son." At this point I'd sacrifice my body. It is, after all, a temporary husk.

"Trust me, I've lost any attraction I once had for you," Richter said.

"It's me you have to placate." Auric licked his lips again, enjoying my reaction. He cackled and jigged, dancing from foot to foot. What strategy to use on the insane?

And then my son spoke up, in a brave little voice honed by far too many hardships. "If you touch Mama, I will burn you, too."

Auric was startled, and actually recoiled. "Goblin," he hissed. But he was afraid.

"You are a bad man like the other bad man, and I don't like you and I don't like it here." Harry put on his best scowl, as if about to throw a tantrum. I moved closer to him and we grasped hands, our courage growing from it. To be defended by a child!

My own strength and determination soared. I'd bring down these men. I'd destroy them, and their nest, and their ambitions.

The dwarf had the confused look of all bullies faced with defiance.

The baron interrupted. "You will touch neither of them unless I expressly allow it," Richter mildly commanded the dwarf, in a manner that showed he expected total obedience. "We want answers, not screams."

"Then let us go," I begged hopelessly. "Our meeting was a colossal mistake for both of us."

"On the contrary. You've studied in Egypt, home of great magic. You learned the African arts amid the slaves of the Caribbean. You've studied in the greatest libraries, and by some rumors have read the Book of Thoth itself."

I was shaking my head. "No, no, you give me too much credit. I exaggerated, to impress you. I led you on. I'm little more than a gypsy reader of the tarot."

"You seek the Brazen Head."

"As an amusement for my husband."

"Whom I will enlist as well. Then I will bend all of you to our will."

Would these monsters really reunite us? With Ethan, escape seemed truly possible. Or would I suck him down into hell as well? My mind hopped like a bird, pecking at flitting hope. "You'll find him?"

"Perhaps. I believe you speculated he might come through Venice. I'll seek him there. Meanwhile, do you wish for reunification?"

"Of course."

"Then you must earn it. And pay me back for my face."

"It was an accident. You were threatening me. My son was frightened."

"First, your husband is going to learn of your imprisonment."

Hope again. "How?"

"News will be sent to Spain, where he is some kind of courier between the navies. You will be reported to be in dire peril. That should encourage him to come, and together we will find the Brazen Head. But without the French."

"We can't lead you from down here." I shuddered, looking at Auric. "Instead you brought us to this midget monster. Why, Baron—or Bishop—or whatever you are? Why this dwarf? Why bring us here?"

"So you can serve the Invisible College while we wait for clues your husband will unwittingly bring. You will seek the Philosopher's Stone by refining gold from base metals."

"No one has ever found the stone that provides immortality and salvation."

"Haven't they? The Comte de Saint-Germain said he had lived for centuries. Other alchemists and magicians have made the same claims, going back to Merlin, Enoch, and Hermes Trismegistus. You will be my chemist, Astiza, and discover and deliver to me the transformation men have sought for ten thousand years."

"I can't. Not in a hole like this. Where am I?"

"The silver mines of Kutná Hora, sorceress," Auric piped up. "A labyrinth of half-drowned tunnels no person has ever fully mapped. A kingdom of darkness. The pit of the underworld. The portal to Satan. The abyss of despair."

"A laboratory," Richter corrected. "And you *will* succeed, because your whelp's life is at stake. Isn't that right, Auric?"

"Boy soup. You promised, master. Should she not produce gold . . ."

"You will succeed, or watch your son boiled and eaten before your very eyes."

I shut them. "Succeed at alchemy?"

"Succeed at magic."

"By threatening me with your little demon?"

"This demon will be your assistant and overseer. Auric knows the dark arts as you know the light. He won't hurt you if you do as I say."

My mind was frantic as a rabbit, darting this way and that. I'd no doubt their intention was to lure Ethan, use him, kill him, and then use me. But I was their prisoner, ransom for my husband. I'd promise to do what can't be done.

"How can I believe you? You said Ethan might be dead. Now you said you'll get word of my imprisonment to him. Which is it?"

"He's a duplicitous agent for both France and England, I've been informed, serving as go-between among great men. If the navies have clashed, he may well be dead. But if he survives, I'll find him."

"How? You're not French."

"The Invisible College is vast and interconnected. France uses us as agents at times, but has no idea that we use France. We must find the Brazen Head before men like Talleyrand do. We must keep it from their conspirators."

"Which conspirator?"

"An agent you may remember. The Comtesse Catherine Marceau."

CHAPTER 20

Your assassin treated you remarkably well, monsieur," someone said to me through a haze of misery and confusion. "Or he was a remarkably poor shot. What did you say, Gideon? A dozen paces?"

"If that."

"And yet the murderer missed every vital organ. You say this Digeon fellow here is good at cards?"

"He's good at cheating with them. Somehow he cut a deck to let me display the high card and keep a cloak. Which I shared with him."

"Skill and luck. Digeon should be a gambler." At which time the speaker probed my left shoulder and gave me a lightning bolt of pain, reminding me I had a new tunnel through my body from a musket ball fat as a grape. Then he poured what felt like liquid fire into the orifice and I flashed fully awake, roaring any number of oaths and thrashing to get out of some kind of enclosure. By the gunpowder deviltry of Francis Bacon, it hurts to get shot! Strong hands held me down.

"These Christians pretend to great piety and then take their messiah's name in vain," my torturer said, commenting on my foul language. "It seems hypocritical."

"To be human is to be a hypocrite, Father," Gideon said.

"Gage!" I gasped.

"Ah, we truly woke him. What was that he said?"

I summoned breath, the mere inflation of my lungs a slog through purgatory. "My name is Gage." It was a croak.

"He's delirious," Gideon assessed.

I shook my head in frustration. If I died, I wanted someone to know who I truly was so word could someday reach my wife, should she live. "I'm not Digeon. My real name is Ethan Gage."

There was silence for a moment. "He must be a deserter," the sadist in charge finally said. "This Digeon is a fraud as well as a cheat."

"He deserts to the front lines?" Gideon objected. "Then this Digeon is a lunatic."

It was time to go all in, given that I was weak as a foundling and desperate for help. My fate was in Jewish hands. "I'm an American savant, a Franklin man," I rasped. "You must hide me from Napoleon. He keeps detaining me from finding my wife."

"I will allow," Gideon allowed, "that he is very odd. No one befriends a Jew. He took my side in a quarrel he had no part in and risked the scorn of the others. Mysterious about his past, too."

"Perhaps he's a Jew himself?"

"I suspect he's not much of anything."

No, I wasn't a Jew. But I've spent time with savage Red Indians, black ex-slaves, Egyptian wizards, Arab adventurers, and the Jew Haim Farhi in Jerusalem, and decided that religion, color, and label didn't make a whit of difference in their performance as human beings. There's good and bad in all persuasions, is my experience. The other thing we share is that we're all a bit peculiar, me especially, but far from unique. I didn't care if this pair were Jewish or Eskimos, if they could help me. I'd have stated this ecumenical philosophy, but instead passed out again.

I awoke once more to the torment of a wagon jouncing on winter's frozen ruts, metal pots banging, axles creaking, and light filtering through cracks in a brown canvas roof. I was lying on a straw tick mattress, my chest and shoulder swathed in bandages, my boots off but the old sword hilt still tucked at my back. I wasn't bound, but since each jolt left me half-paralyzed with pain, I wasn't about to run away, either.

I listened. Armies give a great noise of clanking equipment, tramping boots, rumbling wheels, thudding horses, shouts, complaints, laughs, songs, and the other sounds that tens of thousands of people make when moving as a herd. All of this was absent. Gideon had brought me to a rolling refuge far beyond Bonaparte's forces, and thank Yahweh for that. I'd had my fill of soldiering.

I fell asleep again. And woke.

My feet were close enough to the wagon seat to kick its bottom. "Gideon! I'm thirsty."

My saviors reined up and parted the canvas to let in gray light. Both turned to look at me. I saw an older version of my soldier friend, with the same handsome long jaw, heavy brows, intelligent eyes, and thick curly hair, the elder's tinted silver. Unlike his son, he had a beard and sidelocks, making him easy to identify as a Jewish merchant.

Gideon's father was a peddler to the army, and successful enough to afford a wagon. Many peddlers carry their wares on their backs, but dangling around me were all the things sutlers use to cater to soldiers. There were hides of leather, bolts of cloth, string, rope, buttons, nails, kegs of brandy and wine, tobacco, handkerchiefs, paper, fruit, smoked meats, pickles, sauerkraut, and sugar. There was also a rack with two pistols, a musket, and a fowling gun to protect this hoard and shoot the occasional meal. I saw furs, pawned watches, pewter plates, and iron pots.

"Drink this." I was handed a wine sack. "We're in a hurry." I sucked like an infant, puckering at the sour edge.

Night soon descended, as it must in December. We stopped, my chauffeurs jumped from the teamster seat, and then the rear flap opened and Gideon crawled inside. I slurred something.

"You're not just alive, but a little intoxicated," he observed.

"Not drunk enough. Being assassinated is like being struck by lightning."

"Here, have a taste of this."

It was fiery brandy. I coughed and had some more.

"And this." It was bread softened in beer.

This stew kept me dizzy, but I sipped enough to unclench my throat and roil my empty stomach. I felt feverish and feared sepsis, but at least I wasn't permanently delirious. "You saved my life," I said. "Saved it twice, if we're getting away from Napoleon's army. I was hiding in the ranks from my enemies."

"All we've done is plug your bullet hole. But I killed Cheval. You're lucky he was as bad a shot as he was stupid."

"My own clumsiness, I suspect. I tripped on a furrow just as he fired."

"Then my father was right. You're lucky."

"I'm sorry you had to play executioner."

"I'm not. I would have been his next victim."

"Gideon, listen. I'm having the wretched luck of Odysseus trying to get back to my wife. I'm hoping she's in Prague. Could your father drop me that way?"

The older version loomed into view. "That's already our destination. My son has deserted, too, and will hide in the ghetto until the war ends."

"The Jews will shelter you," I asked, "Monsieur . . . ?"

"Aaron Dray, sutler and financier to His Emperor's troops. Thousands are missing after what's being called the Battle of Austerlitz, and I don't think they'll be particularly anxious to get their Jew back. And by my son's account, no friends will be looking for you, either. Nonetheless, you should consider declaring yourself dead, Monsieur Digeon, or Mister Gage, or whoever it is you are. Unless you're anxious to stand again in line of battle."

"I'm actually very good at being dead," I said. "I'm getting a great deal of practice. Though I hope I'm not actually dying."

"It's a pretty poke through your shoulder, but keep it clean and it will close soon enough. Move too soon and you'll open it to poisons."

I nodded weakly. "Where are we?"

"West of Brunn."

"And the armies?"

"Napoleon has gone northeast in pursuit of Alexander and Francis, though the rumor is that the Austrians are suing for peace. The Allies weren't just defeated; they were destroyed. Europe is in shock. Bonaparte is master."

I collected my thoughts. I was alive, likely to recover, and away from Pasques and Catherine Marceau. If they had followed the army to seek reunion with me, it was either to take revenge for my escape or to get the Brazen Head for themselves. I must not lead them to Astiza. Now we were near Prague. Perhaps the wound had been a blessing. "I owe my life to both of you. Cheval would have finished me with his bayonet. I've some money left to pay you for your kindness."

"Men pay enough for possessions," the elder Dray said. "Kindness should be free. As should life."

"Doesn't cost a penny to come out of the womb," Gideon added. "It's only the grave that is expensive."

"You can use your money to board with a farm family while you recover," Aaron suggested. "Spend the winter sitting by the fire. Lie low until the war is over, American. Then get on with your life, if you have one."

Accustomed as I was to being chased, tortured, imprisoned, and shot at, the charity astonished me. Aaron Dray seemed generous and sensible; he proved that people are capable of surprise, which I suppose is one of mankind's rare redeeming features.

Yet lounging by a farm fire was the last thing I should do, even if I could afford it. I'd been badly sidetracked in my quest for wife and son. Could these new saviors be partners? My mind was spinning from more than alcohol. "That's damned Christian of you," I began, before catching myself. "I mean Jewish. What I mean to say is that I'm grateful, and am going to propose another alternative, a business venture, that offers great challenge and great reward."

"You are in no condition for adventure, Monsieur whoever-you-are."

"I'm a diplomat, a savant, and a Franklin man, and I've been caught up in Napoleon's schemes while working desperately to escape them. I've served Bonaparte before, and was on my way to rescue my wife and son when I was conscripted again into his service. Old enemies from Paris—a comtesse named Catherine Marceau and a rogue policeman named Pasques—came to the army in pursuit of me. So I slipped away to hide in the front ranks."

Gideon laughed. "Like hiding from the jailer by stepping in front of a firing squad!"

"It was a risk, but I thought Soult would be held in reserve. And it was ironic to be shot in the back, no? But I've had stranger things happen. In any event, I'm searching not just for my family but for a medieval relic that a lot of important people seem to want—including Catherine Marceau and Napoleon. Talleyrand, his foreign minister, enlisted me to find it and to give it to him first."

Aaron looked skeptical. "Talleyrand? A medieval relic?"

"The story is that there may be an artificial man that can fore-tell the future. It's worth a great deal of money when we find it." I'm a bit of a salesman, and substituting *when* for *if* is the kind of thing I've learned to do. I didn't tell them that the Brazen Head might have been destroyed centuries ago.

Gideon looked at his father. "A golem?"

This Jewish legend was a well-known tale in Europe. The golem was some kind of mud man, animated by magic, who pro-tected the Jewish ghetto in Prague. It ran out of control, according to my informants in Paris. "Precisely, except completely differ-ent," I said. "This is an automaton built by Albertus Magnus. One legend says it was smuggled east from Paris to Bohemia and awaits rediscovery. My wife, who is astoundingly clever, might have figured out where it is. My boy is a better version of his papa, and brave as Hector. My proposal is that you get me to Prague, we look for Astiza and Harry together, find the machine, and share whatever we sell it for."

"We could take him to the ghetto," Gideon said to his father. "The French would never find him there." He turned to me. "Is this Marceau, and this Pasques, likely to pursue?"

"Yes. I hope they'll believe me dead or deserted, but I doubt they'll give up their own hunt for the Brazen Head. The two are as pestiferous as Corporal Cheval, and considerably craftier. So re-covering in the Jewish ghetto would be greatly preferable to being abandoned at a Bohemian farmhouse." I gave the brightest smile I could, given my prone position and barely stanched wound. "I've been to the Holy Land and have the utmost respect for your cus-toms and religion. I'm something of a scholar when not shooting people."

"You don't seem religious at all. A bit of a rogue, we soldiers judged."

"Ecumenical," I amended. "Pagan on my wife's side. It's all

a little fuzzy, so we like to think of ourselves as open-minded. I'm sure mankind will sort these creeds out someday." I actually thought nothing of the sort.

"Not ecumenical," Aaron said. "You'll be as baffled on your deathbed as the day you were born. No matter. We're offering shelter, not conversion, and you're offering opportunity. A machine that could predict the next Christian riot would be very useful indeed."

"Ask it anything you like. When we find it."

"But how to divide the proceeds, should we sell it?" he went on. "This is assuming we do find your golem, of course, with you wounded and bringing a history of enemies into our new partnership."

I was impressed with his negotiating skills. Most of us don't think our greed through. "My family has been looking for a full year," I bargained. "Perhaps three-quarters for us and one-quarter for you?"

Gideon laughed. "He's asking to be dumped in a farmyard!"

"Actually, there are two of us and one of you," Aaron added. "I've yet to see this wife of yours. So two-thirds for us, and a third for you."

"You're a negotiator as sly as Talleyrand. Divided down the middle, then. That's always simplest." It seemed a little presumptuous to haggle before we'd taken a step to find the thing, but it's simpler to divide the abstract than an actual pile of coins. "I care much more about finding my family than this android, or golem, or whatever we care to call it. So I propose an equal partnership: half to the Gage family and half to the family of Dray."

"Done. And how do you propose we begin this search, Ethan Gage?'

"Get me to your ghetto, a good doctor, and a wise rabbi, and help me make inquiries. I'll show a clue I haven't shared yet."

Chapter 21

Prague bridges the Vltava River in a broad valley, the central square on the right bank and the imperial castle on the left. The streets bend with the river, and the visitor must use church towers to orient himself to the Charles Bridge and its thirty decorative statues. Downstream a short distance is the largest ghetto in Europe, squeezed between market and river. Dark, steep-roofed tenements teeter above ghetto lanes to make narrow canyons, and the crowds are thick with noise and smell. The population waxes and wanes; the Jews have been expelled at least twice in the name of cultural purity, Aaron informed me, and welcomed back twice to lubricate the economy. "Emperor Joseph II, who died in 1790, was such a reliable patron that the Jews named their neighborhood Josefov for him," my new mentor explained.

When I arrived, ten thousand were crammed into a neighborhood fit to house a quarter of that number. Even the cemetery is jammed, the twelve thousand overlapping tombstones marking just the topmost layer of a hundred thousand remains. It idly occurred to me that all soil is corpse powder, animal as well as human, and that we grow our sustenance upon the dead.

The ghetto is a medieval relic. Jews are scattered through most of Germany and Bohemia now, becoming doctors, farmers, artists, and bankers. The craft guilds have weakened, letting Jews into trades, and Jewish women are far more likely than their Christian neighbors to join their husbands in the workplace.

Despite this modernity, the Prague ghetto remains walled, soot-streaked, claustrophobic, and gated. Streets are clogged with carts and stalls. There is almost nothing green except the moss in the cemetery, and stains mark the periodic river floods. The language is a babble of Hebrew, Yiddish, Czech, and German, meaning that even Frenchmen Gideon and Aaron struggled to be understood. There was no room for our wagon in the ghetto, so father and son stabled it near the riverbank and we walked into the teeming streets, me with bandaged shoulder. The exercise was good for me, but my wound was raw and my muscles stiff, so I limped, to considerable sympathy.

My guardians explained I was an American savant with terrible secrets and a wounded hero of Austerlitz. Was there a place I could recover, unmolested by any government? Such a request was understood perfectly.

We were mobbed by the curious, because word of Napoleon's victory caused great excitement. While most in the Austrian empire feared that the battle would be followed by territorial losses and indemnities, the Jewish hope was that Bonaparte would prove to be another Josef, reforming the law and opening the ghetto. Word flew faster than I could walk, and in short order an invitation from the chief rabbi came. Guides breasted the current of humanity so we could be ushered to the New Synagogue, so-named because it had been finished in 1270. An even older house of worship decayed nearby.

The gabled building was deliberately plain, lest it draw envy and attack. Inside, it had the same graceful Gothic arched ceiling as a French cathedral. There was a raised and fenced platform in the center, and steps on one wall led to an ornamental closet with drapes.

"The platform is called a bimah, where the Torah is read," Gideon explained. "The sanctuary on the east wall, closest to Jerusalem, is where scrolls of the Torah are kept in an ark."

"No chairs?"

"Worshippers stand."

I keep seeking a religion to make me comfortable. "What are those slits on the north wall?"

"Women must stay in that annex during services, looking through windows to the rabbi. It's the eastern way."

I know that prophets of all faiths consider women distracting to the message at hand, and I understand the point. On the other hand, I enjoy the fairer sex, and separation disappoints me. My own wife is female, and ten times more spiritual than I am. Making her kind peer through slits in the wall is like denying the cook the dinner, in my opinion. More women front and center would bolster attendance, if they were comely and sang well.

Unfortunately, few people request my religious advice.

Tall, narrow windows let in light, but compared with the baroque excess of Venetian churches, this place was plain as a Puritan. Everyone thinks Jews must be rich, but I saw little sign of it. They dressed simply and worked hard.

Rabbi Abraham Stern greeted us. This man met expectations, being a barrel-bellied, white-bearded patriarch with black robes and cap. Most Jewish men ignore the old prohibitions against shaving in these modern days, but the rabbis remain as bushy as Sinterklaas. Gideon made introductions all around, and Abraham examined me cautiously, reserving judgment. For this I deemed him perceptive.

Since none of us could speak German or Czech, we were fortunate Abraham understood French. "You've come from the battlefield?" he asked us.

"Napoleon is triumphant," Gideon said. "He didn't just defeat the Allied armies—he smashed them. French influence will be sustained far into the German principalities, Russia will retreat, and Austria has been humiliated. Ethan here witnessed the naval battle of Trafalgar, but that French defeat has already been avenged. Bonaparte is like the mythical Greek villain Antaeus, who became stronger every time he was hurled to the ground."

"Reference Bible stories, my son, not pagan ones. I sense you've too much learning from a French school."

"Then I will compare Napoleon to Samson, but with his hair regrown."

The rabbi turned to me. "So Napoleon is Samson. And you look as pallid as that hero after Delilah cut his hair, American."

"I've got a hole through my shoulder and was chilly enough without added ventilation. Now I'm retired from military service and looking for my family."

"In Prague?"

"My wife and son have allegedly been imprisoned somewhere in Bohemia while seeking a medieval relic." This was what Catherine Marceau had written me. She'd hoped to enlist me, and whether her seductions were entirely calculated or she fancied me, I could never figure out. Certainly she wanted to seize the Brazen Head. "I'm hoping to find some word of their whereabouts so I can rescue or ransom them. Have you heard of a beautiful woman with a small boy researching medieval secrets?"

He was clearly intrigued. "There was actually talk of one." My heart soared. "She was called a gypsy, an astrologer, and a witch.

She had Egypt's beauty—and Egypt's mystery. She disappeared. I could make inquiries."

My heart hammered. "I'd be grateful. I've also got enemies trying to conscript me. Monsieur Dray suggested I might hide in the ghetto while we investigate. He also said you might help us with legends about the artifact we seek."

"Which is?"

"An artificial man."

"A golem," Aaron explained, "but built like a machine. Made not of magic, but of metal. Bronze, I think."

"Part of it. Built by Albertus Magnus, the great medieval scholar," I put in.

The rabbi glanced up at the synagogue's vaulted ceiling. "And where is this creature?"

"That's what my wife was trying to find out. Could your stories of this golem and the Albertus automaton have been mixed up?"

Abraham considered us carefully for a while and came to a decision. "There were rumors of your coming. God's ways are mysterious, are they not? To bring this wounded soldier to this synagogue at this turbulent time? And yet there was speculation. Signs in the sky. The cawing of birds. Whispers in answer to prayer. Come, come, into my house. Let's discuss these matters in private."

We were led across a small courtyard to an adjacent building. Steep steps led to a living area with a plank floor, beamed ceiling, and windows that overlooked the ghetto rooftops. Prague Castle rose beyond. The city struck me as one of the most beautiful I'd ever seen. In a world of relentless progress, Prague promised the magic of the past.

The rabbi stoked the fire in a tile stove, put on water to heat, and then thought better of it and opened a bottle of Riesling. Glasses and a pewter plate of kolache pastries were set on the oilcloth that covered his table. Winter sunlight filtered through leaded glass, books gave a studious air, and the sharp, sweet wine was restorative. My shoulder oscillated between dull ache and sharp outrage, and my fitful sleep had left me groggy and grimy. I wanted to rest a hundred years, yet I dared not pause my quest for Astiza. Now I'd entrusted my success to Jews. Rabbi Abraham had bright, mischievous eyes, cautious calculation, and the officious manner of holy men.

"I'm not sure if I'm chasing a treasure or a phantom," I began. "I have a habit of stumbling on odd things, such as the Book of Thoth, Thor's Hammer, the Mirror of Archimedes, or the Crown of Thorns." This raised some eyebrows, but I think they assumed I was exaggerating. "In other words, I've come to accept that the world is a peculiar place. So I ask you plainly . . . Are the legends of the golem real?"

"The legends are real," the rabbi said, taking a judicious sip and smacking the wine in his mouth. He took time to enjoy life's small pleasures. "The golem? The one Rabbi Loew created sleeps in our synagogue attic. Or so they say."

"You've seen it?" Aaron asked.

"Certainly not. I'd never presume to enter. If the creature is there, let him sleep. Rabbi Loew had trouble controlling his creature, and I wouldn't presume to do so now."

Since I, for one, couldn't have resisted peeking, I hesitated to believe him. Was the story just a myth? Yet did not seeing help keep it real? The golem *could* be in that attic.

"But don't you want to use him? I thought the golem protected the Jews from marauding Christians."

"Until he went out of control. The golem was made from the soil of Adam, not mechanical metal, and controlled by incantation, not gears and wires. All this took place more three centuries ago, using sacred magic since lost. The lesson I take is not to toy with God's powers. The more men invent, the more troubled the world becomes. If Albertus Magnus made and lost an artificial man, it's probably for the best."

"The automaton is supposed to foretell the future."

"I'll tell you your future, Monsieur Gage, and mine as well. We will get sick. We will have accidents. We will have sorrow from the loss of loved ones. Someone we love will break our hearts. Armies will tramp, cities will burn, and plagues will erupt, as they have from the beginning of time. And you can't wait to learn this? You need a machine to hurry the horror?"

"Napoleon and Talleyrand believe that's a pessimistic view of the future, Rabbi. They say a machine that could calculate the future could help them avoid disasters and improve what's to come."

"Change the future, you mean. Manipulate it."

"They dream of universal rule, French justice, and a flowering of commerce and art."

"And who in Bohemia is seeking this French enlightenment, delivered on the point of a bayonet?"

"Some Jews are. We've been told your people are excited by his victory."

He looked skeptical. "My people have not thought this through." He poured us more wine. "Bonaparte wants assimilation to bury Jewish identity."

"Which threatens your own authority?"

"The ghetto, my friends, is what keeps Jewish unity alive."

I didn't want to argue religious politics. I had a headache, and this was getting us nowhere. "Don't misunderstand me. I'm not an ambassador for Napoleon, Rabbi, and don't even know if this automaton called the Brazen Head exists. It may be as elusive as the Holy Grail or the Seven Cities of Gold. I'm chased by lunatics, my wife may be imprisoned, and my son may hardly remember me. I've lost my life savings, been shot in the shoulder, and find myself reliant on your mercy, hiding from a treacherous comtesse, a mad and disfigured baron, a policeman as big as a plow horse, and an emperor who periodically threatens to shoot me. The Austrian and Russian emperors are just as hostile. I've been cursed by the Austrians, scorned by the Russians, fled the French navy, been abandoned by my English spymasters, and am probably cursed for stealing Christ's Crown of Thorns. And all this after I announced my retirement." I don't like whiners, but I couldn't help spewing this litany of complaint. I was exhausted.

I was talking to what seemed to be a good man, however, and was relieved to see his skeptical expression soften. He gave a slight, sympathetic smile. He nodded at Aaron and Gideon. Then he gave a broader smile, which was more puzzling, and finally he began to shake. His belly shuddered. There was a guffaw, much to my dismay, and then the other two men joined in as well, laughing so uncontrollably that they could barely keep from keeling onto the floor. I seldom cause such amusement, except among my torturers.

"I don't see what's so funny."

Abraham gasped for breath. "If even half that is true, you must be in league with the devil!"

"I'm trying to escape devils, I tell you. Everyone wants this Brazen Head. My wife is mixed up with it, and I've got to save her life." I felt grumpy.

"We're sorry, Ethan, but there is always comedy in tragedy. It's such an eloquent list of complaints that we may anoint you an honorary Jew. You can start a Society of Job."

"Do you believe a word I've said?"

"You claimed you've got a clue to your quest that you haven't shared yet," said Aaron. "You can trust the rabbi. Come, we've committed to getting you this far. What is it you're hiding?"

I unstrapped Talleyrand's broken sword hilt and brought it out. "I've been dragging this thing through Europe without really knowing why, though I'll admit it's been a handy tool. There's odd luck to this relic. I was given it by Talleyrand just before Napoleon's coronation. The foreign minister thought this might be a clue."

Abraham looked intrigued but cautious. "Swords are hardly in short supply. Why would Talleyrand want a broken one?"

"I don't know, and nor did he. It's antique. It may have a pedigree."

I passed the stubby blade around. Aaron took a look, but it was Gideon who discovered the obvious. "It uses the rose as a pommel."

"What?" I couldn't believe I'd missed this detail. The pommel on the butt of the sword's hilt was smooth silver, but I now noticed that the edge, where it cupped the hilt, was cut in what could be regarded as the edge of a rosebud. The effect was subtle, but elegant and obvious once you saw it. "A good eye, Gideon. It's odd how the rose keeps turning up in my life."

"How so?"

"My wife found a dried rose that led to a mysterious man named Palatine, who persuaded us to try to sabotage Napoleon. An English spy was named Rose, and I fetched her help with a rose. Rose windows in cathedrals and rose symbols among the Rosicrucians. The mystic Christian Rosenkreutz may have stolen the Brazen Head from Albertus, or was given it to prevent its destruction by Thomas Aquinas. Have you heard of Rosenkreutz?"

"Of course. By repute he disappeared here in Bohemia. No one knows where."

Rabbi Abraham took the sword back, dipped a cloth in his glass of wine, and rubbed the stub of blade. I'd never bothered to clean the rust, and in fact the centuries of tarnish had gotten worse when I was at sea. My host, however, began methodically polishing. "Perhaps there's some kind of inscription."

I was embarrassed I'd left this task to others.

Gideon looked over his shoulder. "A letter perhaps. C?"

"More like a moon, it seems to me."

Now Aaron joined them. "No, narrow at one end and broad at the other. It looks like a horn."

Now I hobbled over to look. "A cattle horn?"

"Yes, but as a musical instrument," Abraham theorized. "A battle horn."

"We haven't used that sort of horn since medieval times," Gideon said. "Look, there's something on the other side of the blade. A letter."

It was an R.

The rabbi's eyes narrowed, then widened. "A rose, a horn, an initial. Was Rosenkreutz ever in Spain?"

"By legend he studied there with a sect called the Alumbrados that was outlawed. You think this 'R' stands for his name?"

"Unlikely. No, this is much more interesting. We'll have to consult the texts."

"What texts?"

"First, the history of Charlemagne and the very beginnings of the Holy Roman Empire." Abraham went to his shelves and brought down a fat volume, threading its pages until he found the entry he was looking for. There was a woodcut print of a knight wielding a sword in a great battle, a horn strapped to his side. "This broken sword has spirit, I think. Soul. You can feel it, can you not?"

"Only its edge."

"I can feel the soul of the man who wielded it." He thumped the pages. "This relic of yours is what men have long been waiting for, I suspect."

My head throbbed. "Speak to the point, please. My shoulder feels like nails are being driven into it. I'm addled from weariness."

He smiled. "Congratulations. You haven't found the Brazen Head, Ethan Gage, but you may bear the fragmentary remains of one of the most famous weapons that ever existed. You've heard of Excalibur?"

"King Arthur's sword? I'm aware of Malory's stories."

"Its legend is probably a myth, but the potent symbolism of a great sword is rooted in countless episodes of history."

"How does a rabbi know this?"

"This relic you bring is intimately connected to French history, so much so that mad Rudolf II here in Prague reputedly collected its other half. That's why I looked up Charlemagne."

"You mean Rudolf owned the blade? The missing part of what I have here?"

"Yes, the blade of Durendal, the sacred sword of Roland."

"Roland! The French medieval hero?"

"You're God's messenger, American, and have brought the ancient hilt of the sword wielded by Charlemagne's lieutenant Roland, who died at the Pass of Roncesvalles in 778 while defending the rear of the French army from the Basques. He blew his great horn, Oliphant, for relief that came too late. Wouldn't Napoleon long to own such a powerful symbol?"

He certainly would. He'd hoped to use Charlemagne's own sword at his coronation, but when competing cities offered several lengths of old hardware with claim to the pedigree, Napoleon gave up on identifying the true sword and ordered that a replica coronation sword be made instead. Desired relics have a way of multiplying when money or prestige is at stake. And yet famed swords might well be passed down, and one of them must be real. Could this be the handle of Durendal? "Why would Talleyrand have it?" I wondered aloud.

"He would buy it because of rumors of its power." Abraham came around the table to grasp my good shoulder, ignoring my wince when the pressure pulled at my wound. "Ethan, you've unwittingly brought into this synagogue one of the most momentous relics in the world, and you've brought it to the one place in the world where it can be safely hidden: this ghetto. Just as soon as you find the other half, the sacred blade."

"And how am I to do that?"

"Legend here has long held that it was concealed in the Star Summer Palace, a nearby seat of mysticism and magic where mad Rudolf hid his most important treasures."

"It's kept on display there?" I'd not heard of this place.

"It disappeared. Skeptics question whether it exists at all, but your arrival is too convenient not to be God's will. Your new friends will help you."

I stood wearily and went around to peer, bleary-eyed, at the old book. Yellowed pages, Latin script, and decorative lettering to start each entry. Combative Roland had the fierce and fatalistic look of a man already dead. "After I get some rest."

"Yes, yes, you can sleep here in my quarters. Sharpen your mind before we sharpen the sword."

As I turned away, the light caught something almost invisible on the page, and I ran my finger to pick it up. I thought it a fine thread at first, possibly from the binding, and rotated it between thumb and forefinger. But no, it was only a long, blond human hair.

CHAPTER 22

Harry

I don't like the bad man. I'm sorry I burned his face, but he was hitting Mama. She tells me I did the right thing and calls me her little hero, but now we have to live in a smelly cave. I try to be brave like Papa is, but when Mama cries, I cry, too.

The ugly man knows I don't like dogs. He showed me dogs when they brought us to an old tower, and they barked at me. I didn't like that. I don't like the way the ugly man looks at me, either.

They made us go down long, winding stairs, deep into the earth, and then locked the door. Mama says we're in prison. She says we aren't bad people, we are good, and that the really bad people made the prison. Someday Papa will come and rescue us so we can leave.

The ugly man keeps saying he will burn Mama and eat me, but I am more afraid of the dogs than him. He is short like me. I will burn him, too, if he gets too close, and I think he knows it. He looks mean, but afraid. I've seen Napoleon. Napoleon is never afraid, not even of dogs.

It is very boring here. Mama has helped make me a knight out of old rags and a horse that rolls on wheels she cut from a walking stick, so I play soldier. I saw soldiers with Papa. It's hard to remember, because it was very long ago. When I get tired of my toys, there is nowhere to go and no one to play with. Mama works with furnaces and pots and curly tubes. Nasty juice drips out the end.

She says the world is made up of just a few things, and she is trying to boil smelly soups down to those things. I don't know why. Grown-ups are boring. I want a boy to play with.

My hands hurt because I burned them melting the bad man. I still have bandages. The bandages make Mama feel better. She calls them magic ribbons and tells me to keep them on. Sometimes I can use them to pick up hot things. She calls me a big word I can't remember, but she says it means "helper."

Here is what I remember about Papa. He is very tall, like a giant, and very strong. He can lift me up and hold me upside down. He tickles. He laughs when he's with me, and never cries. Ever. He had a gun that Napoleon gave him. I wasn't allowed to touch it.

Sometimes he kisses Mama.

He took me to fun places in Paris, and once we saw the sun shine through a magnifying glass and set off a cannon. I covered my ears. I had to promise not to tell Mama that we'd gone there. Once I went down a chimney and found candy, and we slept in a church.

We have fun when we're with Papa.

Mama said he ran away to protect us, which I don't understand. I wish he would come. My eyes hurt down here, because it's always smoky. I sleep a lot, but when I wake up it is always night.

I dream about dogs and the burned man.

I want a house with windows someday. I will live there with Mama and Papa, and Mama promises they will only let good people inside.

Each evening, Mama does something to her bowls of drips. She says she can't finish, because then they wouldn't need us anymore. I don't understand. I wish we could just go away.

Mama says she has a plan. She has asked the ugly man, whose name is Auric, to fetch some powders from the big city and bring them here. She says she can't finish without more colored powders. So Auric went away, which is good. The burned man went away, too. But other men keep our door locked and feed us bad food.

Mama tells me stories when we lie on the floor to sleep. She knows lots and lots of stories. They are good ones about gods and goddesses and heroes and princesses.

One of my favorite stories is about a knight named Roland. He was the bravest knight in all of France, and the favorite of the king. One day an army was chasing the king, and Roland and his men stayed behind so the king could run away. Roland and his men were attacked by thousands of soldiers. Roland had a great sword and fought for hours. But finally the sword broke.

Roland also had a great horn. He put the horn to his mouth and he blew a big sound. It was like the biggest sound in the world. He blew and he blew and he blew, asking the king to come back and help him. The king did, but it was too late. Roland was dead. The king cried.

I wish I had a great horn. I would blow and blow and blow.

I would blow until Papa came and took us somewhere bright.

CHAPTER 23

The Star Summer Palace rises from the trees in a game park west of Prague. It is a four-story tower built in the shape of a six-pointed star. The castle thus has twelve vertical walls, a complex and impractical design chosen for magical power.

"The star is called Solomon's seal," Rabbi Abraham said, "after the biblical king. It's made of two triangles, one overlapping the other, and represents the duality of the universe. All things are opposites—light and dark, male and female, fire and water—and yet together they represent unity. King Solomon had this royal seal cast into a ring of supernatural power. Alchemists believe it brings purity and transformation. We Jews adopted it first. Of course, astrologers and sorcerers consider the five-pointed pentagram mystical as well, but when Archduke Ferdinand built his palace, in the middle of the sixteenth century, it was the six points he chose to convey his message."

"Which was?" I asked.

"That's not entirely clear."

"These mystic codes never seem entirely clear."

"That is to reserve their power for those with the fitness to use them responsibly. The palace has been closed for decades, and by reputation it is filled with astrological and mythical symbols. Some of Rudolf's curiosities may have disappeared into this building."

"So it's a gigantic cabinet?"

"The curiosities weren't stored. They vanished. Authorities aren't sure if the building is a gateway to heaven or hell, but whichever of Rudolf's possessions were put there were never found again."

"Perhaps it was stolen. I saw that problem in the pyramids. Sealed tight as a stopper, yet empty as a beggar's stomach. The architects swiped what the pharaoh wanted to take with him, I'm guessing. Except that in the Great Pyramid it turned out there was a different door. Strangest place you ever saw, and I would have been rich beyond imagination if the exit hadn't been so difficult."

My companions looked at me doubtfully. The trouble with having extraordinary experiences is that they're too fantastic to be believed. "The Star Summer Palace had no obvious everyday utility and so was closed up," Abraham went on. "The loss of a broken sword there, if it was lost, has never caused much regret, because there was no proof it was Roland's, or that Rudolf ever put it there. Historians aren't even sure Roland was a real person."

"Like Arthur and Excalibur," I said. "But French foreign minister Talleyrand pressed into my hand the hilt of an old sword he thought I'd find of use here in Bohemia. Which you identify with a French hero fighting in Spain. And the other half is a blade that came into the possession of Rudolf II of the Holy Roman Empire. Which is all very peculiar, yet why would this antique make a difference?"

"Something to do with the Rosicrucians, perhaps," Gideon said. "Roland lived long before the Rosicrucians existed, but maybe Rosenkreutz came across the sword in Spain and incorporated it into his ceremonies. Perhaps he brought the broken blade here, and Rudolf acquired it. Meanwhile, if Rosenkreutz took your golem, he hid it. To open a hiding place, you need a key. This sword Durendal, perhaps, is that key, or could somehow lead us to the key. It's a link between Spain, France, and Bohemia. So we find the blade, steal it, reforge it, and . . ."

"And what?" I asked. "Did my wife go to this Star Palace?"

"We've no rumor of that."

"We're getting ahead of ourselves," Abraham said. "We need to find the sword blade first, and to do that we must break into a locked palace haunted by mystery and legend. If the groundsmen find Jews hunting for Christian relics, what do you think will become of us? Or if they capture the wounded American and enemy alien Ethan Gage, renowned for nefarious schemes?"

They'd clearly researched my background, as well as mastered big words such as *nefarious*. And he had a point. "This is my quest. Direct me to this odd palace and I'll explore it alone."

"With a wounded shoulder?" Gideon objected.

The room was indeed still unsteady. "I can't wait for it to heal. My wife and son need me."

"Nor can you afford to collapse where you don't belong. A poke at your shoulder and you'd betray everything you know, including us."

I *had* learned that a useful response to torture is to blabber and plead. Such realism means they'll never erect a statue to me, but I *am* still alive.

"Get some food and rest," Gideon counseled, "and when you're fitter we'll search this palace together."

"You've already saved my life. I keep increasing my debt."

"Nonsense. You saved me before I saved you. This is part of

our infamous partnership to find the Brazen Head. Let's see it through."

"Partners in infamy. Perhaps we could start a firm with that name. In the meantime, thank you, Gideon. I can use the help."

"And I want to see this sword, your exotic wife, and this mechanical golem." He grinned. "I'll ask it to forecast my own fortune."

We were several days preparing, which helped enormously in healing enough to regain some strength. I slept like the dead for almost three days, and my wound began to mend without infection. Gideon, meanwhile, learned of architectural drawings for the Star Summer Palace in the Capitular Library, at St. Vitus Cathedral. This enormous church in Prague's castle complex includes the tombs of Rudolf II, Saint Wenceslas, Saint Adalbert, and Saint John of Nepomuk, to name just a few. There's a royal mausoleum below, with an entire platoon of less saintly royals, and having spent time in a plain coffin, I appreciated these ornate ones when I visited to research. When my time comes, it would be flattering to be gussied up with marble, silver, and sculpture. The library itself was adjacent in a church tower, and had the smell of paper, ink, glue, stone, and dust that Astiza is addicted to. My spirit wrenched at the scent. I missed her desperately.

As is my habit, I poked about. Across the courtyard from the library is the Old Royal Palace, a warren of rooms built atop Roman ruins. Included is a parliamentary chamber with a stairway big enough to ride horses up, since getting on and off in full armor was not a simple task. A land registry has ceiling and walls painted with dynastic seals and books of deeds thicker than a Bible. I peered out the window, through which two Catholic governors were once tossed out of by Protestant legislators, a Czech custom, called "defenestration," that ignited the Thirty Years' War. Interestingly, the men survived a fall of seventy feet. Catholics said angels saved them. Protestants said they fell into horse manure.

The Star Palace plans gave no clue to where a sacred sword might be hidden. In fact, it was the oddest building I'd ever studied. The first floor is a cellar, and a pyramidal roof tops the fourth. On each level, six hallways and six chambers surround a round central foyer. Windows are tiny. Shapes are not square. Two of the star's points are oriented north–south, and another points toward Spain, but nothing in the drawings gave a clue to the palace's purpose. It has no kitchen, bedchambers, privy, or banquet hall.

The royalty of Bohemia seem quite mad.

In the spirit of lunacy, Gideon and I set out on a moonlit Christmas Eve to examine the place, reasoning that all good Christians would be at home. Snow reflected enough illumination to navigate by, and we carried lanterns to use once we broke inside. The night was cold as witches' breath, bony tree branches thrusting at the stars. The icy crust coughed with every step.

The palace, reached at midnight, was as odd as it had looked on paper. Imagine an ordinary building folded and creased, roof and root, to create a star. The exterior is simple white stucco. There are two or three shuttered windows on each facet of the star, but the facade is remarkably bland. The roof is steep as a wizard's hat, small dormers ventilating its attic. Gideon and I studied the architecture from the shelter of the trees. My nostrils felt frozen.

"It looks deserted," he said.

"Nor do I see any footprints or tracks," I added. We were trying to build each other's courage.

"Not a forbidding building, but not inviting, either. What do you think, Ethan?"

I have, as I've said, a peculiar wife, who gives me insight ordinary men don't enjoy. "Magic. Wise men believe numbers represent the universe, and that both God and men can express those numbers with divine geometry."

A small porch roof marked the door, firmly shut and thick enough to withstand a battering ram. We circled the structure, no larger in its footprint than a large barn, and found no other means of entry. Shuttered cellar windows hugged the ground. The place was tight as a vault and miles from the closest house. Its star pattern reminded me vaguely of a military fort, and while this palace was impractical as a real castle, it still had a fortress feel.

"We should have brought a siege gun," I said.

"Or at least axes and grappling hooks," Gideon said.

I looked up. "We could crawl through those attic dormers if we could get to them, but the walls are straight and slick as the face of a glacier. No ledges, no vines, no creviced stonework, no balconies."

"I did see one possibility," Gideon said. He led me around to a jutting point of wall and pointed to a metal cable running down its apex. "Maybe this could get us to the roof."

My left arm was still in a sling. "Impossible for me. I'm more useless than I like to be."

"Not if I can open the door from inside." He began climbing, his gloves on the odd metal cable and his legs gripping either side of the jutting walls.

I stood back to watch. Gideon scaled the sheer star point to the roof eave, hauled himself onto a roof ridge, shimmied like a monkey, and then let go to slide down a roof slope to a dormer opening. Snow came cascading down with him. Before I could shout instructions he didn't need, he broke through wooden louvers and disappeared into the palace's attic. When he lit his lantern, I could see a glimmer from outside.

I hoped no golems rested there.

I waited impatiently. Gideon would have to find his way to an attic hatch giving access to the rooms below. My shoulder wasn't throbbing anymore, but the ache made me stiff, and cold air didn't help. I looked in the direction of Prague. It was hidden from here, an immaculate snow-covered field giving way to woods. The world looked empty. The stars were ice, and this castle an iceberg. I stamped restlessly. The night gives free rein to imagination, and for a moment I felt as if the trees had moved. There—was that something?

No.

Far in the distance, a dog began to bark.

A thump made me jump. I turned. The massive door opened a crack, and Gideon beckoned me inside. "Or do you want to play sentry in the cold?" He shut the door behind us and slid back a beam, locking it in place.

I lit my own lamp. A short corridor led to a central round hall, with six hallways radiating off it. On each hallway were two doors, leading to the quadrangular rooms that occupied the points of the star. Accordingly, each room had two doors, each leading to a different corridor on either side. They also had two small windows, shrouded by shutters. In the round hall we found three randomly placed hard chairs and two freestanding mirrors, but no other furnishings.

"Not much of a place to live," my companion said. "Two dozen oddly shaped, impractical, empty rooms. No fireplaces, and no sense." The place was cold as a tomb. "Why mirrors, with no boudoir or bedchamber?"

I examined them from different spots. "I'm guessing they reflect the patterns of the architectural geometry. Angles upon angles upon angles. Did you spy a sword?"

"No. If King Rudolf hid it, he did a careful job."

"Let's start at the bottom."

A brick stairway in one of the star points led to a half-buried basement with a central rotunda and the same radiating hallways and odd rooms, making what my mathematician friend Gaspard Monge would call dodecagons. Geometry was clearly the point here, and the point was made over and over.

"If we take away the point dedicated to the stairs," I mused, "we get a five-pointed star."

"How brilliant of you to subtract one from six, my American friend."

"That creates a pentagram. A human with head and out-stretched arms and legs occupies a five-pointed space. Have you seen the figure Leonardo da Vinci drew?"

"And yet the archduke included six. And Emperor Rudolf stored nothing that I can see. All these points seem pointless."

I tried to think like Astiza. "Twelve is a sacred number, like the apostles, and this place has twelve outside walls and twenty-four rooms. If you include the central chamber, each floor has seven spaces, another sacred number. The three aboveground floors have twenty-one, the number of letters in the sacred Jewish alphabet, which I learned while in Jerusalem. My wife is a numer-ologist, and so we chat about such things."

"How interesting your love life is. So the sword is where, wiz-ard?"

"I don't know. It could be buried under the floor." I walked about, looking for signs of a hatchway. The walls were dark, the floor stone. It was a gloomy underworld with no clues that I could discern, except that the echoes were extraordinary. I could speak in a normal voice at one extension of the basement and be clearly heard at the other.

I stamped, seeking hollows, but didn't find any. Just geometry.

"Let's try upstairs."

The ground floor was white, and its ceiling was an alabaster riot of Roman gods in bas-relief. We picked out a centaur, Mi-nerva, Jupiter, Mercury, Nike, Bacchus, Ceres, Hercules, Perseus, and Europa.

"Archduke Ferdinand was the son of a holy Roman emperor," Gideon said. "He'd have an affinity for Rome."

"Look, there's Mars, next to one of the star's chambers. That seems a logical room for a sword."

It was as empty as the others.

We came back to the center, and Gideon pointed up. "There's an ancient hero following a star. Aeneas is said to have followed a star west from Troy to found Rome. In your own religion, the Magi followed a star to Jesus. Does this building represent a guiding star?"

"If so, we're inside what's guiding us, devoured by our own beacon."

"My father would say we are the Ouroboros, the serpent that devours its own tail."

"You've a speculative mind, Gideon. Are you a cabalist?"

"Just a Jew who thinks that people are brought together for a reason. How peculiar that we met, Ethan. We're meant to find something. I think this building is a book to be read, and you're the one to read it."

I was heartened by his confidence, and skeptical of my skills. "Or the rabbi has led us on a wild goose chase. Let's finish this."

The floor above the ground one was yellow, and the topmost or fourth floor was purple. More reliefs and symbols on the ceiling, reminding me of the zodiac the French army had found at Egypt's Dendera Temple. Mystics relish complex obscurity. State a fact and people will accept it as common sense, giving you no credit. Pose a riddle, ornamented with gods and goddesses, and the confusion will be hailed as genius you can charge money for.

What was the point of this palace? The Red Indians I'd encountered saw reality through the prism of a spirit world. Greeks and Egyptians sought understanding through shapes and symbols. Alchemists boil the complex down to the simple.

"These floors represent the elements as understood by Aristotle," I suddenly realized. "Four floors, to represent earth at the bottom, then water in white, air in yellow, and fire with imperial purple. These are the colors of astrologers. The six points are the planets, and the central chamber the sun. The palace is a model of existence. We're standing inside the universe."

"Perhaps a sword could be a compass needle, embedded in the floor?"

"As good a suggestion as any, but I've seen no sign of it. Let's search each level again."

We did so, but the building seemed emptier than ever. Its owner had supposedly constructed it for a lover, but it was one of those male miscalculations. I doubted she'd spend a day in this chill geometry. "If Rudolf or his successors ever stored relics here, I think they've been removed."

Gideon reluctantly nodded. "Unless there's a hidden chamber beneath the cellar, I fear you're right. Yet I feel we're close. Don't you feel it, Ethan?"

Oddly, I did. What were we missing? Earth, water, air, and fire. Planets, guiding stars, halls for gods, death and rebirth . . .

"The fifth element," I said.

"I thought you said there were four."

"Astrologers added a fifth to the Greek tally—the life force itself. It's the mysterious energy that calls us into being. The soul. The spirit. The electricity that fires us. There should be a fifth floor here."

"The stairs take us to only four."

"With a pyramidal roof above. Pyramids have power. What was in the attic, my friend?"

"Nothing that I saw."

In a flash I saw the solution. The subconscious notices what the eyes miss. "But I saw something from the outside that I barely noted at the time. By the gracious wisdom of Solomon, I'm an idiot. What was that cable you used to climb up?"

"Twisted copper wire."

"Attached to what?"

"The peak, I suppose. I didn't climb that high."

"And why was it there?"

"I've no idea."

"My mentor was the late and great Benjamin Franklin. He

shared credit for the invention of the lightning rod with the Czech savant Prokop Diviš, who made one independent of Franklin shortly after the Sage of Philadelphia demonstrated his. Diviš, Ben told me, had the insight to carry the rod all the way down into the earth, where it could discharge harmlessly into the ground. And the Czech experimented shortly after this palace was built. What's the slogan of the astrologers, my friend?"

"I've no idea."

"As above, so below. The sky mirrors the earth. We have the consistency of stars. What we found at ground level, we find above. What you climbed, I'm betting, is the wire leading from a lightning rod at the roof peak."

"So?"

"So perhaps the sword is hidden in plain sight. I can't climb up there with my wound, but perhaps you can. What serves as lightning rod?"

"The sword?"

"Where better to hide something than plain sight?"

"I think I can scale the timber framing of the roof." He climbed back into the attic with his lamp and then poked down his head.

"There does appear to be something very much like a blade jutting from the pyramidal peak of the roof," he reported. "Its base is clasped in a lock with a large keyhole. Lacking tools, I don't know how we can open it."

I took out the sword hilt I'd carried across half of Europe and examined it in the lantern light. For the first time I realized that the stub of blade was too neatly serrated to be merely broken. It had been cut and filed, waiting for reunion. The most profound insights are always in front of our blind eyes. "Here's your key."

Again a wait while Gideon climbed, listening to his thumps and the squealing of old metal. Finally he reappeared. "Astonishing."

He proffered an old blade, blackened and pitted.

And then there was a great boom from the palace door below.

CHAPTER 24

Another crash, and another. The building shuddered. Someone was trying to break in.

"We've been followed!" I hissed, as if they could overhear us through the thunderous thuds as they rammed the stout door. "I saw something in the woods but thought it my imagination."

"We need another exit," Gideon said.

"The roof again, and down the cable! You can help me."

He grimaced. "When the sword as lightning rod came free, so did the wire. I heard it clatter on the tiles as it slithered to the ground below."

I looked at a window on the fourth floor. "I can't jump with this arm. Even if I didn't break something, I'd reopen the wound and leave a trail of blood on the snow." I thought fast. "As above, so below. The cellar windows."

We hurtled down the stairs, the crash of the ram echoing in the stairwell like a bell.

"It will take time to break through the window shutter," Gideon warned.

"Take the sword. I'll delay them and find you."

I stopped at the ground floor, watching the stout door bulge from angry attack. Then I dragged one of the freestanding mirrors to face it. Another I positioned to one side, calculating the reflections in the glass.

Now I waited, curious to see my enemies.

The crossbar cracked, splinters springing and wood twisting. There was a final oath, then a heavy slam, and the bar snapped in two, each end dangling from brackets that still prevented entry. Someone huge heaved against it, again and again, and the door finally shattered completely, disintegrating.

The attacker stumbled in through its ruins. Pasques! I couldn't make out the face, but the bulky silhouette was all too familiar. The Paris policeman had the strength of three men. He'd first accosted me at the guillotine, fought with me at Notre Dame, and confounded me by proving as opportunistic as I am. Now he charged and stopped in confusion.

It was shadowy in the entry, the mirror backlit by my lantern, and in the gloom Pasques saw the menacing reflection of a huge adversary. It took him a moment to realize he was being challenged by his own image.

Other men crowded in behind him. "There! Shoot!" There was the crash of a volley of shots, blessedly emptying their guns. The mirror exploded.

"Fools!" They argued as I dashed to the basement.

It was dark, Gideon's lantern extinguished, but a glance told me which way to go. Light from a broken window gleamed from one of the short corridors, reflecting off the snow. I ran to it. My companion was already outside and reached to pull me through.

I howled. "The other shoulder!"

He switched and hauled as if I were a fish, and I heaved onto the snow. Pain beat like a drum. Ah, well, the wound certainly kept me alert. It would take our pursuers a minute or two to re-load their guns and deduce which way we'd gone.

"You still have the blade and hilt?"

"Yes. I used them to pry off the shutters."

"You carry one shutter and I the other."

"Why?"

"Escape."

We ran across the snowy lawn for the woods. I glanced back, light spilling from the doorway. Shouts in French echoed while boots thudded. Talleyrand's agents were still searching for us inside.

We were just yards into the trees when shots finally rang out. They'd spotted us. Bullets buzzed or whapped, puffs of snow marking their trajectory. We weaved and dodged, wishing the moon would go away. I heard barks.

We came to a long pasture of virgin snow descending toward Prague. The baying and rush of hunting dogs was urgent now.

"Sled!"

We threw the shutters down and belly-flopped with a grunt, me favoring my left shoulder, then we began to slide. The hill was steep enough. Cold air buffeted my half-frozen face.

I heard snarls, a last snapping at my heels, and growls of frustration as we plummeted ahead of the racing dogs. The animals ran, bellies to the white, snow flying, but they began to founder. On the crest behind us men ran up, shouting, and I could imagine them reloading.

By the time they shot again, we'd raced three hundred yards and were still accelerating, their dogs bogged. The reports sounded faint. We slid firmly out of range, Gideon whooping, and managed almost a full mile of sledding before Newton's gravity gave up on us.

We bounded up and ran like madmen until we disappeared into the edges of Prague. Side streets, the castle—we trotted around its periphery and dropped down through the gardens into the New Town, wary of any stranger. We liberated a boat on the Vltava bank to row to the Jewish ghetto. I steered while Gideon pulled, skeins of ice sliding by our hull. We were sweating.

"A close-run thing, American. But who were those men? How did they know we'd be there?"

"I recognized one of them, a policeman from Paris who is an agent of Talleyrand's."

"The French foreign minister has agents in Prague?"

"Agents everywhere, but I first spotted Pasques back in the army. Somehow he learned we'd left Napoleon to come here."

"And the others?"

"His companions, I surmise." That might include the exceedingly seductive, and exceeding dangerous, Catherine Marceau. Somehow they'd tracked me from the battlefield. Had Napoleon seen me after all, at the end of Austerlitz, and relayed my intention to go to Prague? Had they let me lead them to the antique sword? Yet only Aaron and Abraham knew our exact plan.

"We need to get the sword and ourselves out of this city," I said. "Who can we trust?"

"There's my father on the bank, waving to us."

We put ashore.

"Thank God you're back," the old man exclaimed. "I thought you'd been betrayed to the French!"

"We have been," his son said grimly. "We narrowly escaped. But we also found the sword blade. We must hurry to Rabbi Stern."

"But it was Stern who betrayed you."

"What?!"

"I'm dismayed by his duplicity. He wants French political reforms after all, to help the Jews, and decided to cooperate with Bonaparte's agents."

"But he said just the opposite!"

"No one can be trusted when automatons, golems, and politics are at stake. The French told him that the Star Palace might contain what you were looking for, so he directed you there."

The blond hair on the book! I scolded myself. Catherine Marceau had been doing research before us. She'd helped me with research, and I'd helped her by finding the sword blade. Damnation. We were partners again, despite my efforts to avoid it.

"Father, how do you know this?"

"I was making my way to the rabbi's house after bartering in the Old Town when a man called to me in a narrow lane."

"What man?"

"One moment he didn't exist, and the next he appeared as if by magic. I was so startled, I thought he might be a spirit. But his breath fogged in the cold like mortal men."

"Or the devil."

"He said he had a message for Ethan."

"A message! How did he know I'm here?"

"I don't know."

"What did he look like?"

"He had a cowl that hid his features. The alley was dark, and he'd picked a spot where people don't congregate. I feared he was a thief, but he said only one thing. 'Tell Gage that Rabbi Abraham Stern betrayed him to the French. To escape the woman, seek the swordsmith of the Golden Lane. There all will be answered.'"

"All *what* will be answered?"

"That's all he said. He melted into the shadows as suddenly as he appeared. It was as if he was invisible at will."

I immediately thought of Richter's odd gang around Ca' Rezzonico, in Venice. The Invisible College. Which reminded me of another group I'd tangled with, the Egyptian Rite. The only fraternities that seem to seek me are made of stealthy cutthroats, greedy and vile. "That's all? No proof?"

"He showed me two things he said would convince you to come. The first was this, which he said a female French agent had left for you at Abraham's house."

I took the slim volume. It was a French romance fashionable at the Seine bookstalls. Catherine and Astiza had devoured them, and I'd read one or two myself, solely from scholarly curiosity, of course. This one was called *Vulcan's Fire*. Inside was an inscription: "For Ethan."

I flipped some pages. On the frontispiece was a stain that provoked a memory. As spies in Paris we'd used sympathetic ink, a new chemistry to hide secret messages. "Do you have a candle? We need some heat." I warmed the page. Inked was a single word, "Beware." It looked like Catherine's handwriting. This invisible stranger hadn't read it, but Catherine would guess I might.

"This proves nothing," I said, while fearing it proved all. Catherine had collaborated with Rabbi Stern before we arrived, leaving a blond hair on a crucial book about Roland. Yet she'd also left this curious message. Once again I was being ensnared in puppet strings from all sides.

"He gave me something else to pass on. I don't understand its significance, but he said you would." He held out his palm.

It was a marble. Harry had scattered marbles at Notre Dame to make the police slide and tumble when they pursued his mother. I recognized this one from Paris, an agate beauty I'd bought him near Les Halles. I felt the same dizziness I'd suffered from my wound. I snatched and held it to my cold cheek. "My son!"

"This was his?" asked Aaron.

"It *is* his. I remember buying it. That cloaked bastard knows where Harry and Astiza are."

"Then we must go where he commanded. What other lead do we have? A smith on the Golden Lane, a homely dwarf, but apparently well versed in the arts of metallurgy."

"He's heard of Astiza?"

"He sees and hears everything, by reputation. Auric is his name. This cloaked man promised we could trust him."

I looked again at the book. *Vulcan's Fire*. Was Catherine warning about the smith and forge? But would she not be in league with whoever took Astiza? I looked at Aaron. If I couldn't trust Rabbi Abraham, why should I trust Gideon's father? Who was friend and who was foe, and who was allied with whom? I was tired from the long night, dizzy with hope, and filled with foreboding.

"Have you heard of this smith?" Gideon asked me.

"No. But clearly, too many people have heard of us."

"You dare not return to the rabbi's house," Aaron warned.

I sighed, choosing between bad alternatives. "It's time we made our own conspiracies," I said. "Gideon, I need you to follow me to this Golden Lane but not enter the dwarf's smithy. Should I come out alone with a reforged sword, reunite with me. But should I come out as a prisoner, trail us at a distance. I need a hidden card to play in our game, and you must be it."

"Of course."

"Aaron, you're too obvious with your wagon. If we leave Prague, I need you to conspicuously stay here so that whoever is watching us assumes your son and I stay with you. Gideon is safest if no one is certain where he is."

"I understand."

"I'll go to meet this Auric, and hope he knows the fate of my family." I sighed. "We have to put our trust in someone, but just who remains a gamble."

CHAPTER 25

Astiza

Ten thousand years ago, mankind was taught the arts of civilization by the god Thoth and his silvery associates. So teach the adepts of Egypt. At the heart of our complex existence, Thoth explained, is simplicity. In simplicity we find purity, and in purity we achieve communion with the universe. This is the alchemist's quest. He seeks to refine, reduce, and perfect. Dross lead becomes sublime gold, and our troubled beings achieve unity and transcendence. This is the hope.

The smell of this transformation is sulfur, vinegar, urine, and smoke.

The alchemical laboratory to which Horus and I have been confined is a chamber of hell. There's a forge with chimney and a cylindrical brick furnace called an athanor, as tall as a man. Our cell vacillates between the chill of the abandoned silver mines I've been told exist beyond its rock walls and the stuffy oppression of ceaseless fire. I have at my disposal glass vessels of every size and shape, and helix loops of copper to drip and distill. From this I cook chemicals and minerals in a hunt for the Philosopher's Stone, the fabled red rock said to confer endless wealth and everlasting life. Unclear in the magical texts is whether "stone" is literal or metaphor.

My alchemical methods are evaporation, condensation, and fixation. I bake compounds in stone vessels shaped like eggs in the commonsense belief that the universe itself was hatched from an egg. I mimic the gods like little Horus mimics me. I have pots, bowls, hermetic vases, flasks, and gourds, as well as tongs, scoops, scrapers, pincers, strainers, ladles, and spoons. Auric has delivered alchemical glassware blown into fantastic shapes with fantastic names, such as Moon Vessel, Cup of Babylon, Angel Tube, Skull Cap, and Philosopher's Egg. Each condenses and drips in a slightly different way. A double boiler is called a Mary's Bath, and there is a picture of Mary above it, carrying a rose.

Powdery grit coats everything. Metals, stone, and wood are reduced to ash and then dissolved, filtered, settled, skimmed, agitated, boiled, distilled, and strained, again and again. For thousands of years we've known rock ore can yield iron and that the galena from lead ore can yield silver. Why should this progression not continue? Reduce soft lead to its core reality and the result is gold.

Or so the texts promise, in languages foreign and obscure. They are riddled with symbols and are ripe for misrepresentation and error. Some of the writings are called the Language of the Birds, because of the belief that birds sing a sacred language similar to the Enochian of angels. Only Saint Francis of Assisi fully understood them.

The dark art of alchemy is dangerous. Experiments can burn, suffocate, or explode. Moreover, a moment's mistake in a year of reduction can cause the formula to go awry. This mistake can come not just from the hands but from the heart and mind. Thoughts must be measured as carefully as tinctures. In his progression toward gold, the alchemist must make equal progress with his spirit. The wrong intent can literally spoil the broth.

It doesn't help that some alchemists were deliberate frauds and mountebanks. Notables such as Albertus Magnus, Thomas Aquinas, Cardinal de Richelieu, Francis Bacon, and Isaac Newton all made legitimate experiments with alchemy, but the craft also drew claims of gold making that proved as ephemeral as fog. Rulers who bankrolled such experiments were not amused, and Bohemia's prisons were full of failed alchemists. Frederick of Würzburg was so incensed that he gilded his gallows. "There is your gold!" the executioners would shout as the wizards swung, strangling, the taunting color the last thing they would ever see.

Adjacent to the laboratory is a cell where Horus and I sleep, read, and pray. There I've consulted a thousand texts. There's a new book by an Englishman named John Dalton, who has revived the Greek idea of atoms, or particles so small they cannot be divided further. Dalton suggests that these atoms are the true building blocks of the universe. These new ideas are very similar to the old ones of Thoth. I combine ancient and modern in my mind.

In our crucibles we dissolve compounds with elements that can transform base metals to their purer selves. Mercury represents spirit. Sulfur is soul. Salt is body. The salt in tears is crystallized thought, and Harry and I have been weeping for endless months, yearning for release and reunion with Ethan.

Now I sense that our goal is at hand.

I dare not betray hope, lest they be suspicious. I dare not admit to failure, lest they be furious. I keep my jailers at bay with alchemical tricks they interpret as progress. Heat antimony, as Newton did, and the metal turns to crystalline stars. Newton called it the Black Dragon, and my jailers think it precious silver. I tell them it is but a step more toward gold and the Philosopher's Stone, but the last step is the most difficult. Patience, patience! I push them away. At night, when my captors aren't watching, I melt it all down to start again. Every day I delay is a day in the life of my son.

Auric looks at my boy with hideous appetite, his soul as twisted as his body.

So Harry and I pee into a special urn to allow the urine to putrefy. I'm secretly making something to free us from nightmare.

I think I finally know where to go, should we ever escape. In the moldering library where we sleep, I combed every volume of text to try to guess where Christian Rosenkreutz went with his automaton. I studied the rose until my eyes blurred. I pored over maps of Bohemia. I picked apart alchemical chants.

In a book of history about the Thirty Years' War, I came across a drawing of a burned castle that at last answered my prayers. It's the most peculiarly situated and shaped castle I've ever seen.

It's in the shape of ka, the Egyptian hieroglyph for "soul," which I saw etched in the wall in the dungeon of Český Krumlov. Two bent arms, reaching for the sky.

This is our goal. Rosenkreutz haunts my dreams; he has become my inspiration.

Impatience has worn my captors down. They don't trust me, but they grudgingly respect my knowledge. Fulcanelli, the man who is actually Richter, even tried to discuss philosophy again before my cold hatred defeated his overtures. I haven't seen him for weeks now. But Auric came to me with his wicked grin, eyeing my son like a leg of mutton, and asked if word of my husband would spur me to new efforts.

Not word, I said, but *proof.*

Auric said he must visit Prague, and would return with proof. "I will give you evidence—if you will give me gold."

I gave him a list of missing chemicals I said I still needed, acids and chlorides, and asked for a seed of gold to grow a hoard. "Flakes of gold will teach the metal to convert." He cackled and danced and wouldn't give any promises, but for the first time I felt my husband was near. Our enemies had word of him.

Which means he's in danger. And that our tormentors are frustrated and afraid.

Time is running short. In the chamber where Harry and I sleep, illuminated by candles stuck in crevices and ventilated by a crack admitting air from a sky we can't see, there are mysteriously locked cabinets and trunks. Most have so far defeated my efforts at opening them, but one lock I managed to pick. It was a chest the dwarf sometimes goes to fondle, and its brass fastenings are brightly polished from his caresses.

When I lifted the lid, I pulled back a leather cover before realizing it must be human skin.

Beneath were layers of bones on trays of purple velvet, polished by the dwarf's fingers like ivory trophies.

All are the size of small children.

CHAPTER 26

The sword of Roland and the dwarf who was to repair it were equally pitted. The blade was dark and chipped, and the smith was pocked and warty. Auric Nachash's hair was tangled string, his beard wispy splotches, his leather apron spotted with stains, and his hands a scabby red. His hovel on the Golden Lane was noxious, its small forge laboring to exhaust fumes through a slumping chimney. A permanent fog hung in the room. What the waddling creature did exhibit was competent curiosity, handling Durendal with a craftsman's intensity.

"Of course I can fuse hilt to blade," he said. "But the steel is old, oddly discolored, and warped. What happened to it?"

"It was struck by lightning."

He laughed, or rather cackled, nervously jiggling from leg to leg. "Tempered by a thunderbolt? Was that God's wrath or God's favor? And where did you get the hilt?"

"That's none of your concern. Where did you learn to smith?"

"That's none of *your* concern. I'm an unusual man, who required unusual teachers for unusual tastes." He looked at me over the rim of the blade, eyes sharp as pins. They seemed to crawl over my features with the alacrity of spiders. "I instill magic in my steel, Monsieur . . ."

"Franklin. Hieronymus Franklin."

It seemed cautious to use my false name. Aaron had made inquiries and was told that this ugly artisan was rumored to practice dark magic and petty crime. However, there was no one in all of Prague more skilled at metallurgy. Since experience with women convinced me that there was little correlation between appearance and character, I was willing to give the midget magician a chance. Could he know the source of my son's marble? And what monstrous luck if he did!

As precaution, we'd found a hiding place for Gideon in a bell tower that overlooked the Golden Lane. The street itself had a presumptuous name for a gutter gathering of frauds, strumpets, beggars, moneylenders, and magicians. Every old city has a place like that, but I was especially wary in this alley. The street was tight, the hovel odd, and its occupant odder still. He smacked his lips and licked with his tongue when thinking, not noticing the strange sounds he made. His home had bubbling chemicals, jars of dead and aborted animals, and hanks of weed, herbs, and garlic hanging from joists like witches' hair. There was a rude bed, sagging cupboards, and blackened cauldrons.

Adding to my disquiet was the fact that Auric seemed more interested in me than in my weapon, eyeing me like a vintner deciding when to time the crush. I didn't care for the look, and sensed that he didn't care that I didn't care. The dwarf had no doubt gotten plenty of peculiar looks himself.

Best to keep things brisk and businesslike. "Can its strength be restored?"

His gaze swung from me to calculating appraisal. The broken hilt fit the sword blade at the break perfectly.

"Why would you care, Monsieur Franklin? Are you a medieval knight?"

"An expert in antiquities. Even to a collector, what good is a fragile sword?"

"In an age of artillery, what good is a sword at all?"

"Of use when your enemies get close." Best to remind him I wasn't helpless. "And people think this relic is still important."

He fingered the metal like flesh. "Which people?"

"None of your concern, again. Inspired by old legends. Which must exist for a reason."

"Ah, reason." The dwarf nodded, waddling to his anvil. "Reason that I am small and twisted, reason that you are alone and poor, reason that bloodthirsty generals are elevated to lords, and reason that alchemists are mistrusted for nonsense and superstition. We live in an age of reason, where everything is known and nothing understood." He stared back at me. "Do you believe in the unity of all things, pilgrim?"

I thought of Astiza and Harry. "I long for it."

"Belief is part of healing, be it body or steel. I see you favoring a shoulder."

"I was wounded at Austerlitz."

"Serving which side?"

"My own."

He approved of my answer. "Believe in your own recovery. You must not just hope but *know* that restoration is possible. Birth played a trick on me, so I pursue alchemy to repair myself. Dross can become silver. Ugly ducklings can become swans. Enduring pain teaches us to tolerate pain. Inflicting pain relieves pain. I heal myself."

It didn't seem to be working, given that he looked as though his profession was poisoning him. But I've met my share of unfortunates. Some are ennobled by their troubles, and others corrupted. We don't control fate, but we control our reaction to it. Was this little smith tempered, or bent? "I just want to heal the sword."

"You must envision the completed blade in order to restore it. Many an alchemical experiment has gone awry because of a single wisp of doubt. I know a seeker right now who seems troubled. So I put it to you again, traveler: Do you believe in unity?"

I thought of the strange things I'd seen in the bowels of the pyramids, the tombs of the ancients, the sacred tree of the Dakotas, and the voodoo swamps of Haiti. Aye, there's more to existence than we admit. "I don't just believe, blacksmith—I've *experienced* unity. All are aspects of one. I've had exhilarating glimpses of the secret order of the universe. Terrifying ones. Hopeful ones."

"Then you could have answered your own question about the sword's repair." He fingered the blade. "I can tell that this was truly a hero's sword, forged with magic, annealed in holy water, and consecrated in blood. Steel like fiber, woven in the loom of the forge. A hilt as sturdy as a root. A shape to sing as it cuts the air. Sharp as dawn at one time, and indestructible as the stars. It's Durendal, is it not?"

How could he possibly know that?

Auric cackled at my surprise. "Yes, Rudolf was rumored to have put this stub of rust in that peculiar palace—Star Summer, they called it. You have stolen it?"

"Retrieved it."

He held the blade high. "Durendal, Durendal! Even the name is poetry! Seekers have searched for it. And now, to have it on my forge? Oh, yes, I'll restore it. It will whisper its past as I work to create it anew." He held it to his ear. "Once more it will strip skin from muscle, meat from bone, and stir the finest soups. Durendal!"

The dwarf was clearly balmy, while I was clearly desperate.

"How do you know its name?"

"All Prague knows it. And this blade hums to me."

Perhaps the sword truly was a talisman to finding the trail of Rosenkreutz and the Brazen Head. When I did that, I'd find my family, too, or so I hoped. No, *believed*, I corrected myself.

"Then repair it." I deliberately used a tone of impatient authority to keep the lunatic under control.

"For a gold coin, master."

"Agreed." I had the last of Richter's purse.

"I'll have to overlap and weld the two parts. The finished product will be a few inches shorter."

"A shortened sword is better than a broken one."

"The philosopher offers a maxim!"

The little smith bent to his task, using coal to make a hotter fire. At his demand I pumped the bellows, baking myself to a fine sheen. Auric inserted the two broken ends in the coals until they glowed, set them on his anvil and had me hold a chisel at the break while he gave a smart swing with a hammer. We cut two lengthwise slits, one on the long blade and the other on the stub. Then the two pieces were reheated, twisted, and shoved together.

"Not very elegant-looking," I remarked.

"Neither is procreation at its most awkward moments. Patience."

The sword was heated again, brought out white at the joint, laid flat on the anvil, and beaten flat by my squat Vulcan, sparks flying. He doused, reheated, and hammered over and over again, working with sure swiftness. There was a final quenching with an explosive hiss, and then he sighted along the blade and began to smooth and sharpen with file, grindstone, and pumice. Durendal was beginning to look fit for a Roland.

"Satisfied, philosopher?"

I hefted it with my right arm, and then my aching left, before handing it back. I could now suspend such weight. "Impressed."

"Yes, and now the rest of your lesson. You'll need a scabbard. Go to my cupboard for leather and thread and a tape to measure, while I finish sharpening."

I rummaged for supplies and stopped.

In the cupboard was a plain clay bowl. In the bowl was a silver necklace. And on the necklace were two pendants, an Egyptian ankh and an Eye of Horus, a decorative piece inspired by the eye of the Egyptian hawk god.

First the marble, and now this. It was as if Astiza and Harry had inscribed their names. Why had I been led to a dwarf with trinkets from my wife?

I grasped them and turned. "Why do you have relics of my family?"

But I discovered that the newly annealed sword was now pointed at my chest, the dwarf's gaze grim with warning. "Do not move, gambler."

"Why do you call me a gambler?"

"I know everything about you, Ethan Gage. I know you're an impostor, a liar, and I know more about you than you know yourself."

So he'd known my identity from the beginning.

"You're no Franklin man, and no philosopher. You're a spy, an adventurer, a dilettante, a rake, a sycophant to the powerful, a heretic, a treasure hunter, a conspirator, and a libertine."

"And famous, apparently." His list reminded me to create my own.

"I know your wife, I know your child, and I know your real purpose in Bohemia. You're here as a thief, to find and steal another relic."

"You're mistaken."

"You seek the Brazen Head." The sword tip wavered a foot from my chest. I could grab it, but not without slicing my hand and risking a plunge to my heart.

It seemed useless to deny. "How can I steal what was stolen from the French two hundred years ago?" I eyed the sword's point. "Or do you mean Roland's sword, another French relic carried off to Bohemia?" I could overpower this Auric if I could get past the blade, but the cell we in worked was small, giving me no room to maneuver. "And how do you know about my wife?"

"She was here."

At last! Blood pounded so fast that I was dizzy. "Is she alive?"

"Only for so long as you cooperate, Monsieur Gage," a new voice said from behind me, its injured lisp all too familiar. "Your son did not, spoiling my appearance."

I turned with dread and resignation. Baron Wolf Richter held two pistols aimed squarely at my torso. Because I had already been shot once, their muzzles looked even more gigantic to me than usual. Richter himself seemed to have materialized out of nowhere, just like the stranger Aaron had encountered in the Lane. It's an odd trick, becoming invisible, and almost as useful as being dead. In this case he wore dun-colored clothes that blended with burlap curtains I'd assumed screened a pantry. He'd been watching us, still as stone, the whole time.

"So you're in league with Catherine Marceau," I said.

"Hardly. Rabbi Abraham Stern betrayed us by deciding to cooperate with the agents of Talleyrand. We're Czech patriots who believe our heritage belongs to Prague, not Paris. Aren't we, Auric?"

"We're the rightful caretakers of the automaton, if it exists."

"Then you don't support the aspirations of the Jews?"

"The Jews are doing quite well. They don't need Napoleon—or you."

"Where are my wife and son?"

"You can join them, if you wish." The pistols had not wavered, and Durendal was still pointed as well.

I stalled for opportunity. "You really should do something

about your complexion, Baron." I hadn't had time to study the full scale of his disfigurement in Venice, but it looked as if someone had dipped the lower half of his face in boiling acid. By thunder, these two were the ugliest pair of poltroons I'd ever encountered, and that's saying something.

"Your son did this to me, Gage. I've yet to take my full revenge on him."

I was sweating, and from more than the heat. "Harry? My boy is friendly to everything but rabid dogs."

"He's not seen the sun since he scarred me, and never will again unless you cooperate. His sin I can attribute to youth. Your sins to greed and pride. And your wife's . . . I sought you out in Venice out of curiosity and revenge, and you dared steal from me. But I'm much less impulsive than you are. I handle cards better, too." An amused smile, if it hadn't been so twisted by chemicals.

"Harry wouldn't have hurt you if you didn't deserve it. What were you doing to him?"

"I barely struck the hellion. It was a misunderstanding with his mother."

My rage was swelling. "You assaulted her?"

"How could I, when she'd fallen in love with me?"

"What?"

"Ask her yourself. It's quite a tragedy, the three of us. So—do you want to see them alive? Do you want help in finding the Brazen Head? Or will you condemn them by doing something heroic and foolish, ending your life and theirs?"

The door opened. Two more caped men stepped through it, these holding wide-bore muskets. Auric let the heavy sword point drop. Did it give me a chance? No.

"Bind him," Richter ordered. "Wrists to belt, so his captivity won't be too conspicuous when we leave. We don't want trouble in the Lane."

"What do you want? Why don't you leave us alone?"

"Your wife has made some progress on alchemical experiments but is asking for chemicals to complete her concoctions. One is a seed of gold. Do you still have my winnings?"

"They're mine, since you cheated, and no." I wasn't about to give him the last of my meager traveling fund, and, judging from his Venetian palace, he didn't need it.

"Then, alas, she will fail, and it will be cheaper to simply kill your family."

When there is no alternative, surrender and wait. "What do you really want, Wolf?"

"Astiza says she's concocting the Spit of the Moon, whatever that is, to complete her experiments. She wants chemicals, gold, and you, though why she cares for that final item I cannot fathom. As the noblest of our triangle, I propose cooperation. You'll be brought to her, at the price of your purse. No one steals from me. Ever."

"Take the damn money." They'd find it anyway. I took a strip of coins from my boot.

"If she achieves the Philosopher's Stone, you'll be reunited. And together, in the name of legend and science, we'll seek the Brazen Head. The two of you have resourcefulness the Invisible College can put to use."

"And then?"

"You'll join our fraternity forever."

"And why would I do that?"

"To keep me," the little man said, "from cooking and eating your little boy."

CHAPTER 27

The Bohemian city of Kutná Hora is forty miles east of Prague, a day's journey by coach. I rode with the homeliest companions imaginable. They tirelessly informed me that my boy was a whining hellion, my wife a procrastinating temptress, and I a failed schemer, and that we were alive only because we might know lost secrets. We could cooperate or be tortured.

If Gideon spied me being marched from the Golden Lane, he gave no sign. I peeked in hopes he was following, but I saw nothing. I could only surmise he'd been cowed by Richter's gang and its show of strength and gone back to the ghetto, giving up Ethan Gage and family as a lost cause. Couldn't blame him.

Which meant that all I had left was bravado. "My son usually doesn't disfigure people, nor does he typically have the means to do so," I persisted. "What was your meeting all about?"

"An alliance, until your brat spoiled it."

"The rape of my wife?" My fury rose again. "Making a cuckold of her husband?"

"She led me on," Richter said. "It was misunderstanding that led to confusion."

"My boy panicked, it sounds like."

"Malevolence by an urchin. You're lucky, Gage, that your whelp isn't dead."

"Master was trying to be friends," Auric added.

Master! The title was as absurd as Murat's "Serene Highness."

"If you work with us, a great deal of sorrow can be averted," Richter went on, avoiding my question. "The Invisible College works to set mankind on a higher plane with alchemical triumph and knowledge of the future. We represent progress and enlightenment. We're heroes, not villains."

"With extortion, torture, and treachery," I amended. "Is this so-called college invisible because I've never seen nor heard of it?"

"The idea was that of Christian Rosenkreutz. He conceived a secret society of scholars devoted to true knowledge and unhampered by religious restriction. The idea has inspired Freemasonry and the Royal Society of London. Rosicrucian adherents combine scientific inquiry with alchemy, mysticism, and faith. Ours is the Invisible College of the Rosy Cross, a network of scholars sworn to discovery and secrecy. It's a noble cause your wife has been conscripted to."

"A cause with professors who serve as sentries, fire guns, and chase me across rooftops."

"You're the one who played thief, Ethan Gage. I am the wronged party."

"Who cheated at cards, according to Lord Ramsey."

"Ramsey is an old fool, and you are simply a bad gambler."

I longed to finish on the upper half of his face what my son had started on the lower, but revenge would have to be delayed until I found my family. Richter was also biding his time for payback, I knew. He'd never let us survive, let alone go free, and was only waiting to see what use he could make of us before eventual torture and execution. He and I were poised like fencers, waiting for the signal for the real duel to begin. "So how exactly did you broach this idea of cooperation and unity, that time that Harry melted you?"

"With sincerity misinterpreted."

"As I'm confused by a network of scholars that has the furtiveness of assassins and the gunnery of an infantry regiment."

"Unsavory means are required for noble ends. Ask Bonaparte. Except that we are subtler than Bonaparte. What he accomplishes with the slaughter of thousands, we achieve with a few well-placed assassinations. It is completely unfair that he gets an imperial crown for his massacres, while we must hide in the shadows. When we heard the French were in pursuit of the Brazen Head, we knew we must find it first. Napoleon and Talleyrand would use the machine for tyranny. We will use it for enlightenment."

I turned to his froggy minion. "You realize that your master is a complete madman."

Auric's grin was the one they master in hell. "But none likelier to command the future. I'll be a little king, to feed my large appetites."

Satan and dwarf. Equally ambitious.

"How can a machine tell the future?" I asked Richter. "The idea is absurd."

"On the contrary. Albertus Magnus pointed out that we all try to predict the future. That's why we study the past. Would not an omnipotent God, knowing all things and all possibilities, be able to predict what comes next? Of course. And if a machine could be built that turned probabilities into numbers represented by cogs and gears, it could prophesize. But by legend the Brazen Head goes beyond even the intricacy of its own construction.

Albert infused it with something spiritual that pierced the veil into the world beyond this one. Aquinas called it blasphemous. Rosenkreutz called it magical."

"Why was it locked away, then?"

"Great power demands great responsibility. The machine awaits a person like me."

"Perhaps it will only prove frustrating, like the golem."

"Find it first and we shall see. You, me, and your wife together."

My problem was that I was curious, too. To know the future, to avoid danger, to pick the right investment and make the right friends! I didn't just want to escape the Invisible College. I wanted to take the thing they coveted. I forever struggle between idealism and crassness, and so am the most human of men.

As usual I had few belongings. But lashed to our coach was Durendal, the alleged sword of Roland. I was allowed to swing it to exercise my left arm as my shoulder healed, while Richter's "monks" warily watched me with bayoneted muskets. Indulging me amused Richter. The first time I picked up the blade, it felt as heavy as a double-bitted ax, but slowly I worked repairing muscles in my arm, chest, and back. I'd never played with a blade in anything but my right hand, and the ambidextrous exercise put me in my best shape since paddling canoes across half of North America.

"Mules are strong, too," Richter said.

"And stubborn," I reminded him.

Kutná Hora rambles along the side of a ridge above a narrow river valley, the slag piles and abandoned smelters hinting that its bucolic views hide the termite tunneling of silver mines below.

"In medieval times, this was the richest mining district in Europe," Richter lectured pedantically as we rode into the town, which had long been in decline. "Miners delved two thousand feet deep, following veins of silver in a network extending many miles.

But the mines began to play out just as the new mines of Mexico and Peru opened. Then came war, displacement, and fire."

Kutná Hora looked sullen under the gray winter sky. Half the houses were burned-out shells. None of the others looked less than two hundred years old. Potholes were small craters. The few inhabitants who peered at our black coach from grimy windows or dark doorways were as reclusive as lepers. The road twisted and dipped, the city's square so tilted that it seemed about to tip into the mines somewhere below. We passed through the center to a rural dirt lane beyond and followed this to the desolation of abandoned farms, coming at last to a plain, onion-domed church on a lonely hill. The surrounding tombstones poked up like bad teeth.

"When the abbot returned from visiting the Holy Land, he sprinkled soil from Golgotha, where Christ was crucified," Richter said as we climbed out. "His piety led people to be buried here."

"This is where my wife is?"

"Where she will be if you don't cooperate. Come."

The grass was dead and thigh-high. Night was falling on fallow soil and patches of dirty snow, everything cold and bleak.

"Inside."

A weathered door with iron hinges squealed open to an unremarkable interior. The church was empty. Richter gestured with a pistol. "Downstairs."

Under the nave was a crypt. The windows near its ceiling were at ground level, reminding me of the cellar of the Star Summer Palace. This basement was shaped not like a star but like a cross, so that four alcoves or chapels radiated from its center. Except that they were not chapels, and in fact were filled.

Choked with bones.

Skulls made a rubble avalanche. Femurs were stacked like firewood. Knucklebones were pebbles, ribs were woven like baskets, and shoulder blades made shoals. It was like the Paris catacombs I'd visited with Astiza.

"Unfortunately, the church's popularity as a burial site overwhelmed its priests. People brought more corpses than there was cemetery, particularly during the Thirty Years' War. A half-blind monk was given the job of digging up the older bones to make room for the new. He stored the old-timers here."

My quest for the Brazen Head kept brushing up against death. "I'm all too aware of mortality, Baron. Are you trying to make some macabre point?"

"I wanted you to be reminded of the stakes involved."

Then there was a high shout. "Papa!" It was almost a scream.

Harry erupted from the shadows, pulling away from another "Invisible" I hadn't realized was standing there, and came running with arms outstretched. My spirit soared like one of Congreve's newfangled rockets. By the saints, even in one year Harry seemed to have erupted in size, lengthening into a boy not quite five. In relief and joy, I collapsed onto my knees for a hug, gathering him in with my arms as if he were elusive as smoke, and feeling his hot, anxious breath on my cheek. He looked up past me at Richter and Auric. "The bad men are back!"

I got to my feet, scooping him up. "I'm here now, Harry." I almost squeezed the breath out of him, gasping from my own relief.

He sobbed into my shoulder, body shaking, and once more my anger silently boiled. How dare this cabal imprison and terrify my son! More men in robes emerged from the shadows like dark-clad ghosts, and a dozen rogues held pistols and pikes. Harry trembled like a puppy.

"This is what you do to children."

"He's entirely unharmed after mutilating me," Richter said calmly. "Homesick, perhaps, but then his father has never given him a real home, has he? The poor lad has been dragged around the world as his mother's occult slave, turned by his parents into a perfect little monster. Don't lecture me, American."

"Lecturing is not what I intend to do."

"You've no power, and no wife yet, if you'll take the time to notice." He swung his arm, taking in the hillocks of bone. "I'm letting you hold your son as a sign of goodwill. At your wife's demand, I've brought you and your gold to Kutná Hora. *She* asked for your last coins, not I. At your demand, I've brought proof your family is alive. You've robbed me, your wife has shunned me, and your son has harmed me. Yet I remain a man of reason."

I squeezed my boy. "Harry, is Mama all right?"

"She keeps away the bad people." He wept with relief and fear.

"You've made your point," I growled to Richter. "What now?"

"We're going to deliver you and your gold so Astiza will finish her work, now that we have you. When she completes her alchemy, I'll allow reunion and we'll decide the next step. You live as long as you cooperate."

"Where is she?"

"Safe in a laboratory, built in an upper drift of the old mines."

"Decide about what next step?"

"The Brazen Head and immortality, if you see reason. And which of these rubble piles of bone—east, west, north, or south— you join, if you don't."

Chapter 28

Astiza

Since I couldn't see the sky to pray, I prayed to the earth. There's no greater torment than not knowing, and I yearned to learn the fate of my husband. My powers of prophecy had deserted me, and if Harry didn't escape soon, we'd go quite mad. Then the earth seemed to answer. Isis sent me my path. Suddenly the old texts I'd read, the experiments I'd conducted, and the scraps of information I'd gleaned gave a flash of insight. Such revelations are a gift. I had a plan, and with a plan came hope. I began to feel Ethan was near. As if to confirm such suspicions, my jailers became surlier. They're impatient, as if in a race with other villains. I eavesdropped at the door while guards murmured of a battle, French schemes,

Jewish calculation, and refugees streaming into Prague. So I asked for gold.

"You cannot achieve final purification without a seed," I insisted to Baron Richter. "You can't forge the Philosopher's Stone without a dissolution of real gold. Any alchemist knows this. Have the courage to invest in your dreams. Bring me something to work with."

His look was suspicious. He knows I'm procrastinating. And yet here in the pit of hell, what use was gold except for alchemical stews? There was nothing to buy and no one to bribe, and no escape through solid rock. So he agreed, lusting for his great prize.

Then one day they said they needed to take Harry away to meet "a stranger." I screamed and fought, fearing the worst. I imagined my son in that trunk of bones. His death would kill me, and before I died I would turn the alchemical laboratory into my funeral pyre. My captors stunned me with a club, leaving me dazed on the floor, and when I regained full consciousness I was feverish with anxiety. But hours later, I heard the noises of people returning, the lock rasped on the door's metal, and Harry wriggled out of Auric's grasp and ran to me with an excited shout.

"Papa is here to save us!"

There was a clang as someone was thrust into another cell far down the corridor.

"Your husband is here as my prisoner," Richter corrected, stepping into the room. He was wearing his bishop's robe—or, rather, costume—a sword strapped to his side. "It is still possible, madame, for us to work together and for me to show mercy. But only if you do what I expect."

I was dizzy with longing. "I don't believe you. Show him to me."

"We'll never have friendship without trust, Astiza."

I felt the blood crusted on my scalp.

"You had my trust, and betrayed it when you took me to your

mutant blacksmith. You were the great Primus Fulcanelli, seeker of truth, instead of a corrupt and venal German baron seeking small advantage, one of thousands of little men scuttling in the shadows of emperors."

He flushed. "We'll see who scuttles when I possess the Brazen Head."

"I thought *we* were going to possess it."

"*You* are going to find the Stone and turn lead into gold! Or have you already forgotten your promise? Your own son will testify I kept mine. His father is here. Tell her, boy!"

"Papa hugged me, Mama."

I knelt and hugged him, too, while looking up at Richter. "Did you bring me my seed of precious metal?"

"Yes. Coins of your husband's."

Harry turned his own face up to Richter. "Why can't Papa stay with us?"

"I don't trust you together."

I was close to fainting from fear and anger. "Show him to me and I'll do anything you ask. If you're lying, I'll destroy all I've accomplished."

"No! Do what you already promised! Complete your experiments!"

"Show me first or you'll have nothing!"

"Damn you, I'll pen the boy away as well if you don't accomplish something!"

I stood, Harry clutched to my side, my hair grimy, my hands raw, my eyes those of a madwoman. "Show me or I'll curse you all!"

Richter's eyes blazed, his ruined mouth clenched, arms levitating as if readying to strike. But he still had no clues. He snarled, ruined lips twisted over teeth, and then he turned to the men crowded in the corridor. "Show her the fool."

The cell was reopened, there was jostling, and Ethan was

thrust forward, instantly recognizable even though he was only a silhouette in the gloom.

"Astiza!"

"Ethan! Thank the Goddess!" Despite being faint with relief, I managed to whirl on Richter. "I want him now."

An amused shake of the head. "A beauty like you could do so much better."

"Let us stay together, and we'll do anything you ask."

Ethan shouted to me. "Has he hurt you?"

"I'm alive."

"Astiza, we forged an old sword. It may have something to do with Rosenkreutz."

"Silence!"

"Did you bring it?" I asked.

"Richter has it."

"Why is your shoulder bandaged?"

"I was wounded in the war."

What war? I wondered. "Enough!" the baron interrupted. "Put him back." The sentries dragged my husband away, ignoring his struggles and protests.

I was thinking furiously. How to complete the final act? "If I can do the alchemical miracle, you'll let us go?" I asked Richter.

"Absolutely not. But we'll leave here together to find the Brazen Head. Do that and you can go."

I needed to know how much or little Richter knew. "Is it nearby?"

He shrugged. "Bohemia. Moravia. We'll have to hunt."

"A cave?" I was trying to mislead.

"A cave with a tomb." He nodded as if he knew, convincing me that he didn't. "Now you're tantalized, yes? I've let your child live, brought back your oaf of a husband, and even delivered gold. All I seek is partnership. You and I can still be friends." Such a ghastly grin, a slit in scar tissue. I tried to hide my shudder.

"I'll finish," I promised him.

"How long?"

"Not long with the gold. It's the seed I needed from the beginning."

"How *long*?" His dwarf danced behind him, like a child needing to pee.

"A day or two to finish formulating the Spit of the Moon and then transferring its purity. The last step is dangerous, having killed more than one alchemist. Are you ready for risk?"

"My whole life is a risk." Richter blinked when he said it.

"Partners, but nothing more. You must never touch me or my child."

"I'm talking about minds, not bodies." How his eyes lied as he said it! Once he had what he wanted, we'd just hours to live.

And to avenge his deformity, he'd humiliate and ravish me before the end.

CHAPTER 29

I'd bargained my way into prison, but solid rock and iron bars still separated me from my wife. "Let me help her," I tried, speaking through the grille of my cell to Richter. "If we're in alliance against Catherine Marceau and the French, treat us as equals. Astiza works faster when we're together."

"People work faster from fear," Richter said, reciting this as if it were a homily from Franklin. "You'll be reunited when she produces what I want."

My chamber appeared to be a section of old mine tunnel first driven for silver, blocked at one end by a mortared wall and at the other by the bars. It was big enough to imprison a gang, twenty paces long and ten feet high. I had a straw mattress on the stone floor, two candles, a stool, and a bucket to relieve myself. I paced like a caged animal and exercised to continue strengthening my shoulder and arm. I measured time by how my wound healed. I measured my captors by their bearing, studying my guards. They lurked in the tunnel like vermin, not soldiers. Rogues are easier to defeat.

My torture was continued ignorance. They told me nothing. I strained to hear sounds from the rocky hallway where I'd spied my wife, but her wooden door had slammed shut and latched. The muttering of the guards was boring. So I paced and pushed, paced and pushed, always waiting.

I sorted the guards by face to count them, coming up with a dozen—three at a time on six-hour shifts. Auric waddled by occasionally on his way to Astiza's chamber, and once I could hear sharp voices when the door was briefly open. I smiled at the thought of my wife giving the dwarf a scolding. He'd come back muttering to himself, cast an angry look at my cell door, then disappear. I knew he couldn't be trusted. He was an imp, but dangerous.

I waited like a cat in the confidence that Astiza had a plan, and my job was to be ready for it. Meanwhile, news was whatever I overheard. Apparently the Austrians had agreed to an armistice, and the Russians were running for home. In a single day of fighting at Austerlitz, Napoleon had reset the balance of power in Europe.

The Invisible College "monks" entertained one another with tales of lost silver. The mines had sixty miles of honeycomb tunnels, were largely drowned by underground rivers, and delved deep. They'd been hacked by hand, long before gunpowder, and in most places were no wider than a miner's shoulders. Seams of silver had been dug out by men writhing on their bellies like worms. Other places had domed chambers and deep pits where equipment had been staged. The legend was that thieves, embezzlers, or smugglers had secreted their loot below, but no one wanted to venture after it, since the mines were reputed to be home to bats, wolves, bears, trolls, ghosts, and gnomes.

"This alchemical laboratory is an early drift hacked out six hundred years ago," one guard told another. "They sealed off the rest for safety. The entire mountain is riddled as a hive, confusing as a maze, and crumbly as old cheese. Men who went exploring never came out."

"But what if there's more silver down there?"

"Played out or flooded. It's a ruin now."

The tedium of imprisonment continued. And then one day Richter passed by with Auric and went to Astiza's laboratory, where more argument ensued, voices rising. I strained to hear. Finally the dwarf came back to me, holding the sword Durendal.

"Open the electrician's door."

Even though I emerged from candlelight to mere lantern light, I still blinked at the brighter illumination. Auric looked up at me sourly. "The witch needs your help."

"You're referring to my wife, runt of warts?"

"Your pagan priestess of a whore." He shoved me into the corridor, and the guards covered me with pistols, lest I be tempted to shove back. "She's offered you for a risky experiment with noxious liquids. Richter thinks it better that you be boiled than him."

"Why the sword?"

"Magic. She says it plays a role."

Richter was waiting, looking impatient and nervous, hand on his own sword. Something was about to happen. I was pushed inside Astiza's chamber, which was some kind of alchemical laboratory.

"Papa!" Harry tried to run to me again.

Auric intercepted him with ape-like power. When my boy tried to struggle anyway, the dwarf slapped him. "Stay where you are, pustule!" I lunged in fury and got a guard's musket butt in my groin for my trouble, bringing me to my knees. Harry bit Auric's hand, the dwarf howled, and then Astiza snatched our son up and shouted at Richter.

"Another move by that beast and I won't do the test!"

"Auric, get over by the door."

"Give me the whelp to hold, master! Give him to me so that they don't get him back until they do our bidding!"

"No. If that monster touches my son again, I'll smash every vessel." Astiza's tone was quiet, but as menacing as a snake's rattle.

Richter looked at my wife. There was frustration in his eyes. There was also, I saw with disgusted horror, longing. I longed, too—for my old tomahawk, and a chance to settle accounts. But as I grunted and stood, sucking air, Astiza shook her head emphatically at me.

Richter stood erect as a knight. "Enough. Worries about her son could pollute the formulation. You know that, Auric."

"I don't trust them. Any of them!"

"Then stay for the final transformation," my wife told the dwarf coldly. "Watch us if you will. But if you touch my son, I'll transform *you*—into a puff of smoke."

"Don't threaten me," he growled. "Witches can be burned."

"Then leave and let me do my work."

"I'll stay," the dwarf said sullenly. "On the far side of the room. With a loaded pistol. No, two of them, one for each parent. If you don't create gold, I'll cripple you both and then have the boy." He licked his lip.

"Auric, enough!" Richter's voice was a whip.

"This is quite the fraternity you've assembled, Baron."

"Silence, Gage." Richter scowled at his assistant, actually embarrassed by his crude appetites. "Auric, you on one side, the hellion on the other, and Gage and his wife to do the risky work."

"Gold—and immortality. That's our goal, is it not, Baron Richter?" Astiza asked, with soft warning.

"It's your only path to freedom."

Astiza addressed me. "I've been refining the components for

months, but I think I'm ready." I'd no idea what she was ready for. Yet I trusted her.

"For many weeks I've been refining and reducing to isolate the Philosopher's Stone," she explained to us all, "the essential unity behind all elements and existence. I've recently concocted what the ancient texts call the Spit of the Moon, an aqua regia solution to dissolve gold into a crystalline salt. If my studies are correct, this will catalyze the transformation of base metals into fine ones. The next step is the most delicate, the most dangerous, and the most precise. The dwarf must stand clear. Should he interfere, a year of work in this pit will be wasted."

Astiza pointed. "It will be safest over there," she told Auric. He truculently sidled to a new station next to a crude bookcase of raw planks full of heavy tomes. "No, a little further, to be safe. Sit." He squatted on a low stepstool, looking even more ridiculous than usual. To give himself dignity, he leveled his guns.

"Harry, you'll stay behind this table that I've turned on its side." My son obediently went where he was told, no doubt glad to be as far from the wicked dwarf as possible. He didn't show fear, and for that I was proud. Instead he looked at me for guidance, and that made me immensely prouder. I gave him an encouraging nod. He, being not quite five, believed it.

"The rest should leave this chamber," Astiza said. "The reaction I'm seeking can produce a flare of flame and gases." She pointed to a black cauldron dangling from a pulley on the ceiling, the rope holding it in suspension tied off to the bookcase. "Even I dare not get too close."

"Tell me again what's going to happen," Richter said.

"Ethan will carefully push forward the pan reduction with the sword. The noble metals of the legendary blade are required as a bridge to the five elements. He must be quick to crouch if flame erupts."

"And if I'm slow?" I asked reasonably.

My wife ignored me. "The cauldron with the refined Spit of the Moon will tip toward the precipitate, which is a slag of lead seeded with flakes of gold." Having my last coins ground into gold pepper seemed a terrible investment to me, but then, I hadn't read the moldy texts. "There will be a flash of light, a puff of smoke, and, if I have studied correctly, the creation of a red substance that will make gold. If dissolved and drunk, the concoction will extend life indefinitely."

"Why me?" I asked, hoping my wife could hint what she was up to.

"I've sacrificed my face," Richter said. "I decided it's time you risked yours."

"Simply be careful," Astiza said. "You must push the pan just so, retaining contact with the sword. I must measure the pour exactly. If we stumble or miscalculate, there can be injury."

"Could we move all this upstairs, where there's more ventilation?" This cell was a trap, and I wanted a place where we could escape these scoundrels.

Astiza didn't understand what I was trying to do, and didn't back my suggestion. She shook her head vigorously. "Time is critical. I'm told Napoleon has won. French agents will be seeking the Brazen Head. We need to finish and get ahead of them." She turned to Richter. "Close and bolt the door to contain any flare or fire. When the smoke clears, I'll shout."

This plan seemed about as pleasant as pipe smoke in a powder magazine, but alchemists are famed for risk taking. I also knew my wife must be up to something. The others reluctantly retreated just outside our chamber, and the heavy door slammed. We were alone except for a malevolent dwarf with two pistols and a suspicious glint. So I cooperated while she maneuvered me into position, thrilling even to her businesslike touch. We hadn't embraced in more than a year.

She leaned close. "When I command," she murmured, "cut the

rope with the sword and then dive." She stepped away.

So I stood gamely close to a pan of olive-green precipitate as Astiza grasped the cauldron rope to pour. I had no idea what to expect.

Astiza addressed Auric. "After I pour, I'm going to leap behind the table to join my boy. My husband will duck. I advise you to shield your eyes."

He looked at her suspiciously. "No tricks, witch."

"If you wish, wait outside with the others."

"No. I don't trust the three of you alone."

"Then you'll succeed with us or burn with us. Now, for all our sakes. Ready?"

I nodded uncertainly. I'd get one sword swing before Auric let loose with his pistols. I thumbed Durendal's edge to confirm its sharpness.

She pulled to tilt the cauldron. "Harry, stay down! Ethan and Auric, squint!" A plume of purple liquid spewed forth, and I pushed the pan forward with the sword tip to catch the acid as it dribbled, ready to duck. My wife vaulted to crouch next to our son. The liquid hit, and I braced for a roar of flame and puff of smoke.

Nothing. The precipitate hissed, bubbled, and curdled but didn't catch fire. Auric, despite his bravado, had closed his eyes.

Astiza looked at me. "Now!"

I swung Durendal, which was keen enough to chop through taut line as if it were spider thread. The cauldron plunged, gonging like a bell as it hit the stone floor. The line to the bookcase went slack.

Auric uncovered his eyes and stood, pointing his pistols. "Nothing happened."

"Not yet," Astiza called.

"Where is the red stone you promised?"

"Patience, dwarf."

"Why did he cut the rope? Master, it didn't work!" he called. And his eyes, fixed on us, didn't see that the massive bookcase was coming apart. With the line tension released, boards leaned and books began to cascade. More significantly, a carefully positioned heavy iron hammer tumbled off the topmost shelf to fall toward a clay egg the size of a goose.

Auric raised his guns.

I fell flat. So did Astiza and Harry.

The iron hammer struck the container.

There was a concussive roar, and the crucible exploded like a keg of gunpowder. Being trapped in the stone laboratory was like being trapped in the muzzle of a cannon. Air punched my ears, glassware shattered, flame erupted, rock flew, and I dimly heard screams that were not my own.

It was the dwarf.

Everything had gone dark. Rubble slid somewhere, while ceiling bits pattered like heavy rain, bouncing off my back.

Astiza was already up, bleeding, blackened, and triumphant. She used a glowing fragment from the wreckage to light a candle. "Ethan, get the workbench against the door!" I could barely hear her through the ringing in my ears.

My wife jerked me up in choking smoke, and we dragged the heavy bench over a shoal of debris and slammed it against the cell entrance, wedging it so Richter couldn't easily get inside.

I felt half-witted and could barely see in the fog. Auric had been thrown and was still.

"Here, Papa, the pistols." A surprisingly calm Harry was shoving guns into my hands. "Mama killed the bad man, just like she promised." He said it with great satisfaction, and who could blame him?

Good riddance, but what good if we were trapped in a hellhole?

Astiza hauled on me again. "This way!" She pulled me to a

place where the smoke was clearing. Through my ringing ears I could dimly hear shouts outside, and then thuds as bullets blasted into the laboratory through the door, beams of lantern light popping as they fired. The feeble light played over the body of the dwarf, hurled into a corner.

We were already groping the other way. The cell wall had blown out where the crucible had exploded. Beyond was cool air and the smell of water.

"What the devil?" I asked my wife, not for the first time.

"Piss and gold make a fine explosive," she said. "I'll explain in the mines, but Harry and I have been working on this for months."

Her makeshift bomb had blown through the cellar wall, into a mine tunnel. We were going to flee into the labyrinth of Kutná Hora.

There was just one problem. According to the guards, it was a flooded death trap with no way out.

Could Harry swim? Getting an idea, I grabbed the black cauldron.

CHAPTER 30

The smoky tunnel angled downward—not a good sign. It was narrow as a coffin and low as a gun deck on a warship. I banged my head twice, and the cauldron I'd snagged gonged as it hit walls of rock. The three of us held hands, our beacon Astiza's lone candle. Behind, a glimmer showed where fire still burned in the ruined laboratory. The flames should slow pursuit, but they might also consume our air. We could hear shots and great crashes as Richter and his men rammed the door we'd blocked.

"I can't see, Papa."

"I've brought more candles," Astiza said. "Let's get further out of sight and I'll light another."

With better illumination, I saw that the shaft was unevenly hewn from pick and shovel, twisting like a worm into the earth.

"What happened back there?"

"Christian Rosenkreutz made such an explosion in another prison," Astiza explained. "I discovered his formula in old books. It's called fulminating gold, and it has killed more than one alchemist. To make a volatile mixture, you dissolve gold in aqua regia, a form of nitric acid that can be gleaned from urine."

"I peed to make it, Papa."

"We all work together, don't we?"

"We do now that you're home." That Harry called a maze a home shows how low I'd set his expectations. I resolved to do better, should we survive.

"The urine salts have to putrefy for forty days, and then are distilled into crystals," my wife said. "The result, when mixed and purified, is a powder that explodes when struck. I refined enough to fill that clay egg and rigged the bookcase to spill the hammer onto it."

"You're as odd and dangerous as my friend Robert Fulton."

"Useful in other ways, too." She gave me a kiss, hot and hurried. Her lips were soft, her waist taut as a bowstring, and her hair fanned across my cheek like salve. I kissed back, mashing mouths with a colt's enthusiasm, but my son gave an impatient kick as we heard the door give way. There were shouts of dismay as our enemies stormed into the room and discovered Auric. "Later," I gasped. We hurried on.

Astiza led, Harry was in the middle, and I was the rear guard, Auric's pistols in my belt and the sword and cauldron handle clutched awkwardly in my one free hand. My wife selected twists and turns as decisively as if walking a path to her front door, even though we had no map. I didn't argue, taking heart when we seemed to be climbing toward the surface and despair when our flight took us deeper into the earth. I'd already experienced being buried and had no desire to be permanently entombed.

Shouts from our pursuers echoed to tag us. Some of the Invisibles apparently turned the wrong way, and we heard cries of "I'm lost!" reverberate down the mine shafts. Others spotted the faint light of our candles before we turned a corner and they began to sprint toward us. "It's them!"

"Go faster," I ordered.

"We can't go faster."

"Go as fast as you can while I make them hesitate."

"I have chalk," Astiza said. "If we make a turn, I'll make a mark."

Clever girl.

I crouched at an elbow in the mine, my candle in a crevice to minimize its light. Auric's pistols were small, women's guns to fit a dwarf, but lethal enough at close range. Richter's gang came heedlessly on, remembering us helpless and cursing in order to keep up their courage. A torch lit four who drew near. When they got within ten paces, I fired.

A man screamed and pitched backward. Auric's pistol had a pretty punch. Smoke filled the tunnel, the others fell flat, and I fled, the other gun still ready.

I'd no means to reload.

My shot stalled the pursuit. A chalk mark led me to a new branch that curled down into blackness. I dreaded more descent, even while hoping that our bold plunge into the heart of the mines would lose them. Water dripped everywhere, and I splashed through puddles.

I caught up with Astiza and Harry in a few hundred yards.

"Did you shoot the bad men, Papa?"

"One of them."

"I want to go outside."

"As soon as we get away." Yet I could hear running water and feared we were fleeing into a dead end. If the bottom of the mines were drowned, why were we going that way?

"Did they give up?" Astiza asked.

"Perhaps."

Then we heard dogs barking.

"Or not."

"I don't like dogs," Harry contributed.

Someday I'm going to get the boy a nice puppy, but no time for that now. We began to trot. Richter had fetched hounds.

A distant murmur rose to a rumble, and then a roar. We soon saw the cause. Our passage joined another tunnel half-filled with an underground river. It plunged from a cliff upstream, the waterfall meaning there was no chance of ascending. We'd have to plunge into black water and float downstream.

It was hopeless, but so was surrender. The dogs were getting closer.

"Harry, can you swim?"

"I'm scared." He looked miserably at the current.

"I taught him to float," Astiza said. "But he needs something to hold on to."

The baying of the hounds grew louder. Harry was crying. I crouched. "Horus, listen to me. I'm going to shoot one of the dogs, and then we're going to leap into the water. Dogs can't smell us there."

"Can doggies swim?"

"Yes, but they won't follow, I promise." Dogs have too much sense. "You must hold tight to Papa."

He was shaking, cheeks wet, but he looked at me with trust. "Don't let me die."

I hugged him. "I won't." Then, "Astiza, take the cauldron for a moment."

"Ethan, why did you bring that thing?"

"You'll see."

I put my candle on a rock shelf, strapped Durendal to my back, cocked the second pistol, and put my left arm around Harry. I could feel him shake. The baying of the hounds was amplified by the mines into a great echoing clamor of canine excitement. Then there was a blur of movement as they spied our light and charged in excitement, snapping and yowling.

I fired.

The lead animal somersaulted. I hurled both pistols, hearing yips as they struck. Then I plunged with Harry into swift, waist-deep water, my boots sliding on the slippery bottom. Astiza was wading ahead of us, dress dragging, gamely holding a candle in one hand and the cauldron in the other. I eased in to float on my back, gasping from the chill, and held my son to my chest. "Easy, boy. Now we get away from the hounds."

He shivered.

The animals had halted, confused and wary, sniffing the body of their dead companion. Some came to the edge of the water, barking. Harry clutched me as tight as he could. One dog jumped in and Harry shouted in terror, but then the hound thought better of it, turned, and paddled to heave himself out. I heard men's voices, and then shouts of frustration. We floated out of sight.

The water deepened. Astiza was swimming, too, trying to keep the candle alight. I floated like an otter, Harry on my chest.

Then a splash as my wife's candle finally went under, and it was dark—not just dark but as black as it is possible to be. The three of us were carried deeper into the underworld. I reached up and brushed rock. The water was closer to the ceiling. We swirled at the speed of a trot, blind and cold.

"Astiza, are you there?"

"Yes." Her voice was small, with a tremble to it.

To think that medieval miners came into this hell every day of their lives.

"Ethan, the air disappears! Stop!"

I bumped up against her, legs drifting down to find a precarious hold. "Here, take Harry." We were all shivering. I felt past her and ahead. As she said, the ceiling dipped so that there was no air between it and the rushing river. If we went farther, we'd drown. If we went back we'd be tortured and killed. I could still hear the dogs, barking in frustration.

"This is just like old times," I gasped in encouragement, fighting the cold and my own fear of the dark. "We've done this before."

"That pyramid path was engineered. This is a drowned mine. We've no idea how long this river goes. And Horus can't hold his breath very long."

"Somewhere this river will emerge."

"Miles from here."

"You're scaring Harry."

"I don't like the dogs!" he shouted, the sound bouncing.

"We don't have a choice," I insisted. "It ends here, or life has a purpose for us. Do you have the cauldron?"

"It's an anchor, filled with water."

"Empty it."

I could hear the pour as she did so, holding it against the low rock ceiling.

"I'm going to take Harry with me, using the cauldron like the diving bell in the Caribbean. If we invert it, we trap air and give him a little to breathe."

She moaned. "My Goddess, why are you testing me so cruelly?"

"You go first, and we'll follow."

"No," she pleaded, her strength exhausted. "I can't do this to Harry. What if he drowns? We go back and beg for mercy. Beg for him. Our lives for his."

"Don't be foolish, Astiza. There is no mercy. You know that."

"Ethan, I can't . . ."

"Follow your son." And I grabbed the cauldron, took a huge breath, put the cauldron over my little boy's head before he could even ask what I was doing, let go the rock wall, and let us be swept into oblivion.

I had to hope, and dread, that she trusted me enough to follow.

Harry squirmed like a terrier as we rushed, but I held him with one arm and the cauldron with the other, listening to him cough and scream as he choked on the air. I held my breath, silently ticking off seconds as we traveled. I wanted to know, just before we drowned, how long I'd made it.

Thirty seconds. We caromed off a rock wall, I almost sucked in water, and then we were swirling along again, the walls slick as ice. I kicked to hurry us.

A minute. The pressure to breathe was building now, Harry alarmingly slack. Had he fainted? I had no idea if my wife had followed.

Ninety seconds. My chest was a slow burn.

Two minutes. I banged my head against a rock, but the agony in my body worked to keep me from blacking out. Pain arced from skull to heart to lungs.

Eternity ticked on. My body seemed to swell, my nerves crying not so much for air to be sucked in but for what I'd consumed to be released. I let out a train of bubbles.

Two minutes twenty, and I couldn't do it more. I hadn't trained for this.

Two-thirty, then, and I'd agree to be dead. I counted, endlessly.

Two-forty, every fiber screaming, floating upward . . .

My head broke clear and my lungs exploded in release, and then I sucked in another breath, went down, fought up, shoved Harry toward the ceiling so the cauldron clanged but the air was refreshed, then down again in eerie blackness, gulping in a pocket of air. I floated on my back and the cauldron rolled off us and was lost in an instant, my boy frighteningly still, as if dead. I felt the worse but could see nothing in the dark.

Surely my wife couldn't have lasted that long.

"Ethan!" It was almost a scream, and then a cough.

"Here! With Harry!"

By thunder, we'd done it.

And then the ceiling dipped and we were under again, hurled along in a nightmare, but this one was shorter, the length of a room, and with joy I felt Harry tighten against me with a fearful clutch like a cat's. He was alive!

We came out in the dark again, gasping, but suddenly there was a feeling of space above the water, as if we'd slid from old mine tunnel to broader cave. The current slackened.

"Astiza, where are you?"

"Here." She was splashing, trying to find us.

Harry was hacking, proof of life that made me weep.

Far, far away—as far as the stars—I saw a glimmer of light. I thought I was hallucinating for a moment, but the illumination slowly grew. Escape!

We drifted out the cave exit to a forested ravine, branches bare and snow drifting down. Too exhausted to do anything but stare at the cloudy daylight—we'd no idea what time it was—we drifted in a pool for a moment, numb and reprieved, nearly frozen, until our leaden legs grounded in shallows. We numbly stood, shaking with exhaustion and cold. Had we escaped Astiza's prison, only to freeze to death?

"Ethan!"

A miracle appeared. It was Gideon, rising from winter underbrush and stumbling across a rocky bar to help us stagger to shore. He hadn't deserted me after all! Somehow he'd even anticipated our emergence and waited for us.

"How, how . . ." I couldn't even make a coherent sentence. But maybe he could get my boy to a fire. I was weeping with gratitude, so grateful for this second reprieve. Astiza and I dripped, teetering from shock, amazed we were all still in this world. The three of us held one another.

Then other figures emerged from the brush and joined Gideon, pistols and muskets aimed. One was gigantic, another blond, and several looked like French secret police.

"Hello, Ethan," said Catherine Marceau. "At last we are reunited."

CHAPTER 31

Catherine wore a hooded cloak of midnight blue with fur ruff, snow flecking her golden hair like diamonds. Her riding dress was maroon. She wore a dark stone at her throat, brown leather boots with silver spurs, and kid gloves, and she carried a riding crop in her left fist. She was beautiful, clever, persistent, and wicked. French agents pointed half a dozen guns. I was annoyed that I was shaking, but it was from cold, not fear. Mostly.

"I've enjoyed every moment of separation," I replied.

While I'd lusted after Catherine Marceau as any man would, given her voluptuous figure and seductive habit, she'd not only foiled my plan to disrupt Napoleon's coronation but had taken a shot at me with a pistol that, with rare foresight, I'd loaded with black pepper. I got a satisfying sneeze from her, but it was still Catherine who tore our family asunder by forcing Astiza and Harry to prematurely flee from Notre Dame.

She'd later had the cheek to write me at Cadiz, offering alliance to hunt for the Brazen Head, under her own conspiratorial control. "Who is it you work for at the moment?" I asked her now. "Royalists, Napoleon, Talleyrand, or the Invisible College? It's difficult to keep track."

"You know me better than that. Catherine works for Catherine."

I looked at Gideon. "Did you betray us, too?"

"They captured me. I'm sorry, Ethan. I followed you to save you, but I'm failing my half of our partnership."

So I'd dragged him into her web, too. "It's my debt that is mounting."

"We followed from Prague," said Pasques, the gigantic French policeman. He was thick as a wine barrel, had arms nearly the diameter of my legs, and carried the disposition of a tax inspector mated to a paddock bull. "We caught this one lurking at Kutná Hora, sly and sinister like his kind."

"You mean discreet and observant."

"We were far from surprised that you'd fallen in with Jews and deserters, Gage."

"I live to meet your expectations, Pasques."

He grinned with the satisfaction of a cat that has stalked a mouse. "It's taken a great deal of trouble to find you. Yet here we are."

"It does seem serendipitous, does it not? And yet not entirely coincidental. Catherine, I'm guessing you reached Rabbi Abraham before we did?"

"Ethan, you're not always so astute."

"We were directed to the Star Summer Palace after our host consulted a book that was left with a long golden hair. I presume you studied the ancient texts?"

"The good rabbi was persuaded that his interests lie with France. He became an instrument to once more bring us together."

Astiza glanced at me, no doubt wondering about my faithfulness this past year, as I had wondered about hers, given Richter's leering. We'd been imperfect, lonely, loyal, and merely tempted. Or so I hoped.

"Napoleon knew you wanted to go to Prague and recognized you at the end of the Battle at Austerlitz," Catherine related, relishing her triumph. "Did you notice his glance? His eye is an eagle's. Officers made inquiries to find your unit and your friend. It wasn't hard to guess you'd flee to the biggest ghetto in Europe— and be easily manipulated once you arrived."

The cold water that hadn't dripped off me was beginning to freeze. "But how did you know we'd emerge here?"

"Your Jew told us that your witch had a plan to break out."

"Gideon has a name, Catherine."

"He eavesdropped on your meeting with the Invisible College in the Golden Lane. You left Prague with Baron Richter, you didn't emerge from the cells in Kutná Hora, and this is the only known outlet of the underground river that floods the mines. It was far from certain, but then, I'm very lucky, aren't I?"

I looked about the wintry ravine. "Standing with us, still poor, cold, single, and childless, in a muddy dell in the snow."

She refused to react. "Rumor is that you copied the ingenuity I invented in Paris by pretending to be dead in Venice. You flatter me with imitation, Ethan."

"Except the Comtesse Marceau is truly dead." Years before, Catherine had taken a strangled girl's identity and shipped to England pretending to be a refugee royalist, while actually operating as a French spy. It was nothing to be proud about. In fact, I wondered if she'd done the throttling herself.

"And I'll keep you alive, but only if your wife takes me to the Brazen Head." She smiled at my family. "Work with me and I will make you rich and powerful. Defy me and I will debate whether to execute you or give you back to Richter to be tortured. All this trouble would have been avoided if we'd remained partners from the beginning." And to emphasize her goodwill, her agents gestured with their gun barrels to move us off the riverbank and into the cover of the woods.

I felt exhausted. To emerge from drowning to the muzzles of guns? To escape one set of tormentors, only to fall in with another cabal of lunatics? To desert the French army and be recaptured by Napoleonic agents? Astiza and I knew too much, and were cursed by our usefulness.

"This was destined to happen," Catherine went on as we shambled stiffly toward her party's horses. "We were always meant to be together. Weren't we, Astiza?"

My wife, drenched, frozen, exhausted, and defiantly erect, was dangerously calm. "Should it serve the gods."

"We're a partnership," Catherine insisted. "You need clothes, food, and protection from Richter's gang of mystic cutthroats, who are no more true Rosicrucians than the Borgias were saints. Fear not! We represent the French government and the power it projects. Cooperating with us will restore you to Napoleon's good graces. Give him a machine that tells the future and you'll share that future. Always we give you opportunity, Ethan."

I looked at Astiza, who was not only wet and shivering but wasted, cut, and half-poisoned from her long months underground. Yet her dark eyes were bright, and she could be as calculating as Catherine. I'd just seen my wife blow her way through a rock wall, and I wouldn't underestimate her now.

"Our nanny is right," Astiza said to me, not even giving Marceau the courtesy of "governess" in reminding her of our household roles in Paris the year before. "We need help to keep from freezing and to keep Richter at bay. Do you have extra horses, Comtesse Counterfeit?"

She ignored the gibe. "Yes. And money. And tools."

"Then indeed, let's be partners. My clue is a castle that Christian Rosenkreutz may have fled to. It's an educated guess, not a certainty, and I've no idea if the Brazen Head is there. But let's try to find it together."

I was surprised at her acquiescence. Catherine was not.

"Astiza has always been more sensible and practical than you, Ethan. It's a mother's trait. And our destination, Madame Gage?"

"If I told you that, you'd have less need of us. I'll be our guide, but my price is the survival and freedom of my husband, my son, and his Jewish friend. For now, we need to get north across the Elbe River before nightfall."

"When we get to this castle, do you have a key?"

"Ethan does."

This was news to me.

"My husband is more useful than you think," she added to Catherine.

"Oh, I think he's useful." She turned to her six French policemen. "Pasques, take that sword he has and any other weapons. Give the family dry clothes and tie Ethan to his saddle. Jew, I am feeling magnanimous, and have no more use for you. Scuttle back to your ghetto and do not stray into great affairs again."

"I'd prefer to stay and serve my friends."

"And I'd prefer you work with Rabbi Abraham Stern for French interests. Be gone, before I change my mind. Tell him we are near success."

Her agents grinned evilly at Gideon, making plain he had no choice.

"I brought rope for climbing," he finally said. "Can I leave it with Ethan? It may prove useful."

"You may leave it with Pasques. Quickly. Oh, and, Monsieur Dray?"

"Yes."

"Not a word to the other side. I don't wish to have to hunt you down again and kill you next time." Dismissing Gideon, she turned to the rest of us. "Let's get well away from the Invisible College before making camp. How many miles, Madame Gage?"

"Perhaps a hundred to the castle."

"Then there's no time to waste."

We changed out of our sodden clothing, fought our shivers with brandy and sausage, left Dray abandoned on the riverbank, and climbed onto the horses provided by our new escort, Harry riding in front of me. As I watched my new friend fade from view through the light snow, I felt even more helpless. My shoulder ached, my heart was embarrassed by failure, and my son looked despondent. We set out to the north, crossing the Elbe at a ford and trotting through flurries. At least we warmed as we rode.

Catherine eventually slowed her horse to drop back alongside me. "You think me a Fury, Ethan, because I'm a capable woman."

"A dogged one, I'll give you that."

"I do not give up. I can be ruthless, but ruthless only as men taught me. I'm not a comtesse, no. My father was a solicitor, Pierre Avalon, who rose in the Assembly after the Revolution and made too many enemies. Then he fell afoul of the Terror and they imprisoned all of us except my brother, who managed to run and disappear. You think me a spy and impostor. But my parents were beheaded, and I was given the choice of following them or using my beauty to serve the Revolution as a spy. I've only done what I had to do."

"Killing the real Comtesse Marceau."

"No one killed her. That was a foul rumor. She died in her cell of disease. I was an orphan, her title was vacant, and my jailers would have raped me first if I'd chosen the guillotine. So I took her name, fled to London, and pretended to be a royalist. I survived, loyal to myself." She turned to stare me in the eye. "Are we really any different, you and I?"

"I live for my family."

"I had the beauty to marry, but not the stupidity. The last

thing I wanted was to be chattel of an aristocratic twit, either an exiled Frenchman or a haughty Englishman. I had many offers! But I wanted more."

"You're lonely. I've seen it in your eyes."

"I decided on power, and then Bonaparte brought sanity to chaos."

"Dictatorship."

"Order. He and I are alike, too. Survivors. Opportunists. So I was told of a woman researching ancient secrets, told to ally with her wayward husband and get them to Paris. Yet it wasn't I who rebuffed friendship. It was you."

"I'm married. You tempted me like a courtesan."

"Like another opportunity, which you ignored. Don't be priggish with me; I know you too well. Now you're in my power. Your wife is fond of fate, but where has fate delivered you? Back to me. Why? Think about that." She leaned in close. "We ride to find an oracle of the future. But think of your own future, Ethan, and which woman promises you more."

Then she kicked her mare with her silver spurs and trotted ahead. Yes, she wanted me, I knew. But only for the triumph of possession. I also knew she would become bored of any man, like a spoiled child with toys, and toss them away. She had been aloof to intrigue me with challenge, and seductive to undermine my wife. And what did she really desire? To win, but what, and why, she had no idea. Her manipulations were a drug to forestall her own deep dissatisfaction. The most driven are the most cursed.

We avoided any highway and followed farm lanes without inns, so Catherine bargained for a barn where our group could bed in the hayloft. Astiza, Harry, and I made a nest in the straw, with Catherine and Pasques to one side and three rough-looking French agents on the other. A few yards' separation gave meager privacy. Two more stood guard below.

I had one ankle shackled to a barn post.

It was, however, my first opportunity for conversation with my family. I hugged them fiercely and inspected my son's recovered hands, and we briefly reviewed a year of journeying since Napoleon's coronation. Harry said, "Stop going away, Papa," which both warmed my heart and broke it. He was relieved to be out of the cell, profoundly happy that we were reunited—he credited his escape to my appearance, since I'd shot a bad man and a bad dog—and fearful of what was to come. He was old enough to know that bulky men with big guns meant trouble, and young enough to think I could still protect him.

Finally, he fell into exhausted and troubled sleep.

My wife and I kissed again, but our passion was held in check by tension and the proximity of our enemies. I showed her my bullet wound with odd pride, as if being shot in the back was a mark of honor. She touched both scars, front and back, with fascination. Reminders of mortality hypnotize us.

"What's your plan?" I whispered, since I had none of my own.

"I've made a guess from fragmentary hints in old books and the markings on a dungeon wall at Český Krumlov," my wife murmured. "There's no certainty the Brazen Head still exists, but there's a peculiar castle that could have attracted a seeker such as Rosenkreutz. Its architecture is symbolic."

"Gideon and I found the old sword blade in a tower built in the shape of Solomon's seal. The palace was built as a place to speculate."

"Like an astronomical tower," my wife said.

"Yes, except this one looked inward instead of outward."

"What is within is without. What is above is below."

"So what do the stars tell you now?"

"I haven't seen them in many months. It's cloudy tonight. But our destination has a shape that reminds me of the Egyptian hieroglyph for ka, or soul. What better place for our medieval mystic to rest?"

"You think Rosenkreutz is buried there, too?"

"We'll shortly find out."

"And if not?"

She looked at Catherine and Pasques, who were watching our whispering. "Then our usefulness will be at an end. Be ready for a final fight."

The next morning, we skirted the eastern side of Nymburk and followed the river Mrlina northeast, the land slowly rising, with Poland over the horizon. Far ahead we could see the gentle crest of the Krkonoše Mountains. The terrain became more rumpled. The snow gave way to clear weather, the earth like frosting. Catherine announced that we had passed into the year 1806. Then we trotted by the villages of Dětenice, Dolní Bousov, Sobotka, and Troskovice.

From a high pasture, we saw our goal curdled in mist.

"Trosky Castle," Astiza said.

Two rock spires rose from the top of a wooded hill. Atop each outcrop was a stone watchtower. "One is called Baba and the other Panna, meaning 'grandmother' and 'maiden,'" Astiza told us. "Crone and virgin." Linking the two rock crags was a castle wall. "It was built by Čeněk of Wartenberg late in the fourteenth century and passed on to Ota of Bergov. The younger Ota, his son, plundered nearby Opatovice Monastery and by legend hid its treasure under the castle, never to be found. I think Christian Rosenkreutz came here."

"You're certain?" Catherine asked.

"No. But this castle's peculiar shape fits the only clues I have. It burned shortly after Rosenkreutz would have arrived."

It was the oddest edifice I'd ever seen. The geology would have been strange enough, the twin rocks like gigantic fangs. To have each topped by additional towers gave the hill the fantastic silhouette of a horned god.

"You think this was built to mirror an Egyptian hieroglyph?" I murmured to my wife.

"No. But Rosenkreutz might have recognized the glyph and its astrological significance. What better resting and hiding place?"

"It's a ruin. How could he and the automaton be hidden here and remain unfound?"

"Not everyone has the searching ability of Ethan Gage." She squeezed my hand. "Books say there are hidden caverns here."

"I'm done with caves. For all time."

"And yet our path toward heaven requires sojourns in hell," my wife said.

CHAPTER 32

Astiza

Ethan thought me merely calm in our new captivity, even resigned, but the truth was that I was secretly happy, a fact I preferred not to share with our captors. The wicked dwarf was dead, and we were ahead of Baron Richter. After months of captivity in a stinking chamber, fermenting our own urine, I breathed fresh air. My son had healed. My husband had returned. Given such victories, the threat represented by Catherine Marceau was real but manageable. We'd been forced to live with her in Paris, and I knew her too well. She was ambitious, vain, duplicitous, flirtatious, and more practical than cruel. She wanted to use us, not abuse us. Meanwhile, the idea of finally finding the tomb of Christian Rosenkreutz and the

Brazen Head thrilled me. Nothing is more disquieting than straying from destiny's path, and nothing is more satisfying than doing what should be done. After months of imprisonment, we were coming to an ending.

The horned castle of Trosky is a castle of ka, of soul. Once a medieval fortress, now a ruin, it wouldn't reveal its nature to an ordinary visitor. But there was magic to someone like Rosenkreutz. To build one watchtower on a pinnacle is logical. To build two, less than a hundred yards apart, is a sign. The place is a magnet for tumult, and not just Baron Ota and his sacrilegious stolen treasure. The robber knight Sofa of Helfenburk captured the place in a night raid and made it a base for his depredations. Siege and counter-siege resulted in the castle passing to Zitava, Zajic, King George of Poděbrady, the Selmberks, the Bibrštejns, the Lobkowiczes, and the Valdštejns. The pinnacles rise from pools of blood.

We rode up the wooded hill, the old lane to the castle gate overgrown but discernible. Our horses were picketed in the bare trees below the masonry. It was late, the shadows long, the walls cracked and crumbling. When we walked inside the arched gate, their wooden doors long rotted away, there wasn't much to see. Tilted stairs led to rectangular courtyards stretched between the twin monoliths of lava rock. The ramparts were weedy. Many of the stones were blackened by fire. All roofs were gone, and all shelter. I saw no sign of village children playing here, or animals denning. The place was forbidding.

The giant Pasques walked the ramparts, a pinnacle himself in the gloom. He said almost nothing on our journey, as is his habit. But now he descended to confer with Catherine.

"A fine place for a trap." I noticed he leaned closer to the woman than he had to.

"Or a defense." She was oblivious, or indifferent, to the policeman's desire.

"If this is where the Brazen Head can be found," Pasques said, "let's come back with a regiment of agents and a cartload of picks and shovels. I don't trust Gage by half, and I don't trust his wife at all."

"We're in a race with the Invisible College. We don't have time to seek reinforcements. And the witch is our only hope." She turned to me. "A picturesque ruin, but little more than a burned-out shell. Are you trying to make fools of us?"

"Can't you feel it, Comtesse?" I deliberately used the title with a mocking tone. Under the open sky, I felt my helplessness changing to power. "There are places in the world where spirit converges. This is one."

"Does the convergence include an automaton?"

"So anxious you are! What will you ask it?"

Catherine smiled. "When I shall prevail."

"But if you possess it, you have prevailed, have you not?"

"I have other desires as well." She glanced at my husband, enjoying her ability to provoke him—and me.

"As do I," I said calmly, knowing it is my calm that provokes her. "You must help search for the Brazen Head with purity of heart and mind. Where should we look, Comtesse?"

"Under this rubble heap, obviously."

"Yes." I stamped my foot. "Perhaps there are caves. Let's fan out to look for them."

But a half hour's search revealed no entrances, which surprised no one. There were only abandoned pits left by peasants seeking monastery treasure. If it were that easy, the android would have been looted long ago. "Let's look from the watchtower." I pointed to Baba.

"You look for a cave from a tower?" Pasques asked.

"As above, so below, the astrologers say."

The Baba pinnacle was sheer, dark, and rough. Nothing but lichen grew on it. Its wooden stairs had burned or rotted, so Ethan and I climbed like goats while the others watched from below, Harry kept hostage. At the top was a square tower with room for not much more than the two of us, overseeing a panorama of wintry fields and woods. Ethan brought the old sword and we probed the basalt floor, but it was solid rock. I was puzzled. I felt we were in the right place, but it seemed bald of clues.

"Let's try Panna," I said.

This lava outcrop was fatter and not quite as steep, although still lofty. Here the watchtower's wooden roof had burned away, leaving a room that was an open shell. The floor, however, was stone instead of bare rock. Our tapping yielded nothing.

"They'll be angry if we led them to the wrong place, Astiza."

"And not just them." I pointed. I'd looked out over the countryside again. Miles away, the setting winter sun etched a line of black-clad horsemen galloping toward our strange outcrop. They were dressed in black, riding single file.

"It's Richter," Ethan surmised. "He's gotten out of the mines and followed us. Look, one has peeled off, maybe to flank us." My husband studied their approach and then gave that wry grin of determination I'd fallen in love with. "Which is worse?"

"Catherine is greedy," I said, "but Fulcanelli is evil."

"Fulcanelli?"

"His church name, an imposture I allowed myself to be seduced by." I immediately regretted the choice of word.

His smile tightened. "Seduced? What kind of relationship did you have before Richter was burned?"

I flushed, heart hammering. Could I honestly answer that question even to myself? Before Fulcanelli used me, I was using him. "What kind of relationship did you have with Catherine?" I countered evasively.

A long moment, too long, ticked between us.

"What do you see?" Pasques shouted up at us from below, sounding impatient. It was a welcome interruption.

"Baron Richter is coming!" Ethan shouted down. He turned to me. "Maybe they'll fight it out between them."

"Or combine to torment us. Best to disappear, as Richter's henchmen seem to do. But how, how?" I paced the floor. "Truth is usually obvious once you see it."

Ethan studied where I was walking. "The stonework has a pattern," he suddenly said.

The light was poor and the floor filthy, but I scolded myself for not spying it before. I knelt to sweep with my sleeves. "It's laid in the pattern of a rose."

As we hurriedly cleaned, the picture the joints made became more evident. "A lot of bother for a military watchtower."

"But not for a tomb entrance, Ethan." The rose mosaic of large flagstones lay in a circle made by an incision in the rock.

"A rose for Rosenkreutz. But what else?"

The messages of mystics can be as elusive as a forgotten song and as blunt as a blow. "This tower has the name Virgin," I said. "One of many meanings for the rose has been its association with a woman's portal."

"Portal?"

"The opening between her legs. Poets have alluded to roses."

"Ah." My husband was uncharacteristically silent for a moment. Then: "I remember such a line from one of Catherine's romance novels. Just took a peek, you understand. So this is a door?"

"I hope."

"How does it open? I mean, we've had some experience, but . . ."

I thought furiously and finally guessed again, because we had no time to waste. I called down. "Pasques, Marceau! Bring wood for torches and more faggots besides! Bring Horus! Hurry!"

"What's your plan, lovely wife?"

"What opens a rose in nature, Ethan?"

"Well, sunlight."

"And its heat. I want to see if fire has any effect."

"But the castle has already burned."

"Precisely. And why did it burn shortly after Rosenkreutz came here? Was someone seeking entry but didn't know exactly where? And did the fire burn directly against this floor? The roof is burned away." I leaned out again. "I may have found something." And then, "No, not yet!"

Pasques had lit his torch before starting up. The flame could be seen for miles.

Richter's men would hurry.

CHAPTER 33

"Is your wife mad?" Catherine asked me as Astiza fed a ring of fire around the periphery of the tower.

"Eccentric," I said, wondering myself. "Smarter than you or me." Astiza had built a ring of fire on the stone rose, and now smoke and sparks rolled skyward, leaving us slow-roasted on one side and chilled on the other. It was a signal seen for miles, a beacon to anyone approaching.

My wife wiped her brow and addressed our dubious looks. "Heat causes metal to expand. Hot water can be used to crack stones in quarries. Rosenkreutz would recognize fire as one of the elements. Earth, fire, water, and air, all working together."

"If it doesn't open, the Invisible College will besiege us up here," Pasques said.

"We'll drop you on the baron like a boulder," I suggested.

"Only after we've thrown you like a lance."

The smoke began to whiten.

"Steam," Astiza said.

Creaks and groans began to issue from the floor. It seemed to settle slightly and sigh. The incised became more defined, marking the rose from the surrounding stone of the tower. Then there was a whistle that made us jump.

A jet of steam issued from the far side of the tower base like a little geyser, followed by another, and another. Our fire had turned our tower into a teakettle. As the pressure climbed, there was a great clanking and creaking and one end of the rose dipped while the other climbed into the air, a circular section of the tower floor rotating vertically to reveal a shaft. Hot coals cascaded into the pit. The lid stopped to leave a narrow, half-moon entrance on each side of the opening, with just enough room for a human to squeeze and descend.

"The Mansions of the Moon," Astiza murmured. "They mark time, and this door invites us to the future."

"You think Rosenkreutz built this door?" Catherine asked.

"It certainly shows the kind of mechanical ingenuity required to maintain an automaton."

Catherine shouted down orders to her French henchmen to deploy around the castle walls to hold off Richter's deadly monks. She had a pistol tucked in a sash. Pasques had a powerful blunderbuss, a monstrous shotgun that reminded me of Lady Nahir.

I drew Astiza aside. Our earlier conversation had been interrupted, but I wanted answers before we went below. "Richter is risking a battle with French agents over an object that might not even exist," I whispered. "He intercepted me in Venice, kidnapped you, and pursues us in winter. His fervor is out of proportion to the stakes. Why is he still after us?"

"We injured his face, Ethan."

I glanced toward my son, looking down the hole with game

curiosity. It made me proud and terrified that he was taking after his father, but it was an occupational necessity. Secret things tend to be in dark places. "Was it an accident?"

"Harry was trying to save me."

"Save you from what? I thought you were working with Richter—or Fulcanelli—or whoever the hell you thought he was."

She looked away from me. "When we were in the Golden Lane, they wouldn't let us go."

"And Harry threw acid in a man's face?"

She closed her eyes. "He attacked me."

"Who attacked you? Auric?"

"Primus—I mean Richter—tried to rape me."

"What?"

"Ethan, it was a nightmare." She sighed. "He claimed I'd led him on."

"Did you?"

"No. No! Of course not. We did nothing. But I was alone, and I thought he was a bishop, and we'd become friends. I needed help. He misinterpreted. It was very confusing."

My emotions boiled, and not just because this impostor and kidnapper had assaulted my wife. Oh, I was angry, but there was more to it than that. I felt guilty. Hadn't I been flirtatious with Lady Nahir and, before that, with Catherine Marceau? Didn't I enjoy sending salacious signals to pretty women during long absences from my wife? Richter hadn't just attempted rape—he'd unwittingly mocked my own bad behavior.

And it had been left to my son, not yet five, to avenge and protect.

I struggled for words. "I'm so sorry."

"You weren't there."

"Exactly."

"Ethan, it all happened in a moment. Harry didn't even know what he was doing. Richter got what he deserved. That should have ended it, but of course it didn't. And here he comes again."

"Yes."

"Let's find the android. Maybe we can bargain with it to be left alone."

I looked over the broken tower wall. The riders had disappeared into the trees and were climbing the hill. "No. He wants revenge for his humiliation. He wants to possess you, to regain his pride, and then kill you and Harry so the world will never know the embarrassment of how he lost his face."

"Then we ally with Catherine and Pasques. Numbers are our only hope."

It had grown so dark that our faces were masked. "Yes," I said. "Our only hope. You go first." She scooped up Harry and started. "Unless there's another ending," I whispered, too quiet for her to hear.

The others started down iron rungs in the shaft that led into the earth, first Catherine, then Astiza, with Harry in one arm, and Pasques last, Gideon's rope looped over his vast shoulder. He called impatiently. "Hurry, American."

"Start without me, Pasques."

"What?"

"I have something to settle with Baron Richter."

"Pasques, come!" I heard Catherine call from somewhere below.

"Take care of them, policeman." And with the sword of Roland slung across my back, I leaped across the broken wall and clambered back down the outside of the basalt pinnacle to kill Wolf Richter.

And by so doing, expunge some of my worst guilt for too often choosing adventure and pride before my own family, leaving them alone.

CHAPTER 34

The French agents weren't experienced soldiers. One of Catherine's men fired too soon for proper ambush, felling one of Richter's party but allowing the rest to retreat into the shelter of trees under a pelting of bullets, their horses neighing in consternation.

Then gunfire began the other way. I had no gun, only the sword, and so crouched in an old alcove of the castle wall and waited while bullets pinged.

There was a sharp little fight in the gloom. The French seemed to be holding their own, and one shouted, "They're in retreat!" I saw men on Richter's side fall. But then a blast of gunfire from the opposite direction made me jump. Some of the baron's Invisible College monks had flanked the defenders and attacked them from behind. Two of Catherine's defenders pitched over, struck in the back. Another whirled and charged, only to be cut down.

Two more fled, one of them hit and skidding on his deathbed of frozen grass. A monk materialized from the dusk and finished the wounded man with a knife, grunting as he cut.

I thought the last French agent had escaped into the woods, but then I heard shouts and a series of shots in the trees below.

His last cry, and then silence. Finally the sound of a hunting horn, bringing to mind the horn of Roland at his last stand.

All of Catherine's men were dead. The victorious monks who were still alive gathered below the tower we'd climbed. I counted half a dozen, plus the baron.

Now I stepped out, hand on the sheathed hilt of my medieval sword.

This wasn't foolish bravado. Richter and I had one thing in common, an unresolved need for vengeance. I'd never paid for invading his bedchamber and stealing his purse. He'd never paid for assaulting my wife and imprisoning my little boy. We were two cocks in a pit, our swords the spurs. I was counting on a duel.

"Luck let you survive the silver mines of Kutná Hora," I said as I stepped into view.

His men whirled and trained guns on me. They could have shot me down in an instant but wouldn't until the baron gave them permission.

"You should have stayed there instead of overplaying your hand," I went on.

"Monsieur Gage." Richter stepped forward, face hideous, hand on his own hilt, pretending to be puzzled. "Left your wife again?" He looked around warily. "Or is she so tired of your presence that she has already left you?"

"It is I who am tired, and what I'm tired of is you worrying about the presence of my wife." I addressed the others. "Why do you follow a rapist?"

Richter scowled. "That is slander, monsieur. I did not rape your wife. Nor do I rely on luck, either in brelan or the mines. I unreeled line to find my way out of Kutná Hora's tunnels, knowing we'd eventually catch you anyway."

Again I addressed the others. "Ask my son, a mere child, why the monster you follow has a burned face. What precipitated his disfigurement?"

"Gage doesn't know what he's talking about."

"I know that your very presence is an insult to her husband, Baron, that you are an odious schemer, a cheat at cards, a bumbler at alchemy, a failure as a jailer, and stupefied by real mystery. Your only chance at finding medieval secrets was to follow us, since you and your Invisible College dunces here are incapable of discovering anything on your own." I knew rage had swamped my customary prudence, but I longed to finish what Harry had started on this villain.

Richter drew his rapier. It flashed in the twilight as he cut the air, the thin blade a thread of lightning. "All right, the truth then." He bowed like a duelist. "Your wife is a whore, American. She led me on. She's lied to you. Die for her if you wish, but don't die an ass. Face the truth."

"Yes, truth." I drew Durendal with a great rasp. It was a medieval broadsword made for cleaving shield and armor. I cut my own circle in the air, and the sword sang like a choir. "Let our duel decide who's the scoundrel and who the wronged. No guns, and no seconds. We should have ended this in Venice."

He smiled, dangerously so. "I tried to. But you ran and hid in the grave from what I heard. You want to return to it now?"

"I want you to have your own taste of bitter earth."

"He's trying to delay us," Richter told the others. "They've fled down some rabbit hole. But I'm quick with my blade. This won't take long."

I knew he trumped me in swordsmanship. Richter had the quickness of his narrow blade, and under normal circumstances he would quickly have gotten under my guard. I'm a man of our modern nineteenth century, appreciative of the rifle. Still, I had a strategy. I had the weight of steel on my side. His point flicked and buzzed, but my hacker sizzled as I swung, keeping him at bay with arcs worthy of an executioner, if not nearly swift enough to catch him. It was as if I was boxing with haymakers, and Richter jabbing from a distance. He laughed as I grunted. His companions stood in a circle to create an impromptu arena, and we circled in purple twilight, patches of snow and frost casting just enough light to see.

"That antique is obsolete, Gage. You look ridiculous."

"Look again when your head is separated from your shoulders."

"I'm simply waiting for you to get tired." He lunged, hoping he'd distracted me. I clanged away his assault, but not before he cut a shallow furrow across my chest and forearm, ruining my clothing and puckering the skin underneath. Blood welled from the sting.

"Maybe I shall undress you," he said. "As I dreamed of doing with your wife."

So I feigned rage and charged, the clumsiest of bulls, and let him lightly rake me again, this time on my thigh. I howled for effect, but in fact it *did* hurt like the devil. I had to end this before he stabbed me through.

So it was my time for my brelan surprise. My wound at Austerlitz had weakened me, but the weeks since had given me time to exercise my left shoulder and arm. Durendal made an excellent weight, and the left side of my torso had come to equal and then exceed the strength of my right for the first time in my life. My injury had mostly healed, and my power had grown.

I tossed the medieval sword up and caught it with my left hand.

Richter hesitated.

Fencers learn to counter a left-armed opponent, but it takes a moment of adjustment and a rejiggering of strategy. I did not give such time. I lunged, making him back up, and swung. His parry was clumsy, and then his heel caught a stone in the ruined courtyard and he struggled to maintain balance.

It gave me time to lift and cut a downward stroke capable of cleaving him in two.

He blocked and turned my swing, but it was a reed against an oak, and with a great shout worthy of Roland I slammed down on his rapier, forcing its tip to the frozen earth and snapping its blade. Richter cried out as his wrist turned. Now he did fall, scrambling backward on all fours as I came after him, his eyes wide with frank fear.

He collided with one of his henchmen and desperately groped for the man's musket. I leaped forward to kill him before he could point and fire.

Durendal hissed down with a Valkyrie's cry, and Richter only had time to lift the gun barrel against my chop. My sword snapped it in two, the charge going off and the baron howling as fragments flew and sliced. The other monks fired, but I dropped an instant before they pulled. Now their guns were empty.

I lifted my arm to stab the baron, only to find Durendal curiously light.

The medieval relic had shattered again, the blade breaking into half a dozen pieces. I was once more left with a stub. I froze in astonishment, while Richter, the wind knocked out of him and his ruined face pitted with tiny bleeds, seemed equally surprised.

It wasn't just the dissolution of the famous blade that astounded me, however. It was the hilt. The force of the collision had jarred the rose pommel, popping it off. A black protuberance jutted from the end of the handle.

By the soul of Christian Rosenkreutz, it was a key! I'd been carrying it for more than a year without knowing it was there.

No wonder Talleyrand had been told the sword stub was a clue.

All this took an instant to comprehend. I sprang up, Richter out of reach but his monks busy reloading. While they fumbled with cartridge and primer, I sprinted for the basalt pinnacle and its virgin tower. I sprang halfway up just from momentum. Below me, guns swung to aim.

"Leave him!" Richter roared. "He'll lead us to the witch and her treasure!"

Not if I shut the door, I thought.

I heaved myself over a lip of wall, fell to the tower floor, and slipped into the hatchway of two half-moons where the others had gone, hanging on to the iron rungs in the shaft. I could hear the Invisibles climbing, but I had a minute's lead.

Steam had opened the door, but the mechanism was out of fuel. So I reached up and hauled and, with a grind of gears and sigh of pistons, the great lid came down with a crash.

I was in blackness, clinging.

"Astiza!"

"Ethan!" It was a faint call, far below and far away.

To hell with Richter. We'd find the machine, learn our future, and leave all these plotters far behind. The Brazen Head would somehow save us.

A great frustrated hammering began from above. Then there was ominous silence.

CHAPTER 35

I descended through a basalt pinnacle to what I guessed was the level of the castle walls, and then far deeper. The shaft was a natural volcanic vent, its walls frozen, ropy lava. In places it had been hacked wider by men. At the bottom, a rock floor sloped downward. As I followed this, the dark basalt gave way to paler limestone, the ancient volcano having extruded through the earlier ancient reef. Now the tunnel widened, eventually opening into a true cavern. Glossy white-and-pink limestone pillars held up a ceiling big enough for a ballroom. The middle was fifty feet high, but at the cavern's far end, rubble climbed until floor and roof pinched together.

I heard voices and saw a lantern. The four others were examining one of the cavern walls. I shouted greeting, and Astiza rushed to hug me. "I thought I'd lost you again!"

"The baron and I had some unfinished business." I turned to Catherine. "Your men are wiped out, I'm afraid. It's only us now."

"Did you kill Richter?"

"No. Both our blades broke."

"Durendal was shattered?" my wife asked.

"I'm afraid so. I had to shut the hatch after me. They banged on it but quit. Richter will try something else, I'm guessing. We must hurry." I looked about. "We're always climbing into hell, aren't we?"

"This hell is very pretty," Astiza said. "The hanging rock reminds me of glistening, graceful roots."

"I prefer to think of the underworld as a depository," Catherine added, "as rich in artifacts as the bottom of the sea must be for treasure ships."

"I wouldn't have guessed you so poetic," I said.

"I'm a romantic, Ethan."

I was quite sure she wasn't.

"My theory," Catherine went on, "is that this cave network was found before the castle existed. The fortress was built to seal and guard it. They left one entrance where few would think to look—in a watchtower at the top instead of a cellar at the bottom—and left hidden what we've now rediscovered."

"And what is that, my doughty fellowship?" I said it sarcastically, but in fact we were unwilling allies again with Catherine and Pasques. Danger forces strange compromises.

"Show him," Catherine ordered.

My wife took a lamp and walked toward one of the natural pillars, lifting the light. The thick stalagmite, I saw, had been carved into the shape of a woman. Subsequent years and dripping water had softened the carving, but the feminine form and face were still recognizable.

"The White Madonna," Astiza said. "It's a representation of the Goddess, Ethan. It's Isis, Mary, Cybele, and Artemis."

"It's a woman, anyway."

She moved on. "And here's a god." This was a powerful man, bearded, helmeted, carved from a darker hue, and again eroded by dripping water. At first I thought he might be clutching his privates, but then I realized his hands were on the hilt of a grounded sword.

"Not a god," I objected. "They don't need steel weapons."

"Masculine power, then," she said. "All things are dual, and this cave is a repository of symbols." She pointed. Astrological signs were inscribed on the floor. Wreaths of rock wound across the ceiling, carved imps and fairies peering through stone fronds. Grooves on the floor inscribed "golden triangles" of perfect proportion from pillar to pillar. And why did our feeble light seem so bright? Because on the walls were great sheets of bronze that, even when tarnished, reflected a ghostly image of us. Those images were echoed on the opposite wall and back yet again, so that our figures receded into infinity.

"What is this place?"

"An anteroom of the sacred," Catherine said.

"A trap," Pasques said. The giant kept looking around uneasily.

"I think we've truly found where Rosenkreutz came to rest," Catherine said, "but we face a challenge. This way, Ethan."

At the far end of the cave room was a great bronze door, inscribed with symbols. There were circles divided into four quarters, with a symbolic animal or god's head in each. And there were squares divided into smaller tiles, each tile bearing letters or characters from a foreign script.

"The language in the center is Enochian, the tongue of angels," Astiza said. "The ancients knew it, but we moderns have forgot."

"I hope what it's saying is not a curse," I said.

"An invitation, to the right person."

There was also a date, in Latin script: ANNO DOMINI MCDLXXXIV, or 1484.

"The date Rosenkreutz was sealed within," Catherine guessed.

"The Rosicrucians claimed they entered this chamber 120 years later and found the texts that form the base of their organization," Astiza said. "If true, the tomb beyond may be empty."

"Unless they didn't find everything," I said.

"You think you're wiser, Ethan?" Catherine teased me.

"Cleverer, perhaps. We've come this far under terrible circumstances, so fate wants us to find the Brazen Head, don't you think?"

"To harness it."

"Or destroy it." That had been Thomas Aquinas's idea, and he was a saint, an honor to which no one has thought to nominate me.

"That won't happen," she said.

"The door is locked," Astiza interrupted. "We have no tools."

"No gunpowder and no battering ram," Pasques said, with a note of genuine regret. Bashing things in is what men do.

"You could be our ram, Pasques," I said.

"With your head the tip," he replied.

"The lettering could be a code," Astiza said.

"But we have no time to puzzle one, and no magical incantation," Catherine responded impatiently. She kicked the portal. "Your wife promised you have a key, Ethan."

"I will try it." I was nonchalant, and yet mystified that Astiza had predicted my usefulness so confidently. She believes in me more than I believe in myself, which is one reason I love her.

"You really have one?" Catherine asked. She has occasionally proclaimed my usefulness, too, but then been surprised when I confirm it.

"When Durendal shattered, its rose hilt opened and this popped out." I revealed to the others what was in my hand. "Hidden for centuries."

Their intake of breath was audible. "This unlocks this door?"

"Why else all the fuss over an antique sword?" Destiny had become an avalanche, and I was meant to be here and nowhere else. I stepped forward, inserted the key, turned it against rusty resistance, and heard a click. Reforging the sword had allowed it to be swung with power, and the resulting jolt had been violent enough to free the key. People had probably been trying to reunite hilt and blade for a long time.

With a ponderous creak, the great door revealed a chamber beyond. I thrilled to success, and a hundred colors. The others looked at me with respect. Treasure hunting is addictive.

"You're performing well, Ethan." Catherine's praise was the kind used for a hunting dog or stud horse. "My investment in you has paid off."

"My wife gets the credit. We make a partnership."

"You and I are partners, too." She said it lightly, offhandedly, but just slyly enough that it annoyed me. Catherine had been imperiously remote when I first met her, and then dangerously flirtatious when she lived with my entire family. She was instructive yet treacherous, vain yet insecure. Here we were in the devil's armpit, our escape unclear, looking for a mechanical golem a saint had wanted destroyed, and she dropped sentiments like heedless crumbs. I was baffled. Why insult me one moment and play games the next? The French Revolution had broken something in her, I guessed. Her soul. Her sanity.

It was not my duty to repair it. Nor was I going to allow her to toy with our emotions, batting them like a cat. "Let's see if the Brazen Head of Albertus Magnus and Christian Rosenkreutz really awaits."

We stepped inside the new chamber, immediately confused by its complexity.

Then there was a great boom that shook the chamber, a roll like thunder, and a great cascade of rock that sluiced down the lava shaft to bounce down the tunnel at the far side of the room. A cloud of dust rolled out.

Wolf Richter had blown his way from tower to tomb with a blast of gunpowder. He would soon be climbing down to join us.

"We don't have much time," I said.

CHAPTER 36

Trapped," Pasques repeated.

"No," said Catherine. "If we find the automaton, it will tell us a way out."

The room we entered was even odder than the Star Summer Palace, outside Prague. The chamber was made of seven walls instead of the usual four. There was a round stone table on a central plinth in the middle, which could serve as an altar. It was inscribed with designs and pierced on its periphery with oblong slits, like handholds.

"Why seven walls?" I asked.

"The seven planets," Astiza speculated. "The seven days of Creation, the seven days of the week, the seven sins, the seven virtues, the seven sacraments, the seven seals, the seven pillars, the seven sages, the seven alchemical metals, the seven hills, and the seven cycles for Egypt, representing eternal life. Can you feel the power?"

I did feel something, just as I had in the Great Pyramid, but we'd no time for metaphysical musings. Where was the android?

The room was brilliantly painted. Each wall had forty square tiles, five across and eight up, tinted every color in the rainbow and each bearing an alphabetical or numeric symbol, an animal, or an Egyptian hieroglyph. Making sense of the pattern would take a couple of centuries, I estimated. The circular altar was inscribed with four circles, a symbol within each.

"Earth, air, fire, and water," Catherine recited.

Lines on the floor made a complex seven-pointed star. There was no golem and no Christian Rosenkreutz. The tomb, it seemed, had been robbed. We stared with disappointment.

"If the Brazen Head ever existed, it looks like it's gone," I said.

"No," Catherine said. "We'd have heard of its use."

"Maybe it's a myth. Or maybe it really was destroyed by Thomas Aquinas."

"You just said fate wouldn't have led us here unless there was something to find," said Astiza. "Rosenkreutz carried something to Český Krumlov, and he escaped with it. He had to bring it here."

I agreed, and yet we stood, baffled. Pasques looked uneasily out the door at the cave cavern, waiting for an appearance by Richter's men. He swung the chamber door nearly shut, peering through the crack.

"Stand guard with your gun, Pasques," Catherine told him.

"If there's no Brazen Head, maybe Richter will simply let us be," I said, with no conviction.

"He'll still want revenge," Astiza countered.

And then little Harry discovered what we had not. "Drawers," he said. He pushed on one of the tiles and it opened. We tried the same with others, and more drawers slid out. The room was a gigantic cabinet. The one I pushed revealed a rock crystal inside.

Each of the tiles was a drawer a foot wide, a foot high, and several feet deep. They held a bewildering variety of curiosities. There were crystal balls, animal horns, pelts, bolts of silk and velvet, agate bowls, a nautilus shell, silver cups, exotic feathers, crystal stones, tarnished scepters, capes, bone rings, vials of dust, vials of liquid, human skulls, a unicorn horn, splinters of old wood, mirrors, spyglasses, intricate knots, bear claws, a mummified monkey, dried roses, altar cloths, tarot cards, ancient scrolls, and old coins. "Enough rubbish to fill a king's attic," I said.

"An emperor's," Astiza said. "Some of this came from Rudolf, I'd surmise. And it hasn't been robbed, which means the Brazen Head should be here, too."

There were 480 drawers, we calculated, or eighty each on the six doorless walls. But none was big enough for a man-size automaton.

"Rosenkreutz collected from all over the world," Astiza said. "His disciples no doubt continued the tradition. Adepts paid homage to the rosy cross by pilgrimage and tribute. This is like an altar with sacrifices."

Men had died, I thought, in pursuit of clutter in a closet.

And where was my son?

The boy had disappeared. Had he crawled into one of the drawers?

I circuited the room. "Harry?"

Astiza jerked from her trance of speculation and looked stricken. "Ethan, how do we always lose him?"

"He can't have gone far. Harry!" I shouted.

In answer I heard a dreaded call from across the cavern. "It's Gage! Come! We've got them!" The voice was Wolf Richter's.

And then my son. "There's a lever under the table, Papa."

He was short enough to have crawled under the altar table in the center. Before I could command him to come out, he pulled. There was a clunk. And then the altar began to sink, taking my son with it.

Astiza cried out, but Harry seemed unalarmed. He rode the base of the altar down into the earth as if on a descending chariot, the sinking platform the same diameter as the table it carried. It lowered just ten feet to a floor below and stopped with a sigh. I lay down to peer through the hole it had left in our own chamber and saw a round room beneath us. My boy stoop-walked out from under the altar table and looked up.

"Papa, there's a man and a doll down here."

Astiza, Catherine, and I slid over the edge, hung on the lip, and dropped to the altar before hopping onto this new floor. Pasques stayed above to hold off Richter.

The hidden chamber was monochrome instead of colored. Its gray stone was unpainted but engraved with a bas-relief. At first I thought it represented a chain of people, then I realized it was only one. A baby crawled out of a nautilus shell, a spiral similar to what I'd seen represented by the Great Pyramid in Egypt, a geometric representation of the Fibonacci number sequence. A toddler then walked into a forest, and fantastic beasts like griffins and unicorns shared the cyclorama as it curved around. The toddler grew to a girl, the girl to a youthful boy, the boy to a young woman, the woman to a stalwart man, and so on, aging steadily until at the end the figure was stooped, then crawling, and finally sinking into the earth, only an arm straining upward from a pile of dying leaves. The rest was sucked down into the mystery we are all headed for.

"Life's cycle," Astiza said.

"Unless one discovers an oracle to elude the tedious tragedy," replied Catherine. She pointed to the two figures Harry had announced.

One was a desiccated but otherwise intact corpse of an elderly man with long hair and graying beard, dressed in a simple robe and seated on a stone bench, looking across the descended altar. The arid air had mummified him, his skin sunken leather, his eyes closed, his fingers curled.

The other figure, on a bench opposite, was the most curious contraption I'd ever seen. It was a mechanical man with face and breast and backplate of tarnished brass. The android looked serenely back across the altar at what could only be the mummified remains of Christian Rosenkreutz, its guardian. The automaton had legs with a warrior's greaves and arms with a knight's gauntlets, but much of the mechanics of the Brazen Head were exposed, as if its metal skin had been torn away and we were looking at sinews and bones beneath. Here, however, the innards were rods, wires, fine chains, and gears: gears by the countless thousands, many tinier than watch workings. They were connected with springs, coils, ratchets, and levers. Some were wood and others ivory, but most were metal, remarkably preserved by this enclosure. They still glistened with oil. What extraordinary artistry had gone into this golem! It looked like the work of not just a lifetime but a thousand years.

Both husks seemed as preserved as the new wax figures in Madame Tussaud's odd new museum in London's Lyceum Theatre, which I'd seen when arranging to be an English spy.

Where had the expertise to build the Brazen Head come from? Who had taught Albertus Magnus the art of creating an artificial man?

"At last we are rewarded," Catherine whispered.

Astiza inspected the corpse of Rosenkreutz, brushing his brown, bearded cheek with her fingertips. I went to the medieval android. It was lifeless as a puppet with no strings, yet obviously built for animation. A wire from its back disappeared into the floor, as if it were chained or tethered. It reminded me of the cable from the lightning rod.

"Does it talk, Papa?"

"I think he might when he has something to say. He needs something to eat as well. Look how skinny he is." I poked my finger through what would have been the side of the torso, into the innards of the machine. My son laughed at my joke. But how did it work?

For many years I've generated electricity with a hand crank, giving sparks to party and a literal jolt to my former enemy Big Ned with an electrified sword. I suspect that tangible magic will be of real use someday, powering any number of devices that inventors like Robert Fulton might devise. Did this automaton draw lightning—not like Roland's broken sword at the Star Summer Palace, or the great tree I'd found in the Dakotas, but from batteries charged as Ben Franklin had taught me? I saw no crank.

Then I remembered the slits along the circumference of the altar table. They were, I realized, handles on a windlass. I gripped, tugging the table one way and then the other. It rotated clockwise.

"It's stiff with age, but I think this altar might spin in a circle around its axis," I told the women. "Grab hold and we'll march as if raising anchor. You, too, Harry. Pretend we're at sea."

He was delighted by this game.

The altar was stiff at first, but when we gave a heave, it started grinding around with a gasp and a wheeze. As we trudged in a circle, the mechanism below loosened and the table began to spin faster. We heard a faint hum. Finally it spun loose as a top, and all we had to do was stand in place and give it an encouraging shove. We looked at the android. The glass eyes of the Brazen Head began to glow sapphire. "We're waking it up, Harry! I think it wants to talk!"

We were interrupted by a roar from above as Pasques lit loose with his blunderbuss, followed by shouts, cries, and answering shots. Another battle had broken out. There was a pause as both sides reloaded, ramrods rasping in barrels. "Help!" the policeman called.

"Pasques, what's happening?" Catherine asked.

"They approached like wolves and scattered like puppies," he replied. "Get the American up here."

Then more shots, a thud, and finally a yell from the Frenchman and a clatter as his weapon fell. I heard the policeman's body slide to one side. He was groaning. We heard the others approaching.

"Wait in the cavern," Richter shouted to his men.

There was a tread of boots and then the baron strode through a cloud of gun smoke to peer down at us, his acid-eaten countenance a vision from hell. He held two loaded pistols.

"It seems you're useful after all, Monsieur Gage," he said, looking down at our spinning carousel of astrological images, our mummified corpse, and our glowing automaton. "You found what my Invisible College misplaced. And now I will take back what is rightfully mine."

CHAPTER 37

Pasques was groaning. "Have you killed my agent?" Catherine asked. She seemed unafraid of Richter. Two thieves, consumed by themselves.

"We'll see if he bleeds out. He killed and wounded some of my men."

A brief cloud on her pretty face, and then nothing. She tried to feel but had a heart that was numb. She pretended to passion but had no idea what passion was. She had appetites, but they were the appetites of an automaton. "So now it is just us," she said to her opponent.

"It is just me, Comtesse, and the Brazen Head. What happens to you, I will ask the machine." He leaped lightly down onto the altar. "Pray that its answer suits you. Throw down your pistol. The battle is over, and I have won."

"Don't be foolish," she tried, attempting to cast beauty like a spell. "You and I are natural partners. The witch has already led us here. Gage has animated the machine and become superfluous. Pasques is disabled. But you and I can use the android for good." She carefully laid her gun on the altar.

"My good." Richter glanced at Astiza. "The wife we will take as slave labor. She's strong enough to carry the android." Despite his ruin of a face, I could still see lust and longing in his eyes. The man was noble, rich, powerful, a scholar, and here he was with us, grubbing in a hole in the ground for a forecast he didn't need and love he couldn't have. Nor did Catherine miss his glance at a rival woman. *Contentment makes poor men rich*, Franklin has counseled. *Discontent makes rich men poor.*

And I needed to finish what I had started, which was to destroy Baron Richter. Except that my sword was broken, and my hands empty. I glanced at the gun Catherine had set down.

Richter pointed to me with a pistol. "Your husband, Madame Gage, is the most irritating man I've ever met. I'm sure he can be a trial to you as well. I will do you a favor by getting rid of him." He cocked the hammer, and I stood like beef in a slaughter yard.

"Don't be stupid, Richter," my wife snapped back with contempt as stinging as a slap. "Ethan had the key to this place, and he is the only one who knows how to animate the Brazen Head. He's our sole electrician."

Richter hesitated. "Is this true?" he asked Catherine.

"Perhaps." She looked sourly at me. So how could I keep her on our side? How could I use her as she tried to use me?

"Catherine has been our partner since the beginning, Baron," I lied. "We're all necessary if you want to operate the automaton."

He looked from us to the Brazen Head. The machine's face reminded me of the frozen, sober expression of a Greek mask. Could it really foretell the future? The idea seemed improbable, and yet isn't that what astrologers, fortune-tellers, generals, and financiers try to do every day?

Richter strode over to inspect the machine. "So complex! It reminds me of the calendar clock of Prague, but with infinitely more gearing. If Albertus Magnus truly constructed this, it would have been the work of decades. Thank God that Thomas Aquinas didn't really destroy it and that Christian Rosenkreutz spirited it to safety. The idea was that God might have designed Creation, but that once it started, we were living in a clockwork universe, predictable as Newton's laws of motion."

"Life is a very wayward clock," I remarked.

"Events are not the product of chance and free will, but instead are highly predictable if only enough information can be absorbed and analyzed. All the variables of the present can be simplified, codified, multiplied, divided, and ultimately analyzed today and forecasted tomorrow. For example, if we knew the position of every cloud and the direction of every wind, we could predict the weather. Albertus incorporated into gears and levers the patterns of human history, in hopes this machine could tell us great secrets."

"Or protect us as the golem protected the Jews," my wife said. "Perhaps the Brazen Head was built not to suggest but to warn."

"The Jewish golem became uncontrolled. One legend is that he was put to work fetching water, couldn't be stopped, and flooded streets and cellars. A memory of an old Vltava flood, I'm guessing. But the golem was made by incantation. By building mechanical gearing instead of relying on magic, Albertus became a little god, with his own Adam."

"Adam did not obey, either."

Richter came to a decision. "Gage, I trade your expertise for your life. If you were the animator, how would we put this devil machine to work?"

Start with simplicity. I turned to the machine. "How do you work?" I asked.

It blinked, or rather the eyes flashed. My turning toward it, or the direction of my voice, somehow allowed it to sense me. But it was silent. I'd spoken in French, but that wouldn't be the language Albertus used. He'd been a scholar of Latin.

"*Quam operor?*" I tried, turning to my meager store of the language.

Nothing.

I walked over and tapped the brass breast. Again the eyes flashed. It had some kind of sensory apparatus. I tapped knee, shoulder, forehead, mouth . . .

"The gears are turning," Richter reported.

"Spin the altar," I commanded. "Give it more power." So we cranked again, there was a rattle of machinery, and finally a lid fell down from the android's chest and a board of inscribed letters appeared. We would tersely converse by writing, it seemed. The letters spun like dice and then stopped to spell out two words.

"*Quinque quaestiones.*"

"Five questions," Astiza translated. "Is that all it can answer?"

"It has the machinery for an infinite number," Richter objected.

"But perhaps not the electricity," I said. "It's warning us to ration. Or Albertus imposed a limit—to rest the machine or avoid foolish questions."

"What's that smell?" Catherine said.

There was a burning odor coming from the gear works under the altar. Had oil caught fire from our friction? Tendrils of smoke began drifting into the chamber.

"Is this a trap?" the baron asked. His guns came up to cover us.

"We spun too hard and overheated, which is why there is time for just five questions," I hazarded. "Or it is designed to limit human queries. Or it will answer only so much at a time, like the oracle at the ancient Greek temple of Delphi."

"Don't dare trick me, Gage."

"It's the trick of dead Christian Rosenkreutz over there, or perhaps of Albertus Magnus, since this smolder could smoke poor Christian like a ham."

The android clattered and rattled again, the letter cubes spinning. Then it stopped. *"Quinque quaestiones,"* it insisted.

"We must hurry," Astiza said. She marched forward and turned letters on the automaton. "I've been pondering my first question," she reported to us, and decided to ask an eternal one. "What is the purpose of life?" She spelled it out. *"Quid ad mores?"*

"No!" protested Richter. "That's a waste of philosophic nonsense!"

But the automaton was already calculating. Gears whirred, wires hummed, levers clattered like piano keys, and finally the alphabet cubes spun to spell out a single, simple new word.

"Mortem." Death.

"The purpose of life is death? What does that mean?" Catherine said. "It's nonsense. Isn't it?"

I decided it was my turn. I strode to the android. *"Quid ad mortem?"* What is the purpose of death?

The machine clattered again.

"Vita." Life. The answers *were* nonsense.

"I didn't come all this way to play in riddles," Richter complained.

"All right," Catherine said. "One question each, in turn." She moved to the keys. Hers was *"Triumphare velle Napoleon?"* Will Napoleon triumph?

This time the gears spun for far longer. How could a medieval machine know who Napoleon was? And yet it didn't hesitate, but merely "thought" longer than the first two times. And finally it shuddered, the alphabet cubes spun, and it stopped.

"Omnes triumphus ad tempus." Even though I don't read Latin, I got the gist.

"All triumph for a time," Astiza translated.

The smoke was getting thicker, and we had no water or sand to douse a blaze. We'd have to evacuate this pit soon.

"Fools! You're wasting questions!" Richter stewed. He turned to the machine and raised his voice. "*Ubi est aurum?* Where is gold?" Catherine moved the letters for him and the machine began to clatter. The baron watched impatiently. "Finally something practical, so we have coin to hide, power, and refine this creature."

Smoke was filling the room. "The eyes are fading," I said. "It's running down. We should cut it free before it burns."

"No. I want my answer." Finally a clatter. We leaned in to look.

"*In corde.*" Gold is in the heart.

"It's nothing but a medieval parlor trick," the baron said slowly. "There's no wisdom here. Only platitudes. This monster is a fraud! It's built by Albertus to deceive the gullible."

"That's four questions. One left," I said.

"How to live forever," Catherine suggested.

But Harry, whom I'd almost forgotten, shouted his own question. "Will the bad man go away?"

I held Catherine aside while Astiza hurriedly set letters. "*Erit manus abire?*"

"Vile brat!"

But the machine was already grinding and calculating. This time it stopped sooner.

"*Manebit.*" He will stay. And then the machine's last light faded in its eyes and it went still, five questions answered, the chamber polluted.

"Are you satisfied?" Richter sneered. "A perfect waste."

My son was crestfallen when his mother translated. Apparently we were to drag Richter like a ball and chain, if this brass puppet was anything but a joke. Catherine looked at the baron narrowly. And what did that mean for me, the father—to have this lecher and rapist near my wife and son? I felt impotent and defeated after all our trouble. What could I kill him with?

"The fire is going to suffocate us," Catherine coughed. "We have to retreat to the chamber above."

"Not without the automaton," Richter said. "Gage, get it loose."

"It's tied to the floor."

He slashed copper wires with his rapier, sparks flying. "Drag the machine up onto the altar so we can boost it."

I did as ordered. Meanwhile, Astiza lifted Harry to the chamber above and then caught the lip of that floor, swung, and pulled herself up with athletic grace. She leaned down to lend a hand. Catherine uncharacteristically let them go first.

We heaved the Brazen Head up to Astiza. She grabbed to balance it so it stood in the center of the altar.

"You get the lever, Ethan," Catherine ordered. "The baron and I will stand up here."

I hesitated. I didn't want to be underneath with them on top.

"It elevates slowly, Ethan."

So I dropped into the smoke, reached under where the fire had made it hot, and pulled the lever that Harry had used to lower us. There was a clunk, then an agonizing wait, and the altar began to slowly rise toward the floor above.

"Now!" Catherine cried. "Climb on!"

I scrambled aboard, and she held me to balance. As the altar's base lifted clear of the circular chamber's floor, air fed the fire, and flames burst upward. Poor dead Rosenkreutz would be cremated. We'd violated his tomb, stolen his companion, and failed at mastering the future.

An eerie red light picked out our exhausted features, the fire giving off a sulfurous stink. "It looks like hell down there, doesn't it?" the comtesse said.

"We'll put the Brazen Head in an astronomical tower under

the stars of heaven," Richter promised. "Permanently powered. With sensible questions and real answers next time."

"You and I could still be partners," she cooed. "What a couple you and I would make." She reached out. "Take my hand." She put her fingers around his, which were still holding a pistol. He looked at her with suspicion and wonder, this beautiful woman touching a hideously scarred beast, seeing in them something in common. She smiled.

And then with her other she snatched a silver brooch from her cloak and drove its needle into Richter's eye, smirking at his startled howl. The gun came loose. He toppled backward as she kicked, roaring curses, and fell into the red chamber below with a snarl of oaths, the other pistol going off as he hit the floor. Then the altar base came up to seal the hole we'd descended through with a click, returning us to the seven-walled hermetic chamber.

There was a clunk, and a snap, and the altar settled firmly into place. The smoke was snuffed away.

Muffled cries and curses. The lever was on our level, not his.

Richter was trapped.

I waited for her to turn the gun on me, but I apparently still had uses. "Ethan, destroy the mechanism," Catherine commanded calmly.

I crawled under the table and wrenched the lever. It broke with a snap.

Richter's screams of terror were getting louder but were oddly distant, as if he were already a ghost.

The purpose of life is death. The purpose of death is life.

Was it a riddle?

Catherine smiled sweetly at Harry. "See, the prophecy came true, little lad. He *will* stay. Forever." Then she became brisk and businesslike. "Now. Let's not let our trophy fall into the hands of those horrid ruffians waiting in ambush outside this chamber. Pasques, you've bled enough. Get up and protect us."

CHAPTER 38

A lethal contingent of the Invisible College still crouched behind stalagmites, muskets and pistols at the ready. They were unaware of their commander's fate, but were still positioned to block our escape through the tower vent.

"Devise a strategy, Ethan," Catherine ordered, as if it were obvious I'd have prepared a plan that incorporated her decision to murder Wolf Richter by burying him alive. "How will you kill the rest of them?"

"There are too many," Pasques groaned. "Eight or nine."

More than I counted in the courtyard: reserves coming up from the woods? "Trying to fight through would be suicidal." I looked at Pasques. He'd tied a bloody bandage where a bullet grazed his head, which made him look even more formidable, but he was also wounded in the side. A delta of blood had spread on the floor, and he had to be weakening. The rope Gideon had given me was still wrapped around his torso.

"The Brazen Head is a curse," Astiza warned as she knelt to stanch the wound with a scarf. "You saw the desiccated husk of Christian Rosenkreutz, and now Richter has joined him. Let's trade it for escape."

"No," said Catherine. "They'll cut our throats once they have it, to keep their power a secret."

"How do you know that?"

"Because that's what I would do."

"Rather ruthless, Comtesse," I remarked.

"I'm the only one of us who is realistic. Practical."

I'd seen nothing endearing about the monks of the Invisible College. She might be right. "A fighting retreat, then. The floor of the cavern slopes uphill toward its ceiling, but also toward the surface. I hear water somewhere. Maybe there's escape that way."

"And if not?" my wife asked.

"Then I'll sell my life as best I can and you women can plea for mercy by surrendering the automaton. I haven't come this far to give up now. Catherine, give me Richter's pistol and yours on the altar."

"I will not."

"You know I'm the better shot. Trust me, or give up to them."

"Only if you form alliance with me to keep the Brazen Head." She ignored my wife, instinctively trying to attach herself to whichever male was most convenient—for advantage, not friendship.

"We're a family," I offered. "Like in Paris."

She surrendered the guns reluctantly, along with a bullet pouch and powder horn. It was a relief to finally be armed again.

"Pasques, can you still shoot?"

"With pain. But this gun doesn't require much aiming."

"Ready the blunderbuss. Astiza and Catherine can drag the

machine while we battle. Harry, when I tell you, run to the top of the cave as fast as you can. Hide until we come."

"Promise to come, Papa."

The dimness gave us a start. We crept from the bronze chamber door and began climbing the uneven floor of boulders, grateful for the cave's murk while hating its reflective metal mirrors. Their only advantage was that the reflections confused the enemy about exactly where we were. They also didn't know Richter's fate. Harry rambled ahead. The automaton banged and skipped on the rocks as it hung between the women, carried like a casualty of battle. Pasques and I followed, guns ready. There was silence from the waiting henchmen, and then a wary call. "Baron?"

We didn't reply. The farther and faster we climbed, the harder we were to hit. Astiza and Catherine were frantically pulling and pushing the machine. Yet the floor was a chaotic field of boulders that had fallen from the ceiling, and the pitch was steep. Our progress was agonizingly slow.

"What have they done with Richter?" men called behind us.

We didn't answer.

"They are escaping!"

The surviving members of Richter's gang emerged from behind cover, and Pasques's blunderbuss went off with a roar. Our opponents shouted and scattered, and we scrambled a few more yards. Then answering gunfire crashed, bullets chasing us like hornets. Pasques grunted and stumbled, and I knew he'd been hit again. By Thor's thunder, he was a target big as a barn. Ricochets whined and pinged.

I knelt with Catherine's pistol, took a moment to steady my breath, and shot. The closest one collapsed, and the others darted for cover again. A gasping Pasques frantically reloaded.

"Catch up to Harry!" I shouted to the women. The automaton flopped behind them, its expression blank as a marionette's. I let myself drop lower into a crevice between two boulders, ramming and priming.

Our pursuers reloaded as well. The gun duel continued, Pasques and I crouched behind rocks and succeeding in keeping them pinned. Each roar of the blunderbuss set shot rattling through the cavern like pebbles in a can. My shots were measured. I heard another yell of pain from our foes, and then a bullet clipped fragments of rock uncomfortably close to my face. I blinked against the grit, eyes watering, and aimed again.

A shot, and a man went down.

"Remember, the American is a sharpshooter!" Yet shadowy figures were crawling up both sides of the stone cavern, seeking to flank us. I looked backward. The women were almost out of sight, a glint of brass showing near the end of the cave.

"Pasques, time to retreat."

"I'm bleeding from the leg now. A bone is broken."

"Can you crawl?"

He swore. Then, "I can drag myself."

"We can't allow them to get around us."

It was fifty yards to the cavern's upper end, with Pasques a wounded walrus. I'd wiggle and dodge five precious yards uphill, find a scrap of shelter, reload, and fire, forcing our pursuers to duck and pause. They gamely fired back, bullets singing, and I feared that the closer we came to the women, the more likely it was that a bullet would find my son.

The French policeman left a steady trail of blood, using his gun as a crutch and lever. He had no time to load and fire anymore.

Finally we neared the end. Catherine was prone, skirts tangled with the brass boots of the enigmatic android. Harry had to be beyond.

"Is it possible to crawl through?" I asked as we caught up.

"Narrow," Catherine reported. "Your son is exploring, your wife following." She lowered her voice. "Too tight for Pasques."

I felt tantalizing fresh air. "Leave the machine if you must."

"I'll leave all of you before I leave the machine." She wriggled ahead, pushing the android, and it jerked and bobbed as it was crammed into the tunnel. "Astiza, get back here and help!"

I looked at the policeman, my enemy and odd ally. He had a sweaty sheen, teeth clenched, pain immense. He looked at the exit, then at me, and shook his head. "Take the rope." He shed it like skin. "You may need it. Go, go!"

The mad monks of the Invisible College were crawling closer. A brave one traded shots to force me down to load and then sprang up to charge, his bayonet ready. I cocked and shot with my ramrod still in the barrel. It took him in the chest like an arrow, and he pitched back.

"Pasques, your blunderbuss! I'll hold them off while you squeeze."

"It's broken. Go, follow the others. *Now!*"

"You're wounded."

"And slow. And likely to get stuck, greased with my own blood. Join your family. It's too late for me."

Another volley of shots and the policeman cried out as he was hit yet again. Our assailants were converging. It was foolhardy to linger. I crawled past him into a hole tight as a rabbit's burrow. I got my shoulders through only by extending one arm forward and one back, as if swimming. I held the climbing rope that Gideon had given us like an offering and kicked like a tadpole. Astiza grabbed my outstretched wrist and hauled. "Leave your coat!"

I let it slip and finally popped through.

"It's too narrow for Pasques." Ahead I saw dim light and heard rushing water. Deliverance, except what if our pursuers followed?

Catherine forced her way back past me, her body slithering along mine. "Pasques!" she called impatiently. "Now!"

"I cannot fit, Comtesse." It was sad resignation.

"Try!"

"I'm shot through, half-emptied, and too big. The monks are almost on me. *Au revoir*, Catherine, and now I have the courage to tell what I was always afraid to admit before: You became the only thing I ever cared about."

"Pasques, you idiot! Come!"

"I love you, madame. I apologize, but it is true."

"What are you talking about? Are you insane?"

"I always loved you. I couldn't say it before. Dying excuses my boldness."

"Imbecile!" She stretched her own trembling arm.

As did he. But instead of grasping Catherine's hand, he reached up with mighty arms and yanked at the fractured ceiling of the cave. There was a crack as a boulder came loose. The men behind him cried out. More shots came. Then the boulder came down with a crash, there was a rumble of others, and the exit was sealed, dust puffing toward us. Pasques had entombed himself.

We were on one side, the monks on the other. They could excavate, but it would take hours. They could retreat back the way they'd come and emerge from the tower, but that would take time as well.

Time enough, perhaps, to get away.

Catherine backed out, muttering curses.

"He sacrificed himself," Astiza said.

"The fool loved me," Catherine said with disbelief, but wonder, too. It was not an emotion she was accustomed to.

"For that you call him a fool?" I said crossly.

"Love invites weakness." Her own voice betrayed doubt at this belief. "And I deserve a prince, not a policeman." She said it doggedly, dealing with his death in her own warped way. "He was a good companion, but a tool, nothing more. I never told him anything different. I never promised. I never encouraged."

"Yes, you did," I said. "You allowed him to hope."

She sensed our condemnation.

"You think I should cry for an oaf? I'd have saved him if I could. But the Brazen Head is the key—the Brazen Head and me. Thank your pagan gods that I've delivered you with it."

And she crawled back past us, batting Harry aside and yanking on the android. She dragged it like a corpse, or lover, toward the pale light.

CHAPTER 39

We emerged in a rock-walled canyon, its thundering stream white with winter snowmelt. The slowly lightening sky of dawn was a narrow crack overhead. Somehow we'd passed the entire night underground.

There was no way to scale such cliffs with the Brazen Head and a little boy. There was no riverbank to follow, just a flume of rushing water. What we did have was a jam of logs that formed a small pool, the wood frosted.

"Leave the machine," Astiza insisted again. "Thomas Aquinas was right. It's evil. Look at the death it's caused."

"On the contrary," Catherine insisted, with conviction born of desperation. "It will make us rich. Make us queens. We simply haven't asked the right questions yet."

"Time is like this river," Astiza warned. "It can only flow

downhill. To know the future would send time upstream against itself, producing chaos."

"That's quite the hypocrisy from a professional fortune-teller. We don't need your magic anymore, sorceress, we need machines. This is the real future—a future in which we can abandon your magic mysticism for gears and wires that will predict and protect, making life riskless. The age of alchemists and witches is past, and the age of electricians is beginning. Isn't that right, Ethan?"

"I don't feel this is my era, Catherine. I feel marooned."

"The Brazen Head will tell us things scarcely dreamt, and when we anticipate events we'll avoid misfortune and revel in opportunity." Her face was exhausted, eyes wild, but the promise of becoming significant instead of ordinary was within her grasp. "We will be greater than Bonaparte, greater than the Russian czar, greater than Francis. They are not the three emperors, comrades; *we* are, if we keep this automaton to ourselves. We will live as we did in Paris, all of us under one roof, but it will be a palace this time, with a private army greater than that of Baron Richter."

Her vision was a nightmare, of course, a nightmare Astiza and Harry would not long survive. My wife knew this. Catherine didn't want a real alliance, but a temporary triumvirate, like old Roman warlords. Catherine would get rid of my family, possess me like a spider, and devour me like that same spider.

My wife and I looked at each other. We were both thinking the same thing. It was a tempting decision, and we let it hang between us while the whitewater roared. A pistol was still in my fist.

"I have Gideon's rope," I finally said, to break the silence. "It's not long enough to climb out of here, but long enough, perhaps, to lash together a crude raft."

So Astiza and I made one, pulling loose lengths of tree trunks from the logjam on the racing water. We tied five of them into a bundle just big enough to precariously carry our weight. Catherine slumped against a rock and watched us, the idea of contributing beyond her. She ignored Harry, who hunched and shivered, crying silently. The last yards of rope were used to tie on the automaton, but it was a makeshift craft with too little freeboard and too much cargo.

"The worst vessel ever constructed," Astiza assessed.

"But perhaps good enough," I replied, with more optimism than I really felt. "This isn't mountainous country, and this canyon can't extend long. We just need to float down these rapids, find a calm pool with a beach, and swim to a safe shore."

"I'm so tired, Mama."

"Not much more, my love," she said, her voice breaking. "Not much more."

Catherine stood stiffly and moved toward the craft. Astiza blocked her.

"It will float better with one less person," my wife said.

The blond agent was startled. "Get out of my way," she said uncertainly.

"We could leave you here, the cave blocked, the cliff impassable, the river death. We could abandon you, Catherine, as you'll surely abandon us when the opportunity presents itself."

"That is my android! I organized the expedition that brought us here! I assembled the men! I enlisted Pasques! I found the clue to search the Star Summer Palace!"

"Your men are dead. You have no weapon. Why should we save you?" My wife's voice was cold.

Catherine's helplessness was slowly dawning on her. We had no need of her. There were no witnesses. She'd betrayed us and proven herself a murderess. She would complicate any escape. Her eyes were wide, shifting from Astiza's hard gaze to my own. It would simplify everything, and be justice besides.

"Ethan, you can't." Catherine's voice caught as she begged, humiliated to have to do so. "I'll die. I'll freeze and starve."

"I could," I said. Our chances would improve without her. We had too many people for the logs we'd been able to lash.

"Please." It was a sob. She fell to her knees, hands upraised in supplication. "I'm sorry for any discord, our mutual attraction, the problems of politics . . ." It drained away, her teeth chattering from the cold. Her eyes darted.

"But we won't," Astiza said, finishing my thought.

Catherine bowed her head.

"We won't abandon you, Catherine, because forgiveness is more powerful than revenge. Do you understand?"

The comtesse looked up at us again and blinked. She understood nothing except self-preservation. She understood that the French Revolution had executed tens of thousands, that Napoleon's campaigns might result in the death of hundreds of thousands, and that the purpose of life was anything but death. It was survival and triumph. Her look was bleak. She hated the need for mercy. She was propelled by the will to live. Which meant that, for once, she had no answer.

"We need to go before Richter's survivors find us," I finally said.

Catherine walked numbly past my wife to seize the middle position, lying down to hug the Brazen Head. Astiza and Harry balanced on the stern, if you could call one end of a raft that, and I on the bow, the entire contraption dipping ominously in the water.

"Paddle as best you can!" I ordered, which meant thrashing the water with sticks and arms. We pushed off into the current, slipping past the remnant of the logjam we'd plundered. Then we rushed down into the deepest part of the canyon.

It was January, the rocks rimed with frost, icicles hanging, the bare trees up on the canyon rim curved like raptor claws. The river was in flood, Harry moaning as we dashed downstream without rudder or plan. With luck, this sluice of a river would quiet soon, but even as I thought this, its fall seemed to steepen, the current bulging like a muscle. We plunged down into a white pool, car- omed off a rock, and whirled on, trivial and helpless. Catherine shrieked, and I sensed the Brazen Head swinging wildly from one side of the raft to the other, half-loose. I risked my balance to glance back. The comtesse was sprawled across her mechanical man, her thighs grabbing its hips, her face just inches above the rushing water.

"I'm losing my grip! Get us to shore!" she screamed.

"I can't."

Another plunge, the air nothing but foam, a smack as we hit harder water, and then we were through, clinging to the buck- ing contraption for dear life. Catherine, Astiza, and Harry were still there. Freezing water slapped our eyes, mouths, and ears. Ice clotted our hair. We shot into swift but calmer water, an ominous dark gray.

"Is everyone all right?"

"We almost drowned," Astiza gasped. "I barely have a grip on Harry. We need to stop, Ethan."

"Where?"

Indeed, there were boulders the size of hay wagons on the riv- er's edge, but they gave access only to sheer cliffs. It was as if we were trapped in a pipe. So we whirled on, fast as a bird, Harry sobbing, Catherine cursing, and Astiza chanting a prayer.

"Catherine, pull yourself higher. Your skirt is dragging."

She shook her head violently. "I'll lose my grip if I shift. The logs are coming apart. The automaton is coming loose. You did a poor job, Ethan."

We needed to reorganize ourselves. "There's an outcrop ahead. Paddle for that!"

But our raft was unwieldy as a barge, and even though we splashed furiously, we couldn't direct it. We flashed by the refuge, the current quickening.

When would the canyon end?

Then I heard a roar, as ominous as the bellow of a monster's throat.

Looking ahead, I saw the river disappear.

"It's a waterfall!" I shouted. "Abandon the raft! Swim for shore!"

"We can't swim with the Brazen Head!" Catherine screamed.

"Leave it!"

"No!" Catherine twisted to address my wife, her wet hair flying and slapping across the face of the machine. "This is the masterpiece of Albertus Magnus, Astiza, the treasure we've both come a thousand miles to seize. Help me save it!"

"Catherine, there's no time. Abandon the raft."

"Leave it to the river?" She barked a mad laugh.

"Leave it to save your life!" I roared, yanking her shoulder, but she furiously slapped my arm away.

So I deliberately rolled into the frigid water, came up blowing, flung my arm around the waist of my wife as she passed, and pulled her and my son into the stream with me, the raft hurrying on.

"Swim, swim," I cried, "or we die!"

With our weight off it, the raft bobbed higher. Catherine cackled in triumph. She clawed her way up the length of her brass man, thrashing with her arms to try to guide the raft to shore.

Astiza and I were half-paralyzed from cold, but terror can do wonders. We swam as if prodded by the devil's pitchfork, Harry between us, and barely reached a last boulder on the right bank before the ominous lip of the waterfall. My hand slapped rock, slid on wet moss and ice, and then found a crevice and held. My family bumped beside me, my arm lassoing them.

Cold mist rose like steam from the abyss beyond. The raft spun merrily toward the drop.

"Catherine! Don't be a fool! Jump!"

She looked back, torn by indecision. Even she could see there was no longer any chance of navigating the android to shore. The falls were roaring, fog boiled like a cloud, and the cliffs ahead were painted with rime. Showing regret she'd never shown poor Pasques, she finally pushed into the river, shoving the raft and its inhuman cargo away.

Then her eyes widened.

Something caught and yanked her after the android.

Catherine's head snapped, and she floated on her back while she was towed, kicking in frantic fear.

Her hair, those beautiful blond tresses that had taken my breath away when we first partnered, had become wound into the automaton's machinery.

"Ethan!" It was a shriek, a plea, a last expression of despair. She finally had a companion she was married to, wed inextricably in thousands of gears and wires, her hair clogging any attempt to foretell her future.

"The android has me!"

Or she had it. Perhaps it had simply made one last prediction, the one she dreaded.

We hung on the mossy boulder, the current pummeling past. We saw a last flash of foot, whether human or brass I knew not, and then heard a faint scream as Catherine Marceau and the android rode the thundering cataract down.

Finally there was only the pounding of the river.

We shuddered, and not just from cold.

We still had just enough strength to drag ourselves out of the water and up onto the rock. Harry was squeezed between, squirting water like a sponge. It drained from mouth, nose, and ears. We pumped him to keep his spark alive, thrilled by his every cough. We were all near dead.

And yet we'd escaped. I knew this as firmly as if a fortune-teller had proclaimed our fate. The Brazen Head had indeed given a future to my family—and taken it from Catherine Marceau. I felt escape, relief, and a somber depression that everyone's desire had come to nothing. We'd discovered a miracle, but we had let it sink away.

Deliverance also gave me a flicker of energy. I spied a crevice and ledge in the cliff face, which we could follow toward the forest above. The canyon was lower here, diving to follow the plunge of the falls, and climbable. We crept up a slit of wet rock, trembling with exertion and panting with hope. A slip meant death for all of us.

So we held on.

We crawled onto flatter land with the joy of shipwrecked sailors—gone from Richter, gone from Catherine, gone from the Invisible College, and gone from the madness of war.

"Some farmer will take us in," I whispered. "We'll hide."

"I love you, Ethan." Astiza's tone was utterly spent, our lips too numb to kiss.

"I love you. You saved Harry for all these long, terrifying months. Your alchemy saved all of us in Richter's prison."

"Now let's save our marriage."

Shakily we stood. We could see the falls, a long, dizzying plunge into a black pool rimmed with foam and ice. We watched for life but saw none. The shaky raft had disintegrated, and the metal man would be an anchor that dragged its lover down. Catherine was at the bottom of the pool somewhere, forever in its embrace.

All triumph for a time, the Brazen Head had foretold.

I carried Harry as tightly as a puppy as we worked away from the river, our exertions keeping us alive. The light was growing, and we might even get some January sun.

It was over at last. My family back, my enemies vanquished.

I stopped a moment simply to suck in great drafts of breath.

And then a nasal voice gave challenge.

"Where have you hidden it?"

The voice made Astiza jump and Harry cringe, but at first I couldn't see its origin. My eyes flickered along the spine of the ridge as if hunting for deer.

"You didn't think you could keep it for yourselves, did you?"

With sickening realization, I cast my gaze lower. The sun hadn't reached this part of the forest, and so the dwarf was still in shadow, but his calm menace reinforced my memory of gnomish malevolence.

"Don't worry about the boy," he added. "I've got a way to get him warm."

"Auric!" My wife's voice was a wail.

"You thought you killed me, didn't you, witch? Maimed me with your evil trick. But I'm not one to die."

He stepped forward, or rather staggered, a cross between a waddle and a limp. If Richter had lost his lower face, Auric had lost his right side, the very bones of his jaw caved in and his triumphant grin missing half its teeth. His leg was twisted, his hands burned even more horribly than before. Yet those hands gripped a new set of small pistols.

I realized that he'd been the rider I saw splitting from Richter's group, sent to guard against any escape through a backdoor in the castle.

"Why can't you leave us alone?" My question was as hopeless as it was pointless.

"I swore eternal vengeance, Ethan Gage. Burned, crushed, bleeding, and I knew I had only one purpose left in life. I insisted to Richter that he bring me on a pony, and when the others blundered ahead into the castle and fired off enough shots to win at Austerlitz, I wondered what other escape you might find. You're a worm, but a clever one. A knife to a farmer's eye won me word of an old cave entrance, and the place on the river where you'd either exit or die." He looked past us. "Where's Catherine?"

"Dead. Drowned."

"Richter? The others?"

"Dead too."

"And where's the Brazen Head? Where did you leave it?"

"There is no Brazen Head, Auric. It was all for nothing."

"I don't believe you. Catherine Marceau would have killed you if there weren't an automaton. My master would have killed you. They needed you only as donkeys."

"Let us go. It's over."

"Oh, no." He lifted the pistols, the pain of the effort twisting him even more. "It's only beginning. You can tell me, and pray I let your child die quickly. Or resist until I take him for roasting, and find the automaton on my own."

"Auric, please," Astiza pleaded. "Redeem your soul before it's eternally damned."

"There is no soul." He cocked the hammers. "That's the real secret of alchemy, sorceress. No soul, no ka, no spirit, and no stars. Only power."

And then there was a sound like the thrum of bird wings, and the dwarf's head exploded.

CHAPTER 40

Astiza

Life has its own symmetries. Sometimes things are meant to happen. Sometimes deeds bring their own rewards. And so it was that Gideon Dray saved my husband yet again, saved me, saved my son—with a stone hurled with biblical vengeance.

One moment Auric Nachash was going to shoot us; the next he was brained with a rock the size of a pigeon egg, hurled by a sling that Ethan's Jew had fashioned from a strip of old leather. It was David and Goliath all over again, except this Goliath was a considerably smaller target. And it was the back of his head, not the front, that shattered into pieces.

The pistols fell into the snow.

Hate had kept the dwarf alive after my explosion, but whatever Auric had once meant to be had died long, long ago.

We were shocked, of course. Our executioner had been slain by an agency as sudden and unexpected as a lightning bolt. Neither of us quite knew what had happened, but then Gideon called out cautiously, "Ethan?" When my husband managed a wheezing bark in reply, he emerged from the trees and came toward us.

Dray let his sling trail in one hand and hefted the rock up and down in the other, contemplatively. He kicked his victim to make sure he was dead, then stepped forward to hug us.

"By what miracle?" my husband managed.

"I've been trailing the little ogre since yesterday afternoon. I'd no weapon to help in the castle gun battle, but I was appalled Auric had survived. I decided to track him, since the dwarf seemed to have a very certain plan of his own. I used a dead monk's belt to fashion a makeshift sling."

"Where did you learn to wield it?"

"Jews are prohibited weapons. It's why we needed a golem. And without one, we learn to fight with fists, teeth, rocks, and slings. I've practiced all my life, even after joining the army. I was determined not to be helpless if the regiment ever ran out of ammunition."

"Thank the gods," Ethan said. "Or goddess," he added, with a nod to me.

"I believe it is simply 'God,'" replied Gideon. "You owe Yahweh allegiance if you keep calling on me for rescue." He looked around. "Are there others?"

"Some may emerge from the castle and hunt for us."

"Ah. I sent that bunch flying in the other direction. Pulling a cowl over my head, I pretended to be a simple priest, telling them I saw a fugitive family run the opposite way in the snow. It will be some hours before they realize my deception."

"We owe you for all time," I said with fervor.

"No, madame, a good deed does not require repayment, or it is not truly good. Yet someday perhaps you can do your own good deed for me or my people, and that will be payment more proper." He squatted. "And you, Harry, are you all right?"

My boy looked at our friend solemnly, his tears dried. "The bad man is finally dead."

"So he is." Gideon stood, looked about, and looked back at Ethan. "And where is it? I trust you found it?"

"Found what?"

"The Brazen Head."

As strange as it seems, we actually needed to be reminded of what he was talking about, so traumatic was our encounter with the dwarf. Then we hesitated. Should we admit to its existence? We were embarrassed at its loss, but also protective of its watery grave. It would never be found by anyone. Except, perhaps, by us.

"It turned out not to be useful," Ethan finally said. "It spoke in riddles."

"What kind of riddles?"

"Nonsense things. Catherine destroyed it."

He doubted us, as any intelligent man would, but he also didn't seem to lust for the machine. The Jews already had a golem, and wisely left it in an attic.

He inventoried our condition. "Every time we meet, you are soaked. Do you like being coated in ice?"

"I think we are done with swimming."

"I doubt it. But you need shelter and a fire. And rest. And food. Here are some crusts of bread."

We ate like the starving animals we were.

Then we began a slow, weary walk—keeping to the trees, our eyes wary of more surprises—toward a wisp of smoke in the distance that might mark a friendly farm. The scraps of food warmed us sufficiently to keep going.

"And are they riddles, Ethan?" I murmured to my husband

as we walked along, talking turns carrying an exhausted Harry, who'd lapsed into sleep. "Do you think the Brazen Head was useless? Is that why Albertus let Rosenkreutz take it? Or was it evil and brought here to be locked away? Was it too powerful a seer?"

"Not a seer so much as a repository of wisdom," my husband said to me.

"You found wisdom in its answers?"

"Certainly all men are successful for a time but are ultimately defeated, every one. By death if nothing else."

"Yes," I said. "And surely the truest gold is within our hearts. The only gold you can never lose, and never spend without it being replenished."

"Richter will stay in his little hell forever. He and Rosenkreutz together, eternal in their own way. The Brazen Head predicted that."

"But the purpose of death is life?" I asked. "And the purpose of life is death?"

"I spent several weeks dead while in search of you," Ethan said. "I shared a coffin, heard the dirt thrown on, and wondered the meaning many times in the thunder of navies and tramp of armies."

"And?"

"Look at these winter woods. A graveyard of leaf and fern, but death that is necessary to bring forth the next round of life. An eternal cycle, as reassuring as a rainbow or calendar or clock. We all die, Astiza. But in that death, we become immortal. Not just supernaturally, but in nourishing and making way for the next round of life."

I smiled at his conversion. "Ethan, you sound like a priestess."

"Catherine would finally call me a realist."

"We *make* life, too." I nodded toward our soggy son, on his shoulder.

"It's too bad we can't relax like the animals do," Ethan mused, "and accept the cycle. We're forever dissatisfied."

"If we didn't strive and worry, we wouldn't be human, would we? We'd be an android, like the Brazen Head."

"So what do we strive for now, my dear wife?"

"Rest. Refuge. Renewal. To finally stay together as a family."

He smiled. "To be common for a change."

But neither of us is. That is our blessing. That is our curse.

CHAPTER 41

My family and I hid for three days in an isolated farmhouse, Astiza nursing Harry back to good health. A rider came, inquiring about fugitives, but Gideon paid the farmer to say he'd seen no one. Neighbors said that black-clad strangers had been reported following the river and scouring the ruins, but there was no report of discovery. Finally, they left.

"Where will you go?" Gideon asked me.

"West is France and the sphere of French influence," I said. "South is where I first encountered the agents of the Invisible College. So north and east, I think, until we decide what to do. We'll aim for the Baltic and take ship for the life we deserve."

"Paid for how?"

I laughed, ruefully, at my poverty. So much striving, for so little gain! Except I had a wife, child, freedom, and experiences that can't be bought. I was rich in the things that count.

"I'll gamble. Astiza will tell fortunes. Perhaps we can find honest jobs as well. Something that draws less attention, I hope. I once had a fortune in England but lost it to bad investments. My mentor Franklin said it is harder to keep money than to earn it in the first place."

"My father is adept at keeping it. Here, take a hundred talers to get started on your way."

"No, you've done too much, my friend, and our quest has put both of your lives in jeopardy. Keep it for the Dray children, when you have them."

He laughed. "What wife would want me?"

Almost any on the planet, I thought, but didn't need to say that. While great men climbed and fell, Gideon would abide, gleaning his father's wisdom.

"What will you do, my Jewish friend?"

"Return home with Father, I think, and expand our business together. Nor do I think this recent war will be the last, and there will be other armies our employees can follow. Find a patron, Ethan. It's an advantage having someone who can help."

He took his leave on a late January afternoon in the year 1806, and we stayed a final night. When we rose, we found he'd left the hundred talers, and that he'd purchased a horse and sleigh for us besides. The goodness of one man can balance despair over the mendacity of a hundred.

Harry was sick after our river dousing, and, given the mortality rate among children, we worried a great deal. But he recovered, and then bounced back with the vigor small ones have. He had nightmares but talked little of his months of imprisonment. He chattered instead about the farm animals and new adventures. I hoped the alchemical prison would become a vague memory as he blossomed into boyhood. The days slowly lengthened from the darkest time of year.

Finally we set out, traveling north into a Poland that had been dismembered and absorbed by Russia and Prussia a decade before. As I learned to drive our sleigh on snowy roads, I considered our options. One was to be ordinary, doing small things and rejoicing in our smallness. Perhaps I could establish an American trading company in Tallinn, or assemble a cargo for Philadelphia in Copenhagen.

But another was to capitalize on my expertise. All the world was talking of Napoleon, the terrible Prometheus. He was reforming hero to some, predatory dictator to others. And while my adventures had brought me little material gain, they had brought me a wealth of experience. I knew Bonaparte in his many moods, had observed his armies, and understood some of his success and weakness. I'd died, risen, and come away with unusual perspective.

The Russian government in St. Petersburg was famed for hiring foreign savants from the West to modernize its institutions. Did I need a patron? I'd passed through the lands of two emperors. Perhaps we could fetch up for a time in the nation of a third, Czar Alexander. He might not like me, but he certainly could use me.

"Gideon said the most successful advisers have been made Russian nobles, with grants of lands and palaces," I said. "It would be amusing to be rich for a while."

"Or at least warm," my ever practical wife said. So we slid northward, goal in mind, bundled in furs as we passed through endless silver forest. We paid for shelter in the log huts of peasants each winter night.

Armies had stood down for the winter, Napoleon as dominant on land as he was thwarted on the ocean. All his plans to invade England had come to nothing. All of Britain's plans to overthrow him had left Bonaparte stronger than ever. The world would wait now to see how strong his empire would be, and whether the Prussians would still resist. He cast light and shadow like the sun.

So we traveled unnoticed and unmolested, sled runners hissing on ice. But on the fifteenth day of February, on a snowy road just south of St. Petersburg, we finally encountered a troop of cavalry. We steered our sleigh to the side of the road to let them pass, hoping we wouldn't be bothered. Except that I recognized the splendid posture of one as they galloped, decided to take a chance at happiness, and called out to my old rival.

"Prince Dolgoruki!"

The riders reined up and the noble squinted. I stood and took off my fur cap to reveal my features. The prince gave an order and the hussars wheeled to surround us, hooves kicking up a surf of snow. My own horse shied nervously as their steeds boxed us in, their nostrils blowing steam.

"By the beard of Saint Basil, is it the American scoundrel? You dare put yourself within reach of my sword?"

"Adviser," I corrected. "Historian, seer, electrician, and military consultant. With my family, seeking asylum from Bonaparte." I bowed. "Ethan Gage, American savant, at your service. With Astiza of Alexandria." She nodded. The soldiers, who couldn't understand our French, looked impassive.

Prince Peter Petrovich Dolgoruki, the very same man I'd conducted to a conference with Napoleon before the Battle of Austerlitz, regarded me warily. The disastrous defeat had aged him in the two months since we'd talked.

"You travel to the losing side, Gage?" he asked in the same French, the language of the Russian court. Their nobility aped the manners of their enemies, admiring France as much as they feared it. "I thought you'd tied your fate to the frogs."

"I was conscripted, not recruited," I said. "And the balance of power has been upset with Austerlitz. Napoleon is a tyrant, his ambition boundless. I know him as well as any man alive and am prepared to offer my expertise to a monarch seeking to best him." I tried to smile winningly.

"You mean he dismissed you." Dolgoruki was not entirely stupid.

"I deserted to care for my family. Now, after Austerlitz, I believe my knowledge will be better appreciated in Russia. I'm neutral, as I said, but perhaps of use to Czar Alexander. Good card player, too."

He looked at Astiza and Harry. "This is your family?"

"My wife and son. We've been reunited after many trials. Consider them evidence of my friendly intent. No spy brings his family." Well, I did, but no need to go on and on about our oddities.

He leaned down to address Harry. "So you're an adventurer like your father. You're a brave little lad, aren't you?"

"We killed the bad men."

The prince's smile was tight. "Not the most awful one. Not yet."

"Will you introduce me to your sovereign, Prince?" I said.

"I'm sure he'll remember you," Dolgoruki said sourly, "and your deceptive diplomatic mission with the sly Savary."

"I was pressed into service and said nothing false. I tried to warn you."

He knew this was true. It was Russian rashness, not the diplomatic posing of Ethan Gage, that led to disaster at Austerlitz. "And your mission to us now?"

"Do you want to beat Napoleon? I can tell you how." A cheeky promise, but the first step toward recovering our fortunes was to get in the Winter Palace door. Should I play our cards right, we'd have an empire to protect us, respite from travel, a good home, and maybe a puppy for Harry. We'd make our fortune and go home to America. I might even write a book.

"You are impudent."

"Opportunistic. Improvisational. And my wife is a scholar and priestess of Egypt, offering the wisdom of the ages."

"Is this true, madame?"

"My husband and I met when I helped my master take shots at Napoleon. His regime tore my family apart, and now we're trying to put it back together. Please, Prince. Give mercy. And my husband a chance."

He shook his head, persuaded, as so many are, by her beauty and my bargaining. "War makes strange allies."

"And strong friends," I encouraged.

"You'd betray your former master?"

"Napoleon was never my master. And he must be contained to achieve peace, both of nations and of my family. Fascinating fellow, but as troublesome as the devil. I understand he's his mother's child."

Dolgoruki was too proud to befriend a commoner, but perhaps if I achieved a title . . . My imagination always outruns my accomplishments. Finally he shrugged. "We'll let the court decide your fate." He turned to his men. "Colonel!"

"Yes, Your Excellency?"

"A salute to our new allies! And back to St. Petersburg, as escort of this . . . embassy, of sorts." Now that a decision had been made, the order was crisp and princely. There was a thrilling rasp as the sabers came out and were shouldered in salute, Harry wide-eyed at the hedge of steel. Dolgoruki was making plain who was in control. "In desperate times, even Ethan Gage may be of use."

Had we finally found safe harbor? Russia sprawled from where we conferred to the Pacific and Russian America. Distance enough from Napoleon.

"Now we can seek refuge to truly make our marriage," my wife murmured. "Perhaps it is over at last."

I cracked the whip and our sleigh slid back onto the frozen road, the soldiers forming an escort around us. A cry of command, and off we raced, the cavalry setting a brisk pace for our normally uninspired horse. Within the hour, St. Petersburg loomed into view.

We paused to take it in. The place was only a century old, built on the bones of a hundred thousand slaves, and invented from scratch like my own Washington. It had canals to rival Venice, frozen to white ribbons. It looked new, ambitious, ostentatious, and huge. The prince rode back and reined up next to our sleigh. "While the nobility speaks French, you should begin to learn Russian as well, Ethan Gage. To start, try, *Ya durak*."

"*Ya durak?* What does that mean?"

"I am a fool."

I scowled, but the prince leaned in conspiratorially. "You're about to enter the greatest capital in the world, in the greatest country, of the greatest people." He evaluated our rags. "And finally see your fortunes turn."

I looked at the golden domes and spires of the Russian capital, glowing in the late winter sun of 1806. For the first time in years, I thought this might prove true.

As with other Ethan Gage books, many of the places, events, and characters in this novel are real. The three emperors fought at Austerlitz, as described, and the French did capture Tabor Bridge with a ruse claiming an armistice. The Austrian, Russian, and French officers cited are taken from history, including the flamboyant Murat. His claim that he avoided personal killing was made shortly before his execution in Italy, after the collapse of Bonaparte's empire. Also taken from history is the curious talisman that Napoleon shows Ethan in his tent.

Josef and Paulina Schwarzenberg did put on performances in the theater at the castle of Český Krumlov. As Astiza predicted, Paulina met a tragic end. Visiting Paris in 1810, she burned to death in a fire at a ball.

The medieval legend of a Brazen Head, built by Albertus Magnus, that could foretell the future is drawn from history, as is the legend that Saint Thomas Aquinas destroyed it. The legendary background of Christian Rosenkreutz is also authentic, and the description of his tomb is taken from speculative accounts. Rosicrucian chapters exist today, including a museum and study center in Palo Alto, California. The suggestion that Rosenkreutz took the Brazen Head, however, is the author's invention.

Ca' Rezzonico, in Venice, the theater at Český Krumlov, Prague's Klementinum and castle, its Jewish ghetto, Trosky Castle, and the silver mines of Kutná Hora are all open to visitors today. The church of bones, or Sedlec Ossuary, which is described, is more elaborate than in Ethan's day, because it was after the events in this novel that nineteenth-century monks arranged some of the bones into bizarre decorations and chandeliers.

The alchemical books, beliefs, methods, practitioners, and sayings used in this book are taken from history. A tower in Kutná Hora has a replica alchemical laboratory in its basement. The risk of explosion in these chambers was very real, and the gold fulminate that Astiza concocts was particularly dangerous.

As bizarre as alchemical beliefs might seem today, the quest for the Philosopher's Stone represented the birth of modern chemistry. Alchemical belief in fundamental elements has been confirmed by modern science.

The Battle of Austerlitz was Napoleon's greatest victory, confirming his domination of Europe. While estimates differ, the Allied losses—approximately 27,000 dead, wounded, and captured—were three times French casualties. The heavy sanctions imposed on the Austrian empire, however, ensured that war would continue. One can only wonder at the course of history if Napoleon had stopped military campaigning, consolidated France's position, and concentrated on domestic reform. Each battle, alas, planted the seeds for the next, and his eventual downfall.

And Durendal, the sword of Roland? While there is an alleged fragment embedded in a wall in Rocamadour, France, most authorities consider this a replica. The reader can decide whether Ethan Gage found the real sword, then shattered it once more, and where hilt and key may be today.

ABOUT THE AUTHOR

WILLIAM DIETRICH is the author of twelve novels, including six previous Ethan Gage titles—*Napoleon's Pyramids*, *The Rosetta Key*, *The Dakota Cipher*, *The Barbary Pirates*, *The Emerald Storm*, and *The Barbed Crown*. Dietrich is also a Pulitzer Prize–winning journalist, historian, and naturalist. A winner of the PNBA Award for Nonfiction, he lives in Washington State.